THE BEAR CLAW TALES

BEAR CLAW TALES 1-4

C.D. GORRI

Sign up for my newsletter and get the latest on my releases, giveaways, freebies and more:

www.cdgorri.com/newsletter

WELCOME TO BARVALE!

Hello Readers!

Come inside and meet the Devlin brothers! In order of their stories, we have *Marcus*, *Taylor*, *Daniel*, and *Nate*! Four Bear Shifters on the hunt for their one true and fated mates! Get to know the movers and shakers behind the infamous *Bear Claw Bakery*, maker of the finest baked goods this side of the Atlantic! I hope you're hungry, cause we got cream claws and honey drizzled goodies for all!

Let's help these four growly men hurry up and find their mates before their wild side becomes too much to *bear*! Enjoy!

Del mare alla stella,

C.D. Gorri

**Continue the journey with The Barvale Clan Tales!*

BEARLY BREATHING

BEARLY BREATHING
BY C.D. GORRI

For anyone who believes in true love, this one is for you!
del mare alla stella, C.D. Gorri

USA TODAY BESTSELLING AUTHOR

C.D. GORRI

Bearly
BREATHING

A BEAR CLAW TALE 1

BLURB

He's looking for his mate. She just wants to have fun. Will Leya and Marcus find their destiny one hot summer night?

Sweet and curvy, Leya Tremayne is tired of being a shoulder to cry on for the men in her life. Determined to shed her image, she goes on a tropical vacation with plans to let her hair down!

She meets Marcus Devlin and is instantly attracted to the devastatingly handsome stranger. He is exactly the type of man she needs to help her build her new image! Can she handle a one-night stand with this rugged Bear Shifter or will she lose her heart in the process?

Marcus Devlin is looking for his true fated mate. After months of searching, he is just about ready to give up when destiny lands in his lap. *Literally.*

After rescuing the beautiful blonde tourist from an untimely accident, Marcus knows instinctively that she's the one. He just has to convince her!

A Message from Taylor, One of the Devlin Brothers...

Hi there,

My name is Taylor. I'm the youngest of the three Devlin Brothers. Now, this is a secret, but I feel like I can trust you, so I'm just gonna say it. We're Bear Shifters. Werebears if you prefer.

My oldest brother, Marcus, has been a real sonofabit-, well, he's been one cranky ass bear! He needs to find his one true and fated mate to soothe his beast or there's a chance he might go feral!

That would really suck for us, seeing as how we've just hit the bigtime with the family business. We're the owners of Bear Claw Bakery, you might have heard of us! The best non-GMO savory breads and sweets in the country! Heck, maybe the whole damn planet!

But don't take my word for it. Dive into these pages

and see for yourself! And if you see Marcus, maybe let him give you a sniff, just in case you're the one?

Oh, steer clear of Daniel! My poor big bro got his heart crushed. Yup, he was left at the altar by his fiancée! Let's just say the experience left him one bitter and angry dude. He hates women.

Yup. I'm the nice one in the bunch. But don't get any ideas. I am a confirmed bachelor for years to come yet! No rush to mate here. Especially not with Krissy Sposa, our home store manager. Despite what the curly haired bear seems to think!

Anyway, back to Marcus, he's the one looking for love. I gotta get going, I have a hot date with a sexy redhead.

TTYS!

-Taylor

PROLOGUE

Marcus rolled his shoulders and waited impatiently for the familiar buzz that preceded his Change. It was early yet. The evening sky was still bright with the setting sun. Too light for what he was about to do, but he didn't care. He needed to do it *now*.

He tore off his apron and stepped out of his flour-caked sneakers, kicking them onto the rubber mat that sat against the exposed brick wall of the hallway that led to the ovens.

He'd have to remember to tell the cleaning service to hose down the mats before they left at night. He made a mental note, but that didn't slow him down in the least.

Marcus turned sideways so he could fit smoothly

through the back door of the bakery and half-jogged down the steps. He sniffed the air, ignoring the sweet smell of flour and yeast as he loped towards the stand of trees just behind the employee parking lot.

He ran his eyes over the area, checking one last time to make sure he was completely alone, before stripping out of the remainder of his dough splattered clothes.

The bakery was hot as fuck on any given day, no matter the season. Today was no exception. Tiny rivulets of sweat clung to his skin, but the cool air that met it caused him to shiver. *Or was it caused by something else?*

He sucked in a deep breath. Change was coming, his Bear sensed it. Not the kind that swapped skin for fur, this was something else. *The weather perhaps?*

Just another week or two and the unseasonably cold spring would be over, replaced by the intoxicating heat of summer. Marcus loved summer.

Actually, what he liked most about his home in southwestern New Jersey was the change of the seasons. Except lately.

This winter had been a long one and, as for spring, it was nonexistent. He felt restless and barren as the landscape. Small, unfulfilled buds covered the trees. They looked hard and small, dead even, incapable of holding the life he knew that dwelt deep inside.

He longed for the lush green of the summer months. With it came the frenzy of his fellow woodland creatures as they went about their lives of hunting, gathering, making homes, and making babies. *Fuck. Babies.* The thought alone used to be enough to have him breaking out in hives. *But now...*

This line of thought was not helping with his current state. Anxiety filled his veins. He exhaled and shook his head, freeing his shoulder-length hair from the confines of the tight braid he preferred when baking. *It's time.* The voice inside him growled, but Marcus resisted.

He didn't want things to change. He liked his life. Business was good, his family was healthy and safe. He had deep roots right there in town. What more could he want? *Mate. Must find a mate,* his inner beast growled.

His family was long and well-established in the area. He had duties to both his business, his brothers, and his Clan. But could he fulfill them without giving up a part of himself?

Marcus knew his history well. His great-great-grandfather, Ignatius Devlin, moved to Barvale from

Ireland over two hundred years ago seeking fortune and a better life for himself.

After he'd landed, he started as an apprentice baker to the one man willing to give an Irishman a job. Years later, after marrying the man's daughter and inheriting the shop, he founded the Devlin Clan.

Family legend said the young baker's wife was curious about her husband's nightly runs through the woods. He'd avoided her questions with success until one night when their first child promptly turned into a bear cub after refusing to go to bed when his mother ordered him to.

Old Ignatius had a lot of explaining to do that night, afterwards, harmony reigned in their house, and the bakery was re-christened the Bear Claw Bakery.

The Devlin Clan owned and operated the Bear Claw Bakery to this very day. In fact, his father had recently retired from the business and was ready to do the same with his role in the Clan. *More changes.*

Marcus and his brothers had immediately thrown themselves into work. He had to prove not only to his father and brothers, but to himself, that he could do a good job. And he had. Only, just lately, he felt as if time itself was breathing down his neck. His Bear was restless.

It wasn't because of Bear Claw Bakery, that much he knew. Marcus had baking in his blood. There was nothing on God's green earth that compared to the heady rush he got when he breathed in the wholesome fragrance of freshly baked bread and the other sweet and savory goods that made the Bear Claw one of the best in the industry.

The old family recipes that had been passed down to them were revered by the brothers. They were responsible for keeping their products fresh with bold new innovations in flavors and by using only the best non-GMO, organic ingredients.

His father had smiled indulgently whenever they talked about their new take on old family recipes. *As if he had ever used inferior ingredients! Bah!* But the world was changing, and chefs and bakers the world over had their work cut out for them in so far as selecting only the best for their products.

Marcus dusted the flour off from his hands and grunted. Success aside, something was missing from his life. Something soft and supple with sweet curves and a wicked tongue... *Fuck, not now*, he thought.

The image of a faceless woman with a body made for him entered his mind and he felt himself swell instantly in response. *No.* He was damned if he was going to admit that what he craved, what he lusted after was a woman. *No, not just a woman.*

Women were not exactly flocking to his bed, though he'd had his fair share. He was a good-looking guy, but his days of sowing his wild oats were long gone.

One night stands simply held no appeal. *But having one woman, the right woman, might.* Marcus squinted against the setting sun and rubbed his hand over the middle of his chest.

He was acutely aware of the emptiness there. Like a hole had suddenly popped up right smack in the middle of his heart. He'd been fighting it for months now. But tonight, it hit Marcus like a ton of bricks.

He couldn't outrun it any longer. *You need a mate.* The second he acknowledged it, his Bear roared in agreement. He wanted to balk at the very idea of it.

That his Bear should demand he find a mate before the man was ready! It made him damned angry. *Shit.*

He just didn't have the time to find a mate. Not now. He was too busy. But when he had the time, it shouldn't be too hard, he told himself. He knew that women found him attractive.

Marcus was the eldest of the Devlin trio. He was taller than his two brothers, though they too shared his bulk, and he had an easy-going nature most of the time. He worked hard, his body evidence of just how hard.

All three Devlin boys were heavily built, each one covered in sinewy muscle. They were big as, *well*, as *Bears*. Shifters in general were well muscled, but Bears were downright brawny.

It didn't stop the ladies from flocking to them. When he was younger, he ate up the attention, but nowadays it just felt wrong. He was tired of one-night stands. And he had plenty to offer a mate, now that he was coming around to the idea.

He was handsome, with his chiseled features, full lips, and preferred bit of scruff on his face. He was financially sound, and the bakery was doing amazing.

Unlike his two younger brothers, Marcus had inherited his mother's mane of dark brown hair. He kept it long and plenty a woman enthused over the natural silkiness of his locks. *Yes.* He was enough to tempt any female.

Not just any female. A mate. My mate. Fuck, fuck, fuck. He'd never been interested in more than a casual affair with women. But he realized this was bound to happen sooner or later.

At least he could be objective and choose one before he fell under her spell. Lord knew he didn't want to wind up like his brother, Daniel. Poor guy was still eating his heart out after his fiancé left him at the altar for another man.

"Fuck me," he growled out loud.

Sure, he'd tried dating more and more the last few months, but there were slim pickings out there for a guy like him. He disliked aggressive women, and the types that frequented the bars and restaurants that he and his brothers used to hang out in were more than that.

Christ, last night a long-legged blonde had walked right up to him and put her hand right on his dick before he even got her name. Not his type at all.

Taylor, the baby of the family and his mama's pride and joy, had been too happy to take over from there. Marcus left early and came right here to work off his annoyance.

Ten hours by the ovens in their main distribution baking facility and, *still*, he was agitated. *Need to Change. Now.*

He rolled his neck and relaxed his crouched stance. Mate or no mate, he needed this time right now to unwind. He was more than a little anxious to stretch his legs.

He refused to think about what would happen if he couldn't find her. His Bear roared at the thought of going *feral*. Unmated *Bear Shifters*, or *Werebears*, were a threat to their entire way of life.

The fact that supernaturals walked amongst humans, or *normals* as they were called, was a secret that must be kept at all costs. Each group had their own way of enforcing this rule, and there were other agencies that helped track down and take care of anyone who was a threat to that and a handful of other absolute rules.

Fact was, a feral Bear had no place amongst society. In short, Marcus would be hunted and later put to death if he went feral. A strong probability if he remained unmated.

This odious task was usually carried out by the Alpha of the Bear Clan in question. For him that would mean his father. *Fuck.*

Okay, time to Shift, he told his inner beast. He visualized the thick, dark fur and the hefty weight of his other self.

His body trembled in response to the magic that responded so readily whenever he called forth his Black Bear. He was easily double the size of any normal black bear and right then, every single inch of him was on edge.

The next day, he was leaving Barvale to visit one of the new Bear Claw Bakery locations. His job was to evaluate the site and make sure it was up to their specifications.

He'd leave all this business of finding a mate till he got back. This new store was the perfect excuse for a few days of relaxation. Just what he needed!

As the eldest, he got first pick when it came to travel. He'd use this as a mini vacay. After all, it was his business plan that led them to lease spaces in Stein Luxury Hotel & Resorts.

Bear Claw Bakery had over a dozen locales up and down the east coast already, but with these new mini storefronts in the popular hotel chain, they'd launch into an entirely new level of renown and fortune.

Famous locally and in the tri-state area for their wide selection of organic, non-GMO, freshly brewed coffees and teas, not to mention their made-to-order fresh fruit or veggie smoothies, Marcus knew they'd benefit any tourist establishment.

They also served a delectable assortment of freshly baked bread, muffins, cookies, pies, pastries, croissants, and other goods throughout the day.

He was thrilled with the prospect of Bear Claw Bakery becoming a household name. Of course, the new mini bakeries in the hotel chain had shortened menus, but they were damn good ones. Marcus made sure of it.

His brothers had helped him decide what products they'd sell at these smaller bakeries. Of course, baking would be done on the premises. That meant finding chefs. Good ones.

Marcus had spent months interviewing and training the right people to manage the new locations. Finding experienced chefs was handled by Daniel. The Bear may be a woman hater now that his fiancée had dumped his ass, but he could sniff out talent fast as lightning.

Taylor, his youngest brother, came up with the idea to feature fresh local produce in their stores according to each location. Marcus and Daniel readily supported the decision. *Real ingredients for real people.*

All three brothers took turns to visit the new locations, and there were just a handful left. Marcus' turn was next. And not a minute too soon. This mate business was making him nuts. He couldn't wait to land in paradise!

He booked the hotel room for an extra week

instead of the normal day or two the trip usually entailed. He couldn't remember the last time he just relaxed. He was long overdue.

This time tomorrow he'd be sitting on a beach with a tumbler of *Clover Bite*, his favorite brand of artisan whiskey, and soaking up the glorious sun. But right now, he needed to Change.

His Bear hated to fly. The idea of soaring thousands of feet above land was ludicrous to the beast inside him.

Marcus found it best to let him out before a long trip. *Alright, buddy, let's run,* he said to himself and let out a short roar as his body changed to that of his hulking Black Bear just before he took off into the woods.

CHAPTER
ONE

Leya Tremayne sipped from her glass of chilled Chardonnay and listened to her impeccably dressed boss over their shared appetizers.

She sighed and nodded her head in all the appropriate places, but her mind was a million miles away. *I can't believe this is happening.*

When her big, handsome boss asked her to accompany him to dinner, she'd had a minor heart attack. All her daydreams over the past few months were finally about to come to fruition! Or not.

She'd been certain her luck had changed, but after nibbling on a stuffed mushroom, not her favorite appetizer by the way, and watching him order a fruity cocktail that made her shudder, he started confessing his real reason for asking her out. *This cannot be happening to me again!*

"You don't have any plans tonight, right?" he'd asked while perching on her desk earlier that evening.

Like the desperate jerk she was, she nodded her head and agreed with him. Even though it was Friday night and damned presumptuous of him to ask her to go with him on such short notice.

Oh well, she thought, *that's what you get for being obvious. Still, at least I'll get a nice dinner.* Those had been her thoughts when he first brought up the subject of his super sexy, super skinny, and somewhat bitchy girlfriend.

Several blue cocktails later, he was still rambling on about his relationship with the tall, model-thin, Tris Beverly, and they hadn't even ordered their food yet.

Leya sighed miserably as she tried to appear sympathetic. *Hmm. More like just pathetic,* she rolled her eyes. Was she doomed to be a shoulder for guys to cry on forever?

"She said I was insensitive!" he said and took another swig from his *Blue Hawaiian.*

What kind of a man drank a Blue Hawaiian at an Italian restaurant for Pete's sake?

"I'm sure she didn't mean it, Gary. You're the least insensitive man I know," Leya said with an appropriate amount of concern in her voice.

She really wanted to end this nightmare of a dinner, but she didn't want to offend him. The man *was* her boss.

Unfortunately, he seemed to think she was also his therapist. She sighed and looked longingly at the next table. *Ooh, shrimp scampi over linguini! Totally drool-worthy.*

Gary asked another question, and she nodded hoping it was the correct response. Her stomach grumbled.

He continued on and on, so, *yes must have been the right answer. Good guess*, she thought and sipped some wine.

Her stomach continued to grumble. Reminding her the half a mushroom appetizer was all she'd eaten since lunch.

Typically, it did absolutely nothing to quell her appetite. To put it bluntly, Leya liked food. She looked down at her ample figure. *Well, duh.*

"It's just that Tris is so hot! A guy would be crazy not to want her, right? But-"

"Uh huh, but Gary-"

"See, I knew you'd get it, but she..."

While he droned on, Leya gazed longingly at the happy couples enjoying dinner. *Why am I here?* She'd worked for Gary for two years, and though they'd been friendly, he never asked her out.

Clearly, he was head over heels for Tris, and she was a fill-in. She paused as his perfectly manicured fingers captured hers.

Startled, Leya stopped at the sudden feel of his absurdly soft hand. *No fireworks, but maybe...*

"If only I could have fallen for a shy and vulnerable girl like you, huh?" He winked and took another swig of his bright blue drink, oblivious to the way his words sliced through her heart.

Leya knew her limitations. She was nothing like the thin, beautiful Tris. *Nope.*

Leya had an ongoing love affair with sweet rolls and mocha lattes that showed. *Okay*, she was overweight, and she knew it.

She exercised regularly and tried to eat sensibly, but sometimes it was difficult. She worked long hours and often ate on-the-go.

Working as an administrative assistant in the big city was non-stop. The job had quickly lost its luster, but she stayed because, well, she'd been afraid to leave.

She had crushed on her boss since meeting him.

Forever it seemed, but finally, *tonight,* she realized he'd never notice her as a woman. He saw her as a secretary and a buddy. *A shoulder to cry on.*

She withdrew her hand from his. Maybe they could have salvaged the meal, but Gary didn't even signal the waitress.

She didn't get a chance to order as he sent the woman for drink after drink! He just kept guzzling his *Blue Hawaiian* and moaning about his girlfriend.

Well, at least one good thing would come of this. She sighed and ran a hand over her pulled back hair.

Leya had to move on. She sighed as she paid the bill, Gary having forgotten his wallet at work. He stood to say goodnight and nearly toppled the table over. *Just great.* She'd have to see the jerk all the way home. *Ugh.*

"I can drive perfectly, I'll be fine. Always drive myself," he grumbled.

"No, really," she insisted.

After about ten minutes of refusing, Gary agreed. As if that wasn't bad enough, the man had suddenly caught a case of *the hands.*

The entire taxi ride, he'd tried to cop a feel, which wasn't all that easy to avoid in such a confined space. His too-soft hands groped her over her clothing no matter how many times she shoved them down onto his own lap.

"That's enough, Gary. Okay, we are here. Thank you," Leya said to the driver as she paid the fare.

"No problem, lady, you sure you don't need any help with him?"

"Um, no thanks, it's okay," she smiled at the man's kindness and exited the cab to find Gary sitting on the curb, attempting to take off his shoes.

"No, don't do that here, Gary!"

"Why not? I'm tired, and my feet hurt!" His whine hurt her ears, and she wondered how she ever imagined herself in love with this baby-man! *Another fantasy bites the dust*, she thought and rolled her eyes before hefting him off the curb.

"You're almost home now. Come on, upsy-daisy," she struggled under his weight as she helped him into the elevator.

Leya used the wall to try and keep him upright, but she lost hold of him when one of his hands suddenly dropped onto her blouse.

"Leya, Leya, *Leya*, you know, you have got one giant pair of boobs on you-"

"Mr. Trainer! Stop that!" She pushed his hand off, mortified by his behavior.

He started to slide down the wall, all the way to

the floor. She had half a mind to leave him there, but being the responsible idiot that she was, she forced herself to help him up again.

She gritted her teeth and grabbed his hand to stop its wandering only to have him push his face way too close to hers.

The smell of sickeningly sweet alcohol made her want to vomit. She turned her face to avoid his slobbering kiss.

"Come on, Leya, *Leeyyaa*, maybe I should *lay ya? Lay ya, Leya*, ha, ha!" He snickered loudly.

She was tempted to drop him where he stood. *The rat!* But she made it this far and she'd see the asshat inside. *Ugh.*

"Mr. Trainer, please remember you're my boss, and this is unprofessional!"

"*Puhleease!* Everyone knows how you feel about me, you know, Tris was even jealous, and I couldn't believe it! I mean look at her and look at you! I told her, Leya is a good secretary, but I am not into chubby virgins!"

Heat burned her cheeks at his drunken admission. Did he really see her as nothing but a fat secretary who'd be so desperate to take what he was offering? *OMG!* And what did he mean *everyone knew?*

Mortification was making it difficult for her to breathe. He continued as if unaware of her sudden stiffness and pallor.

"You're fat, but not bad looking," his hand roamed again, and she was almost too stunned to move, "yeah, I mean, why not, I could take one for the team. So Leya, want me to *lay ya*?"

"What?!" she screeched.

"Come on, maybe I can show you what you're missing, I can knock that halo off your head, a pity-fuck now and then is good for the soul, they say," he giggled like a schoolgirl and dropped his hands to grab her ass. *That's it!* Before she could react, the door opened to reveal a pissed off Tris.

"What the hell?"

"I think this jackass is yours!" Leya said.

"Oh, baby, there you are, I was just, uh-"

"Gary your hands were on her ass!"

"Come on, Tris, you know she doesn't do it for me. She's a fatty nobody, but you're the one I want," as he fumbled with his apologies, Leya, narrowed her eyes and unceremoniously pushed him.

Gary stumbled forward, caught off guard. He surged forward and knocked over Tris. They both stared at her from their positions on the floor of his apartment with their mouths hanging open.

"Leya?"

"You little tramp-"

"*Nuh uh*, you don't get to call me names. That's it, I have had it. Mr. Trainor, I quit!"

With those words ringing in her ears, Leya Tremayne took the stairs two at a time. She stood outside trembling in the chilly night air as she hailed another cab. The noise and lights of the big city were nothing more than a blur through her unshed tears and the noise in her head.

She went home to her apartment and the first thing she did was turn on her laptop. After sending two short but sweet emails, one to HR and one to Gary.

She informed them both of her decision to quit without notice and thanking Gary for his generous agreement to giving her two-weeks' pay up front. *Take that you jerk*. She also gave them instructions on where to send the few personal items she left in the office.

Afterwards, Leya looked around her rental. It was a decent size, but it was sparse. As if she'd just moved in. She sighed and closed her eyes as she realized she hadn't made a single *real* friend in the two years since she'd left her parents' home and travelled to the big city to work for that jerk!

She was tired of being unappreciated and *pitied*! Leya sucked in a breath, willing herself to calm down. What she needed was a fresh start! But first, a little rest and relaxation.

Minutes later with an airline ticket and hotel room booked, Leya let out a long sigh.

Paradise, here I come!

CHAPTER

TWO

Marcus breathed in the warm, hibiscus-scented air and smiled. His Bear chuffed and snorted in his mind's eye. The huge beast happy with their little escape. *Paradise!*

A little business mixed with a few nights on the beach was just what the Bear ordered! He'd worry about finding someone to settle down with later. *Ugh. Settle.* He hated that word.

Once upon a time he would have wanted something else, something like Ignatius and Dolores Devlin had! His great-great grandparents were rumored to be truly *matebonded* as only *fated mates* could be.

Such an occurrence was a rarity among Shifters.

33

His father told him the tale of their love when he was just a cub. But Marcus didn't believe in fairytales anymore.

His mother and father had a strong no-nonsense kind of marriage until his mother died. His father mourned her in his way, they all did. It had been three years now.

His father retired from the bakery, but he still ran their small Clan. He was whole after his wife's death, leading Marcus to believe that his parents were not a truly matebonded couple. They were not fated mates. Maybe it really did only exist in fairytales?

He shrugged. *So, what?* He just needed someone to fill this ache in his chest, to settle his Bear, then his life could continue like it had been. But first things, first, *vacation time.*

"Welcome, Mr. Devlin!"

"Hi, Mr. Gordon," Marcus had been in contact with the hotel manager the past few days organizing his stay.

He nodded and took the man's hand careful not to squeeze it too hard. Mr. Gordon was a *normal.* Marcus looked around the huge lobby of the hotel and smiled. The open concept was fluid and very modern, unlike most of the other hotels, he stayed at.

This one had undergone renovations recently, and Marcus approved. The lobby was large and clean. *Inviting* was the word that came to mind.

The guests seemed to think so too as they milled about with wide, happy smiles on their sunburnt faces. This was going to be the perfect place to relax before he went back home and resumed his search for a mate. Mr. Gordon motioned for a bellhop to come and take Marcus' bags.

"Shall I show you to your room, Mr. Devlin?"

"Let me drop in on the store first. I've missed Mrs. Leeds."

"Ah, certainly, sir! The Bear Claw is a most welcome addition, and the guests are raving about it!"

"Great to hear, Gordon."

"Certainly! I will send your things up ahead of you."

"Thanks."

"Anytime, sir!"

Marcus nodded and turned to the shining glass doors of the Bear Claw Bakery. When he entered, he was greeted with the familiar scents of their famous morning honey buns and sweet raisin rolls.

His smile grew broader as his impeccable sense

of smell told him Mrs. Leeds followed his instructions regarding their signature recipes to perfection.

"Mr. Devlin! I see you've come to check on me!" a booming, accented voice reached his ears.

"I see you've added that coconut honey bun we've been discussing to the menu? I'll take two to go and a large iced coffee, black, darling!" He greeted the older woman with a warm hug and friendly smile.

"Oh, yes! You will love it, I am sure! Right away, sir!" She smiled at him and swatted him playfully when he tugged open her apron strings.

"You tease, now if you go wandering round the island this visit, you just watch yourself, a pack of wild dogs was seen just last week over at your favorite lookout point, Mr. Marcus," she told him and giggled like a girl when he kissed her round cheek.

Her hands went to tidy her pretty, gray braids as she moved quickly behind the counter and told a young man to fill his order in her native tongue. She smiled at him with all the warmth of a grandma to her young cub and he grinned like one back.

"Thanks for the warning, dear."

Cheerful music played through the speakers, as Marcus quickly checked the equipment over. After taking a few notes and listening to some of his feisty manager's suggestions, Marcus took his bag of goodies and his iced coffee and left the store.

He was proud of Mrs. Leeds. She'd been an unemployed housekeeper when she came in for the interview. Older than what he would have liked, she was proud and determined.

He'd been dubious about her skill, but he soon found that she not only had a head for business but in the kitchen, her fingers were pure magic.

Later, she brought on two grandsons, a daughter, and her brother, to work for him. He liked the idea of the place being run by a local family, and he readily hired each one of them.

In just a few days, the Leeds family learned how to run and operate the small branch of Bear Claw Bakery. Marcus and his brothers had been thrilled!

They were loyal, hardworking, and, they were Shifters, not unlike him and his brothers. The Leeds were Cormorant Shifters, a type of bird native to the island that evolved to be expert fishermen.

Mrs. Leeds and her kin were excellent additions to the Bear Claw Bakery family. Marcus was more than happy with their performance. He paid well, unlike most jobs on the island, and he offered benefits too. Yes, indeed, Marcus liked his new hires.

He lingered in the shop a few minutes until Mrs. Leeds went back to the ovens. He sipped his coffee and stood up to head for his room.

Shit, he thought and patted his pants pockets. He never got his key! *Ugh.* With a sigh, he yelled goodbye to Mrs. Leeds and headed back towards the concierge.

He took a deep breath, shaking his head in the process. A hauntingly sweet aroma filtered into his nostrils, stopping him suddenly in his tracks.

What the-? His Bear stood up in his mind and roared. Loudly. *The fuck, dude?*

His Bear was not hearing him. The more than eight-hundred-pound beast was literally doing somersaults and roaring so fucking loudly that Marcus almost fell to the floor with the force of it.

What was the source of that amazing fucking smell? Like honey and flowers, a sweet heady musk that made everything else pale in comparison. This scent was everything!

He needed to find it. *Now. Must. Want. Need.* The elusive source of the fragrance was driving him nuts. He inhaled a great deep breath. He took it down inside of himself and savored its flavors. *Warm and sweet. Sexy as hell. MINE.* That one word had his knees buckling.

He turned towards the head concierge. The scent was stronger in that direction. It was like heaven. All his favorite things. Honey buns and lavender. It was like *home* and *warmth*, *sex* and *need, possession* and *sweetness* all rolled into one.

His head turned and he stilled. A predator that had found his prey. The source of that delectable honey and lavender mix. The fount of that tantalizing scent was very near.

Perhaps behind the large plant that obstructed her from his view. *Need to find her now.* And it was a *her*, that much he knew.

His blood thundered in his ears as he sought the source of his torment. *Yes.* It was a woman. At least he thought so, but it was hard to tell under that hideous frock she wore.

He frowned as he took her in from head to toe. This was the cause of his heart pounding so hard he thought he was having an attack of some kind? *WTF?* He breathed in again, yup, it was her.

At first look, she was nothing special. She was in her late twenties, medium height, but what stood out besides the tendrils of blonde hair that escaped the ugly ass bun she'd tortured her locks into, and the no-nonsense set to her shoulders, was an outfit so utterly unflattering that the words butt-ugly would be a kindness.

The woman was talking to one of the hotel greeters, but he missed the sound of her voice as he pondered why someone would wear *that*? Did she have no sense of style? Was she color blind?

"Hello, welcome to Moongate Island!"

"Thank you, um, can you help me?"

Marcus was staring. He couldn't help it. The woman smelled like heaven, but she looked like hell. She wasn't ugly, well, not that he could really make out her face, but her outfit was decidedly unattractive.

Mine, his beast growled. Apparently, his Bear didn't give a fuck about her lack of style. She'd be naked most of the time anyway. Naked he could do. He supposed he could live with it. If he had to. He frowned at her.

Puke-green slacks hugged her legs and hips, *long legs and well-rounded hips*, he was happy to note, but the color was hideous. Thankfully, she somewhat covered the glaring pants with an oversized, long-sleeved blouse.

Unfortunately, said blouse was printed with huge flowers in pink, orange, and that same puke green. Whoever designed the shirt must have stolen it off a 1970s sofa reject. *Yikes!*

He started to turn away, he'd best think about how to approach the unfortunately dressed woman. but he'd moved too slow. She spotted his blatant interest. *Fuck, now I have to talk to her.* He was pissed as hell at the thought, but then he saw what the plant and her sunglasses had hidden from him.

Startling blue eyes in a heart-shaped face met his. *Holy shit!* He was a goner. *Fucking beautiful.* She glared at him and her lips pressed into a thin line before she ignored him. His Bear roared at her disinterest.

Had she just dismissed him without a second glance? No fucking way. But that was exactly what she'd done.

She turned back to talk to the concierge. Marcus growled and stared at her even harder. *Turn around and look at me,* he willed, but she did not budge.

Ugly clothes or not, she had the most beautiful eyes he'd ever seen. They were the color of a September sky. Clear and bright, they were easily the bluest eyes he'd ever witnessed. *Utterly breathtaking.*

His stomach tightened as he inhaled her scent. *Tupelo honey with the faintest hints of English lavender.*

He imagined she'd taste just as sweet on his tongue. *Grrr.*

He felt his Bear's possessive growl tremble through his body. His fingertips ached, and his gums itched, his Bear desperate to make an appearance. *Uh oh.*

He should get as far away from her as possible. The thought was met with more rumblings from his Bear. He wanted her now in his den where he could stake his claim.

We must leave her for now, he told his inner beast. *She is a normal and doesn't know of our kind, best not frighten her,* his attempt to soothe the Bear was met with anger and impatience. Finally, he dominated the Bear with a single growled thought. *Back off.*

His self-preservation instincts were nothing compared to his Black Bear's drive for him to find his mate. *Fucking terrible clothes or not, this woman is mine. MINE.*

Still, he knew better than to frighten her. Marcus exhaled, but couldn't stem the slow growl that crept up from his throat. Her eyes jumped back to his and he covered up the noise with a cough. She frowned.

Time's up, Romeo. I need to get out of here. He should really move, but his legs refused to work.

The urge to gather her up in his arms and sniff

her from head to toe was damn near overwhelming. He unconsciously stepped closer to the woman. His Bear rumbled with happiness at her nearness.

"Can I help you?" his mate asked. He felt his cheeks heat and realized he'd been caught ogling her. He grew even redder as she regarded impatiently.

"I said, can I help you? Mister?" Her voice was husky and rich, music to his ears, but it was her wide eyes that held him hypnotized.

"Mr. Devlin, your key!" his attention was brought back to Mr. Gordon who was waving his card key in the air. *What the fuck am I doing?*

"Sorry, excuse me," he murmured and quickly turned away from her.

No way. We're not doing this here! He fought the Bear for dominance and won. Though his chest was heaving with the effort.

He turned to Mr. Gordon and gathered his key, nodding at her on his way to the elevator. This time he managed to avoid eye contact.

His Bear snarled and growled at him, but he refused to listen. He was here for two things, work first, then relaxation. Not to find his fucking mate in some *normal.* She was a badly dressed tourist on vacation for shit's sake!

Too late, fucker. She is the one. Normal or not.

His Bear seemed to smirk at him. Hints of her honey sweet scent filtered through the cooling system of the hotel and Marcus groaned. He was so fucked.

CHAPTER

THREE

Leya sighed and took in the incredible view of the ocean from her room. Moongate Island was situated in the Atlantic, but this was unlike any water she'd ever seen on her brief trips to the shore.

It was crystal clear and almost teal in color. The waves tickled the sand with foam, and dozens of tiny little fish swam just a few feet from the hotel guests.

She longed to go down to the surf and frolic and play. Leya watched the couples scattered all over the sand. Each one an island unto themselves. She sighed, a little green with envy.

Oh well, at least I'm here. She had to stop daydreaming about finding true love. It clearly wasn't gonna happen for her.

Instead, she needed to concentrate on the paradise she'd landed in! It was all so beautiful, and she could see every inch of Moongate Island from right there!

By some lucky twist of fate, she'd learned that the bargain rate room she'd booked was uninhabitable when she arrived. Some water damage or some such thing.

The hotel manager insisted she accept a luxury suite without any additional charges to make up for it. Leya happily agreed. She was due some perks in life, and a free upgrade was a fine way to begin her vacation.

After her disastrous encounter with the gorgeous stranger in the lobby of the hotel, she was determined to enjoy herself. *Oh boy, was he hot!*

Of course, she noticed the huge man when his blatant stare had become obvious. Of course it wasn't all coming up roses, for Leya, the man had a fierce scowl on his perfect face as his eyes bore holes into her.

She doubted it was anything good that kept him staring. Then she had to go and open her big mouth, but whatever. He had no right to give her dirty looks! Just because he was hot as hell and she was, well, *her.*

Okay, so she wasn't exactly used to big, good-looking men staring at her and as a result, she hadn't been the friendliest when she spoke. He'd apologized and skedaddled out of there as fast as his long legs could carry him.

Oh well, nothing was going to come of that encounter anyway, so why mourn the loss? Leya shrugged to herself. For some reason, she'd missed the big guy when he'd walked away.

He was so out of my league, she stopped the thought. Leya had to get over this whole she wasn't good enough thing.

How often did she come across a man who made her heart pound and her mouth water? Not fucking often. *That's it,* she scolded herself. *No more hiding!*

"Here's to the first day of the rest of my life," she smiled and sipped from her complimentary champagne.

Not a big drinker, her first impulse had been to refuse the gift basket from the hotel staff. She was glad now that she didn't. The bubbly drink soothed her nerves. It was like sipping sunshine.

She walked to the large bedroom and unpacked her carry-on luggage. What had she been thinking? Leya frowned at her clothes.

She picked up item after item, tossing them to

the polished floor. *I dress like an old lady.* So many years wasted trying to hide her ample figure under oversized tunics and slacks. She resembled a piece of furniture most of the time!

The green outfit she had on was a gift she'd received last Christmas. She hated it, but since it fit her, she figured why waste an outfit. *Oh Leya, you should've thrown it away!*

Society spent billions in the fashion industry convincing women like Leya that they should hide their bodies. She knew it was wrong and biased, but thin was in! And she was not thin in any way shape or form.

She caught herself in the mirror and cringed. *No wonder tall, dark, and studly stared. I look like an old cat lady's couch!*

She tore off the offending clothing and tossed it across the room. *Uh! I know, a swim might cheer me up!* Leya had one swimsuit and groaned as she put it on. *Dear Lord!* She shook her head in disgust. *Well, this is what you get for ordering from a catalogue.*

It was the wrong color. The wrong size. And it made her body look short and puffy. Her bust was uncomfortably pushed down, and her butt looked enormous. *OMG! I am a mess!* She frowned as she turned around in the mirror.

"No freaking way," she put back on her ugly green outfit and left her room. *First thing on my vacation-to-do-list, shopping!*

She was looking through her wallet when she walked right into something. It was hard and immovable. *A wall, perhaps? In the middle of the hallway...*

"Oof!" Leya swayed, but strong hands reached out to steady her. Large, rough hands, *hmm*, definitely not the soft manicured hands of her ex-boss.

She'd thought about him with nothing but distaste for the last twenty-four hours. But all those thoughts went right out of her head as those strong hands that steadied her, suddenly pulled her closer.

She tilted her head back, eyes going wide with a mixture of surprise and, *oh yes*, desire. She was helpless to do anything but stare as the gorgeous giant from the lobby bent his head to her throat and *sniffed*.

"What are you-" before she could finish her question he straightened and stepped back.

"Easy there, you should watch where you're going. You okay?" the man's voice was as rough as his hands.

Not unpleasant, just deep and very, very masculine. She squirmed under his gaze and wondered if it was possible to die of humiliation twice in one day. But back up a sec...

Did he just sniff her? Maybe she imagined that? She looked up into impossibly dark brown eyes and was once again stunned silent.

His eyes were like molten chocolate, the sinfully expensive kind. The planes of his face gave way to full luscious lips that she'd just bet tasted like heaven. And he had the cutest little dimple in his chin.

He cleared his throat and her gaze went back to his. Was that a smile playing at the corner of his mouth? She couldn't be sure, captivated as she was by his now, nearly black eyes. Recognition flared between them, and Leya gasped.

"Uh, sorry, I was just going to get a new bathing suit-" she shut her mouth abruptly.

"Were you now? Well, you be careful," he grumbled the words and turned away from her.

Leya shivered unconsciously against the sudden cold that came with his departure. She could have kicked herself. Could she have acted any more like an idiot? *Ugh.*

She looked down at her dowdy clothing. Maybe if she didn't dress like a circus tent, he would've done more than just glance at her and run away. *Yeah, right.*

She narrowed her eyes and shook her head. She was not going to let a man, *any man*, dictate how she felt about herself. She wanted to change her wardrobe for herself.

Not because Gary had called her fat, or because this gorgeous stranger left her tongue-tied. With new determination in her step, she took the elevator and headed to the exclusive boutique.

"Can I help you find something, miss?" the question was asked by an older woman with a brilliant smile as Leya entered the hotel's one boutique and scanned the rows of colorful dresses and flimsy underthings.

She had never tried to dress for anything other than camouflage, and she had no idea where to begin.

"Yes, I, uh, think I could use your help," she smiled and told the woman what she wanted.

The saleswoman seemed to be blessed with a perfect eye for her body shape and coloring! An hour later, Leya had several items lined up for purchase and was still trying on more.

"Ah, miss! Yes! Yes, this is the one for you! The yellow looks wonderful with your lovely hair, it accentuates your blonde highlights! Oh, mama those men out there best be on guard!" The lightly accented voice of the woman who ran the *Island Body Boutique* smiled and complimented Leya.

For the first time in her adult life, Leya felt wonderful. She turned around in front of the full-length mirror and could hardly believe it. The cut and color of the swimsuit looked amazing on her full figure. She'd have never guessed yellow for her hair and skin tone, but the woman was right.

She added the swimsuit to a similarly cut red one along with a few sundresses, and some of those flimsy panties and bras she would normally have never dared to buy.

Leya grinned wickedly. She had money in her savings and had never splurged on herself. She justified the purchases as necessary for her vacation and her new life motto! Leya was going to please herself this trip! *Yep, this is gonna be great!* Gleefully walking down the hall, she went to her hotel room to change.

She'd spent three hours total in the boutique! Thank goodness the hotel sported a Bear Claw Bakery! Liandra, the saleswoman, had gotten her an iced mocha latte about an hour ago. Otherwise she'd have been dead on her feet.

It was too late to swim, but there was always

tomorrow! Liandra told her about the light buffet and live band at the tiki lounge right on the beach, it was there every night from five till midnight. It was seven now, and Leya had skipped lunch in favor of shopping.

She smiled. *Second thing on my vacation-to-do-list, let my hair down!*

FOUR

She's here. Mate. Mine. Claim. Now. Marcus' Bear was practically bellowing in his mind for him to go get the woman.

The beast had no problem recognizing her as his mate. Ugly clothes or not. Not that Marcus really gave a shit about what she wore. She had the most beautiful eyes he'd ever seen. *Shit! She's a normal.*

What was he going to do? The woman was a stranger, a human for fuck's sake! He couldn't just walk up to her and say, *hey there, my name is Marcus, and I can change into a big furry bear, who by the way, has chosen you for his mate, so do you want to come home with me and get to work on making some babies?* This was so fucking bad.

Marcus paced back and forth across the wide

floors of his luxury suite. His Bear roared again. *Quiet!* He demanded. He needed to think. To come up with a plan.

Hell, he needed a fucking drink too, but first he needed a minute to regain his control. His Bear was too close for him to leave the room.

It took all his strength and concentration to wrestle his Bear back to a relatively passive state, but Marcus knew it was too late. He'd sniffed his mate, and he wanted her. *Now.*

The buxom beauty didn't know it yet, but she was his. *Time for that plan.* Oh, he had one alright. The first thing he wanted to do was peel off those ugly clothes to see just what she was hiding underneath.

Then he wanted to run his hands all over her. Quickly followed by his mouth. Then his tongue. *Yes.* Licking was good. He'd make sure his mate was ready. Hot and wet just for him and he'd lick her sweet, sweet honey. Swallow it all down. *Grrr. Mine.*

Easy now. His Bear roared. Clearly the beast thought he should move his ass. *No. Slow it down, pal.*

He should figure out his approach before he started imagining the curves that he instinctively knew his mate was hiding. He'd make sure she knew just how beautiful she was to him. That would be a fucking priority.

Marcus groaned. He closed his eyes, reciting multiplication tables. He tried to ignore the way his dick instantly flared to life at the mere thought of his mate's lush curves. *Fuck*, his shorts were getting damned uncomfortable.

He knew he was in serious trouble if just imagining what her body would look like caused him to react like a green teenager. If her body proved half as lovely as her face, he knew he'd find heaven there.

She was made for him. *Literally.* There was no doubt in his mind she was his one true and fated mate. He smoothed a hand over his chest, his heart hammered away regardless of his efforts to calm down.

He simply couldn't stop thinking about those sexy as hell eyes of hers. They had to be the most intense blue he'd ever seen. So blue they looked violet.

But what else? A mate was for life. Surely, they'd have more than just sex between them. He wondered if her mind was as quick and bright as her eyes promised.

The brief physical contact he shared with her in the hallway when she'd walked into him was enough to shoot awareness to every single one of his nerve endings.

He was shaking like a boy just remembering the feel of her! *Would she be as soft as her shapely curves promised?* Sure, she tried to hide them underneath that ridiculously oversized blouse she wore, but Marcus knew better.

He was just as anxious to know her mind. She'd been aware of him, he could smell her arousal, but she'd retained the ability to speak. *Unlike him.*

And the way she took him to task in the lobby for staring? She was feisty! He liked that. Marcus couldn't wait to verbally spar with her. Almost as much as he couldn't wait to get his hands on her.

Marcus wanted to strip her slowly and run his hands over every single inch of her. *Fuck, eight times fifteen equals...*

It was no good. Math was no match for the pull of his mate. His Bear was going into overdrive. He wanted her now, beneath him, hard and fast. He wanted to bury himself inside her, to feel her sheath him as perfectly as he knew she would. This woman was made for him.

His Bear was too riled up to be gentle. He wanted to rip off her clothes and stake his claim in the worst possible way, but that would be nuts.

He knew nothing about her! Marcus ran a frustrated hand over his face. His father had warned him in his youth that meeting his mate would be unlike anything he'd ever felt.

He'd listened dutifully to his father, but he never expected anything like this. He spent all of three minutes in the woman's company, and he was like a horny teenager, hard as a fucking rock and aching like a damned cub!

Fuck! He needed time to think and plan his next move. And yes, he'd definitely be doing that over a drink. He left his room and held his breath as he passed her door. The last thing he needed was a whiff of her tupelo honey scent.

He barreled through the hotel doors onto the private beach. The cooling sand felt good under his feet. His flip-flops dangled from his fingers as he kicked along the surf.

Sunset on the island was beautiful, though he rarely had time to enjoy it. Even now when he took the time, it was bittersweet. Marcus had no one to share the moment with.

Claim her. He sucked in the salty sea air and stared out at the horizon. He'd be thirty-five this coming winter. He was alone except for his brothers and their business.

It was high time he settled down and had a family of his own. Maybe he could get used to the idea that he'd found his mate after all?

Marcus was sweating despite the cool breeze coming off the water. He unbuttoned his shirt about halfway down, but he still felt too warm. It was all this business about his mate. He needed to leave it for today. Maybe he could approach her with it slowly.

He ordered a tumbler of *Clover Bite* from a passing waiter. He gave the guy a big tip when he came back just moments later with his glass of artisan whiskey over two moon shaped ice cubes. He tossed it back and closed his eyes as the sweet, yet fiery liquor burned its way down his throat. *What was he going to do?*

He shook his head and sat down on the wrought iron chair and stared off into the distance. The sounds of laughter and music faded as he thought of how he would go about getting her to listen to him, but he had no real idea. This was new territory for him.

More laughter erupted from the bar, but he ignored it. Marcus hated crowds, but he didn't relish the idea of having to walk a half mile every time he wanted a refill. So, he settled for a lone table and chair down the few stone steps off the patio where the hotel's one and fabulously crowded tiki bar sat. At least the waiter would see him from there.

He shook his head and ignored the revelers. *Normals* had a way of turning even the most innocent evenings out into some sort of frat party nightmare. He wanted no part of the drama.

Judging from the hooting and hollering coming from the direction of the bar, another victim just walked in. He shook his head. Poor little lamb, she probably had no idea she just walked into the lion's den.

Oh well, it was none of his business anyway...

FIVE

Leya sucked in a breath as she stepped onto the stone patio of the hotel's most popular outdoor bar, the *Moongate Tiki Lounge*. She exhaled as she took in the décor.

It certainly felt like paradise! Not the cheesy replicas she'd come across in the city at any rate. No, this place looked as if it had been carved into the landscape. Plants and blooming flowers erupted in a riot of color in every available space.

There was a mini waterfall behind the main bar, and that was lit with stylish multi-colored LED lights. Primitive masks decorated stone walls and enormous torches lit up every corner.

A live band played a vibrant reggae beat that made Leya wish she knew how to dance. Still, she smiled and swayed to the rhythm as she walked over to an empty chair.

This was exactly what she wanted in a vacation! She threw her head back and took in the stars and the cool breeze coming off the ocean. The night was magical! She bit her lip as she took a step further inside the exotic paradise.

Her dress was a deep blue color that brought out her eyes. It was shorter than anything she had ever worn before with a fitted bodice and flare skirt.

Judging from the frankly appraising glances of the people she'd passed on the way to the bar, it was apparently as flattering as Liandra had said. *Not that she cared about other people's opinions*, she told herself firmly.

The dress was fun and flirty and made her feel good. That was all that counted. Yes, she did feel kind of exposed, but this was the first day of her new adventurous life. A new wardrobe was a requirement!

And this dress was certainly new! The elastic bodice and off-the-shoulder cap sleeves didn't allow for the heavy minimizer bra she often wore. The bulky beige thing was now in the trash can of her hotel room with most of the clothes she'd brought from home.

Leya shocked herself today when she added several, teeny, tiny bits of lace that passed for under garments to her purchases at the boutique. Again, necessary, she told herself.

Each one of the twenty-two-dollar pairs of underwear were needed to accommodate her new wardrobe! The matching bras were simply a given. Some of them hardly covered her ample assets, but Liandra assured her she looked good. And she believed her.

She bit her lip and looked down at the cleavage spilling from her top. *Too much too soon?* A whistle brought her head up, and she was shocked to see a group of young men drinking at the bar waving and trying to get her attention.

They weren't her style, but she wasn't rude by nature, so she waved back, but she managed to find an empty seat far away from them. It was probably best to ignore them.

She found an empty seat a good distance away and set about having a good time. *Operation let my hair down is a go!* After some pleasant conversation with the bartender, and a few other hotel guests, Leya realized she was actually having a good time.

"What else can I get you, sweet lady?" the happy

bartender asked her with his pleasantly accented voice, and she smiled back at him.

"Do you carry any *Bite*?" she asked.

She was happy to note that they did and ordered a glass for herself. She was talking to an older couple from Chicago who were on the island for their twentieth anniversary when the bartender placed a brightly colored cocktail in front of her.

She scrunched her nose. Leya hated the overly sweet drinks. *Especially after Gary.* Leya preferred her favorite brand of top-shelf whiskey served over ice in a short glass any day to the candy named concoction in front of her.

"From an admirer, miss," he said and winked.

Leya eyed the blue cocktail distastefully and asked him to send it back with her regards, but *no thank you.* She didn't think anything of it until someone grabbed her arm and spun her around in her chair.

"Hey, now, that drink was from me! Now, I'm sure you didn't mean to be rude. Let me introduce myself, my name is Alec, now tell me, did it hurt?" The young blonde man held her arm tightly in his grip. He reeked of alcohol, and his speech was slurred as he spoke. Leya yanked her arm back and narrowed her eyes at him.

"Look, I appreciate the gesture, but I'm afraid I don't take drinks from strangers."

"Well, okay now, Miss Goody-two-shoes, but you didn't answer me, I said, did it hurt?"

"Excuse me?"

"When you fell from Heaven?" he looked back at his buddies who were busy snickering and whistling from their end of the bar. Leya had enough of this nonsense. She dropped a bill on the counter and turned to the older couple she'd been chatting with.

"I'm sorry to leave so soon, you two have a nice anniversary," she said. *Maybe bars weren't good places to start adventures after all*, she thought to herself.

"Hey, what about me?" *Mr. Grabby* followed her across the floor and took hold of her elbow this time. Leya did not like that at all. She'd almost gotten away too! *Ugh.*

"Look, pal take your hand off me," she said and tugged her arm, but it was no good, blondie was stronger than he looked.

"Now, look here, you don't want to embarrass me in front of my friends. Come on, let's dance," he grabbed her hip with his other hand and tried to drag her against him.

"Ooh, hey, I don't want to dance with you!"

"Sure, you do, come on," he rubbed against her suggestively to the hoots and cheers of his pals.

"I said let go!" She yanked herself back with more strength than she realized. *Oh crap*, and that was when she lost her footing.

"Damn it!" She yelled as she tipped backwards, wind-milling her arms. The force of her pull with the strength of gravity all worked against her as she felt herself fall backwards, down the three stairs that led to the beach.

She closed her eyes and braced herself, but instead of the jarring impact she expected, Leya landed on something hard. *Hard, but warm.*

Day-um. Leya gasped and looked up into familiar brown eyes.

"Didn't I tell you to watch where you were going?" His teasing voice reached her ears, a low grumble over the sounds of the tiki bar.

The things that voice was doing to her! *Oh my!* Her rescuer looked down at her with an amused expression on his face. If it wasn't for the way his dark eyes raked over her body, she'd think he was laughing at her.

"Oh, um, I-"

"Hey, lady, damn, I just wanted to dance!" The

blonde looked down the stairs in horror at her near miss and Leya scowled.

She lifted herself into a sitting position, but firm hands held her waist where she would have stood up. She ignored that. *For now.*

"Steady now," he murmured, his lips tickling her ear. She ignored the thrill that went through her and focused instead on the young clout who made her fall.

"I don't want to dance with you, you-" she was visibly shaken. Her rescuer spoke to her, close enough she felt his warm breath on her neck send shivers down her spine.

"Mind if I handle this?" he asked, and at her nod he turned.

She watched as his expression changed from teasing sweetness to pure threat. He addressed the cocky fool who'd grabbed her without moving her from her place on his lap.

"Son, you best turn around back to your friends if you know what's good for you," he said in a deep voice that practically growled in his throat and made her knees turn to jelly.

"No problem, man!" The younger man backed away hands raised.

"Well, this is cozy and all, but suppose we see if you can stand up alright?"

Leya felt her face heat up furiously. She was still sitting on the guy's lap, for Pete's sake! She was probably crushing him.

"I am so sorry! I must be hurting you!"

"Hurting me? A little thing like you? Darlin', I could sit like this all night. I just want to make sure you didn't get hurt when you fell," his gaze dropped, and she heard him suck in a breath.

"Oh, uh, no, I'm fine, but I am not little-" she looked down and saw why he was having difficulty breathing. Her elastic top was pulled down, and her breasts were almost completely bared to his and everyone else's' eyes. *Yikes!*

"No, baby, you are not," he growled.

She yelped and stood up quickly. Scrambling off his lap and tugging the fabric back in place. She didn't even realize the hand he kept solidly on her waist.

She tried taking a step back, but he stood up too. His hand firm and solidly on her body. The feel of him singed her through the layer of material. She didn't feel intimidated by him. *No.* She felt warm all over. She wanted to lean into his touch.

Oh Lord, Leya shook her head and looked up at

him from her high-heeled sandals. The man was huge! He had to be well over six-feet tall, and twice her width! There wasn't an ounce of fat on the guy.

He looked like a bodybuilder or football player or something. He was so big. She actually did feel small standing next to him. That was a novelty in itself! One she would love to get used to.

"Um, thank you so much," she whispered, unable to break the spell of his intoxicating stare.

"I'm Marcus," he said. His eyes sparkled in the moonlight like onyx as he looked down at her.

"My name is Leya."

"Like the princess?"

"Yeah, sort of," she laughed even though she'd heard that one a time or two in her life.

"Your folks George Lucas fans?"

"Yes, well, my dad really, but my mother insisted the spelling be different. It's L-e-y-a."

"Beautiful," he said, and again her knees turned to jelly.

"Thanks. It's a cool name I guess."

"I don't mean your name, though that's lovely too."

"Oh."

The fingers on her waist became caressing, leaving little flames of excitement wherever he touched. She could feel the heat coming off of him through the thin layers of her dress as he swayed closer to her.

This was new, she thought, *different and magical.* She didn't have much experience with giant good-looking men, but she was definitely game to try.

The sound of the waves crashing drowned out the band from the bar. Or was that the sound of her blood pounding inside of her head? Leya didn't know, she only knew she felt hot and swollen all over.

Leya wanted, *oh yes,* she wanted alright. *Him. She wanted him.* She never did have much luck when it came to men, but for some reason, this man, here and now, felt so right to her.

She licked her lips and watched his eyes follow the movement. He seemed to tense. The rumbling sound from his chest increased. She watched as he closed his eyes and exhaled before pinning her with his gaze.

"Have dinner with me?"

"Yes," she said immediately.

She knew it was fast, fast and crazy, but it felt right. He took her hand in his large, callused one and together they walked towards the hotel.

"Do you like seafood?"

"Yes," suddenly she was reduced to one-word answers. *You dope, talk to him!*

"Great," he smiled at her.

It was one of those thousand-watt smiles she'd only ever read about, sexy and sinful. Full of secrets and promises. She felt her heart turn over in her chest. No one had ever looked at her like that.

He had straight, white teeth and a small dimple on the right corner of his mouth. His hair was a deep, dark brown and fell in rakishly handsome waves to his shoulders.

His eyes were darker by a shade and reminded her of the expensive Blue Mountain coffee she infrequently indulged in. The expensive drink was rich and sweet, lacking the bitterness of cheaper blends.

I wonder if he tastes like that. Smooth and rich. She felt her cheeks warm and realized she must be blushing furiously. He didn't seem to notice, *thank goodness,* as he approached the hotel manager.

He squeezed her hand, and ten minutes later they were seated in the hotel's most exclusive restaurant. She smiled in appreciation.

"Uh, what do you like?"

"Oh, well, obviously I like everything," she felt her cheeks heat up again and looked down at the table.

"Why 'obviously'?" he looked genuinely confused, and Leya could have kicked herself for her stupidity.

Now, wasn't the time to bring up her weight problem, though he could see for himself that she had one. *Best just say it.*

"Oh, well, I mean, you know, I'm not, I mean," she took a breath and looked directly at him, "It's obvious I enjoy food." Leya frowned when he sat there quietly as if waiting for her to continue. *What more needed to be said?*

"I'm not thin, you know," still nothing, "Fine, I'm fat! Okay?" she hissed at him. Damn the man for making her spell it out! And she had such high hopes too...

Her face was burning, and she bit her lip wishing she could take back the last few minutes of their time together.

Leya had never felt such a powerful attraction to a man before, and she had to ruin it with her idiotic confession. He wasn't blind, he could see what she looked like! *And yet he still asked you to dinner.*

As she mulled over whether or not to bolt for the door, he placed his large hand over hers and leaned forward dwarfing the small round table where they were seated. She had no choice but to look at him as it seemed he wasn't going to release her hand until she did.

Oh boy, might as well get this over with, she thought before looking him squarely in the eyes. She'd been friend-zoned often enough to read the signs.

He was definitely about to tell her she was a great gal and didn't need to worry about her weight with him. *Yadda yadda.* She swallowed her disappointment and sat facing him.

If only he wasn't so good to look at. *Oh well.* As if reading her thoughts, he dropped his gaze and boldly swept his eyes over the mounds of flesh that were revealed in the snug top of the dress she wore.

Leya felt hot all over from that stare. His brown eyes darkened to almost black as his stare seemed to penetrate the tabletop, the dress, anything that was in the way.

It was as if he was looking at her naked. An idea that she found she didn't quite mind. *Well, that's certainly different.*

"Leya, I don't know who's been feeding you that line of garbage and, believe me when I say I would gladly pound every single one of them to a bloody pulp if you'd like, but first things first," his voice was gravelly and deep.

She could hardly keep up with what he was saying, especially, when his thumb was running over the top of her hand in slow seductive circles that made her want to drool. *Spit it out, buddy, before I embarrass myself!*

"*You* look exactly the way a woman should look. Baby, you are incredible," his voice went even deeper as he traced every visible line of her body with those molten eyes of his.

Leya released the breath she'd been holding. Her entire body seemed to sizzle with awareness. Small trembles danced along her skin under the heat of his penetrating gaze. *Did he mean it?*

He sure looked like he did. He didn't release her hand, not even when the waiter came and left their menus on the table. She hardly noticed, captivated by what he'd said, what he was still saying with his eyes and that wicked thumb of his.

He wants me. Me! She felt hot all over at the realization, powerful and indescribably sexy for the first time in her life. Desire flared between them. No doubt, her entire body was turning beet red under her clothes.

Even her breasts seemed to warm and swell at his words. He moved his thumb to the soft side of her wrist, and Leya's lips parted. When had a touch, any touch, never mind one as innocent as this one, caused such delicious friction inside of her?

She waited as he leaned even closer to her. *Okay, not friend-zoned, but what now,* she thought. Marcus looked as if he was about to say something, but the waiter interrupted them.

He leaned back in his chair, but not before lifting her hand to his mouth and kissing her fingertips. He lifted the menu and spoke. His voice a deep rumble that sent shivers down her spine.

"Do you mind if I go ahead?"

"With what?" She sounded breathless, but she didn't care. No one had ever looked at her or talked to her quite like that.

"With ordering, for the two of us?"

"Oh, sure, that's fine," she smiled.

It was old-fashioned, but Leya kind of liked it. Besides, there wasn't a dish she'd met that she didn't like. She sat back and listened as this gorgeous stranger proceeded to order for them both. Well, she quickly learned he had good taste in food at least.

He ordered a chilled seafood tower that promised exquisite delicacies such as raw oysters, clams, boiled shrimp, crab legs, and lobster claws. Next, they were to sample some of the hotel's famous conch chowder, followed by broiled Chilean sea bass served with a creamy spinach risotto on the side.

Then he finished the order with two chocolate soufflés with vanilla sauce for dessert. He had to order those ahead since the kitchen needed time to prepare them.

"Wow," she said.

"What? Did you want something else?"

"Um, no, I think even I might have trouble putting all that away!"

"Whatever you don't want, I'll finish, I have quite the appetite," his barely veiled innuendo sent a wave of heat right to her belly and lower.

The mood lightened a touch when the first dishes arrived. They laughed and talked throughout the entire meal. She loved the way he served her himself, shooing the waiter away when he would have done the job.

It was as if he took pride in filling her plate and when she was uncertain if she liked something, he lifted the fork to her lips himself to allow her to decide before he served her more.

"This is incredible," she said as he poured her some more of the delicious dry white wine he'd ordered.

"Yeah, I love seafood, and it's impeccable here,"

he popped a shrimp into his mouth, and she squirmed as he licked the tips of his finger, smiling at her the whole time.

"So, uh, do you travel a lot?"

"Sometimes. Lately, yes."

"For work?" She asked, curious about him.

"Yes. This is kind of a working vacation. But what about you?"

"I was an administrative assistant for a PR firm in New York, but, uh, I just quit my job actually."

"Really? Why?"

"Well, it's kind of embarrassing."

"Tell me, anyway, Leya," he seemed genuinely interested, and she'd yet to get it off her chest.

She could trust him, she decided. It was fast and crazy, but she really felt she could. That settled, she went ahead with her tale.

"So, I very stupidly had a small crush on my boss," the small growl from the other side of the table had her eyes shooting up, but the sound quit before she could question it, "anyway, he turned out to be an enormous jerk," she noticed him tense, but he didn't interrupt her.

She continued, and before they were finished eating, she'd told him the entire story. Even the embarrassing bits.

"Not to be a dick or anything, but I'm glad."

"That my boss was an asshat?"

Confusion warred with anger over his blunt statement. Why would he be glad someone had treated her so shitty?

"Hell yeah, I am glad, Leya. If he'd been half a man, kind to you, or nice in any way, then you wouldn't be sitting here with me. Of course, I'd happily kick the shit out of him for insulting you that way."

Happiness welled up inside of her at his admission. He seemed to feel pretty strongly for having just met her. That was good. It meant whatever magic was making her feel this way, wasn't one-sided.

How long does it take to fall for someone anyway? Fall in like, not love. Too soon for love.

"That's a good answer, Marcus," he returned her smile.

"So, I've decided to make this vacation a series of new experiences for myself. The first thing I did was dump my suitcase and buy new clothes. You might have noticed the way I looked when I first arrived-"

"Not to sound like a jerk, but I noticed you-"

"Oh no, in the green-couch outfit? It was

hideous!" She hid her face and grimaced when he gently tugged her hands down.

"Not that I'm complaining about that sexy dress you have on, because fuck yes, it looks a damn sight better than that green outfit, but the truth is Leya, the way you dress isn't as important as who you are."

OMG. New panties needed at table five! Heat pooled in her belly and travelled to her core. He was absolutely perfect. *The things he said! The way he looked. How he made her feel. My oh my, maybe, just maybe...*

"I guess I always dressed according to what fit me. It's not easy being a plus size in a size zero world."

"I don't know from sizes. I just know you look amazing. You should wear what makes you feel good about yourself."

"Even if it leaves some parts of me exposed?" She blushed as she looked down at the ample cleavage on display and noted the way his eyes riveted to that exact spot and his lips parted.

"Honey, covering any part of you up is a goddamned crime."

"I'm glad you feel that way, Marcus, it makes what I'm about to ask you a little easier."

"What's that?"

"First, you should know I'm almost twenty-seven years old."

"Okay-"

"I'm not done yet. I've been waiting my whole life for something special to happen. I admit, I thought about having a *vacation romance* on the plane over."

"Yeah?" he swallowed, she followed the small movement with her eyes, continuing before she ran out of courage.

"I'm through waiting."

"Uh huh."

"Twenty-seven and virtually untouched."

"Wait, you mean you're a virgin?"

"Yep."

"How is that possible?"

"Not for lack of trying," she laughed and felt her cheeks heat up.

"Excuse me?" He coughed into his napkin and she continued before she lost her nerve.

"In high school, there was Steven. He was shy and cute, and the one time we got into some heavy petting his mother walked in, and you can guess what came next."

"Poor Steven." She couldn't be sure, but she swore Marcus' eyes glowed when he said that.

He looked as if he wanted to tear *poor Steven's* head off. She took a sip of her wine and lifted an eyebrow. He nodded, and she went on.

"Then, in college, I tutored Judd, a football player with a habit of well, being *early* to the party, if you catch my drift."

"That's too bad for Judd."

She tilted her head to the side and nodded. He seemed tense. But he nodded again despite looking as if he wanted to say, *fuck off Steven and Judd.*

"After Judd, was Thomas, a music major. He started off as nice and attentive, but I later discovered he had some strange ideas about women. Let's just say I told him to take a hike before we even got to third base."

"Poor Thomas," his voice got even deeper.

"A few dates here and there in the years that followed were not promising. Then there was Gary, who I told you all about."

"Oh yeah, Gary. I'd love to meet him in a dark alley."

"Anyway," she laughed, "now I have a problem."

"What's that?"

"I'm tired of waiting. I want to make *something special happen.*"

Marcus swallowed again, and Leya bit her lip. *What the hell? You waited long enough already.* Much longer than any of her old friends from school or anyone at her former job.

This vacation was supposed to be her turn to run wild before starting her new life. She got the wardrobe, onto the next experience.

"What are you saying?" He asked in that deep, sexy voice of his. The one that made goosebumps break out all over her body.

Oh, but the man definitely had a voice. A dark, deep timbre that made her mouth water and her core ache.

"What I am saying Marcus, is that I want to make that something special happen *with you.*"

"Check please!"

CHAPTER
SIX

Marcus stood up abruptly. He grasped Leya's hand, signed for the check and practically ran out of the restaurant.

Holy fuck!

The shy little woman he bumped into earlier that day had nothing on the vixen he'd been trying so desperately not to drool over all through dinner.

Her laughter drifted up to his ears like music as he tugged her along the corridor barely able to hide his desperation.

Before the elevator doors closed, he had her back pressed against the wall. *Fuck yeah.* He'd been dying to get his hands on her lush curves ever since he'd laid eyes on her.

The feel of her warm body, soft and pliant,

submissive, underneath the hardness of his, made him tremble like a boy. *Slow down.* He ordered his Bear to be still.

The beast pushed against his skin. He wanted to claim his mate. Marcus growled as he rubbed his hands over her arms and then to her face. He brought his head down and rested his forehead against hers, barely able to breathe for wanting her.

Still, he needed to give her this one chance to say no. His Bear bellowed, but Marcus ignored him. It would be her choice or not at all. That made the Bear go quiet, but he felt his anxiety. It mirrored his human half's.

"Leya, if you were only speaking in hypotheticals you better say so now," his voice was gruff as he insinuated himself between her thighs and held her firmly by the waist.

"Oh, no, Marcus-"

"Huh?" he wanted to roar, but then she smiled and pulled him closer.

"I meant it, *I want you,*" she licked her lips and pressed her body against his in an erotic invitation that was almost as mesmerizing as the slow smile that curled the corner of her pretty little mouth.

Blood thundered in his veins, and his heart

pounded in his chest. *Holy fuck, she wants me.* His bear roared in triumph.

Marcus lowered his lips to hers. Finding his mate was something he expected to take a long time, a tepid experience at best, but as her lips shyly responded to the soft pressure of his, he felt a rush of passion so strong it was like a fucking tsunami. *Mine.*

Marcus wanted to be inside of her. He wanted to cover her in his scent, embed his teeth into her shoulder. *Mark her.*

He wanted to bring her to his den, in his bed, and not let her get up until she was too weak to stand. Instinct and hunger almost got the best of him, but reality dawned as she whimpered in his arms. His mate was a *normal* and a virgin. He had to go slow.

She'd need time to get used to the idea of being a Bear Shifter's mate. Time that his Bear had no desire to give her. *Mine! Now!*

"Marcus, please" she whispered and bit his bottom lip when he stopped kissing her.

He groaned and deepened the kiss, thrusting his tongue between her two plump lips. He wanted to take his time, to cherish, but his body had other ideas. *And so, did she.*

He delved his tongue into her warm mouth and

took what she offered. She was so damn sweet. *Like the tupelo honey, she smelled of.* He was going out of his mind.

And his little mate answered his every demand with some of her own. Virgin or not, she was sensual and seductive. He wanted to give her everything he had.

Marcus wrapped her up in his arms and pressed her to him. The hardened nubs of her breasts rubbed his chest. He couldn't wait to taste them.

What was it she'd said about herself, that she was fat! *Fat? Fuck no!* His woman was perfect. Her body was a study in femininity.

She was soft and strong with dips and valleys that would require long hours to explore thoroughly. And he intended to begin as soon as possible.

He traced her soft and gently rounded stomach with his fingertips, then circled her tiny waist with his hands. Next, he ran his palms over the womanly flare of her hips and back around to knead her luscious ass.

He growled deep in his throat as he continued to probe and explore her mouth in the confines of the elevator. Squeezing her plump globes, he hauled her off her feet causing her to whimper and moan.

Marcus' Bear pushed against his skin. He gripped

her waist, deepening the kiss. Her shapely legs were long with thick thighs, just the way he liked them. They ended in dainty feet with her red painted toes peeking through strappy, high-heeled sandals.

Oh yeah, his Leya in those sandals with nothing else on, her delicious legs wrapped around his waist or hiked up over his shoulders. The hardness in his shorts throbbed and he wondered if he'd even make it to the room.

She pressed closer to him, her small hands tangling in his hair as she pushed her breasts against his chest. *Damn*, if she wiggled one more time, he just might embarrass himself!

Like Judd the stud? Fuck no! His Leya was going to experience some satisfaction before he went at her like some fucking horny teenager!

He ran his hands up her rib cage until they rested just under her breasts. Heat from her body seeped into him, and he could hardly wait to lower his head and get his mouth around one pert nipple. At the sound of her frustrated moan, he slowed his kiss.

Not yet, baby, he thought. Nibbling and teasing her plump lips, he slowed down until he was doing nothing more than rubbing her lips with the softest of touches.

She followed him with her mouth, wanting

more, wanting him, and it made more than his head swell.

"Look at me, baby," Marcus stared as her lust glazed eyes slowly opened.

He made sure she was watching as he cupped both her fabulous breasts in his hands. His Leya's eyes widened as sensation registered and her swollen lips parted on a moan.

Marcus growled out loud then and seized her mouth like a pirate plundering the richest of treasures. She tasted of the wine they shared at dinner and something sweeter, headier, that made him groan.

"Oh God," she moaned as his hands travelled south. He cupped her throbbing sex over her clothes. Heat seeped into his skin.

Her panties were thin and damp and more than anything he wanted to rip them off. *Roarrr.* She dropped her head, allowing him access to her long neck and that soft dip just below her collarbone. He grazed her flesh with his teeth, tracing the hollow with his tongue.

She whimpered as he lifted the hem of her dress. He rubbed her mound with the heel of his hand. Loving the tremble that coursed through her body.

She made a deep, mewling sound. Marcus

groaned in response. He wanted to make a meal of her right there.

The ding of the elevator sounded, and the doors opened. He swung her up into his arms. Thank God, the hall was empty. He hated the idea of anyone else seeing her like this. All soft and unguarded. *And his.*

She was so sweet, his mate. Sweet and sexy. *Hot as fuck.* Marcus wanted nothing more than to take her right there. To bury his cock so deep in her tight, wet heat that he'd need a fucking map to get out again. *Mine. Mate.*

The roar in his head was so loud he could hardly hear her moan as she struggled to press closer to him. Her lips found his neck and he growled as she sucked on the skin there.

She wants you, take her. He'd never experienced such desire, never thought the promise of such pleasure was possible. She slid down his body and opened the room to her suite.

Her soft hands travelled tentatively over his chest and stomach, tracing the outline of him through his shorts. He growled and tossed his head back, loving the feel of her as she touched his body.

He wanted her more than he wanted air. Which was why it shocked the shit out of him when Marcus found himself standing just inside her hotel room with the door propped open.

"Aren't you coming in?" her lust filled eyes met his, a questioning look that made his heart squeeze.

"Not yet, baby."

"But-"

"Honey, I don't know what kind of fucking idiots you used to date, but right now I'm thanking God for them. You were cheated, but I'm not going to cheat you, I want you-"

"I want you too-"

"And I am so fucking happy to hear you say that, but not like this, not in a mad frenzy. When we make love, and have no fucking doubt that we will, I want you to be sure. I want you to be ready."

"But I am-"

"What you are, baby is too damn hot for words. You're killing me," he said when she pressed into him and dropped a kiss on his throat.

"I thought you were going to show me what the fuss was about, Marcus? Changed your mind?" She looked up at him with her heart in her eyes, and he could have roared aloud.

"Never that, baby," he rubbed his fingertips along her throat and up to cup her face, he needed her to focus, to *hear* him.

"You're mine, Leya Tremayne," he growled and pressed his lips to hers.

"Marcus?"

"I'm looking forward to showing you what the fuss is all about, baby. I'm gonna fucking dream about it all night."

"Then why are you leaving?" Her frown was so damned adorable he wanted to nibble on her lower lip.

She didn't know it yet, but he had no intention of leaving her anywhere. She was his. For good. He just had to convince her of that.

"Baby, I want to do this right. Will you let me?" he nibbled her ear and kissed her jaw, nearly forgetting his decision to slow it down a bit when she moaned.

"Oh fuck," he groaned. Maybe he could leave her with something more. It might just kill him, but what better way to go?

He pressed his mouth over hers, walking her backwards to the wall. Marcus growled, delving his tongue inside her hot mouth as his hands found her again under the skirt of her dress.

The little scrap of silk she wore did nothing to disguise her heat. He gripped the fabric and tugged, tearing it from her lush body.

Fuck yes. She was wet and hot. Needy for him. *Only me. Mine.* He slipped his fingers over her lips, parting them. He traced her moist softness, swallowing her moans as she whimpered and turned boneless in his arms.

Leya gasped as he slipped on digit inside her tight heat and stroked slowly. *Oh fuck.* He circled her swollen bud causing her to grind against his hand.

She moaned, and he increased his pace, fucking her with one finger while toying with her swollen clit with the other. In and out, swirl and tug, again and again until he felt her shiver and grip his neck in a tight embrace.

Her back arched and she cried out. Marcus growled, his cock instantly hardening, responding to her soft cries. His fingertips itched as his bear pushed to release his claws.

Biting wasn't the only way Werebears claimed their mate. No, they scratched, bit, fucked, coating their mates in their scents. It was primal and instinctive. His Bear wanted nothing more than to mark her. *MINE!*

His entire body thrummed with desire. His human side fought his Bear to remain in control. *Fur can't bring her pleasure,* he reasoned with the Beast. The Bear was only too happy to let his human half see to her needs. He just wanted to claim her already. A sentiment the man echoed.

Marcus nearly caved into the demands when her soft hands gripped his wrist, urging him on. He shook like a boy, almost breaking the promise he made to himself. He wanted to plunge right into her moist heat, barely stopping in time.

This is for her. All for her. And it was worth every bit of torture as her breathing grew frantic and her cries more desperate. He felt the instant she shattered beneath him and his Bear roared in triumph! Pleased to give his mate such pleasure.

"Marcus," she moaned, and he let her ride out her orgasm. Promising himself there would be more soon. *Very soon.*

He slowed the kiss. Coaxing her shivering body back down to Earth with soft, soothing touches. The scent of her musk mixed with his scent filled his nostrils. So fucking good. *Grrr.*

"But you didn't?" She was gasping for breath, confusion marring her azure gaze.

Marcus kissed her softly, savoring her flavor on his lips. She was perfect for him.

"Baby, that was all for you."

"Marcus, I told you, I'm ready-"

"Sweet, you have no idea how difficult it is for me to walk out that door," he started.

"Then don't, stay with me," she pushed into him. Her soft body tempting him beyond reason.

"Leya, I promise, we're going to do this together, sweet. Just let me set the pace, you won't regret it."

"How can I after what you just showed me? Never before, Marcus," she looked down and bit her lip.

"Was that your first time, baby?" he whispered in reverence.

"No man has ever made me feel like that," a blush crept across her cheeks, but he'd be damned if she was gonna be embarrassed.

"You're a treasure, love."

"You mean you're not, turned off by that?"

"No fucking way. If the assholes who knew you were too selfish to see to your needs, they never deserved you. I'm so honored, baby, you picked me. Thank you so much for giving me *this* here and now. I promise you; this is just the beginning."

"Are you sure I can't?"

"Not tonight, sweet. Trust me."

Doubt filled her blue eyes. Marcus frowned. He wanted to rake his claws against the idiots who'd made her feel insecure. The ones who passed up the chance to be with her. At the same time, he wanted to thank them for saving her just for him.

Possessive much? Hell yeah! Still, he wanted her to see herself as he did, a beautiful, sexy, and vibrant woman, someone who deserved to be loved for who she was.

A "vacation romance"? Hardly. She was fucking his. Forever. *Fated mates.*

What about your big furry secret? That was a separate issue. Leya had to accept that he truly wanted her as a woman first, then he'd work out when to introduce his Bear.

"Okay," she said, and he saw the moment she decided to trust him. He exhaled and squeezed her waist, thanking God she said yes.

"I'll be here first thing in the morning to take you out on our second official date."

"Second?"

"Well, yeah."

"Okay," she conceded, "dinner counts, even if we didn't eat."

"Oh, baby, I ate. I devoured that sweet mouth of yours, little one," he grinned and nipped her lip making her smile and shiver in return. *Good.* She should always smile.

"We'll go swimming, then I'd love to take you hiking to this little spot I found last time I was here."

"Does this hike end with a nice view?"

"Breathtaking," he answered, but he wasn't talking about the hike.

"Sounds good," her lips tilted up in a smile that stole the breath from his body.

Dazzling. He pressed his mouth to her lips and kissed her softly before nudging her further inside and closing the door. Marcus groaned.

Fuck. Time for another cold shower.

SEVEN

The morning sun blazed overhead. Leya smiled. It was crazy to think that a company, *Stein Luxury Hotel & Resorts* to be exact, owned the whole island. Sure, it was only a small island, but still. *Amazing*, she sighed as she looked at the abundance of life that flittered before her.

To think she'd only just discovered *Moongate Island* on a travel website the night she'd quit her job! *Must've been fated,* she mused. The fact she'd gotten a tremendous deal on the entire vacation was just a bonus.

She was always bargain hunting, even though she had more than enough in her savings account. A hold-over from her youth when she used to flea market shop with her Nana in Winter Springs, Florida.

Seriously though, she deserved this bit of luxury. It was her first time splurging on herself and, so far, so good.

She'd done more here in one day than she had in all her years in New York. New clothes, new outlook, and enough courage to proposition a hunk like Marcus into taking her virginity!

I can't believe I asked. Who am I kidding? I can't believe he said yes!

She should be embarrassed, but she wasn't. Leya woke up this morning still riding the wave of her first ever man-induced orgasm. She'd blinked happily until she recalled they hadn't exactly gone all the way.

Then the nerves settled in. She almost called the whole thing off. Too embarrassed to breath, she'd even checked out airplane tickets. But before she could click anything, *he* knocked on her door.

She'd been nervous as hell, but he knocked again and called her name. So, she answered. And there he stood, looking gorgeous as ever. It took minimum effort on his part to get her dressed and ready for a morning on the sand.

It's about damn time, her inner biological clock said as she unbuttoned her cover-up. The gauzy fabric was so thin it was almost sheer and even though it fell to her ankles, long side-slits made it almost indecent. She bit her lip.

Buying new clothes was one thing, wearing them was another. She never dressed to emphasize her curves. In fact, she always tried to cover them up. *Not anymore!* God gave her an appetite and boobs for a reason. *No more hiding.*

She straightened her shoulders. No need to worry with the way Marcus was eyeing her, *like a starving man looking at a banquet*, she mused. True, there was something threatening in his dark gaze.

Something wild an untamed. *Gosh, Leya, you sound like a damsel in one of those books you read on your phone during coffee breaks!*

Still, it didn't make it any less true. His eyes almost seemed to glow in the sunlight. A liquid molten pool of chocolate she was longing to dive into. Instead of scaring her, she felt excitement sizzle under her skin.

And yet, other than a peck on the cheek when he picked her up, he hadn't tried to kiss or touch her. He'd been the perfect gentlemen. *Darn it!*

He'd suggested coffee and sweet rolls from the

Bear Claw Bakery in the hotel lobby on their way and she readily agreed.

She was shocked upon her arrival to see one of her favorite places in the city right there in paradise! Bear Claw was the absolute best. Marcus grinned widely at her proclamation and ordered them both large coffees and a few pastries.

He carried their food in a small bag to the semi-private cabana he'd rented for them on the beach. The lounge chairs were fitted with soft foam cushions and plush towels.

Long gossamer curtains fluttered in the breeze as he arranged their fare on the small round table that sat between the chairs.

"The sun is warming up, why don't you get comfortable and we'll have some breakfast," he spoke casually.

As if he wasn't suggesting she take off her cover-up. Leya narrowed her eyes as he busied himself doctoring his coffee. This wasn't her room with the lights off. This was broad daylight. *Hop to it, girl. Like ripping off a band-aid.*

She eyed him under lowered lashes as he pretended not to watch her. He was good at that. Making her feel at ease when she really wanted to run and hide.

Swimsuits were not her favorite attire. No chubby girl liked to be reminded of her physical imperfections, and nothing brought them out quite like a bathing suit!

Even though the new one looked, well, *different*, she still felt exposed. Every dimple and curve, every ounce of extra wiggle and jiggle would be on display. *Oh damn!*

She looked at him and hesitated. Talk about Beauty and the Beast, only he's the beauty. *Shut up inner dialogue!*

She couldn't help but sigh. He looked damn good in his blue swim shorts, and rippling sun kissed muscles. The sheer size of him was incredible.

His chest was spectacular with just the right amount of dark curling hair. His powerful legs were covered with the same hair. Unlike those guys who skipped leg days, there was nothing off balance about Marcus. He was a perfect male specimen.

Not just that, he was thoughtful, smart, and wickedly funny. She liked his sly sense of humor and the way he was always touching her casually.

Holding her hand when they walked, her elbow when he held the door open, brushing back her hair when it blew in her face. He made her feel small, feminine, protected, *desired*.

Feelings she was beginning to like. Feelings he might reconsider when confronted with her size. *Quit being a baby*, she sighed as she undid yet another button. It was almost *go time*. She let her mind wander to take it off the inevitable disrobing.

He could have any of the women on that island judging by the covetous eyes that followed him when they walked to the beach that morning. *But he chose you.*

With the last button undone, she closed her eyes and let the cover-up slide off her shoulders and down to the warm sand. The sun heated her skin, yet Leya shivered for a second.

She slowly opened her eyes to find Marcus with one hand on a cup of coffee and the other on a packet of sugar. His eyes, like liquid onyx, ate up every inch of her in the two-piece yellow suit.

Her entire body thrummed under his heavy-lidded stare. She knew the suit looked better than any she'd tried on. It emphasized her curves, but instead of making her feel overweight and self-conscious, she felt deliciously feminine.

A noise cut the silence, it was low and deep. Unrecognizable above the surf and wind, and the noises made by the other tourists milling about.

But none of it mattered to her. There was only Marcus and the way he was looking at her. His eyes grew impossibly dark and she arched her back unconsciously.

Enjoying the way his eyes widened, following the movement. For the first time, Leya felt powerful in her womanhood. She swore she heard that sound again. Wait, it was emanating *from him. Was he growling?*

His face grew hard and angry as he looked past her, and she turned her head to see what interrupted what had truly the been the most erotic few minutes of her life thus far.

Marcus was staring down a man, older and obviously married with his wife and kids in tow. Leya could have just died! The man stopped dead in his tracks and was staring at her with his mouth hanging open.

Well, he was until his wife bopped him on the head and yelled at him to get moving. Leya laughed out loud. *Marcus was acting jealous of her!*

"Do you like it? I bought it yesterday," she said to distract him from the poor family man.

"What, baby?" *Ooh, she liked it when he called her that.*

"My suit. Do you like it?" She turned around in a circle in front of him and almost giggled when he took her hand and gently pulled her down next to him.

"Darlin', you look as sweet as a jar of honey and just as good to eat," his tone teased, but his eyes were full of promises. *More promises.*

He dropped a hard kiss on her lips and pressed a cup of coffee in her hand. Her tongue darted out and caught his flavor and she moaned. He tasted so good.

"Thanks," she smiled.

"Uh. You like sweet rolls? These are a specialty!"

"Oh yes, I told you, I love *Bear Claw Bakery*! It's my favorite!"

"Really? You weren't putting me on?" he asked with his head cocked to the side. He was adorable like that. Kind of like a puppy.

"No, I swear, I get my coffee there every day back in the city."

"Well, I am glad to hear it."

"Why?" She asked taking a nibble of the sticky sweet roll. The sun was causing the honey to run. Leya smiled and licked a drizzle from her skin.

"Cause its mine," he said as he ate one roll in two huge bites.

"Whoa! And I thought I liked these! But what do you mean? Like, do you own a branch or something?"

"No, not a branch. We own the entire corporation. *Bear Claw Bakery* is strictly a family operated business. In fact, I came here to see how the new store was doing."

"You mean you own *Bear Claw Bakery*? The whole thing?"

She stood up and knocked over the table holding their food. *OMG. I am completely mortified.*

"Leya? You okay?"

"Sorry. Excuse me," she hurried away, forgetting her cover-up in her haste.

She ignored his calls as a staff member hurried over to clear away the mess. *You idiot! You propositioned not only a ridiculously good-looking guy, but a freaking mogul as well!*

The sound of footsteps behind her made her move faster between the towels and lounge chairs. But it didn't matter, she was no match for his long strides. A hand on her elbow slowed her down and she squeezed her eyes tight.

"*Leya!* What's going on? Why are you so upset?"

She was huffing and puffing like she ran a marathon, and his chest barely heaved with the effort it took him to chase her down. *He's a freaking millionaire!*

"Look, I had no idea who you were last night, and I hope you don't think I did that on purpose? That I, you know, somehow knew who you were and let you order all that expensive food and wine and well, that I came on to you because of *who* you are-"

"Leya, of course I know that! You are the least mercenary person I know. Besides, I asked you to dinner first. But when all is said and done, I hope you did say yes because of *me*. God knows I want you for *you*."

"But-"

"No buts, don't walk away from me over this, please," he looked at her in earnest, his fingers holding her in place as if he was afraid, she'd slip away.

"Marcus, this is crazy. I'm not in your class-"

"Stop that! This is the twenty-first century. This thing between you and me is about us alone. Let's see where it goes, okay?"

"Okay. I'm sorry I panicked. I just didn't want you to think I manipulated you-"

"As if you'd do such a thing," his voice sounded husky, and she detected just a hint of vulnerability.

"Come on. Let's finish breakfast?"

"Alright, Marcus," she could swear he looked relieved.

Silly, but then he tensed once again when she added, "I just don't like lies. I want to make sure there's no misunderstanding between us. I mean even if this is just a vacation romance, I want it to be honest, alright?"

"Anything you say," he murmured, his fingers caressing as they danced along her arm and she almost missed the glint of possessiveness in his eyes before he replaced it with a charming smile, "Let's eat then swim."

After they ate, having ordered more rolls and coffee from the hotel staff, they ran towards the surf and played like children in the cool, clear water.

Marcus was full of energy. He swam like he was born to it. Splashing and showing off around her. Leya gasped when he lifted her up out of the water and tossed her in the air only to catch her in his big, strong arms.

He never seemed to tire. What's more, he never paid any attention to anyone else. He only had eyes for her.

She was completely dazzled by his attention. He

teased and joked with her, softly coaxing the real Leya out from hiding. It had been so long since she just let go. But she could finally be herself, *with him.*

They lounged on a double raft in the mild waves. Him sprawled on his back and her lying on her side just looking at him.

He glistened like a bronzed god in the surf. All golden and muscular with dark hair that was starting to get gold highlights in the tropical sun. *Beautiful,* if a man could be that.

She exhaled and bit her lip, wishing for more than his gentlemanly handling of her. The idea of pressing herself against his hard, wet body in the skimpy suit she wore made her pulse race.

Not that she would do that with all those people around. *The reason for his restraint possibly?* She could only hope so. Hours later, they dragged the raft back to the sand and let the waves tickle their toes as they built a rather sad looking sandcastle with their hands.

"It's too top heavy," she said as he piled on the sand.

"Well, maybe, but I kind of like that," he looked at her with narrowed eyes, and she swatted him when she realized what he was talking about.

"You have a dirty mind, sir!"

"Only when it comes to you, sweet Leya," he said with a growl and captured her lips with his.

"Finally," she whispered into his mouth and kissed his salty lips. The soft whisper of his tongue against the seam of her lips had her sighing his name, giving him an opening.

It was a sweet and sensuous caress, arousing as hell, even though only their mouths touched. He sucked on her top lip and nibbled the lower one with his teeth.

Marcus' long tongue expertly stroked her mouth as he thrust inside. She sighed deeper, falling more and more under his spell with every slow slide between her lips. She needed more.

She reached for him just as a wave came and crashed over them both. Saltwater and sand filled her mouth, and she sputtered laughing at the entire incident. Marcus pulled her up to stand, but it was too late, they were both a mess.

"Come on let's rinse this off," he laughed and swept her up in his arms. He dove under the next wave holding onto her with a gentle, reassuring strength.

Leya sucked in air as he came up with her still

cradled against his chest as if she were something precious. He brushed a strand of hair back from her cheek. The water was cool and refreshing, but Leya felt as if she were standing on hot coals.

"Hey," he said looking at her through his dark, wet lashes.

His eyes were dark and velvety, almost liquid as he watched her mouth. The sun beat down on them from up high, but Leya hardly noticed. The air seemed to sizzle, alit with a magical electricity only for them.

Oh no, she gasped, and eyes widened. His hands tightened on her. *No. NO. NO!*

How could I fall in love with him already? But she had. She knew it in the answering rumble of his chest. He kissed her mouth softly then carried her to their cabana.

He walked looking at her, oblivious to the stares of the few people scattered on the sand. They all seemed to melt away, blending into the background with the music and the wind.

The whole world just faded away. All she saw was Marcus. *Oh, so tempting, Marcus.* She itched to touch him. She ran her hand along his square jaw and reached back to tangle in his wet hair, then she pulled him closer.

He tugged the curtain closed and laid her down on the lounge chair.

"Kiss me, Marcus," she said against his mouth and lost herself to the feel of being in his arms and diving into his kiss headfirst.

EIGHT

Shit. No lies or misunderstandings. A "vacation romance". Good job, idiot!

Marcus tried to shut out all the nagging doubts in his head as he'd held Leya in the cool Atlantic waters. They'd frolicked and played for hours. *Like cubs.* He grinned thinking about the day they'd have their own.

Oh fuck, picturing his sweet mate swollen with his young was going to end with him having a raging hard-on in his swimsuit. *Not a fucking option.*

He'd been back to reciting multiplication tables when she pulled his head down to her lips and asked him to kiss her. Then he was lost.

He didn't lie as a rule, but man, did he have a

secret. A big one. *About nine-foot-tall and eight hundred pounds give or take.*

After he managed to get that conversation out of the way, how was he going to convince her that she was his *fated mate?* The one being in the universe made just for him and vice versa? That their little vacation romance was destined to last a hell of a lot longer? *Like a lifetime longer.*

Marcus exhaled slowly as they walked out of the cabana hand in hand. She was so fucking perfect. The feel of her soft fingers interlaced with his was amazing, more than he'd ever dared hope for.

He gazed down at her bent head as they walked back to their rooms, her blonde waves blowing in the breeze, the scent of honey wafting into his nostrils. His mouth watered. She was so beautiful.

But that wasn't why his blood thundered in his veins, not the whole reason anyway. Leya was smart and kind, funny and honest. The more they talked and spent time together, the more he wanted, no needed, to be around her. She was quickly becoming necessary to him.

Mine. Mate. Marcus would have argued with his Bear for acting like a Neanderthal, but the truth was, his human side couldn't agree more. *I have to tell her the truth about myself. And soon.* His Bear growled in agreement, eager to meet his mate in the fur.

Marcus exhaled to quell the nerves in his stomach. *Damn. I'm a Bear and yet I'm nervous as a mouse.* He bit back a groan. The sun dipped lower in the beautiful skies, and he turned to her. An idea started taking shape in his mind.

"We still goin' on that hike?" Leya smiled up at him as she donned her cover-up and slid her feet into her sandals. The lobby was air conditioned and would be cool after their time outdoors.

"Definitely, sweet," he said.

His eyes were riveted to the side slits of her sheer dress. The garment flowed over her soft curves, almost hitting the floor. Those glimpses of her tanned legs were just enough to make a man wonder...and wonder.

Just how high did those legs of hers go? How would they feel wrapped around his waist? Would they squeeze him when he took her? Grrr. He had every intention of finding out.

"Alright, I'm in! So, what should I wear?"

"Um, shorts and sneakers should be fine. Bring a change of clothes too in case we decide to, uh, camp out. Would you be game?"

"Of course," she smiled and agreed without hesitation. A fact that made his Bear chuff in happiness. *She trusts us to keep her safe.*

"Great! I'll grab some food and supplies. Meet you at your room, okay?"

"Awesome, I'm starving," she laughed.

"Me too." *But not for food.* He pressed his lips to her palm and tasted her sweet skin as he handed her into the elevator.

"I'll be by your room in about an hour, okay."

"Okay," she bit her lip. Marcus was unable to resist a light brushing of his mouth over hers before the doors closed. He smiled to himself as he set about getting ready for that night.

A little while later, they traipsed through a mini, tropical wilderness, miles away from the hotel. Marcus had explored the area on his last visit. As a Bear, he loved being out in the wild.

His natural curiosity had him trekking all over the island the first few times he proposed to open a shop at the exclusive resort. Moongate Island was gorgeous.

Lush and tropical, with one small local fishing village and the resort as the only inhabited areas. The rest of the grounds were as nature had intended. With a few changes left by the people who had explored over the centuries of course.

Marcus discovered the spot he wanted to share with Leya on one of those treks a few months ago. He couldn't wait to experience it with her. It would be like seeing it for the first time again. *The first of many shared experiences*, he silently hoped.

The overhang was reached by a rocky path and overlooked the Atlantic Ocean. But it was a different side to the deep blue than they experienced at their hotel. Tall, rough waves pounded against the mountainous side of the island. The noise was loud and thrilling to hear. Like listening to thunder from the source.

Funny, how it reminded him of the sound of his own blood rushing in his ears whenever he stood close to her. He exhaled as he waited for Leya to tie her sneakers and join him.

"Oh, Marcus, this is beautiful!"

His chest swelled with happiness. Leya seemed genuinely eager to go on this hike with him. When he'd suggested they camp their overnight, he was equally surprised when she agreed.

Her trust in *him*, in his ability to keep her safe and his good intentions, humbled the mand and filled the Bear with pride. She was his. His to care for, to love, and protect. *She just didn't know it yet.*

"I'm so glad you wanted to do this. I wasn't sure you'd like this kind of thing."

"You know, not all chubby girls hate exercise."

"Okay, about all this fat nonsense-"

"Marcus, come on, it's not as if I don't know I'm fat-"

He turned around in a move so fast she didn't even have time to guess what he was doing! He plastered her against his body. Holding her by the waist in his steely grip.

Every nerve ending was on edge at being so close to her. Feeling her body, even through layers of clothing, smelling her sexy honey scent as her arousal drifted into his nostrils was almost more than enough to wrest control from his hands. He closed his eyes, attempting to hide the Bear.

This was dangerous, being so damn close to heaven! He pressed his hips forward unable to help himself, and in truth, not wanting to. Her body was soft, rounded and perfect for him. A foil to his hardness.

He growled deep in his throat as he nuzzled her neck and found her lips with his, allowing her to feel his current physical state. A state that hadn't changed since he'd laid eyes on her.

"You feel this?"

Her eyes grew darker in her arousal, her honey scent all the more potent. His voice deepened, instinctively answering her need. It would always be like that. His Bear's first thought to please, protect, and care for his mate. *Mine.*

Marcus moved his hands, caressing the silky skin of her arms and neck. *Damn*, she felt so fucking good. His breathing became rough as he tried to focus.

"For the record, *you are perfect.* And I didn't think you wouldn't like hiking because of your weight. I was thinking more like girls, bugs, and no bathrooms didn't mix. The only *chubby* thing around here, is this," he pressed his hardness against her soft belly and saw heat flare in her blue eyes, *oh fuck.*

"Leya, this happens anytime I get within a few feet of you. Hell, all I have to do is even think about you and I'm hard as a fucking rock. You are so beautiful, baby, I'm having a hell of a time remembering my promise not to rush things."

"I never asked you to promise that."

"I know, but I promised myself, I'd give you some time to decide for sure. Because once we do this, baby, there is no going back."

There was already no going back, but he didn't want to scare her. His Bear roared angrily. He was never giving his mate up regardless of what his human half may have implied. *Easy*, he told his beast.

"Okay. Um, so tell me about this place, while we set up camp," she said and bent down to their supplies.

"Okay. This side of the island is completely mountainous and unspoiled. No one lives nearby," he said and unfolded the tent while she removed two rolled up sleeping bags from her bag.

"Why not?"

"Well, the natives here live in a fishing village," he thought of Mrs. Leeds and her Cormorant Shifter family and smiled, "They're pretty damn amazing and supply all the fish to the hotel restaurants. Anyway, this part is deserted as there are rumors of wild boars and packs of feral dogs roaming the hills," he frowned when he saw her eyes go wide.

"Don't worry, sweet, I won't let anything happen to you."

'I know that. Sorry for being silly, it's just I was bitten by a dog as a child and sort of never got over my fear of them."

Marcus frowned hard. His bear wanted to find the offending mutt and rip its fucking head off. *Grrr*.

"Marcus! I was nine, really, it's okay!" She

laughed, and his Bear was soothed once again. A happy Leya was good. *Yeah. Keep her happy.* That was the plan.

"Sorry," he continued, "alright, well, mostly folks stay away because the volcano, though dormant, it's due for an eruption. At least that's what the locals say, but they've been saying that for a hundred years or more."

"They do, uh, track volcanic activity though, right?"

"Of course," he smiled.

They talked about the little things for the next twenty minutes over their lunch of cold fried chicken and a chilled tropical fruit salad.

Marcus packed up the leftovers and piled them into the insulated backpack he carried along with their tent, some more food, emergency supplies, and fresh water. It was seasonably warm, so he didn't worry about a fire.

They sat in companionable silence for the next few minutes. *This is easy*, he thought shocked by his admission, *being with her feels natural, like breathing.*

He asked about her family and friends. He knew about her job already.

"I'm not close to my parents and I have no siblings."

"Really?"

"Well, dad wanted a boy and mom was indifferent. I think she didn't like me because I wasn't like the other girls, you know? I didn't look like them and I never wanted to be a cheerleader or girl scout."

"It's their loss, I mean it," he said and took her hand. Her brilliant blue eyes never failed to hypnotize him. Like sapphire pools he couldn't wait to dive into.

"I have two brothers and it's just my dad now, but we are all close. We run *Bear Claw* together," he didn't want to dwell on his brothers. He wanted to focus on her.

Like most Shifters, his family was close. *Too close at times*, but he couldn't imagine it any other way. Most Shifters craved community, leadership, a natural pecking order. Their cubs would grow up safe and secure. *Leya pregnant with our young...*

"My parents never understood why I chose the city. I just needed a change. But I guess they were right. I'm tired of life in the Big Apple, but I don't want to go home either," she fiddled with a stick she found lying on the ground while she spoke, "I'll worry about finding a new home when I go back. Anyway, how about you, Mr. Bakery-mogul?"

Little do you know, my love, you have a home

waiting for you. In me. He had to focus on her words to come up with a quick response. *Fucking daydreaming again, pal? Claim her.* His Bear seemed happy to taunt him.

"Oh, come on, I'm just a simple baker, Leya."

"Yeah, right. Anyway, where do the baking Devlin's hail from?"

"My family lives in Barvale, New Jersey."

"Is that by Maccon City?"

"Yeah, just west of there. How did you know?"

"My company had a client there, Lane Liquors Corp. You know it?"

"Yes, I do! I am a fan of *Bite*."

"Really? Me too!"

They laughed as he took two small bottles of the local craft beer that he stowed in the cooler. Leya grinned and lifted hers to her lips and he exhaled. He didn't know if she liked beer, but took a chance she'd enjoy the light, fruity blend the hotel served.

Marcus was so focused on her that he let his guard down. He should have been paying more attention to his surroundings. A mistake that was soon brought to light when the unmistakable sounds of growling reached his sensitive ears.

"Um, Marcus," she squeaked. Leya's eyes popped

out of her head and he followed her gaze to two snarling beasts that moved in front of them.

"*Shit.* Okay, Leya, get behind me," he slowly stood, doing his best not to provoke the animals.

When he was satisfied, she'd listened to him, and moved behind him to the entrance of their tent, Marcus began sliding to the left. He wanted to direct them away from their campsite.

The sound of a third feral dog sneaking up behind them was not lost on him. *Fuck.* The scent of Leya's fear was making his Bear nuts.

"What are we going to do?" she asked. Her worry sliced through his hesitation. His protective instinct going into overdrive.

He knew what he was going to do as he eyed the three huge dogs that for all their scavenging ways didn't seem the least bit underfed. He just hoped she'd understand.

The animals were huge, scarred, and vicious if their snapping jaws and snarls were anything to go by. Marcus narrowed his eyes. *Time to share some secrets.*

"Leya, I need to show you something."

"Now?"

"Trust me."

"What do you mean? Why are you getting undressed?"

He unsnapped his shorts an pushed them down along with his shirt and sneakers.

"Just remember, I'll never hurt you, got it?" She gulped, and he took that for a yes.

He had no choice now anyway. A second after he uttered those words the first dog lunged to attack. And he was headed straight for Leya. *Roar!*

Marcus focused on calling his Bear. That familiar pull of energy was welcome indeed as the sound of his mate's scream did nothing to soothe his beast.

Touch her and die! Mine!

CHAPTER
NINE

Oh, crap! What the-?

Leya's eyes bulged as she watched the man she'd been falling in love with, shed his clothing in the face of three huge mongrels. While she didn't mind the view, the timing was kind of off.

Surrounded by three snarling dogs was not exactly how she wanted to see her first fully naked man. Not that being amorous was what Marcus had in mind. Her gorgeous giant stood in front of her as if to protect her, butt-naked, as it were.

Then something began to happen, something definitely out of her realm of knowledge. It was as if the air around Marcus's body shimmered and warped. Under her watchful eyes, *fur*, thick, black-brown fur sprouted all over his body. His rapidly growing body. *A Bear! Marcus is a Bear!*

The huge Black Bear in front of her roared loudly. His jaws created the deafening sound that seemed to scare off one of the dogs. The other two weren't so bright.

Heat and rage poured off the Marcus-bear and Leya backed up to the tent looking for something she could use as a weapon without taking her eyes off the scene in front of her. *Sunblock? Seriously.*

The two remaining dogs seemed to take her movement as aggressive, and they attacked Marcus. Leya, clearly out of her mind with fear, tossed the can of spray suntan lotion at one of the dogs and yelled at him to go away as the other dog took a bite at his hind leg.

Marcus really didn't seem to like that. He swiped at the dog with his enormous paw and sent him flying. The second dog, having gotten up despite the sunblock, must have realized he was no match for the Bear and ran down the incline after his buddies.

Marcus gave chase, but only for a few feet. He pawed the ground and bellowed in the direction the dogs ran, but nothing answered. He turned back to her. His familiar brown eyes roamed over her, and she realized he was making sure she was safe. Warmth pooled in her belly as she took a step forward, her hand raised.

"Marcus?"

His answering chuff made her giggle. *A Bear? OMG. Marcus was a Bear!* The enormity of the situation seemed out of her reach for the time being. She was full of awe and wonder.

The kind she used to have when she read too many books as a child. Her early days were filled glued to the pages of books about magical beasts and daring adventures! She spent hours on end daydreaming about the day something wonderful would happen to her. *Looks like it finally did.*

Marcus sat down on his furry rump as she tiptoed closer. He chuffed again, Bear lips opening and closing as if tasting the air. He allowed her to tentatively run her hands over his dense fur.

He was so soft! Leya sighed as she felt his energy vibrating through his body. She pulled back meeting his eyes in wonder. Standing before her now was no longer a Bear, but a very naked, very aroused, Marcus.

"Are you alright?" His voice was a deep grumble

barely above a whisper. It sent shivers down her spine.

"Am *I* alright? What about you? Oh, that mutt bit you!" She exclaimed noting the blood running from his calf.

"Don't worry about it, I heal fast."

"We need to clean that," she said and turned to the tent. His voice still reached her as she looked for something to clean the wound with.

"Did uh, did you really throw sunblock at one of them?"

She nodded, feeling a little foolish now that the adrenaline was subsiding. Leya ignored her embarrassment and grabbed some wipes from the bag. She blotted the cut which was already miraculously knitting itself together.

"Leya?" he knelt down too, halting her ministrations, "You sure you're okay?"

"Yeah but, um, what are you? I think you should tell me now, don't you?"

"Okay, well first, this is why I waited to, *you know*, with you, because, *fuck*, well as you just saw, I'm a Bear Shifter. My family, the Devlin Clan, are Shifters going back to forever I guess, but that's not the most important thing I have to tell you."

"It's not?"

"No. My sweet, brave Leya, I, that is, it's widely believed that Shifters have predestined mates. When we meet our fated mates, *we know*, there's an instinct, a *connection* between them, mostly that doesn't happen until the mates consummate their vows to one another. Sometimes the connection is so strong they *mate bond* without having, *er*, sex, but that's the real way they sort of declare they are mates, *oh fuck*, I'm doing this all wrong-"

"So, you are saying what? That we're mates?"

"Uh, yes?"

"Oh. You don't sound sure."

"I'm fucking sure," he moved so quickly she couldn't follow it. One second, he was a few feet away, the next, he was right in front of her.

"You. Are. Mine. Leya, I know this is a lot to take in and that you have no reason to believe me, but I swear to God, I am crazy about you. I feel things for you that should be impossible-"

"You mean like you, turning into a Bear?!"

"No, well, yeah! I guess-"

"So, you mean it should be impossible for you to feel anything for someone like me?"

"God no! That's not what I mean at all! *Shit*, I'm sorry. I mean that it's impossible to expect you to feel anything for me. And now I probably fucked it all up cause you're perfect and I'm this fucking animal!"

"Okay, Marcus, I think we need to start from the beginning."

"Fine, just let me get my shorts on-"

"No, you just sit right there and start talking."

He wanted to growl, to roar, to punch something, anything to get that horrified look off her face. One thing he never considered was possible rejection.

Oh crap. The dirt under his bare ass was hot from the late afternoon sun and the pebbles sticking to his cheeks grated. It wasn't that he minded sitting there in the buff, well, *not exactly*, but how was he supposed to answer questions when his cock was sitting at half-mast? As a Shifter, he was hardly bothered by nudity, but the smell of her so close was driving him fucking nuts.

Not being able to touch her? *Fucking torture.* In those tiny cut-offs and that fitted tank top, she looked good enough to eat. *Talk about good ideas!* She sat back on her feet facing him and unconsciously thrust her perfect breasts forward. *Drool.*

He could almost imagine what she was thinking behind those gorgeous blue eyes of hers. *How could she not know how perfect she was?* He had to wipe that confused frown off her face. For good.

"Just to recap, you're a Bear and you think I'm your *mate?*"

"I know you're my mate."

"And it's possible we have some sort of close connection, but we haven't bonded yet because we haven't had sex."

Swallow.

"Um, yes."

"So, if we have sex then we are what, like married or something?"

"Yes. Sort of. We will be officially *mated.* It's better than married to Shifters. Once I have claimed you, you can be damned sure, I will never let you go, and every other male around you will know you belong to me, but of course, a legal marriage would be prudent too."

"Okay, *Captain Caveman,* hold up a sec, are you saying you want to marry me?"

Swallow again. Hard. Fuck.

"Yes. Absolutely. I want you, Leya, *only you*. As my mate, as my wife, forever."

"Okay, then, there is only one way to see if this is true or not," she stood up in front of him.

Her skin seemed to glow against the rising moon as she took the band out of her hair and let the soft blonde waves fall down around her shoulders. She unbuttoned her shorts and Marcus hissed in a breath.

"What are you doing?"

"Unzip that sleeping bag, will you?"

He moved mechanically following her orders, but his eyes never left her. She stepped out of her sneakers, stuffing her socks inside, and placed them inside the tent. His hands stilled on the sleeping bag as she stood just inside the opening.

He tensed in his crouched position, eyes riveted to the movements of her hands as she unzipped her shorts and pushed them down her long legs. Marcus' throat went dry. Before he could move, she had her tank top over her head, revealing lace-covered mounds of flesh to his starving eyes.

"What are you doing?"

"I'm taking my clothes off, Marcus."

"Why?"

"I thought that was obvious," she grinned, her hands moved to the front clasp of her demi-cup bra.

Before she had the chance to unfasten it, he was there. His sweet, sexy mate was taking her clothes off. *For him.* Marcus shivered like an inexperienced cub, taking her in his arms as if she was something delicate and precious. *She is.*

"Are you sure you want to do this?" he asked. Part of him was afraid she'd say *yes*, the other part of him wouldn't move a muscle until she told him to. Her big, blue eyes looked up at him, trust and something else, something warm and all-consuming glistened in their depths.

"Yes," she said, "Marcus, I'm sure," her blue eyes roaming his face as she raised her hands and pulled on his head.

"I won't be able to stop," Marcus' voice was a low growl. Longing and need threatened to consume him. *Never like this*, he thought as he struggled to hold on to his Bear.

"I don't want you to stop. Please Marcus, no more waiting. I want you," she went back to the bra, but his hands swallowed hers and gently moved them aside.

"Let me, baby," his voice echoed through his body. More Bear than man, he had to will his skin to stay put as he, *oh-so-gently*, peeled the lacy fabric from her glorious skin.

Better than any Christmas or birthday present. Those were always too hastily unwrapped to be really appreciated. Yes, this was something to be savored. For his mate, he would not rush. He'd go slow. Even if it killed him.

His blood thrummed in his veins, heart pounding as, inch by inch, he revealed her gorgeous form. Her skin was smooth and unblemished. She was suntanned from their day on the beach. A lovely shade of gold, like honey. *Grrr.* His Bear growled as he tested her softness beneath his searching hands.

She arched her back in silent submission. Her eyes grew heavy-lidded with desire. The scent of her arousal made his mouth water. He couldn't wait any longer. Marcus bent his head.

He took one plump nipple in his mouth while pinching the other with his fingers as he tasted her. *Sweet as honey. And mine. Roarrr.* She shivered in his arms and moaned his name, her hands tugging his long hair, pressing him closer to her sweet flesh.

She tasted so fucking good. He burned for her. *Finally*, he had her in his arms. Joy and possession welled up inside of him. His lips left her breast to find her mouth. Their kiss was deep and passionate.

Tongues tangled, teeth nipped, and hands roamed. *Honey and lavender, sweetness and spice.* His Leya was all woman, more than a handful for the mighty Bear.

He fucking loved it. She pressed herself against him, hips swaying as she moaned her delight in the feel of skin against skin. Her boldness and the innocence that lurked underneath made his dick swell and throb against her soft belly.

Fuck. If she kept that up, he was gonna come all over her. His Bear rumbled as her sweet musk filled his nostrils. *Mate.*

"Finally, my sweet Leya," his lips found her neck and he nipped her none too gently.

"Marcus," she moaned, "I think I'm ready."

"For what, baby?"

"To see what all the fuss was about."

His whole body seemed to vibrate at the depth of passion in her gaze. He lowered her onto the sleeping bag and loomed over her. He was determined to give her everything she wanted, but first, he needed to taste all of her.

"And I'm gonna show you, baby, but the Bear wants a taste first."

Her eyes widened with questions, but he let his body do the talking. His hands traced the curve of her arm up to her bare shoulders, his mouth followed, dropping kisses along her sun-kissed skin that seemed to glow in the moonlight.

Marcus forced himself to blink just to make sure she was real. She looked like an angel and smelled like heaven. *Tupelo honey and lavender.* Her scent filled his nostrils. He caught her flower petal soft lips with his, then took them between his teeth and nibbled delicately.

His mate was a virgin, fresh and untouched. His. She clung to him sweetly with her mouth opening slowly for his tongue, answering his need with her own. She was ripe and ready for him.

Her entire body seemed to vibrate beneath him. She moaned low in her throat, and if possible, he grew even harder at the raw sound. *Mine.*

His open mouth pressed kisses down the crevice between her breasts. He'd be back later to properly indulge himself with the sweet mounds, but for now, he had other places to tease and taste. Marcus needed her hunger to match his own before he took her.

His hands roamed over her luscious curves. Leya was a fucking goddess without her clothes. Big enough to fill even his hands and sweet as the honey his Bear craved.

Her passion was a delightful surprise. She met

him kiss for kiss, touch for touch. Never shying away from him. No, his mate dove right in, submitting to him, but not leaving him in charge. Her nails scratched at his back, lips and teeth nipped his skin, hands cupped his ass. She was eager and responsive. *A hot-blooded siren in his hands.*

Marcus wanted to make everything so fucking perfect for her. She pulled on his hair, but he didn't mind as he knelt between the open v of her legs and moved the naughty little piece of lace that barely covered her to one side.

She bucked under his exploring fingers. He used his hands to part her lips, the cropped curls teased his skin and he groaned aloud when his tongue snaked out to steal a taste.

Leya moaned in response. Her hips jerked as he lapped at her warm, throbbing center. Unsatisfied with his access, he tugged on the lacy panties she wore. The fabric tore right off her supple body with a sound that sent tremors through him.

He pushed forward, causing her to spread her legs wider. *Oh, I fucking like that.* He lifted her left thigh and draped it over his shoulder digging his fingers into the soft flesh at her hips.

Mine. Roarrr. He thrust his tongue into her tight hole, growling when her muscles clenched. He could almost imaging how she would feel surrounding his dick. She was so hot and tight. It was going to be amazing.

Fuck yeah. But she had to come first. *Yes*, Marcus needed that very much. He swirled his tongue around her quivering bundle of nerves. Long kisses, deep licks, and a few pulls on her tiny bud with his lips had her calling out his name.

His Leya tried to buck him off, but he held her in place with his hands and stroked her from ass to clit with his long tongue. She tasted like ambrosia and he couldn't get enough of her. He felt the second she reached her pinnacle, her pussy clenched and spasmed around his mouth. Her juices dripping, he lapped up every single drop. *Fucking delicious.*

"That's right, baby, feel it," he growled against her, reveling in her pleasure. Pleasure he gave her. *Grrr.*

Marcus watched as she slowly opened her eyes. Leya breathed with her mouth open, chest rising with each inhale, glorious breasts bouncing in the sway. *So beautiful.* He rose to his knees, ready to worship at the altar of his mate. *Mine.*

"Leya?" He voiced her name like a question as he positioned his cock against her swollen lips. She was so wet for him, and so fucking hot. Still, the choice was hers.

"Marcus!" She called out and opened her arms. Fingers clasping him and drawing him down to her sweat-slicked body.

"Mate," he growled and pressed inside.

Marcus felt her barrier and was filled with a fierce sense of possession and pride. *Untouched. Mine. Only mine.*

"Look at me, baby," he said as he pushed his hips past her maidenhead. He claimed her in a roar that filled the tent.

Her body froze in the midst of his deafening yell and he forced himself to still.

"Marcus, I don't think you fit-" she panicked and squirmed underneath him, but he did not move.

"Relax, sweet, allow your body to adjust to me. Like a stone falling into water, you can take me, baby, you were made to," he stared at her, lost in her blue gaze and felt the second she relaxed and accepted him into her.

She was so tight. *Perfect. Made for him.* Her body softened and opened around him, then he began to move. He felt her enjoyment in her pleasure filled cries and the way she raked her nails across his back and shoulders as his body moved over hers.

Fucking music to his ears. The pain only adding to his pleasure. Leya twined her arms around his neck and panted. *Leya, sweet, sexy Leya. Love. Mine. Mate.*

Blood thundered in his ears; his Bear roared inside. Every thrust of his cock he seemed to touch more of her inside. Stroking her walls, heightening their pleasure. His cock pulsed in time with ever squeeze of her channel. *Fuck, soon now.*

Their scents mingled, entwined, and a new one emerged. Theirs. *Yes,* that felt right. It was the scent of their mating. One she would always carry. As would he. Marking them both as taken, *mated forever.* Marcus groaned as he thrust deep inside her quivering warmth.

She pulled him down for a soul scorching kiss that made him tremble. He needed her to come one more time before he could reach his pleasure. Marcus grabbed her legs, and she followed his lead, locking them around his waist. He slipped even deeper inside of her. *Oh fuck. Gonna come. No, not without her. No fucking way.*

He found her nub with his hand and rubbed with his callused thumb while he pushed himself deeper and faster. Tiny nails dug into his shoulders and his mate threw her head back and cried out his name.

He felt her pussy ripple in her climax, sucking his dick with her sheath.

Finally, he felt the pleasure of his own orgasm rip through his body. *A million fireworks, a comet orbiting the earth, a fucking supernova.* Coming inside of her was all of these things and more. He roared her name as his hips jerked out of time, pumping his seed into her heat with every quivering movement.

Mark her. His Bear growled and Marcus felt his fangs distend. He leaned forwards and she tilted her head, granting him access. His teeth slid into the flesh at the side of her neck like a hot knife through butter. He reveled in the coppery liquid that poured down his throat, pressing his teeth in deeper in the way of his kind.

Marcus claimed Leya as his mate for all the world to see. He put his mark on her body, while her sex tightened around his shaft and milked him for all he was worth.

"Mine."

EPILOGUE

The plane ride back to the states was long. *Too long.* At least it felt that way to Leya. She smiled and leaned her head against Marcus' shoulder. Her *mate* grumbled softly and opened his eyes to place a kiss on her forehead.

"Can I get you something?" Her stomach tightened at the sound of his deep, sexy voice.

"No, I'm good," she replied still smiling.

"Okay, I'm just gonna use the restroom. Be right back, baby." He got up and she admired the six-foot plus view of him as he squeezed down the aisle to the first-class restrooms.

They had almost the entire section to themselves, except for an older couple. The woman looked at Marcus then at her and nodded her approval. Leya bit back a giggle. He was a damn fine specimen of man. *And Bear. Her Bear. Grrr.*

Leya stretched in her seat. Her body was deliciously sore. She'd used muscles she never even knew she had the past few days! Heat warmed her face as she thought about how she'd gotten in that state.

And now I know exactly what the fuss is all about! She smiled at her own little joke. Marcus spent the remaining days of their vacation showing her exactly what she'd been missing on the king-sized bed in his suite, *and the shower, and the floor, and the kitchen table...*

Still, she couldn't get enough of him. *Her very own Bear! Her one true, fated mate.* According to him, what they had was rare and special. *Something to be treasured.* He vowed to do just that, to *treasure her* every single day of their lives together.

As far as she could tell that meant he felt the need to protect, provide, and possess her. *The three P's.* She giggled at her silly thoughts. Leya was a realist of course.

She knew relationships took time and effort on both sides. *Compromise, patience, love, and understanding.* All things she was ready to try with him. Marcus was incredible.

Her heart swelled with emotion as she thought about how her life had changed in just a few days. Sure, it was fast, but how many chances did a girl get to be claimed and mated by a sexy Bear Shifter who made her feel loved? She was grabbing onto him with both hands!

She'd never been impulsive or reckless, but this was *her life*. Her mind was still flying high, but *her heart*, her heart told her that he was worth it. He was the one. Her only one. She believed everything he told her.

How could she not after she watched him get all furry and fangy to save her from that feral dog? She had watched him risk life and limb for her and had no doubt he'd do it again. He loved her. The truth of that statement warmed her, hell, it made her shiver too.

The idea that *she* was loved. Big, dependable, boring Leya Tremayne loved by Marcus Devlin of *Bear Claw Bakery*. And she loved him right back. That was all that mattered.

Her eyes found his as he walked back over to his seat beside her. He put his arm around her back, and she snuggled into his side. One of her favorite positions when they weren't doing *other* things.

"So," he breathed in her hair as he spoke. He

seemed to love sniffing, kissing, and petting her. He was a very physical being. She loved it.

"The moving company should be finished packing your apartment up today. They'll deliver everything by the end of the week. That okay? Need to run up there and get anything?" Marcus asked while holding her securely in his strong arms.

She ran her hand over his t-shirt covered chest and smiled as he rumbled beneath her touch. *He liked being petted too*. She sure had enjoyed exploring his body with her eyes, hands, and mouth that morning. With any luck, she'd be back to exploring him in just a few short hours.

The diamond that winked up at her as she rubbed his pectorals had been an amazingly wonderful surprise after they'd mated, an occurrence he assured her was more unique than she knew. According to him and Clan law they were already married, but being a *normal*, he knew she would want a traditional wedding. *Flowers and all.*

After that brief discussion, he'd gone out for a few hours and came back with a string quartet, dozens of flowers, chocolates, champagne, and a huge diamond engagement ring. *Her Bear was a romantic!* She was so ridiculously happy. Leya couldn't stop smiling.

"What is it, baby?" he asked with one dark eyebrow raised.

"I'm happy," she told him.

Marcus grinned broadly, his handsome smile stealing her breath away. He captured her lips in a searing kiss that made her toes curl and she moaned softly as he pulled gently away.

"That's good, baby, because I am going to do everything I can to make sure you never have a reason to stop smiling. There's just one thing I forgot to warn you about-"

"What's that?"

"Well, you see, I mentioned my two brothers," he began.

"Yes? Daniel and Taylor, right?"

"Well, Daniel is the middle brother, and uh, he *kinda* hates women."

"What? Why?"

"You see, it's not his fault. He was supposed to get married and his fiancé left him standing at the altar."

"Oh my! No wonder, he hates women. But will he hate me?"

"No, baby, you are *mine*. He will love you." The *or I'll kill him* went unsaid.

"Then there is Taylor, and well, he's the baby

brother. Kinda spoiled by my parents before mom died, but anyway he won't be a problem. Unless he tries anything in which case, I'll rip his arms off and feed them to him."

"Geez, Marcus! You know I love you, and I'm sure Taylor will see me as nothing but a big, big sister!"

"None of that now, sweet, or I'll have to spank you for talking bad about my mate."

"Spank me?" She licked her lips and watched his eyes darken. *The idea had merit.*

"Not here, baby, we're landing. My brothers are getting us from the airport. They're probably already here," he said as he made sure both their seatbelts were fastened.

"So, you ready to meet the family?"

"Oh, I'm *bearly breathing* with anticipation!"

They both laughed at her joke, and she tilted her head up for his kiss. Love, happiness, and excitement for the future, *their future*, coursed through her veins.

"I love you, Marcus," she whispered into his mouth as he kissed her sweetly.

"I love you, my beautiful mate."

The end.

BEARLY THERE

BEARLY THERE

A BEAR CLAW TALE #2

by C.D. Gorri

For my ARC Team! You are the best!

del mare alla stella, C.D. Gorri

C.D. GORRI

Bearly THERE

A BEAR CLAW TALE 2

BLURB

She knows he's the one, but he is fighting it tooth and nail, or in this case, claw!

Krissy Sposa has been dreaming of her mating to gorgeous Bear Shifter, Taylor Devlin, since she was a teenager! But the sexy blonde Shifter is determined to remain a *play bear* despite her belief that they are fated mates.

Taylor has known the curly haired she-Bear ever since she started working for his family at the original Bear Claw Bakery location. Sure, he knows about her school-girl crush, but there's no way he is going to give in to temptation. No matter how sweet she looks with flour on her shirt and cream filling on her lips, Krissy Sposa is off-limits.

When a lone Bear comes sniffing around Krissy, Taylor has a decision to make. Claim her as his own or watch her get swept away by a handsome stranger!

A Message from Marcus, One of the Devlin Brothers...

Hello Clan-mates,

Leya and I are pleased to announce our engagement to the entire Barvale Clan!

As the oldest of the three Devlin Brothers, I am also pleased to announce that I am stepping into my father's shoes officially as Clan Alpha as he's ready for retirement.

He's off to see the world and as peaceful as things are here, I don't foresee any problems. Of course, anyone who is not happy with me taking up the reins has the right to issue an official challenge for the position at the next Clan gathering.

Now, we've got some in house changes. My youngest brother, Taylor, is our new Keeper. He will make sure Barvale Clan law is upheld and all incidents reported for posterity. If you have any Shifter related issues, please see him.

Now, I know Taylor seems like nothing but a play bear, but my baby bro is a force to be reckoned with when the need arises. He may seem all sweet and cuddly, but he's got some wicked sharp teeth, I guarantee. Do yourself a favor and read up on our laws before you try and take him on!

All you single ladies looking to catch a handsome Bear may want to watch out as well. Taylor's a charmer, but he's been known to break a few hearts. He is a confirmed bachelor, and that is directly from the Bear's mouth.

So please, do not bombard his work email with requests for dates or hook-ups. That address is for serious Clan or Bakery business only.

Speaking of which, Bear Claw Bakery is doing phenomenally well, and as such, we are investing some serious money back into our Clan! The health and well-being of our Clan is of the upmost importance.

We will begin with a complete overhaul of Barvale County Park. You can expect to see brand-new, cub-proof, playground equipment going up in the next few weeks!

More in-house changes include my brother Daniel as

our new Clan Enforcer! Do yourself a favor, don't do any bad shit that brings him knocking on your door.

Lastly, we will be hosting an engagement party in just a few weeks where I will introduce you all to my blushing bride! A warning one and all, be on your best behavior with my fiancée.

See you real soon!

-Marcus Devlin, Alpha of the Barvale Clan and CEO of Bear Claw Bakery

PROLOGUE

K rissy Sposa gritted her teeth and tried her best to remain calm. She'd been working up her nerve to ask Mr. Devlin, her Alpha and the owner of Bear Claw Bakery, for an after-school job ever since she was just a kid.

Krissy was almost thirteen now and she knew she'd be great at whatever it was they asked her to do! *She just had to be.*

Her mother wasn't doing all that well lately. She'd gotten fired from her part-time job and Krissy knew it was because the cancer was back.

She sucked in the cold air as she thought about how her mom suffered. And always silently. She'd tried desperately to hide her condition from her two daughters, but it was no use.

Both girls were Shifters. Their noses told them the truth before her mother could get the denial past her lips. Certain things had smells. Like fear, anger, pain, sadness, and lies. Some of these she'd attributed with her mother for far too long.

"Please help my mom get through this," she whispered her prayer to whatever gods were listening.

Her heart squeezed in her chest. This morning's bout of nausea had ended badly and, not for the first time in her young life, Krissy cursed her father for running out on them.

There was no one to explain about the changes she was experiencing. The fiercely protective sow that had risen up inside of her this past year. No one but her *normal* mother to teach her to control her Bear.

He was the one who passed on his supernatural side to her and Luisa, her younger sister. Not that either of them remembered the big Bear Shifter past his name and a vague recollection of his face.

Gianni Sposa wasn't a one-woman kinda guy. He'd upped and left when Krissy was still in second grade and Luisa, had still been in diapers. *The jerk!* Not that it mattered. Her mom was awesome!

Kind and loving, Patricia Sposa tried her best to

raise two Bear cubs on her own. When her husband left her, she sought advice from the local Clan Alpha, and he'd taught her the basics.

For a normal with two rambunctious Bear cubs for kids, she did an excellent job. Working as a school librarian she was always there for the girls, but she'd had to leave her position after this last round of chemo had left her incapacitated.

They had no choice but to replace her and since they still needed to pay bills and eat, she'd gotten a part-time job at the grocery store. But they had to let her go that morning after she'd been unable to show up once again. Her family was suffering, and Krissy was desperate.

Her feet ached with her quick, repetitive pacing. She'd been at it for an hour now. People filed in and out of the busy storefront of Bear Claw Bakery, the absolute best bakery and coffee shop around, while she contemplated her options.

They were few and they all sucked. What choice did she have? Shy Krissy had to go in! Quiet and awkward, confrontation was something she actively avoided. Too big to go unnoticed, and too insecure to strut her stuff like the other she-Bears in the clan, she'd endured the childish ribbing of her classmates and Clan-mates alike.

At five foot eleven inches tall, she towered over most of the boys in her class. All round, ninth-grade had been pretty terrible so far. Especially since she'd skipped a year in grammar school and was younger than everyone else.

Of course, the stress of high school came in second to everything else going on in her life. Christmas was just a few weeks away. Poor Luisa had her heart set on a new bike! But their mom could barely keep food on the table. With two Bear Shifter daughters, it was a difficult job.

No matter how scared she was, or how much Krissy hated the idea, she just had to go see her Clan Alpha. She needed a job and fast. It was the only way her little family was gonna make it.

With her back straight and her eyes cast downward she turned to the wide double doors with the words *Bear Claw Bakery* etched on them in gold.

She was going to demand an audience with Alpha Devlin! Her plan was going to work! If only she'd just looked up.

"Hey! Look out!" Krissy's sensitive ears recognized the high-pitched shriek of Barvale High School's one and only head cheerleader, Margot O'Conner, but the screaming normal wasn't fast enough to stop her from turning right into a six-foot plus brick wall.

Heat crept up her face and she knew she was blushing horribly. *Oh no! I can't believe I did this!* She closed her eyes tightly, wishing for all she was worth that the ground would simply open and swallow her.

A deep and pleasant chuckle reached her ears. Then the one boy in the whole world Krissy never thought would ever speak to her leaned over and offered her his hand.

"Ooof! Are you okay?"

Taylor Devlin, the youngest son of the Alpha and the quarterback for Barvale High's football team towered over her from where she now sat on the frozen ground with his hand outstretched. He was smiling gently at her, totally cool and unruffled by the havoc she'd just caused.

Her mouth hung open as she tried to wipe off the soggy, *utterly ruined thanks to her*, remnants of the drink and honeybun he'd been eating from her jacket.

"Come on, let me help you up," his playful grin, despite the coffee staining his varsity jacket, made Krissy lightheaded.

"Uh, thanks," she nodded and took his proffered

hand, trying not to look at the scowling beauty next to him.

That was his type, petite and perfect. The two of them were like high school gods. All golden and glowing with perfect skin and hair. They'd never noticed her in the halls or the cafeteria. Barely even acknowledge her existence.

A circumstance that she presently thought wasn't so bad. Definitely better than this! Humiliation burned her cheeks. Krissy wished he'd just forget about her and move on, but to her surprise he kept hold of her hand!

"Uh, I am really sorry," she began, but Margot cut her off.

"Well, *no duh*, loser! You should, like, watch where you're going!"

"Hey now, that's unnecessary, Mar. Uh, tell you what, you go ahead to the field, and I'll catch up with you later," he dismissed the cheerleader and picked up the smashed cup and napkins. Without a backwards glance, he took Krissy by the elbow and herded her inside.

She couldn't believe it. Taylor Devlin just ditched Margot O'Conner to help her inside. *No freaking way!*

Focus, you are here for a job not to drool over football players.

"You're Clan?" he asked in a low voice, with that same jovial smile on his handsome face. She nodded dumbly, unable to use real words just yet.

"Just had your first Change?"

Another nod.

"Have you been inducted?"

Krissy shook her head this time. Her induction was coming up soon. She'd had her first Shift, *or Change*, but with her mother being so ill, she hadn't gotten around to scheduling it yet.

"So, what's your name?"

"Uh, Krissy. Sposa. Well, it's Kristianne Sposa."

"I'm Taylor. So, *Kristianne Sposa*, what can we do for you?"

"Oh, um, I need to speak to Alph- I mean *Mr. Devlin* about the 'help wanted' sign in the window, and I guess about my induction too. Uh, my mom hasn't been up to a meeting," she murmured and felt her cheeks grow hot under his curious stare.

"Dad's not here, but you can talk to Marcus, my older brother. He's the one who's in charge now anyway. Come on, I'll introduce you. We'll get you a job and get your induction all squared away, alright there, *Dimples*?"

"Dimples?"

"Yeah. You got one right here," he pressed a spot to the right of her lips, and she went rigid.

"You don't mind, do you? Kristianne is a big name for such a little girl."

"Um, no, it's okay," she said and walked past him as he opened the door. *Hmm. No one ever called her little before.*

"Then *Dimples* it is," Taylor Devlin smiled, and Krissy's Bear sat up straight in her mind's eye.

She breathed deep as he walked past to open yet another door further inside the bakery. The scent of fresh cut grass and forest filled her nostrils.

She'd never encountered a smell quite like it. Fresh and clean. Welcoming even. Like coming home after a long hard day. One word reverberated through her entire body. *Mine.*

She stopped dead in her tracks and tried to still the panic welling up inside of her.

"What's the matter?" Concern marred his perfect face as he waited for her to step through the door.

"Uh, nothing," she stuttered but walked quickly through.

"Alright then, Dimples. Let's get you situated."

She knew then, her life would never be the same.

"*Dimples?!* Come on Krissy, where ya at?" the loud rumbling Bear startled her into clicking the wrong key on her laptop. *Ugh.* Why was *he* here?

"Dimples! Marcus sent me to sign the order, he's shacking up with his mate tonight, and I'm already late for my date," Taylor Devlin's voice boomed out from the front of the bakery all the way to the back office where Krissy had been holed up since the storefront closed at six that evening.

She was only supposed to stay after for a few minutes, print the orders then leave them on the counter for Marcus to sign. But as usual, she'd gotten sidetracked by work. The sound of a cell ringing had her ears perking up.

"Hey! Yeah? Sorry, I am running late, but you wear that little red number and I promise to make it up to you. Uh huh."

Of course, the golden boy had a date tonight. When didn't he? She sighed and looked at the clock. Nine o'clock on a Friday night and she was still in the office! *Some life you have!*

She shook her head and stood up stretching her long limbs. She enjoyed working at this location for a lot of reasons. One was that she didn't have to sit at a desk for all hours of the day.

Here she got to interact with real people. The forest behind the ovens was great for an afterwork Shift, and she was close to home! So, *yeah*, it was perfect.

Not to mention she could eat her heart out over Taylor Devlin from up close. *Guess I'm a glutton for punishment. Groan.* Ignoring his continued shouts, she walked around her desk and rolled her shoulders. It wasn't her fault he got roped into actually working tonight! First time in how long?

"Dimples!"

Stupid friggin' nickname! It was better suited for a pet. Something you called a kitten or guinea pig! Her Bear bristled at that.

No matter how many times she complained, he

never called her anything else. But that was Taylor for you. He barely even noticed she was there half the time.

Still treated her like she was a kid. She exhaled slowly, willing her anger and humiliation to die down. *Easy girl. Just finish up your work! Stupid billion-dollar company.*

The brothers kept their main offices in the original bakery, despite the building in nearby New York City that held the rest of corporate. Which was also why she still worked there.

Money hadn't changed the brothers and in a way she was glad. Bear Claw Bakery was a family run business and, though she wasn't technically family, she was still damn proud of the place. She'd seen them rise after all.

"Dimples!"

"One second," she murmured. She didn't need to yell. Like her, Taylor had supernaturally enhanced hearing. He just yelled to piss her off. *Jerk.*

She hurried to finish plugging in the right quantities. Taking inventory was always a bitch, and she had dozens of locations to account for. She was the general manager for all the bakery branches in the tri-state area not to mention she oversaw the other managers across the USA.

Krissy was damn good at her job. She loved the responsibility and the trust the brothers had in her. She would never leave them willingly, despite her humiliation at last year's office Christmas party.

Bear Claw Bakery had saved her life. Literally bailing her and her family out when she was barely a teenager. The Devlin family had done more for her than her own father.

Krissy pushed all thoughts of the past out of her head and hit print. She waited for the old wireless multi-function to get fired up and to start spitting out paper.

The machine took forever, but Marcus wasn't particularly into tech and he saw no need to replace it. He was the big boss as it were. New Clan Alpha and CEO of *Bear Claw Bakery*. He'd been voted in on both offices by his brothers.

Marcus Devlin was as trustworthy as they came. And he was the one who usually stopped by the office once a week to sign the necessary papers.

The other two were in and out less and less frequently. Each of them trusted Krissy. *Like a sister.* Her Bear chuffed at the thought. She didn't feel *sisterly* to all of them. To Marcus and Daniel, sure. But not to Taylor.

Her Bear had insisted from the first time she saw

him that he was theirs. *Mate.* A wave of mortification swept over her as unpleasant memories from this year's holiday office party surfaced in her consciousness.

She'd made the fatal error of telling Taylor after ten too many shots that he was her mate. Of course, he'd let her down gently. *But still.* It was a humiliation she could've gone her whole life without. *Fucking shit.*

"Where the papers at, Dimples?" Taylor Devlin loomed in the doorway to her small office.

A golden-haired Bear of a man with a deceptively lean build. He wore black leather boots on his feet and no jacket. His button-down shirt looked like it was made just for him. *Probably was.* She knew all too well that he had muscles on his muscles underneath the shirt and stylishly deconstructed jeans.

They were Clan after all, and though it was bad form to ogle Shifters when necessarily nude to perform their Change, she may have snuck a peek in every now and then. She was single, not dead.

And Taylor was mouthwateringly good too look at. She clamped down that part of her that wanted to roll belly up and be petted by him and gestured towards the printer.

"Papers coming out now, boss," she said and

tossed a pen in his general direction. Of course, he caught it without even looking.

"You sure we need all this in the Springfield store?"

"Yeah. We just signed a contract with a local wedding planner. She's been ordering huge amounts of our pastries and coffee by the pound for these amazing wedding breakfasts she organizes."

"Ugh. Don't say wedding or I'll break out in hives. It's bad enough with Marcus and Leya around here. We don't need you mooning over wedding bells too!"

"As if," she said and forced herself to ignore the pain that shot through her heart at his cold words. *Jerk.*

"Alright, Dimples, here you go."

She nodded and reached a handout to grab the papers from him forcing herself to keep her eyes downcast on her keyboard. *Don't look. It only hurts more when you do.*

"You know," he hesitated, and she felt his eyes on her. Krissy didn't need to be told from his slow, measured gaze, that he was looking over her work uniform of a plaid shirt over jeans. No doubt, he found her lacking. *As usual.*

She knew what she was. *A Bear.* Tall and big

boned. She stood almost six-foot tall, weighed about a hundred and seventy-five pounds of some muscle, but mostly flub. *She worked in a bakery for fuck's sake!*

Yes, she had *T* and *A*, but she was too insecure to flaunt it. Choosing jeans and flannel shirts over anything else to wear at work. The bosses didn't mind. They were like her *brothers* after all. *Oh damn. FML.*

"It's Friday night, Dimples. Don't you have a date?"

"Sure. I have two actually," she sassed and tried to smile, but failed.

"I'm serious, you're too young to work all the time-"

"Taylor, I am fine. Luisa isn't home yet from med school, and mom is recovering from her latest round of physical therapy. The hip replacement was only a month ago. She needs me."

"How is she? Did she like the flowers?"

"Yes. She did. That was very thoughtful of you. Now, I'm going to scan and send these documents, then I am going home to relieve the nurse. You have fun on your date," this time her smile was genuine. *Of course it is, my heart is genuinely breaking.*

Taylor nodded and with a small wave, walked out of her office without looking back.

I can't do this anymore, she thought sadly as she stood up an hour later to go home. She locked the place down and waved to the bakers in the back as she grabbed a half dozen rolls fresh from the ovens before taking off for the night.

Taylor Devlin might not think of me as mate material, but surely someone out there would. Maybe it is time to move on.

She pondered that thought all the way home.

"Earth to Taylor! Bro, you haven't said a word throughout this whole meeting," Marcus stared down at his little brother with unflinching concern in his dark brown eyes.

Daniel grunted, but did not add to his brother's comments. Waiting for Taylor to enlighten the group instead. He figured his baby bro had some female troubles and he was best left out of any discussion involving women.

Especially after his heart had been torn out of his body by his ex. *Grrr.* His Bear riled too easily at the remembered pain and Daniel shut it down before shit got away from him.

As Enforcer to his brother and the Barvale Clan, he needed to act the part with the temperament befitting his station. He turned his blue stare onto his youngest brother and watched him. *Hmm.* Something was on the guy's mind.

His handsome face was scrunched up in thought and he waved a hand in the air as he turned to both of his older brothers. It was only the three of them gathered around the large mahogany table at the Clan Den.

It used to belong to their father, but as Alpha, Marcus now lived at the enormous fifteen-bedroom cabin that sat in the middle of the hundred and eighty acres of forest and land, including the freshly stocked Lake Ursa, the Devlin family owned.

There was a single road that granted access to the Den and the other smaller guest cabins that dotted it, but it was all private access. The Clan took security very seriously.

In fact, Daniel had doubled their efforts with new state of the art cameras and alarm systems made by Draco Fortis. Best in the business as far as he was concerned.

"Taylor!" Marcus' voice jolted the youngest Devlin out of his reverie.

"Yeah, um, so I was thinking about Dimples-"

"Finally," Daniel muttered, and Taylor shot him a curious look.

"What? No! I mean, she works really hard and takes care of her mom while her sister is in med school, maybe we should do something for her?"

"You mean, like why don't you take pity on the girl already? We all know she's been crushing on you since forever," Marcus glowered at Daniel for his tactless comments.

"What? It's true! I mean throw her a freaking bone already, Taylor, man, the girl drools after you," the Enforcer raised his hands in mock surrender as Marcus growled at hm.

"Dimples is like *our* little sister and I won't have you talk about her like that," Taylor shouted.

"Oh yeah? What are you gonna do, pretty boy?"

Marcus raised his eyebrows as he watched both his younger brothers act like cubs. *Ugh*. The agony and triumph of being the toughest, most dominant, *AND* most mature brother.

"Okay! Alright! Daniel, shut the fuck up. Taylor, you might be on to something. Now, we just gave every one of our employees a raise and new full, comprehensive health coverage. Maybe we can do something a little more personal, that does not involve Taylor sacrificing himself-"

"Some fucking sacrifice, did you see the way our 'baby sister' looked at the office party last year. The *chesticles* on her? Holy shit, Krissy Sposa is all grown up and *day-yum!*" Daniel was baiting him. He knew it. But Taylor couldn't help but respond.

He'd always been protective of Dimples. Ever since he bumped into her pacing outside the bakery all those years ago. The fact his brother was talking about her like she was some chick you picked up in a bar made him see red.

He picked up the spoon he'd used to stir his tea and honey and looked it over. *Yes, he drank tea fuck you very much.* Then he flicked it over the table hitting Daniel right between his eyes. Fucker deserved it.

"That's fucking sticky, you asshole!" He growled then stood up, ready to tackle the shit out of his little brother, but his Alpha stopped him with the full-on force of his station reverberating in his deep voice.

"Enough! Sit! Now, shut the fuck up about Krissy's, uh, *assets*, Daniel. Taylor you knock it off too. I know you think of Krissy as our baby girl, but Daniel has a point. She is an adult and, yeah, you're right also. She does work too hard. Tell you what. Let me talk to Leya about it," his voice softened as he said his mate's name and both younger brothers rolled their eyes.

"She's been feeling a little antsy about making

friends and since she's going to start working for us anyway, we might as well throw them together before I formally introduce my mate to our Clan. Speaking of which, on to Clan business," Marcus' voice floated in and out of Taylor's hearing as he pondered what his older brother had said.

Taylor exhaled a deep breath. He didn't know why Daniel's remarks bothered him so much, but they did. The miserable fucker was always throwing out snide comments about Taylor's so-called man-whoring ways. Called him a play-bear and everything. *Dick.*

So he liked pussy. What the fuck? It was a free country. Barvale and the surrounding towns were stocked with some prime women. They knew the score. When he met a woman, contrary to popular belief, he did not lie to get them in bed. He laid out his terms, and if the woman agreed, well then good. If not, he moved on. Anyone he got involved with had a good time. No harm. No foul.

He'd always been a *however-many-women-at-a-time* kind of guy. Nowhere near the age where he felt the need to find his mate and settle down, he saw no reason to change his ways.

Not like Marcus. He was grateful to the powers that be that his big bro had found his fated mate.

Hell, he even marveled at the idea that he'd met his destiny on a tropical vacation! *Sounds like a plan.* It just wasn't for him.

Daniel had been ready to tie the knot years ago, but after she-who-shall-not-be-named left him standing at the altar, *literally*, he'd sworn off women.

Both stances were too strict for Taylor. He liked women. He just didn't like commitment. *Fucking Daniel.* That prick had to mention the Christmas party where poor Dimples had had way too much to drink.

Who knew she'd look so damn sexy while chugging back liquor and shaking her ass to some truly hideous holiday music? But she had.

She wore a velvety black dress that clung to her generous curves and had many-a-tongue hanging out that night. Hell, he'd almost decked John from accounting for trying to squeeze her ass on the dance floor.

For the first time in recollection, her curls had hung loose down her back instead of in their usual pig tails. The scent of jasmine and vanilla floated around her.

She'd looked shocked as hell when he'd grabbed her hand and spun her around the dance floor. *And yes*, being the gentlemen, he was, he'd stopped them under some strategically placed mistletoe. It was a Christmas party, so yeah, he gave into temptation to taste her soft pink lips.

He'd been shocked as hell to find himself desperate for more than one pass after that chaste meeting of mouths. Raging desire had coursed through his veins and he'd pulled her away from the crowds to a dark corner where he could experiment with his newfound attraction to his little Dimples.

And fuck him, he'd been attracted! He'd sported a full-on boner from just that small taste. His heart had thudded in his chest and his Bear roared in his head, but it had all come crashing to a screeching stop when she'd whispered that one dreaded word to him in the darkness. *Mate.*

Panic gripped him and he'd forced himself to let her go. *Poor Dimples. Poor him.* He'd never been so hard in his life. He'd hated himself for doing it, but he'd had no choice. He wasn't made for *happily ever afters* and she was.

Taylor had let her down gently. He'd ignored her teary-eyed nod and the calm way she accepted his rejection. As if she'd already known he couldn't possibly want her. The lie tasted foul on his tongue, but either she'd been too drunk to notice, or too inexperienced to call him on it. *And thank the gods, because he couldn't have resisted her if she'd offered herself a second time.*

He'd forced himself to be nonchalant the next time he saw her. And he had no regrets. He went back to living his life on his terms. Happy as a Bear in the woods. *Right?*

Of course, he made the right decision. Their relationship was back to normal. She hadn't quit her job as he'd feared she would. In fact, she acted as if those frantic, shared kisses had never happened. A truth that he didn't even realize bothered him until right then.

No. That's dumb. This is for the best. We're friends. She's like my little sister.

Even as he had this little conversation with himself, he noted his Bear sitting up and shaking his head at him from that place in his mind's eye where his beast waited. *Grrr.*

THREE

Krissy dusted the flour off her jeans as she stepped around the counter. Dodging the various employees that moved restlessly gathering orders and making smoothies and lattes, she contemplated her options for the day. It was after ten in the morning and she'd been at work since six without breakfast. She was starving.

"Excuse me, Frankie," she moved past the young freckle-faced girl who smiled nervously at her. She was a freshman at the local community college and a member of their Clan.

She reminded Krissy a lot of herself when she came in for the part-time job. The oldest of two kids from a single-parent home, she helped support her mom and younger brother with her job at Bear Claw.

She smiled now at her decision to hire the girl on the spot, noting how hard Frankie worked. Choosing a pecan crusted honeybun and a large mug of specially brewed dark roast coffee, Krissy sauntered over to an empty table and opened a reading app on her cell phone.

Sometimes she needed a few minutes to just let her mind unwind. *A good snack, an even better book, and I'll be right as rain.* Ready to tackle the shit ton of emails waiting for her inside her small office.

The old-fashioned bell above the door rang, but Krissy ignored it as she read, nibbled, and sipped. It wasn't until someone slid the chair out across from her and sat down that she looked up.

"Uh, *hello?*" Krissy recognized the blue-eyed blonde with the radiant smile as Marcus' fiancée.

"Hi! Krissy, right? I'm Leya, we met the other day," the woman practically overflowed with happiness as she shook Krissy's hand.

Krissy found herself wanting to squint against such an unabashedly blinding display of joy. *How nice to be happily mated*, she thought, ignoring her own feelings of melancholy.

"Yes, I remember, is there something I can do for you?" She closed the app and sat straight adopting a formal expression.

"Oh, no, no, please, don't be so formal. I was just stopping by to invite you to come out with me-"

Another jingle over the door had Krissy's head swiveling around before she could respond. *Why would the bright ball of energy that was Leya Tremayne, soon-to-be-Devlin, want to hang out with her?*

Before she could ponder a reason, she spotted the person she'd been hoping to avoid. Taylor Devlin in his very fine flesh. Twice in twenty-four hours. *Must be a record.*

"Hi Taylor!" Leya gushed and waved him over.

Krissy frowned. He did seem to be looking for someone. She was surprised when his emerald green eyes sparkled in her direction.

What the heck was going on? First, Marcus' fiancée was here asking her to hang out and talking a mile a minute, then Taylor came in looking for her? Usually, the brothers spent days at a time away from the office, knowing she'd take care of things. This was all highly unusual. *Was she being punk'd?*

"Anyway, you want to come with?" Leya seemed so earnest, and yet Krissy had no idea what she was talking about.

How could she concentrate when six-and-a-half-feet of blonde god was walking towards her?

"Who's coming with who?" He asked and realizing what he said was unable to hide the crimson blush staining his cheeks. Krissy could have died right there. *Um, me please? No! Bad Bear!*

"Why Krissy and I are going out to do some shopping! Right, Krissy?"

Before she could refuse the claim, Krissy watched as Taylor reached over and snagged a piece of her honey bun while guffawing at his almost sister-in-law. Her eyes narrowed as she listened to him. *The ass!*

"Dimples? Shopping? Yeah, right. She buys her flannels and jeans by bulk, don't ya, Dimples? *Shopping?* As if she'd leave work for that," he chuckled and grinned at them both in a way she *used to* find irresistibly charming.

Right then, Krissy wanted to kick the big blonde jerk right where it hurts! *How dare he!*

"Actually, she's right. Good thing you got here in time Taylor. We're about to get a huge delivery and it needs to be signed for. You don't mind, I'm sure. Oh, and put this in the bin," she handed him her garbage and walked straight out the front door, Leya on her heals.

"But Dimples, I gotta-"

"Well, looks like we're off! Later, Taylor," giggled Leya. She jumped up from her seat, a ray of pure sunshine, and gave her almost-brother a squeeze.

"Bye now! Be a good boy and sign for the delivery! Oh and Marcus said to meet us later at *The Thirsty Dog* for a little party, 'kay?"

Krissy barely overheard what Leya said to the bane of her existence as she stepped outside into the early spring air! What's more, she really didn't care. *Is that really what he thought about her?*

He spoke as if she was some kind of hopeless workaholic! Like she lived in her flannels and jeans! Like she had no interest in being a woman! How could he?

Cause he's right, her Bear hated arguing with her human half, but sometimes, the animal had to call it like it is. Krissy scowled as she looked down at her completely inappropriate for the weather attire.

But can't he see beyond my clothes? To the Bear and the woman underneath? The question threatened to choke her, as did the answer. *No. he can't and he doesn't want to.*

After the kiss they'd shared at the Christmas party, Krissy had been certain that he saw her as a woman now. Maybe not like the women he preferred to date, *but still.*

I am such a fool. That stupid, fateful night! If only

she could go back in time and talk herself out of it! How she'd taken care with her dress and hair. How she'd had more to drink than usual.

Of course, that had been after her mother took a bad tumble on some ice in the grocery store parking lot. Patricia Sposa was getting older and she wasn't physically well to begin with. The fall had taken a lot out of her.

The stress of her mother's impending hip replacement and the recent relapse of the ovarian cancer that plagued her was simply too much. Of course, the excellent health care the brothers' provided completely covered the operation and rehabilitation. But at the time, it seemed impossible.

She'd foolishly tried to drown her troubles away in shot after shot of the delicious *RumChata* liquor. *Literally*. She just wanted to be young and carefree for one night.

Of course, Taylor was there. Always something of a playboy, *notoriously so,* he'd stood like a beacon amongst his employees. The night club they'd rented was beautifully decorated, very upscale and inviting.

She'd worshipped him from afar for years. Hiding right under his nose. For all his supernatural capabilities, the blonde Black Bear Shifter had remained ignorant of her affection for him. She drank, danced, and flirted that night. Trying to forget for just a little while the load of responsibilities she bore every single day.

Surely, the Fates decided to pity her that night. Taylor himself had asked her to dance and spun her round and round the dance floor. And she'd loved every minute of it.

Her heart thudded in her chest, her body heated, falling more and more under the potent spell that was being near Taylor Devlin. The entire time spent in his arms, her Bear had growled the one word she'd gotten used to hearing whenever he was near. *Mate.*

Then she did the unthinkable. She told him. Spilled her guts to the pussy-hound of a Bear and had to sit there while he politely told her she was mistaken. She'd had too much to drink and Taylor could never be her mate. *EVER.*

The painful memory was almost too much to bear. She stifled a gasp, not knowing where she was walking, but she slowed her pace when a small hand on her arm had her looking down into the sympathetic eyes of Marcus' mate.

"Hey now, Krissy, I know my almost bro-in-law can be an insensitive jerk, but don't let him get you down."

"Um, I'm sorry, Leya. I think I should go home"

"Wow. You do care about him, don't you?" Leya's shock made Krissy laugh through her tears. She wiped them away quickly, allowing herself to be tugged by the smallish woman to her car.

"I, uh, I think I just realized he's never gonna *love* me," Krissy said the word as if it was dirty. A nasty trick the world played on her, making her think she could have him.

"Oh Krissy! Look, I'm so sorry honey. I love Taylor, but he's a dog! Now, you are not going home."

"I'm not?"

"Nope! We are going shopping! Besides, you know what they say, there are plenty of fish in the sea! Or maybe I should say, *bears in the woods*?!" She giggled and Krissy found herself responding.

"That is terrible!"

"OMG, you're right! Don't tell Marcus!" Leya laughed again and Krissy understood how Marcus could fall for this bright and happy woman.

"Now, the best way to get over any man is to shop till you drop! Are you with me?"

Krissy looked down at her worn jeans and faded shirt. *Flannels and jeans by bulk, huh?* Fuck that.

"Yeah. I am ready."

"Great! Jersey girls are so lucky with the whole no sales tax on clothing thing, I've lived in the city so long I forgot! Now, I have been dying to get down to the *Full Moon Outlets* ever since me and Marcus landed after our vacation!"

"Sounds good to me!"

"Yay!"

With an excited squeal of rubber on pavement, Krissy said a mini-prayer as Leya hightailed it onto the highway. Marcus' little normal mate drove them to what was sure to be the most thorough shopping experience of Krissy Sposa's life.

"Where the fuck are you, Taylor?"

"At the bakery! Your mate dragged poor Dimples out the door to do some shopping with her today."

"So?"

"So? Well someone had to stay and sign for the shipment of new mixers. These fuckers cost fifty grand each! Now, I'm stuck overseeing all thirty of them, plus the extra handles, get divided and sent to the other locations."

Laughter flowed over from the other end of the line and Taylor frowned. The fucker was laughing at him!

"You know *this sucks*, Marcus! She shouldn't be doing this alone. I had to carry like ten boxes of equipment to our vans for distribution myself. Does she normally do this shit?"

"Fuck, Taylor, that's been part of her job since she was seventeen! She's a Bear not some delicate freaking flower," his brother growled, but Taylor didn't like the implication.

"Marcus, this isn't right. It's too hard for her-"

"Oh Jeez! Look, shut the fuck up, alright? We got an issue," Marcus switched to his Alpha voice and Taylor was all ears.

"What's up?"

"I was out with Daniel and a few of our guards patrolling the perimeter around the Den," he paused, and Taylor stiffened. Something had his Alpha worried.

"I scented something strange. A stranger, actually. Ursine, for sure, but it was *different*."

"What do you mean?"

"I don't know. Like us, but not of our Clan. Still, there was something familiar about the scent."

"As *Keeper*, I've been studying our laws. Anyone, Shifter or normal, seeking refuge in our territory is required to announce him or herself-"

"It was male."

"Okay, well still, the laws state he must formally seek permission to be here. Otherwise, we are well within our rights to defend our territory and to hunt him down."

"Yes, well, let's hope it doesn't come to that. We will give this stranger a few days to announce himself."

"Are you sure that's a good idea?"

"For now. Okay, work and Clan business aside, you're still meeting us for drinks and wings tonight at *The Thirsty Dog*, yes?"

"You know it's Saturday night, right? I mean I have better things to do than to watch my brother and his mate, though if Leya is looking for a little something from your younger and sexier brother for comparison-"

"I'll rip your damn arms off and feed them to you first, *dick*. Look, it's not just us. Daniel's gonna be there."

Taylor's eyebrows rocketed to his hairline. His brother was rarely seen in mixed company these days. *Maybe he should go?* It was true, he had a date. But the woman he'd promised to take out was more than a casual acquaintance.

A blast from his past, actually. Margot O'Conner, former cheerleader and sometimes fuck buddy, had waylaid him at the pharmacy where he'd gone to restock on some, *er*, necessary *protection*.

He was clean as they came, Bear Shifter and all, but he had no intention of making any little Devlin's by accident! Anyway, he'd taken her hint and asked her out.

Hint meaning the way she'd pressed her body fully into him and grasped onto his forearm. *A little trip down memory lane maybe.* He'd regretted the decision later and meant to cancel.

She could be a bit much. Her tendency to be possessive and throw tantrums was unappealing, but she still looked good. Maybe he could share a few beers with her and his brothers tonight?

Yeah. She could meet him there. That way if he didn't feel like scratching that old itch again, he could part ways friendly-like. He was just tapping off the text with the change of plans to Margot when Marcus' voice brought him back to the present.

"Ok, good, by the way Krissy will be there too and a couple of the guys." Meaning his brother's guards would be there as well. The Clan Alpha always had guards with him when he went out amongst normals.

Did he say Dimples was going? Now, why would she do that? Despite her antics during the holidays, she hated drinking. As far as he knew, she liked work, and, well, work. *Huh. Odd.* He knew so little about her. For some reason, that bothered him. A lot.

"Okay, uh, my date will meet me there. Anyway, I'll see you later."

Taylor couldn't quite erase his frown the rest of the day. He'd meant to stick around for an hour or so, until Krissy got back. Then he'd find out if his brother had just been messing with him.

Surely, she didn't have any intention of going to that rowdy Werewolf run bar on a Saturday night. She was sure to be harassed by a bunch of half-drunk Shifters, or worse, *normals* looking for an easy lay.

His growl surprised him, but he controlled himself before anyone else seemed to notice. He cleared his throat and grabbed an iced tea from the cooler in the back.

It was cool outside, low sixties, but he felt as if he was burning up. He breathed in the air, the smells of fresh baking bread and sweets painted the air and his beast reveled in it. It was truly a nice evening. Even if he was sweating balls and felt all antsy.

He checked his phone; it was getting late. *She's not coming back to work.* The realization filled him with shock. Shit, maybe she was having car trouble? He dialed her cell phone, worried about her well-being he told himself. It went right to voicemail.

Shit! She could be stuck somewhere on the highway waiting for a tow truck with no gas, no phone! *Fuck.* Before he got through the door, he remembered she'd left with Leya. If there was an issue with a car or anything else, Marcus would have taken care of it.

Grrr. What is wrong with me? Taylor ran his hands over his face. He felt anxious and unsettled. A weird sort of anticipatory sensation began somewhere in his gut. Completely out of sorts, he grunted.

This was all her fault! Dimples wasn't supposed to be out gallivanting with his brother's mate. She was supposed to be here. Tucked away at the bakery, where he knew she was safe! *Dammit.*

Disgusted with himself Taylor got up from her desk. The scent of jasmine and vanilla hung in the air, too powerful to ignore. *Fuck.* He needed to get away from there.

He needed space and fresh air. It was only six, he didn't have to be at *The Thirsty Dog* for another two hours and it was about a half hour away. He had time for a run!

Fur pushed through his pores and his beast grumbled happily. *Wait.* He rushed outside and walked past the graveled employee parking lot to the woods that sat behind the bakery. The ovens gave off so much heat he felt it burn into his back as he passed the familiar building.

The flour and yeasty scent perfumed the air and drove away the disturbing fragrance of jasmine that had somehow started to make him a little woozy.

Tucking himself behind a close copse of oaks he immediately shucked off his clothing. Within seconds he felt that familiar hum of magic lengthening his muscles and snapping his bones. His beast pushed out from within, flexing and growing, stretching him until he stood on four legs, a huge, off-white Black Bear.

Taylor's fur was so much lighter than both his brother's it was almost comical. *A blonde Black Bear!* He'd had to deal with a lot of shit from his brothers and some of his peers in the Clan when he was younger. Shifters often tested the dominance of others to establish hierarchy in a Pack or Clan.

Because of his white color, he was often targeted. Taylor learned early to use his size and wiry frame to his benefit. He was not as bulky as some male Bears, but he was generally faster. They soon learned that white fur or not, his Black Bear was a force to be reckoned with.

His brothers wouldn't have allowed him to grow up as anything less. Animalistic tendencies demanded he be able to defend himself, and in time, protect his mate and cubs. So, yeah, he trained.

His parents never coddled their sons, but he recalled his father telling him stories of special *white* Black Bears when he was a kid. It always soothed his ruffled fur after a round of teasing from his peers. Kids could be jerks sometimes.

His brother Daniel was blonde in his human form, like Taylor, but even his fur was more of a dark brown, lightening on his head and neck to a golden glow. Neither of them had Marcus' deep black coloring.

Dad had told Taylor that his unique coloring made him a *Spirit Bear*. Rare in the natural world and even rarer in the supernatural one. Taylor learned to be proud of his uniqueness. And when it was called for, he'd beaten the shit out of anyone who dared taunt him.

Sure, he was more a lover than fighter. He left most of the violence to Daniel nowadays. *Go figure.* After all, he was the Clan Enforcer.

Even Marcus loved a good tussle now and again. But Taylor was more into books than fists, and yeah, *women too.* He was the original *play-bear* of the bunch. Took to girls like a fish to water just about as soon as he could talk.

His Bear chuffed at the phrase. *Touchy much?* Taylor ignored the animal's faint protest and encouraged him to amble forward. He tried to find his fur at least once a week, but admittedly, it had been awhile. He needed this. The release of his Change.

There was nothing like the quick rush of energy and the fullness of Shifter magic as it filled his limbs. Settling him like nothing else, his Bear rose up from deep inside.

A frequent reader, he'd perused a few accounts in the old Keeper's journals of Spirit Bears. The Devlin's produced one other a hundred years back, but the cub had died young. The victim of a hunting accident.

The journals were like memoirs of a sort. A kind of *captain's log,* only instead of the Alpha, they were recorded by his chosen Keeper. He'd been honored when Marcus chose him. People tended to think him flippant. Not that he gave them any reason to see beyond the façade. *Dimples knows the real you. Remember the collection of Shakespearean plays she gave you for your birthday last year?*

The books were old, and leather bound. A unique

edition, they were over a hundred years old and illustrated with fine gold etchings. He'd loved them. Odd how she knew that when no one else seemed to.

The Bear turned his head and began ambling through the forest. His mind wandering as he went. Reading about his ancestors from the point of view of the Bears who'd led before him was simply amazing.

One account that he'd found particularly interesting was written by Connor Devlin, his great-uncle. The Bear Shifter was as much of a ladies man as Taylor himself, but the way he'd described his Change, well, that was breathtaking.

It spoke to Taylor in a way that not many things could. Uncle Connor, as it were, recounted each nuance of the shift in what could only be described as pure poetry. And the consequent feeling of being grounded, well, Taylor could totally relate to that!

In fact, today's shift was to help him do just that. His Bear grunted as he slowed his pace. The animal was distracted lately. Taylor tried not to think about why. A certain curly haired face popped into his head, but he pushed her out just as quickly as she'd appeared. *No. No freaking way.*

He paused in his tracks, lifted his furry head to the trees, sniffing as he went. Intent on easing some of his anxieties with a nice hard run, but first he needed to perform a thorough search of the grounds. He breathed deeply, using his supernaturally enhanced bear sniffer to test the area.

Suddenly, he stopped dead. A low roar blossomed from deep in his chest. There was a sharp, tangy scent in the air. One he didn't recognize.

Stranger. His Bear walked round testing the area for signs of the intruder. There it was again, stronger the closer he got to the bakery. Whoever it was, he was long gone. The scent was a few hours old at least.

He swiftly changed back to his human form and shrugged into his clothing. His Bear on high alert, he couldn't shake the feeling that there was something familiar about that scent.

Taylor dialed his brothers. *Damn.* Both calls went straight to voicemail. He spied the time and frowned.

Fuck. It was later than he'd thought. He hopped into his black custom Range Rover with its pure white leather interior and zoomed down the road. *Shit.* His date was gonna be pissed, unless she'd changed drastically from high school. *Doubt it. Oh well, home first then bar.*

Freshly showered and changed, he grinned as he

pressed down on the accelerator. Thrilling at the immediate response of the pristine engine. *A good car purrs for her master on the road like a good woman does in the bedroom.* His Dad could be a bit sexist in his views, but damn if he didn't say the funniest shit.

Most people were surprised when they saw his car of choice. It was not some two-door flashy sports car, but rather, a fully equipped, luxury sports utility vehicle. But fuck them. He was no one's stereotype, and New Jersey saw some pretty fucking fierce weather.

Hot summers, cold as fuck winters, blizzards, hurricanes, thunderstorms, droughts, you name it. The Garden State was unpredictable as fuck, too bad the jokes about it weren't. Not that Taylor gave a shit.

He was a Jersey boy to the core and proud. His family had immigrated from Ireland a couple hundred years ago and came right to the place he called home. They practically named Barvale for fuck's sake. It literally meant *bear town!*

He'd never wanted to live anywhere else. Even with their newfound status, the Devlin boys hadn't even considered uprooting the original storefront and moving to some posh Manhattan building or trendy Boston brownstone. That was for their corporate employees. *Delegating was the shit!*

Fuck Manhattan or Boston. This was home. Taylor, Marcus, and Daniel had each pitched in to turn the lucrative family business they'd inherited early from their dad into a billion-dollar corporation.

Bear Claw Bakery was everywhere. They served their goods in hotels, on airplanes, in movie theatres, schools, universities, cruise ships, and several dozen amusement parks across the world. That was a lot of fucking honeybuns if he did say so himself.

Of course, they hired the best of the best to help run their empire and maintain their local, hometown feel. *Like Dimples.* She was amazing. A great employee. *Hell,* she'd practically grown up at Bear Claw.

Yeah. She was like family. That's why he couldn't understand when she'd gone and turned a simple kiss into something it wasn't. *Stress?* Maybe.

She did work hard and, her home life had never been easy. Not with caring for her mom who was ill more often than not, and practically raising her younger sister. Luisa was a pip. She'd worked summers for her sister as an assistant but hated the job.

After college she'd opted for medical school and got in. Tuition was a lot. But clever Taylor had introduced the Bear Claw Bakery Scholarships that year. Coincidentally, Luisa was one of the first recipients.

He frowned remembering how pissed Krissy had been. It was only after some quick thinking that he'd saved his ass. She thought he was making a dig at her not being able to support her family, but he'd assured her that had nothing to do with it.

The brothers paid her a handsome salary, he knew that. But it didn't go far with a family of three to support and the countless doctors' bills despite the generous insurance coverage they provided.

Regardless, he'd gotten her to calm down with a little charm. Who knew she was so proud? Then again, he should have known it. She was so dedicated and trustworthy. She really was the best.

He hoped Marcus did the right thing today setting her up to hang out with Leya. She was probably angry that his brother's mate made her stay away for so long.

Yeah, poor Dimples. She probably just wanted to go home. No way she'd want to go out for drinks. Dimples didn't drink. She'd be so out of place in her flannel shirt and baggy jeans at *The Thirsty Dog* on a Saturday night.

Poor thing, maybe she wouldn't be too mad. He could ask her to dance and make amends. He had a sort of date, but she was an old friend. Margot wouldn't mind.

Besides, it was only Dimples. She was like a sister. *Wasn't she?* For some reason his bear huffed at the description. He checked the time and squirmed in his seat.

Ten minutes to go.

FIVE

Krissy slammed down the shot glass and sucked hard on the lime. She giggled a little as the cool citrus juice chased the hot alcohol as it slid down her throat leaving a trail of fire in its wake.

It took a lot for any Shifter to feel the effects of alcohol, and for a Bear Shifter more than most. Their size, the speed of their metabolism, and supernatural magic saw to that.

She'd never taken advantage of those particular fringe benefits of being a Shifter. *Until now.* Spending a real girls' day for the first time in her life left Krissy a little shell shocked.

She'd spent more money on clothes than she ever had before in her entire life! Not that she couldn't afford it. The brothers paid well, but she was still paying off her sister's school loans, and there was the house, and her mother's medical bills.

Still, she deserved a little something for her efforts, didn't she? Guilt threatened to overwhelm her, but she pushed it away. She wasn't used to this.

Krissy just never bothered treating herself before. Well, that all changed today! She looked down at herself and smiled. Her skintight, designer jeans were artistically ripped in strategic locations to show glimpses of her smooth thighs and calves.

Who knew her legs could look that good? And her butt! OMG! She almost died when she saw how great her ass looked in the clingy blue jeans!

The material was soft and strong. *Kind of like her.* They hugged her frame perfectly! Outlining her assets and making her feel great in the process. She'd probably cry about the money tomorrow, but right now she was more than glad that she bought not one, but several pairs by the same designer.

An off-the-shoulder peasant blouse that ended just above her belly button complimented the jeans. She had to admit, she looked downright cute! Something that at five-foot-ten inches tall and a solid size fourteen, Krissy had never felt about herself! But dammit it was way past time she did! *She was cute and sexy! So there, world!*

The men who sat at the bar laughing and smiling at her while they downed more shots seemed to think so too. She knew a few of the guys. Were-wolves mostly. But there was one man who stood out. He was handsome as sin in a desperado kind of way.

Her senses told her he was a Bear too, but he was a stranger to her. Definitely not Clan. He'd arrived at *The Thirsty Dog* shortly after she and Leya had. Almost an hour ago now. Cautiously friendly she returned his smile then studiously ignored him.

The two women started with some margaritas before moving on to shots. They toasted Leya's upcoming marriage, and New Jersey's awesome no taxes on clothing before collapsing on their stools in a fit of giggles.

The sheer joy and exhilaration of the day made her feel like she was floating on cloud nine. *Okay, maybe that was the tequila.* With her newfound brav-ery, she looked over at the big hunk of Bear she'd been eyeing and sent him a shot of the locally distilled artisanal whiskey, *Summer Bite.*

To her humble surprise, he accepted! The hunky dark-haired stranger even raised the shot glass in her direction before downing it. Krissy had never been so happy. Of course, then again, she'd sampled several shots herself by this time. *LOL or was that YOLO. Never mind.*

Her sluggish mind wasn't working too well, but she didn't care in the least. Krissy was having fun! *Ooh look, more shots!* The bartender, a cute Werewolf names Jordan, winked at her as he set up another round of shots. More tequila. And enough for three!

He nodded towards the stranger. Obviously, the shots were from him. At her smile, he strode towards them. Confidence and more than a little interest evident in his swagger, he tilted his head at the two of them.

"Ladies," he murmured, eyes on Krissy as he spoke.

"Uh, I'm gonna go sit at the table and order some appetizers, Krissy, Marcus will be here soon. Why don't you, uh, sit here and get to know your new friend?" Leya bit her lip and winked at her, nodding to the huge dark-haired man before scampering off to a nearby table.

"My name is Nate," the stranger offered his hand. It was large and warm, swallowing hers up as squeezed it for a second longer than necessary. He smiled sheepishly at her raised eyebrow and she noted his eyes were a deep forest green.

"I'm Krissy Sposa," she said and nodded to the shot.

"Shall we?" He lifted one of the tiny glasses handing it to her, then took another.

Nate clinked them together and murmured cheers, before they both started the ritual of lick, salt, drink, suck. Giggles erupted from her mouth as he winced at the tartness of the lime.

"So, what are two pretty ladies like you doing here all alone?"

"We're not alone. At least we won't be. My friend's fiancé is on his way."

"*Her* fiancé? So you're single then?"

"Um, yeah. Yes. I am single. You?"

"Darlin', would I be talking to you if I wasn't?" His accent was different, though she couldn't place where.

"Can't say as I know you well enough to answer that, *darlin'*," she sassed back.

"Okay, I get it. I'll just have to prove myself. Now, you mind if I ask you something?" He leaned forward and she breathed in his scent. Definitely a Bear. *Not our mate,* her Bear growled, but she pushed the beast away.

"Okay, but I'm warning you, I'm not an easy mark."

"I never thought you were, darlin', not with those eyes and that mouth."

"What do you mean?"

"You're quite the looker Krissy Sposa, now about my question?"

She laughed and leaned in closer breathing in his pleasant musk. *No thrills*, she noted with disappointment. Still, Krissy admired his smooth manner and giggled at the traces of Western accent in his deep voice. *Stranger indeed.*

He was good to look at, glimpses of his deeply tanned, muscular body peeked out from his black t-shirt. He looked dangerous, and sexy too.

His dark hair hung over his forehead in a thick wave. A very attractive man. *But not our mate.* Krissy ignored her Bear and allowed Nate to turn into her from his bar stool.

Her sow bristled at his touch, but she allowed it. Curious to see if she could respond physically with another man. It wasn't unpleasant, but still, she felt wrong. *No. Don't go there. You are single, unmated, and you deserve to have some fun.*

Nate's legs caged her in on either side and she leaned forward to hear what he was saying over the noise of the bar. It was band night. A group of musicians were tuning their gear, getting ready for some good old-fashioned rock and roll.

Krissy appreciated a live band now and then. She also liked having a handsome man pay attention to her. *Nothing wrong with that*, she told herself. She laughed at Nate's jokes and didn't pull away when he twirled the end of her newly dyed and styled hair around his long finger.

"What's that smile for?" Nate asked.

"Oh, I was just thinking that I am having a nice time."

"Are you now?"

"Yeah, I am. I don't get out very often. You know, responsibilities and all."

"You look like a responsible person, darlin'."

"What does that mean?"

"Honey, it's in your eyes and your posture. You're genuine, Krissy Sposa, and if you don't mind me saying, you're pretty as all hell. You sure you ain't got a man hidin' somewhere, waitin' to pounce on little old me?"

"You little? No, seriously, I am very, *very* single."

"Well, seems to me Krissy Sposa that there are some pretty dumb men up in here. But their loss, is my gain, darlin'! How about another round?"

She laughed out loud and nodded her head. *Yes.* Krissy was having fun. She smiled and accepted the shot glass from Nate. He leaned in closer and whispered in her ear.

"Ever do a body shot?"

"A what?"

"Well, darlin', you hold your glass here, and I wrap my arm around yours. Yes, just like that. Now, you hold my glass in your pretty little hand, right about there. I'll hold yours here. Then I lick your sweet little wrist, just like this, and add a little salt-"

"And I lick yours?" Her eyes sparkled with mischief as she did the same maneuver to him.

"You catch on quick there, baby girl, now on the count of three, we lick, we drink, and then we suck," he wiggled his eyebrows and she giggled again.

Krissy never did anything like this before! She felt wild as she basically made out with a total stranger in public! The way she saw it, she was long overdue.

This guy, *Nate*, might not be her *one*, but he sure as hell was fun and attentive! He was hot too, and he looked at her like she was the only woman in the bar. Doing a couple of body shots with him sounded like a really good idea!

The music began pounding and he swayed a

little closer to her. Heat from his body spilled onto hers. They didn't belong to each other, but she wasn't looking for her fated mate tonight. She knew where the asshole was, and he didn't want her.

Determined to enjoy herself, she nodded when she was ready. On the count of three she and Nate grinned then, *lick*, *drink*, and, oh my, *suck*!

Nate slipped the lime between his teeth and pressed it into her mouth. His salty sweetness mixed with tequila and lime met her lips in a searing hot kiss. *Whoa!*

Krissy did what any red-blooded woman would do when a hot guy offered her his lime.

Krissy Sposa opened wide and sucked for all she was worth. She was enjoying herself too until an earth-shattering roar erupted from somewhere behind her.

"What the-"

"Fuck!" Taylor scrambled out of his SUV and walked through the doors of the very crowded bar.

It was usual for a Saturday night at *The Thirsty Dog*, especially since they started having live music on the weekends. He hated being late, and from the seventeen texts he'd gotten on his drive over, he knew his date was already there. And she was pissed.

"There you are!" Margot zeroed in on him as if she had specialized Taylor-seeking lasers in her cold eyes. *Damn.* He frowned in mild annoyance.

She looked aggravated. He frowned at her too tight leather pants and corset top. She looked like she was at a damn vampire costume party for fuck's sake. She always did like too much make-up and perfume for his tastes. He'd forgotten that about her.

He preferred light flowery scents with a hint of vanilla. *Like Dimples.* Where the hell had that thought come from? He pushed it away and forced himself to smile at Margot.

Though he could not stop his wince as she kissed him hello. At least he managed to tilt his head to the side, so she caught his cheek instead of his mouth. For some reason, his Bear was not happy with the overdone woman or with him for his attention to her.

He nodded at the tall, sleek looking woman who accompanied Margot. She was strikingly beautiful. Pale and thin, perfect features. She looked like a model.

Willowy and graceful, the polar opposite of his so-called date. He appreciated her beauty but was surprisingly unmoved by it. Once again, an image of Dimples crossed his mind.

His Bear hummed in appreciation. *WTH? Where do these thoughts keep coming from?* He shook his head and pretended to listen to whatever Margot was chatting about. But he really had zero interest. Something was humming around his head, distracting him. He looked around expectantly.

"I said this is my cousin, Lacey. She's the model, remember I told you? I saved us a table over by the bar," Taylor nodded at Margot's cousin and tried not to be annoyed at the way she pulled him along behind her like some errant child.

"Look, Margot, my brothers and Marcus' fiancée are meeting us here, so give me a chance to find them-"

A huge hand on his shoulder had him whirling, but he calmed down when it turned out to be one of said brothers. Daniel and Marcus were both there, to his surprise. He greeted them and leaned in to listen over the din of noise in the crowded bar.

"Where are the girls?" Marcus' voice was a deep growl.

Taylor suspected the crowd was getting to him as he searched for his mate. *Never come between a Shifter and his mate.* It was like Shifter Etiquette 101. He stood aside and scanned the crowds for the woman, hoping to soothe his agitated Alpha.

Taylor shrugged not seeing them. Then he looked ahead, towards the bar and exhaled. He pointed to a table where Leya was currently sitting, *alone.*

She seemed okay, looking at her phone and munching on a nacho. *Where the hell was Krissy?*

Surely, she didn't leave the soon-to-be Alpha female of their Clan by herself?

The fivesome started moving towards Leya's table. He smiled at his new sister and looked away appropriately when she and Marcus embraced. It seemed wrong to watch somehow. Like voyeurism.

The two of them just melted into one another. Two halves that were suddenly whole in the tender *hello* they shared. So obviously suited, the irrefutable fact they were fated mates was evident in spades.

Taylor felt himself overcome by a twinge of jealousy. *He wanted what they had*, he realized. And with surprising preeminence. His Bear roared inside his head. Taylor acknowledged the animal was searching, looking for his mate too.

Poor thing. Taylor shook it off. He turned to look at Daniel. He was stiff and uncomfortable, and it showed. It surprised the shit out of Taylor that his taciturn bother was at the bar to begin with.

Socializing was something the grumpy Bear avoided ever since the event-which-shall-not-be-discussed happened. He'd become a sort of recluse in the time since his near-wedding.

Taylor was secretly happy the woman had walked away from his brother. Daniel was a deep soul. A good brother. A *great* Clan Enforcer. He was solid and dependable.

His ex-fiancée had been a money-grubbing world class bitch and a half. And Taylor did not say that lightly. In fact, he despised anyone who maligned women in name or action. However, that one deserved the title.

The first hint of her true character had shown when she'd demanded a bigger ring than the one Daniel had proposed with. Shit just declined from there. Melinda had flirted with everyone within a ten-foot radius of her when Daniel wasn't looking.

The woman had even propositioned him. *Taylor*. He was so disgusted, he'd tried to tell his older brother, but Daniel had been blind to it. A broken jaw had convinced Taylor to drop it at the time.

Afterwards Daniel had apologized, but Taylor didn't mind. His brother had suffered humiliation after humiliation with that woman. So, *yeah*, now he was entitled to a little privacy. But he hated to think he was wasting his life on regrets.

So, *yeah*, Daniel joining them was a huge big deal. A cause for celebration. Taylor was extremely happy to see him, but he couldn't figure out why Daniel was snarling at Margot's cousin. Lacey sure was beautiful. Tall and thin, not really his style, but she was fairy-like and elegant.

She didn't look anything like her petite and bossy cousin, Margot. She didn't act like her either. That was kind of a plus in her favor though as far as Taylor thought. *Damn. What was he doing agreeing to go out with this woman?*

It was too late now to get out of it. Besides, he was more interested in his brother's strange behavior. Lacey looked almost hunted. *Interesting.*

Taylor ran a hand through his thick blonde hair. He'd always been a good-looking guy and he'd used his looks to pick up women for years. He should have come alone tonight. Not with some chick he dated back in his high-school. His palms were sweaty, his head ached, and his heart thundered in his chest. *Where the hell was Dimples?*

Margot was talking about her day and how things went wrong at her nail appointment. Apparently, the stylist did a poor job trimming her cuticles. Not that Taylor cared. Like at all. But he smiled charmingly and pretended to listen as he tipped back his beer. His mind wandered to his absentee manager once again. *Dimples. Where are you?*

"Anyone need anything?" Marcus asked as he got

up from his seat and kissed his bride-to-be before heading over to get more drinks from the bar.

Taylor shook his head, not caring what Margot wanted at the moment. The place was crowded, and the waitresses were nowhere to be seen. He took the opportunity to ask Leya a question.

"Hey, when did Krissy leave?"

"Leave? What do you mean?"

"Well, where is she? I assumed she left?"

"No! She's at the bar, right there."

Taylor turned around and scanned the bar. He saw a bunch of guys and a few women. There were some Wolves he knew from the local Pack, a couple of Bears from his Clan, a few normals, and some lucky guy kissing the neck of a seriously stacked brunette. *Dayum!* She was fine as hell!

He especially liked those blonde tips at the end of her wavy hair, and her sumptuous peach of an ass outlined in a pair of impossibly tight jeans. That lucky son-of-a-bitch had his thumbs hooked right into those jeans on either side of her ample hips. He sat open-legged and had her pressed up against his front so tight Taylor wondered if she could breathe! *Hot damn!*

He could imagine the silky soft skin that lucky SOB was brushing with his fingertips. Taylor's chest tightened as he continued to look at the gorgeous creature.

Her waist dipped in to show a perfect hourglass of a figure. Breasts heaving as she giggled, practically spilling out of the low-cut blouse she wore with pretty little thingies all over it. *Flowers?* He didn't know or care. It looked fucking hot.

Now, Taylor didn't generally poach on another man's territory, but he couldn't look away. She was so gorgeous. *And familiar.* Somehow, the way she was standing seemed to tickle something in the back of his mind. *Damn!*

He couldn't see her face from this angle. The beefy dude she was draped over was whispering into her neck and he was blocking Taylor's view. Marcus came back, hands full of drinks, and momentarily blocked his view. *Fucker.*

Taylor moved around him as the couple swayed against the crowd. The man's hands tightened on her waist, moving her dangerously close. His hands smoothed over her hips, flirting outrageously with the beautiful creature.

Taylor knew the signs. Obviously, the man was some new player in town. Not really strange for the Jersey Shore hot spot. But he couldn't stop his eyes from going back to the woman. *Who the hell was she?*

There was something about her that he swore he recognized. *Impossible.* Taylor knew every pretty woman in the area. Hell, he'd fucked most of them too.

A fact which suddenly pissed off his Bear. He wasn't a total dick or anything. The women he slept with knew the deal. He didn't promise happy-ever-after. True, he rarely called for a repeat performance, but they knew that beforehand.

Anything he did with a woman was by mutual design. But he forgot every single one of his old conquests as he stared at the long-legged brunette with the blonde tips standing in the arms of another man at the bar.

He'd definitely remember that one. If by nothing else, then by that ass alone. His Bear growled deep in his mind's eye. *WTF?* Taylor stiffened.

He felt Leya's eyes on him. Marcus pushed something at him, and he absently accepted the cold bottle from his brother. He put his empty one down, his eyes never leaving the good-looking couple.

Completely ignoring his date and everyone else around him, Taylor frowned. Inching forward, he tried to place where he knew that woman from. Then, suddenly, she turned her face towards them.

"What the fucking fuck?!" Glass and beer flew

everywhere as Taylor shattered the bottle in his hand.

"Jeez! Taylor, you got me all wet!" Margot stood up gasping.

"Um, I better go with her. I'll tell a waitress to come clean this up," Lacey stood up and followed her furious cousin.

"Bro?" Daniel ignored the two women and focused on why Taylor had lost his shit. Following Taylor's gaze, Daniel sat up straighter.

"Easy there," Marcus held onto Taylor with a firm grip, his Alpha voice controlling his brother's Bear when all he wanted to do was rip that fucking guy off his Dimples. *Roarrrr!*

"Let me go, Marcus!"

He barely recognized his voice as he growled the demand. He felt something hot and wild surging in his chest. Jealousy? *Yeah.* Rage. *Fuck yeah.* And, was that, lust? *Gulp. Yes.* For Dimples. *Oh shit.*

"Calm the fuck down, Taylor! What's wrong with you?" Marcus' question grated on his nerves, but not more so than Daniel's comments.

"Holy shit! About time Krissy goes out and gets some!"

"Shut the fuck up, Daniel!" Taylor growled.

"Is she doing anything you haven't done a

million times? What's wrong with her having a good time? Why you so mad, bro?" Daniel's argument was compelling, but Taylor still didn't like it.

"Who the fuck is that guy?"

"Does it matter?" Marcus asked.

"No. *Fuck*. I don't know. Besides, what the hell is she wearing? And what happened to her hair?"

His Bear was pacing in his mind's eye. Taylor had never felt this way before. The room felt too close, the air too thick. His Bear hung his head in shame.

Was that his best come back? What is she wearing? The truth was there was nothing wrong with Dimples' clothes or hair. She looked good. Like seriously good, as in hottest most fuckable woman in the place!

High fucking praise, if he did say so himself. Taylor just didn't want anyone else to see her like that. Dick-move on his part? Abso-fucking-lutely.

His Bear agreed with him on that point at least. No one should see her like that. *Mine.* And that fucking guy? The one whose arms were about to be broken? Yeah, him. He needed to go. Like yesterday. *Grrr.*

"What's the matter with what she's wearing? We went shopping, got our hair done and every-thing! Doesn't she look great?" Leya, his sweet little soon-to-be sister smiled up at him innocently, and Taylor wanted to roar again.

Not that he did. He knew better than to mess with his Alpha brother's woman.

She was right though. His Dimples looked ravishing. Dressed up like that, she was sexy as fuck. *But* he frowned as he took in her appearance from the newly frosted hair to the bottoms of her stiletto heeled sandals, *she doesn't look like Dimples!*

Where the fuck was his Dimples? His reliable, sweet, innocent, Dimples? With the flannels and the pig tails? The one who wouldn't be at a bar letting some strange fucking guy grope her! GRRR.

"Dude! Get a fucking grip. Krissy is a big girl now. And, *dayum*, can I just say I am shocked as shit, bro! I never knew she looked like *that*," Daniel let out a low wolf whistle.

Marcus held on to Taylor's elbow a little tighter. That didn't stop him from whipping a fork across the table and catching Daniel in the shoulder.

"Ow! Fuck, that's twice, Taylor!"

For the first time ever, Taylor wanted to lay into both his brothers. His fingers itched with the urge to release his claws and his skin tingled all over. The Bear wanted out.

"She sure fills out those jeans, doesn't she bro?" Daniel persisted in being a dick.

"Shut the fuck up, you asshole!" Taylor growled, ignoring Marcus' increasingly tight grip on his arm.

Taylor wrestled internally with his Bear. The animal half of him was freaking the fuck out. All it wanted to do was rip into the bastard who was rubbing his paws all over Dimples like he had every fucking right. *Who the fuck is that guy?*

"I don't know, his name's Nate. He bought us a round earlier, but I wanted to save this table, so I came over here and Krissy stayed to chat with him. That's okay, right Marcus? I mean, she's a Bear, it's not like someone is gonna mess with her, right?" Leya asked.

"Of course, it's okay. Krissy is an adult. Right Taylor?" Marcus' command was not lost on Taylor, but he was having a hell of a time calming his Bear in spite of it.

"Well, they've been hanging out over there for like an hour or so, while I waited for you, baby," Leya bit her lower lip and looked at her mate. Marcus gazed adoringly back at her and Taylor wanted to scream again.

Fuck. What was happening to him? His protective instincts were going into overdrive. Not to mention the sudden possessive feelings he was having towards one curvy as sin employee.

And, oh yeah, he was hard as fuck! Hell of a time to get a boner. His jeans were growing increasingly tighter every time he glanced at her *assets*. His entire world was upside down and it was all because of her! Dimples was driving him mad.

He closed his eyes and exhaled searching for his usual calm. Taylor was the easy going one of the three brothers. Jealousy and mind-numbing desire had never been part of his repertoire. *Never like this.*

"Uh oh," Daniel's murmur had Taylor's head turning around to the *cozy couple*. And his head damn near exploded.

"MOTHERFUCKER!"

He tore out of his brother's grasp just as that son-of-a-bitch slid his tongue past Krissy's delectable lips. The fact that she was a willing participant didn't even enter his mind.

Taylor was on the guy in two seconds flat. He sniffed as he grabbed the stranger's huge, meaty shoulder and shoved. *Bear!* Oh good. He was a Shifter too. Taylor grinned, ignoring Dimples' startled gasp. At least he didn't have to pull his punches.

This close he was briefly distracted by the light jasmine vanilla scent that was all her. A distraction that cost him a punch to the side of his head. *Goddammit*, she smelled and looked way too fucking good.

He'd have to spend some time with her to see if she smelled that good everywhere. *Yeah. Good plan.* His Bear agreed. First, he needed to kill this fucker.

Her lips were soft and plump with that just-kissed look. *This fucking prick!* He turned back to the fight he'd started and threw a solid left-hook. One good thing about having brothers, Taylor knew how to take *and* throw a punch.

Screams and chaos erupted around him, but he ignored it all focusing on hitting the grinning fucker right in the jaw. The stranger grunted and took the hit well, barely sliding off the stool.

He was bigger than Taylor originally thought. Stronger too. He didn't fall down, but his steps faltered as he swung and missed. *Mine! Protect!*

Taylor's animal roared with pleasure at the thought of being able to battle another Shifter for her. *Fighting over Dimples? Fuck yeah.* Now it was his turn to falter. What the holy fuck was he doing?

"Taylor!"

"Duck bro!"

Krissy and his brothers were yelling as the bar's two huge Werewolf bouncers came bounding over to hustle the battling Bears outside. Taylor was still stunned at the insistent cries of his Bear as he breathed the fresh air before taking another hit in the stomach. *Mate! Mine! Protect!*

He didn't have time to sort out his animal. Taylor had just taken the last punch he was going to take. The not-too-distant sounds of sirens reached his ears. He needed to hurry up and get his shots in before his fun ended all too soon.

He stood up and growled his fury at the strange Bear. The man's beast shone in his brown eyes and he smiled tauntingly at Taylor. Then all hell broke loose.

SEVEN

"No Sheriff, I have no idea who that man is, I simply saw him accosting my employee, and I reacted regrettably. I am happy to pay for any damage to the establishment that our disagreement caused," Taylor spoke through gritted teeth. His jaw was bruised, and his head pounded.

It took six guys, big fucking Shifters, to pull him and that asshole apart. After they'd been all but shoved outside the two men had unleashed hell on each other. Taylor still smelled the coppery scent of blood from his own split lip and other various cuts and bruises.

He was happy to note most of the blood on his clothing was not his. True, he was the prettiest

Devlin, but he fought like a goddamn bull, or er, *bear*, when the occasion called for it.

Marcus was settling their tab and apologizing to Mike, the owner of *The Thirsty Dog*. He was a Werewolf and, though the place catered to Shifters, normals did frequent it as well. So, *of course*, they called the fucking cops.

The Maccon County Sheriff's Department policed all of Maccon City. They even made their way to Barvale on occasion. Taylor was acquainted with the Deputy on call, a young Werewolf named Tony D'Amato.

He was a good man, if a little green. He grinned as he took Taylor's statement. *Fucker.*

"Okay. I think that does it. Now, you wait here, Mr. Devlin," he nodded and walked away jotting down some more notes.

Taylor couldn't believe this shit. Dimples was glaring daggers at him from where she stood off to the side being questioned by another officer. All he did was protect her!

Grrr. His Bear bristled at him for upsetting her. Well, what was she mad at? She should be thanking him!

"Bro, you ready?" Daniel asked after talking to the officer.

He'd learned that the guy he hit, Nate Cordoza, was visiting the Garden State from Texas. He was looking to relocate and happened upon *The Thirsty Dog* "looking to make some friends". *Yeah. Right.*

"Bro?"

"What? Don't I have to wait?"

"Nah, he's not pressing charges. Marcus invited him to the Den to meet with us."

"What? Why?"

"Cause he's a fucking Bear, asshole."

"He's the one! The one I scented earlier tonight behind the bakery! This fucker has been stalking us, Daniel!"

"What? Alright look, you can explain later. Come on. Krissy, you ready?" Daniel called over to where she stood.

She nodded at Daniel and drew herself up to her full height. *Holy shit.* She was tall and curvy in all the right places. *How had he never noticed?*

Her long legs outfitted in those sexy designer jeans with that utterly feminine top hugging her ample breasts made Taylor's mouth water and brain turn to mush. He tensed as she moved past him. Vanilla and jasmine tickled his nose. *Fuck. Now what?*

"Thanks, Daniel. I appreciate it. I'm ready. Leya left with Marcus, and she forgot to give me her keys.

So, I don't have a ride," she said by way of explanation.

He watched her fervently, waiting for her to meet his gaze. He was shocked when she wouldn't. That wasn't like her. Dimples was one of the most honest and candid people he knew. She was exceedingly bright and honest to a fault.

"You don't have to explain to us, sweetheart. Of course, we'll drive you home," Daniel answered her with a small smile on his lips.

He glared at his brother over her head as they headed back towards the car. Taylor raised his hands in question. *Asshat.*

He walked stiffly behind the pair of them. For the first time in his entire life, he felt uncertain. It was an uncomfortable, nagging, itching kind of a feeling. Needless to say, he didn't like it.

His Bear roared in his mind's eye so loudly he couldn't even think. He'd ignored Margot the entire night. Left his date hanging without even a backwards glance, and he had a fist fight! Both actions were highly uncharacteristic of Taylor.

Imagine, him engaging in violence over a woman! Not caring if anyone heard him growl or watched the inhuman speed and strength that imbued every single one of his punches.

He recognized the man as a Shifter and thanked the gods for that. But the thing was, he wasn't sure he would've cared otherwise. And that was bad. Very bad.

He would've killed a normal with hits like that. Hell, Taylor had been completely out of control in that moment. His Bear was running the show as much as he could without fully Shifting.

What happened to set him off? Then he pictured it. That guy sticking his tongue into Dimples' willing mouth. Once again, he saw red.

He halted in his tracks. One word. One word alone echoed in his brain louder than any other. *MINE!*

Shit. He thought back to that night at the office party. How she'd been so sweet and pliable in his arms. How she'd opened up to him, like a bud flowering for the first time. She'd trembled and sighed into his mouth, sweet and soft as honey.

The taste of her still lingered in his mind every time he closed his eyes. Her jasmine vanilla scent tickled his senses.

There was something about her, something about a woman who was comfortable in jeans and flannels but smelled like flowers that drove him a little wild.

Why hadn't he acknowledged it before? The answer was simple. He was scared. Now, he felt nothing but regret for how he'd treated her that night.

Looking back, turning her away when she called him *mate* had been the hardest fucking thing he'd ever done. Lost in their shared kiss, unable to name the feelings she'd invoked, he'd done what he always did when shit got hard. He fought his feelings and ran.

He grimaced. *She'd had it right the first time. Mate. Sweet mate.* He only hoped he hadn't completely ruined his chances.

Taylor just had to talk to her. He needed to tell her how he felt. He slid into the back seat next to her, ignoring her gasp of surprise and Daniel's raised eyebrows.

The ride back was going to be about half an hour or so. *Plenty of time to talk this through.*

Daniel cleared his throat and flipped on an AM news station. He hummed as he drove, and Taylor was grateful for his attempt at giving them privacy.

"Dimples look-"

"No."

"But I need to explain," he wanted so bad to make her look at him.

She sat stiffly in her seat. Her head turned

towards the window watching the asphalt as they drove. He could feel her anger rolling off her in waves. *Shit.*

"Dimples," he tried again.

He lifted his bruised hand and made to touch her, stopping when she stiffened. They both sat still, not daring to move. He took that as a sign to continue.

"Why, Dimples?"

"Why what?"

"Why'd you go and do all *this*?"

He reached out with his battered, shaky hand and cursed himself for the fool he'd been. His fingers slid over her silky waves of her hair, ending at the platinum tips that glowed like silver in the moonlight.

"Women get their hair done Taylor, it's not a big deal."

"And this?" he tugged on the droopy cap sleeve of her peasant blouse, causing it to fall and reveal more of her silky skin.

He gulped and felt his beast rise. *Damn, Dimples, you are so fucking beautiful. How did I never noticed?*

But that's not true, he suddenly realized. He had noticed. He just never acted. He couldn't. Not when he was such a *play-bear*, running from bed to bed without so much as a returned call afterwards.

Gods, he hated that fucking nickname. His women knew the deal, but for the first time in his life, he felt ashamed of his behavior.

Dimples was worth so much more. He wished he could erase his past, but there was no turning back the clock. He made his bed, now he had to hope to the gods she still found him worthy.

He tested the softness of her blouse between bruised fingers and inhaled her sweet fragrance. How he wanted to bury his nose it in, lose himself in her scent. Desire was like a punch in the gut. It was nearly his undoing.

Sensitive to the sound of his exhale, Krissy looked up and met his eyes. They were so bright and clear. *Hazel*, but more amber than brown, mixed with a mossy green that was as warm and inviting as the woman herself.

Such a wealth of emotion in the deep pools of her eyes. He could happily drown in them.

"Taylor? What? They're just clothes. Sorry to disappoint you, but I'm still just me."

"How could I ever be disappointed? You are beautiful, Dimples. I've just never seen you dressed like this-"

"So, that's your excuse."

"What?" He felt the temperature in the car drop a few degrees. She shoved his hand away and glared at him.

"So I dress up a little and that gives you the right to you lose your fucking mind?"

Both men sat up straighter. Taylor's mouth hung open, and Daniel's eyebrows were so high they almost disappeared in the waves of blonde hair that fell across his forehead.

Dimples rarely lost her cool. She never yelled, and she hardly ever cursed. She definitely didn't go around saying *fuck*. *Wrongo*. Apparently, she did, and she was just getting started.

"I've worked at Bear Claw Bakery for years, Taylor! *FUCKING YEARS!* You never ever look at me! You barely even register that I'm there! Now, for the first time EVER, I go out, get dressed up, meet a hot guy at a bar *ON MY OWN TIME* and suddenly you act like some sort of crazy protective older brother?! *WHO THE FUCK DO YOU THINK YOU ARE?*"

Brother? What? Ew! No! His Bear bellowed at her gross misinterpretation. The beast demanded he correct his mate right now! Taylor's head pounded as he tried to keep up with both his animal's indignation and Krissy's outrage.

"No! That's not it at all!"

"Well, I don't know what it is, Taylor, but you completely fucking humiliated me in there! I mean, where do you get off hitting a guy just for talking to me!"

"Oh *talking*, is that what you were doing? He had his fucking tongue down your throat, Dimples!"

"Ooh! Don't you call me that! You don't get to use nicknames with me like we're friends or something!"

Okay. That stung. Of course they were friends. He'd known her for years. Hell, she was family. And now, well, she was *more*. *What?* Oh, she was still yelling at him. *Fuck.*

"It is none of your business who sticks their tongue anywhere on my body!"

"What are you talking about? *Who's been using their tongue on you?!*" That riled his Bear even more.

Taylor couldn't keep the growl out of his voice and that earned him another scathing look. *Fucking shit.* But he couldn't help it! The thought of Dimples with a man, *any man,* made him go fucking mental. He saw red. He wanted to beat up the entire damn world. He was so screwed.

"Oh, please! I am not about to explain my sexual

exploits to you! And I sure as hell don't want to hear yours!"

"What?!"

"You know what, it's been a real shitty couple of years, guys, so you know what? I'm taking tomorrow off. Thank you for the ride, Daniel," she moved to open the door, but Taylor grabbed her hand. He refused to let go until she looked at him.

"Dimples? *Kristianne?* Please, I have to talk to you," he pleaded with her.

He breathed in, scenting her anger and sorrow. *Fuck.* Knowing he was responsible for the hurt and sadness was killing him. *Please*, he thought, *look at me.*

She was a Shifter, like him, she would be able to tell his sincerity, but it seemed that after all these years she'd had enough. With one final tug on the door, she slipped out of his grasp.

"I don't want to talk to you, Taylor, not now. Maybe not ever. And I changed my mind about tomorrow, I am taking the whole week off. If you don't like it, fire me!"

"Please, don't walk away. I need-"

"It's always been about what you need, or what mom needs, or Luisa. What about me? When does someone see to my needs?"

Shame warred with shock at her heated response. She was right. He'd been a selfish asshole. But he wanted to, no needed to make it up to her. She just had to listen.

"I'm finished. You hear me? Done."

"Dimples-"

"Leave me alone, Taylor," she closed her eyes on his name, and simultaneously closed the door in his face.

He watched helplessly from the back seat of his car as she walked across the lawn. His heart squeezed tight in his chest as he watched her.

She was so beautiful and proud with her back straight and head high. So strong on her own. She's had to be.

Shame threatened to consume him as he watched. But he couldn't turn away. His eyes followed her, step after step, up the sagging front porch. Her childhood home had seen better days, but he noted the repairs she'd made over the years.

Shit. He was a total fucking bastard. He made no move to follow her inside, swallowing the lump in his throat as he continued to torment himself watching her. *You are a complete prick, Taylor Devlin.*

Dimples had worked so hard for so long. Countless weekends and nights. Hell, she used to beg for overtime even when she was just a kid. She'd studied at night, got her degree in business management, and still managed to take care of her mother and sister.

She was a nurturer. Taking care of her family was all she knew, but it didn't stop there. How many times had she made chicken soup for sick employees or Clan-mates? How many times had she helped them with personal problems?

She was always doing stuff for other people. She'd moved on from being the Barvale Store Manager, to the General Manager for the entire region years ago, and yet she still did all the little extras. She involved Bear Claw Bakery in several community outreach programs.

She even had an arrangement with the neighboring Maccon City's Macconwood-Nighthawk Teen Outreach Center for seasonal hires. She took at risk teens in, mainly Shifters, and gave them jobs. A real start in life where most had never had a break. Some of those kids remained with the company, turning into their best employees!

He'd never realized before how much she gave of herself. She was so generous. She deserved someone who could give her back some of that love. Someone to walk proudly next to her, not treat her like a fucking booty call!

We can do that and more, his Bear growled at him. Taylor was beside himself. On one hand, he wanted her so bad he could taste it. On the other, he knew she deserved better than him.

Sweet loving Dimples deserved the best. After years of giving everyone everything she had and never complaining about it, she deserved the fucking moon and all the stars.

We can give her the moon and we can make her see stars, his Bear insisted. *She is ours. Mate. Mine.*

Taylor growled in frustration. How could he have been so fucking blind? He looked at the faded siding and the chipped paint on the porch and growled again.

She deserved better. Marcus was more than generous with salary and benefits. He saw to it their employees were well taken care of, especially after their company had gone through the roof. And Dimples had always been more than an employee. She was dependable, reliable, trustworthy.

Hell, he could be himself around her. He didn't always have to smile and be charming. He could be a real Bear, growly and grumpy, and she still stuck by him. Over the years, she'd shown more integrity and loyalty than anyone he'd ever known.

Employees looked up to her and came to her with their problems. She dealt with temperamental vendors and foreign investors alike with diplomacy and skill. Sure, she preferred to hang around the office in jeans and flannels, but she was efficient and completely irreplaceable.

Hell, Dimples was a huge part of Bear Claw Bakery. She was the heart, he realized.

She was his heart. Oh fuck, he really fucked this up. How many times had he taken for granted simple things like asking her to fill in for him? To take on even more responsibilities?

There he was, living his life, not a care in the world. *Alone.* No one to care for and protect. *But you can care for our mate*, the Bear insisted.

She never took a break. Never even asked for time off, unless her mom was sick. He'd been too selfish and stupid to notice. *Fuck. Fuck. FUCK.*

"Dude, she needs some space," he hardly realized Daniel had started the car again before he drove off towards the Den. *Away from her.*

Taylor nursed his aching jaw and turned in his seat. His eyes riveted to the window where he knew Krissy's bedroom lay. He'd been in it once. To bring her some college text books she'd left at the office a few years ago.

Krissy hadn't been home yet, having stopped at the pharmacy for her mom first. Mrs. Sposa had let him in.

He remembered the beige wallpaper with the tiny pink rosebuds all over it. The white, four poster bed and the delicate, rose colored cover. He recalled thinking that for a jeans and flannels kind of girl, she sure liked pretty things.

Her shelves were lined with poetry books and regency romance novels. She had a collection of small wooden boxes on her dresser, some of them sat open with little doodads inside. A couple of pictures were stuck in her mirror.

Silly shots of her with her mom and sister, and one of her at the bakery with Taylor and Daniel. Marcus had taken the picture. He remembered the day well. She'd been accepted into the night program at the local college and she'd been so surprised she cried. Taylor had done his best to make her laugh. He asked her to smell one of their signature cupcakes then smushed her face in the frosting, resulting in a food war.

Covered in cake crumbs and buttercream, he and Daniel had draped their arms over her shoulders.

Marcus had shot the picture. Boy, they'd laughed about that for days. She still didn't trust him around the cupcakes.

It had been a good day. Memories like that one swarmed his brain. He couldn't imagine life without Dimples. *How could he not have noticed that she was his mate?*

Then he realized he'd always known. Deep down, his Bear had always recognized her, but his human had pushed her away. *Cause I'm just the fun guy. No real depth. Nothing to offer.*

"That's bullshit, Taylor," Daniel said his eyes burning into Taylor's.

Fuck. He'd said that shit out loud. His brother had heard his weepy bullshit excuses. His cheeks burned and he knew they'd be dark pink. *Shit.* He wiped a hand over his face.

"She deserves better than me, man. I've been a total fucking asshole. We both know it. I've fucked around with so many women, and she's seen it all. How will she ever believe I'm serious?"

"You gotta make her, man. Look, Taylor, you're my brother and I love you. We both know I don't know shit when it comes to women, but I know one thing. Krissy has loved you for years. That's not something that just goes away. Give her a few days. Alright? You'll think of something."

"Yeah. Alright. Thanks, bro."

Hollow-chested and miserable as all hell, Taylor trudged into the Den feeling like he just went ten rounds with the Devil himself.

The real devil, not that jacked-up douche he went to high school with. New Jersey had its very own Devil living in the pine barrens not forty minutes away from Barvale, but Taylor shrugged off the wayward thought as he closed the front door.

The second he stepped over the polished entryway; he went on alert. He sucked in a breath and growled. *That scent. The Bear. The fucking guy who stuck his tongue down Krissy's throat! He's here. In. My. Home. WTF?!*

His angry steps resounded through the hallway as he walked towards the kitchen. *Yup*, there he was. Sitting at the table like he owned the fucking place.

Taylor stopped short and bared his teeth. His Bear rising in his mind's eye, fists clenched against the claws that were begging to come out.

Marcus' eyes snapped to his and Taylor wavered under his Alpha's stare. He knew his brother was pissed. No need to make him angrier by Shifting then and there.

Leya didn't like anyone to Change in the Den. But how was he supposed to react when the man he wanted to skin was sitting in his fucking house?

The stranger, he recalled his name was *Nate something or other*, sat there with a guarded expression on his face.

Him? Hot? Dimples thinks this douche is hot! His Bear growled at the reminder.

It took one second of observation for Taylor to begrudgingly acknowledge the man was not unattractive with his tanned skin, dark eyes, and brooding expression.

Of course, he was the opposite of golden-blonde, green-eyed Taylor. Stocky where Taylor was lithe. Serious-faced where, Taylor was always smiling. *He was charming dammit, not broody like this guy. Fuck. And Dimples was attracted to him?!* That did it.

"What the motherfucking fuck is this fucker doing here?!" Taylor exploded into the room.

A single, raised hand from his brother, *his Alpha*, stopped him in his tracks. *Motherfucking shit.*

Taylor growled. The dick had Krissy's scent all over him. Jasmine and vanilla mixed with the stranger's own smoky ursine fragrance. He wanted to rip the fucker's head clear off his neck. *Grinning bastard!*

"Stop. Now. Sit down, Taylor, you too, Danny."

Daniel took the seat to Marcus' left and Taylor slid into the one on the right. The air in the room was thick with tension.

He noted Danny had adopted his no-nonsense Enforcer face. *Good.* He hoped the fucker sweated under that gaze. *You have no idea, pal.* Having been on the receiving end of said stare, Taylor knew just how ruthless Daniel could be.

"Daniel, Taylor. I know you've met our mystery guest here earlier, but let me introduce you officially to Nate Cordoza," Marcus rarely used his controlled Alpha voice when it was just them in the Den.

Taylor reckoned it had more to do with the man sitting at the end of their kitchen table than anything else. He took no offense. An Alpha's job was to control potentially dangerous situations for the well-being of the entire Clan. His brother was a good Alpha.

He watched as Marcus' gaze never left the strange Bear Shifter, wondering at his brother's odd behavior. Then he knew, because two words left Marcus' mouth that Taylor would have never guessed in a million years

"Our brother."

Disbelief and fury warred within Taylor, but

before he had a chance to speak Daniel leapt across the table and had the newcomer by the throat.

"What the fuck did you say?"

"Daniel!" Taylor yelled.

"Let him go!" Marcus' voice rang with power.

For some reason, Taylor found himself with his arms wrapped around Daniel's waist, hoisting him off the man who claimed to be their brother. They left him on the floor while Taylor backed Daniel into the far corner.

Nate gasped and rolled to his knees, sucking oxygen in greedily. Daniel, Marcus, and Taylor were breathing heavily as well. Bits of broken chair crunched under his shoes as he went to the sink to run some water over his mostly healed face.

"It's true. We share the same blood," Nate stood up and eyed the three men wearily.

"Alright, alright! Sit the fuck down and you two stay calm. We need to hear what he has to say!" Marcus barked the order out and Taylor stiffened. *Shit.* He was right though. They needed to hash this shit out.

With one chair down, they still had enough for them all to sit. Clary, their housekeeper was gonna be pissed as hell though.

The Barvale Clan Den had seen its fair share of

rumbles, but never in the kitchen. That was Clary's domain. The older woman was widowed at an early age, but she helped raise the Devlin brothers and still took care of them to this day.

Yeah, Taylor mused, she was going to be pissed. But he wasn't going to let any errant thoughts distract him. This was serious. He donned his Keeper persona and focused on the stranger.

"I've scented you behind the bakery. You've been watching us."

It was a statement not a question, but Taylor noted the surprise in Nate's eyes before the other man nodded.

He inhaled and frowned. It was all so clear now, that intangible thing that had bothered him since he'd walked those woods hours before. He'd failed to understand the significance earlier that night, but now he knew.

The strange Bear's scent that he'd sniffed out early that evening had riled his Bear because of the familiar, or rather, *familial* notes in it. His Bear had recognized *family* even as his human half shuddered to think what that meant.

"Please. Start from the beginning," Marcus said and sat back with his face an impassive mask.

Taylor felt pride swell inside his chest. His

brother was already exercising the kind of leadership skills it took his father years to learn, according to his Keeper's journals.

Taylor sat back and trusted in Marcus' judgement. He stilled his racing heart and did his best to remain calm. He was his Alpha's Keeper and it was his job to listen and record the events of the night.

"Let me begin by saying, I come from a small Clan in eastern Texas. We're no more than fifty Bears. There's a lot of land there, not like here so we aren't close-knit."

"Fuck, just fifty of you?" Daniel asked.

"Well, now they're down to forty-nine. I was sort of kicked out. Too much *trouble*," Nate raised his eyebrow as if waiting for them to argue the point.

He continued his tale, speaking frankly and openly to the three virtual strangers who were his half-brothers, if he was to be believed. *Hmm.* Another brother?

Yes, his Bear answered. Taylor reluctantly appreciated the truth in Nate's statements. He had a third brother. *One who kissed Dimples. Grrr.*

He shook his head to rid himself of the image. That was for another time. Nate was talking about his Alpha now. There was no obvious disrespect, but Taylor could tell he did not like the man. He repeated how his mother had refused to leave the area and the Clan she grew up in.

"Are you a full Black Bear?" Marcus asked, his animal glowing through his dark eyes. The tension rose in the room, but quickly dissipated.

Marcus was a strong Alpha, his natural dominance bringing the other Shifters present to heel, so to speak. Not a bad thing actually, Taylor reluctantly admitted to himself as he rolled his shoulders to calm his agitated animal.

"Half Black Bear, half Grizzly. I'm a tad furrier than the average Black Bear Shifter and larger too. There were some in my old Clan that had an issue with me being a mixed breed. I had to prove myself many times during my life in Texas," Nate grunted the answer.

"Well, you're in my Clan now and we don't fuck around with any prejudice here. Anyone who shows themselves to be a bigot or all-around asshole usually answers to Daniel here. He's our head Enforcer. Taylor's our Clan Keeper. And as you know, I am the Alpha."

Nate grunted in reply. He kept his eyes carefully trained to the side of Marcus' face. Not meeting the Alpha's gaze was a wise choice. *Well fuck, he's smart too*, Taylor thought.

"Are you here to challenge me, Nate?" Marcus' timber was deep with his rising Bear.

A show of dominance now and again was not uncommon amongst Shifters, but Taylor was still somewhat shocked.

"No. That's not why I am here. I've just lost my mother, my old Clan hates me, figured I'd leave before they kicked me out anyway. I headed up North on a whim to see if I could find out who I really am," he scowled self-deprecatingly.

Taylor felt a tug of sympathy for the guy. As Keeper, he had inside knowledge of the inner workings of Bear Clans. He knew that what Nate was saying was true.

The Black Bear Grizzly Shifter was seen as a threat by his old Clan. Their sorry excuse for an Alpha didn't want to take on Nate and lose so he'd allowed their bigotry to push him out. *Dishonorable fuck.*

"Look. You know I'm not lying about this. My mom passed away. I never knew my father. I found this letter among her papers when I was cleaning out the house after it was *suggested* to me that I move on," he reached into his pocket.

Everyone tensed. Daniel went deceptively still, ever ready as an Enforcer should be. They all relaxed when Nate pulled out a faded envelope creased with wrinkles.

It looked old and worn, as if it had been read multiple times over the years. He handed the envelope to Marcus, but Taylor read the return address before his brother flipped it over to take the letter out. The postage stamp was from Barvale, New Jersey. *Fuck.*

"I'm going to read aloud," Marcus grumbled, "'*Dear Rosita, I wanted to write you to try and express my feelings about our weekend together. You gave me peace when I thought I'd lost all hope. You are the most generous woman I have ever met, and I will cherish the memory of you always. It was your sweetness and kindness that made me see I have to try and work things out with my wife. I will never forget you. Please call me if you ever need anything. Always, Iggy D.*'"

"Shit," said Daniel.

"So, Iggy is your father, right? Well, is *Daddy* home then?" Nate rapped his knuckles on the table and looked at his three half-brothers with a rueful grin on his face.

"Uh, no. Dad is travelling in his retirement. Look, this letter is hardly proof-" Daniel started, but Taylor interrupted him.

"He's telling the truth," Taylor gritted his teeth.

He hated the thought, but he knew Nate was telling them the truth based on the journals he'd been reading.

"Dad's old Keeper has a record of his early travels. He spent a lot of time in the West, after Daniel was born. You're from the Flint Clan?"

"Yes. I mean, I was, I am sort of Clan-less at the moment."

"Fuck that. Don't you recognize his scent? It's ours, mixed with his grizzly side. He's our brother, Marcus, he belongs here," Taylor addressed his oldest brother.

"Wait a second. Now you want him here? You just tried to kill him outside of *The Thirsty Dog*!"

"I didn't try to kill him," Taylor growled, embarrassed.

Nate stared back and forth between the men as if they'd gone nuts. The tension still remained in the air, but it eased with every breath. He was a dominant Bear, but not even close to Marcus. *Yes.* This was an Alpha he could respect.

"Look, I'm not trying to start anything here. Just thought I'd meet the man that sired me, and I don't know, maybe see if I could fit in. I'm not some teenager looking for a home. But I am a Bear Shifter, and you know I would be better, my Bear would be better, more cooperative, if I had a home with a Clan," his face burned bright red and Taylor scented his discomfort.

An unfamiliar urge to protect the Bear that he'd wanted to kick the shit out of only an hour ago filled him. *WTF?*

"Yes. That is true, Nate, and until we can reach our father and come to a decision, you are welcome to remain here. We will call it a trial period. If there are no problems and you want to stay after that, we will have an induction ceremony, does that work for you?"

"Really?"

"Yes. We need to wait for Dad to confirm your identity, but I believe, based on what our Bears are all telling us here, that you are indeed our half-brother."

"Uh," Nate started, but Marcus continued, ignoring the interruption.

"We will help settle your Bear either way, Nate. Now, *welcome*. This is our Clan Den, but it is also our family home. Visiting Bears stay here sometimes. The Devlin's live here. *My mate* and I live here. There are currently several empty bedrooms."

"Uh, it's nice?"

"You'll stay here in Barvale."

"Okay. Thanks," Nate moved to stand, but Marcus levelled a look that sent him back to his chair.

"I mean, *here*. As in, you are staying in the Den, *little brother*."

Taylor laughed at the baffled look on Nate's face and the pissed off one on Daniel's. *Hmm. Another brother. Well, well.* He didn't really know why he trusted the Bear all of a sudden, but his beast was telling him to. Taylor decided he'd ignored the animal's instincts for too long now. He was going to listen from now on.

"Look, there's a private entrance to this room, over here. Thought you might prefer that for now. There are some smaller cabins on the property as well, but they aren't furnished," Taylor talked as he showed Nate to one of the huge bedrooms in the basement floor of the Den.

The strange Bear was a little tense, as if he didn't know what to expect of the three Devlin brothers. *Nate Cordoza.* Taylor rolled the name around his head.

His Bear had no ill feelings towards the man, if anything the animal was glad to have found family. Especially since he believed his new brother would not go after his *mate* now that he knew they were related.

"Look, Taylor, the woman from the bar-"

"Dimples? What about her?" Taylor tensed.

"Yeah man, my bad. She didn't smell mated or I would never have hit on her like that," Nate ran a hand through his long, dark hair. He looked about ten years younger. *Unsure and abashed.*

"Um, we're not *mated.* That is, *uh,* fuck. It's complicated," Taylor opened a drawer underneath the bed and pulled out clean sheets and pillows, he and Nate proceeded to make up the bed and he continued.

"We've known each other for a long time, me and Dimples, you know? Like since we were in high school. Suddenly, I don't know-"

"Dimples?" Nate asked and Taylor growled. *My Dimples. Mine.* Nate raised his hands in surrender.

"Nah, man, I get it. You just realized she's your fated mate, bro, and the Bear went a little crazy. Shit's totally normal. I've seen it happen a time or two."

"Uh, yeah. I guess. I mean *fated mates?* I don't know, I never believed in that kind of thing until Marcus brought his girl home. Anyway, she's pissed as hell at me right now."

"I bet," Nate grinned.

"Look, did your mom ever *say* anything about my dad to you?"

"No. when I asked her who my father was, she'd say shit like he was the sweetest man she'd ever met, but he had responsibilities. She never told him about me."

"Damn man, I am sorry. It might have been fun though, having another older brother growing up."

"How do you know I'm older?"

"Age?"

"Twenty-seven."

"Ha! I'm twenty-six! Besides I read the journals. I know what years Dad was visiting the Flint Clan."

"Makes sense."

"Yeah. See you tomorrow, old man," Taylor nodded and left him there to settle in.

A mate and a new brother in one night. Holy shit.

EIGHT

"What a day," Krissy groaned as she hurried to grab a few of her reusable grocery bags from sliding off the front seat of her pickup while she turned onto her street.

She'd expected a phone call or something the day after the incident at *The Thirsty Dog*, but surprisingly not one person had reached out to her after the debacle. The second day after the incident, she'd been kind of antsy, but she busied herself with some much-needed household chores.

Predictably, she thought of Taylor while she'd worked. He'd seemed intent on speaking with her the night of the fight, but he hadn't made one move towards her the day after. As it turned out, he did not attempt to reach out the second day either.

She broke down and texted Marie, the older woman who ran things at the Barvale store to see how everything was going. To her utter shock, Marie texted her that Taylor was filling in for her during her stay-cation.

Krissy had balked at the idea. Taylor couldn't be trusted to remember half of the things she normally did. But Marie insisted that he was there, and he was doing a bang-up job. She'd shrugged and put down the phone.

That was a while ago. In total, she'd been gone from Bear Claw for five days. And they hadn't even cared. Business carried on without her. *They didn't need her.*

Oh no! She missed her job. Krissy actually loved the bakery. The smells and sounds, and the routine. She dealt with vendors and all sorts of staff all day long. It had been unsettling, the quiet of being home alone.

Her chest felt tight as panic set in. Did she blow the only job she'd ever had? Maybe the brothers realized they didn't need her now? *OMG.* Was she actually fired?

She didn't even want to go down that road.

Instead, she headed to the Barvale Pharmacy and Convenient Store and picked up her mother's prescription.

She also bought a few feminine necessities. Nothing like a steady menstrual cycle to remind a girl she was unmated and never having babies.

Ugh. Her Bear roared in her mind's eye. *We have a mate. A good, handsome mate. Our body is good, healthy, getting ready for cubs. Claim him. Make cubs.*

Krissy shushed her beast. She always had to keep a firm leash on her Bear. Especially when Taylor was around. The silly animal insisted he was her one and only, but she knew he didn't reciprocate her feelings.

Regardless of how much his behavior the other night resembled jealousy. *Yes. He was protective. He is a good mate. Mine.*

NO! Shh. Easy girl! It's just period hormones. We'll settle in with some of this brownie batter ice cream and that new Gosling flick, in another day or so we'll be good as new.

Her Bear chuffed at the shameless use of her favorite treat to dissuade her from thinking about Taylor. *And cubs. Mostly Taylor.* Ice cream always did the trick!

Krissy hummed to herself as she drove down the quiet, oak lined street that led to the small Victorian she grew up in. Her maternal grandparents left the place to her mom when Krissy was just a little girl.

Thank goodness! Who knew where her mother would have wound up after her husband abandoned her and their two daughters? He'd left just a few weeks after she'd first been diagnosed with cancer. *The rat!*

Krissy admired her mother's grit and strength. Cancer was a mean son-of-a-bitch and it didn't discriminate.

Patricia Sposa had been given more than her fair share of woes, and yet through it all she'd remained kind and supportive. Not to mention grateful for all of Krissy's hard work.

Well, she didn't want her mother's gratitude, she just wanted her to be well. She said a silent prayer in her head for the mother who'd raised her.

Briefly distracted, Krissy slammed on the brakes when she saw a familiar Range Rover in her driveway. *Grrr. Now? He's here now? Ugh. What the heck did he want?*

She grimaced as she looked at the boxes of feminine products she'd stocked up on at the pharmacy. *Oh well. I'm sure he knows about this stuff by now.*

She struggled to find some inner calm but kept going back to the other night. As if Taylor Devlin hadn't thoroughly humiliated her enough, now he was here in person. Probably to fire her! *Great. Just great.*

"Hey Dimples!" His deep baritone called out to her and she shut her eyes against the wave of attraction that assaulted her every time he spoke.

She couldn't help the way she felt. But she'd had plenty of practice hiding her body's natural reaction to the big blonde Bear Shifter. After all, she'd been crushing on him for over a decade now.

Krissy bit back on her arousal and focused on the nippy spring air and the fact that her cramps were back with a vengeance. *Damn period.*

She grabbed two of the heavy sacks and headed for her stairs, ignoring Taylor as she went.

"Hey, let me help," Taylor moved with the natural grace of most Shifters.

His hair was styled the way she liked, longer on top and buzzed on the sides. His face clean shaven and handsome as sin. She smelled the residue of shaving cream and realized he'd just come from the barber.

Hmm. That was odd. It was Thursday. He never went on a Thursday. She shook her head and focused on gathering her jacket and purse.

Lithe and lean with the build of a rodeo cowboy,

he grabbed the rest of her shopping from the floor of the truck and silently followed her up the cracked driveway to her stairs.

She studiously ignored him as she walked up the wooden porch steps, praying they didn't snap under their combined weight. She'd been meaning to get those fixed, but she never seemed to have the time.

Not that she was embarrassed of her home. Her mom did the best she could and with Krissy's help, they'd finally paid off the mortgage that year. It wasn't easy with Luisa's med school bills, but she was proud of that.

Sure, the Devlin's were way above and beyond her humble origins, but that was their problem. Not hers. If Taylor didn't like it, he could reverse his fancy SUV right out of her driveway and head back home.

Millionaires to start with, the brothers had turned their small bakery into a billion-dollar business in just a few years. With their combined Ivy League educations and natural charm, they'd stormed the business world, taking Bear Claw Bakery from humble hometown baked goods, to a household name.

There was a Bear Claw every hundred feet in New York City, not to mention the deals they'd just signed with several major hotel chains and cruise ships to provide baked goods and fresh brew to their customers. You could even buy their non-GMO, all natural, cinnamon bun dough in the supermarket thanks mainly to Taylor and his insistence that what they had was better than anything else out there!

All three brothers were amazing, and she'd enjoyed being part of the team during their rise to fame and fortune. They'd always treated her well. *Like family. But,* she sighed as she set her bags down on the counter, *I'm not family, I'm expendable.*

"Mom! I'm back!" Krissy called into the main section of the house, doing her best to ignore the big blonde Bear who stood behind her with his arms full of her groceries.

She felt her cheeks heat as she realized he'd been holding the bag with her tampons on top. She turned and motioned for them and he grinned.

Taylor released the bags to her outstretched hands, his fingers grazed hers sending jolts of electricity down her spine. His green eyes never left her.

"You're pretty when you blush, Dimples," he murmured as he moved into her personal space.

She tried to back up, but the counter was blocking her way. *What was he doing?* She could hardly breathe as Taylor traced the arch of her eyebrow down the side of her face with his finger.

"You smell so good," he leaned down, and Krissy gasped. *Was he going to?*

"We will finish this later," a noise from the foyer had him stepping back.

She hadn't even realized her mother was slowly padding into the room! What was he doing to her?

"Hi, dear. Hello, Taylor. I was just about to make some tea," Patricia Sposa walked towards her daughter looking frail as ever.

Still recovering from her recent hip replacement, her movements were slow. Krissy frowned as she watched her mother try to lift the kettle off the stove and moved to do it for her.

She smiled and kissed Krissy's cheek then moved to sit at one of the tall chairs at the kitchen island. This most recent relapse with her cancer had resulted in aggressive radiation and chemotherapy treatments that left her feeling drained most days.

Krissy's heart contracted when she thought of just how much pain she experienced daily. The cancer had been in remission for close to seven years now! That was a miracle in itself and she knew to be grateful for the little things, but how she wished she could give her mother some of her Shifter healing abilities.

"Hello, Mrs. Sposa, you look ravishing today!" Taylor's deep voice shook her from her musings and she mechanically went about filling the kettle and preparing tea.

"Oh, Taylor! Stop it! Now, my Kristianne is the one with all the looks here!"

"Mom!"

"On that I wholeheartedly agree, Mrs. Sposa, but she gets it from you! Dimples is always stunning. Now, these are for you, madame," with a flourish that was *so Taylor*, he produced a bouquet of flowers and a pastry box full of goodies from Bear Claw Bakery seemingly out of thin air.

He must have brought those in with her other bags, but Krissy had been too busy to notice. He was just that damn good.

She sighed and put away a few of the perishables while Taylor charmed her mother. Waiting for the kettle to boil, Krissy filled a ceramic tea pot with the loose jasmine tea leaves her mother preferred.

She took some cups and saucers out of the cupboard. Teatime was done right at the Sposa house.

She smiled and thought of all the little tea

parties her mom had thrown for her and Luisa. She took down a flat ceramic platter painted along the edges with delicate blue flowers. She arranged some of the pastries Taylor had brought for them on it. *He brought honey almond bear claws, my favorite.* She smiled.

Surely, it was just a coincidence, but for a second, she pretended he knew what she liked. That he'd cared enough to notice. And for some unknown reason, that thought made her so mad! Krissy growled and bit her lip. She looked to see if her mom had heard it, but the older woman was still chatting as if nothing was amiss. To Krissy's relief.

Taylor, of course, had heard her growl. His green eyes flashed with his Bear. He frowned as he watched her, but she ignored him and placed honey and sugar on the island countertop. How could she fight with him when he was making her mother smile and blush like a girl again?

The tea kettle whistled blaringly and the Shifters in the room cringed. *Yikes.* Darn supernatural hearing! Krissy turned off the flame and poured the boiling water into the tea pot breathing in the floral aroma of the brew as she did.

"Krissy, would you mind bringing mine to my room? I think I'd like to sit in my recliner and watch the cooking channel while I have my tea. I hope you won't think I'm being rude, Taylor?"

"Of course not. In fact, would it be okay if I walk with you? I need to use the restroom anyway."

"Why, that would be very nice! Krissy?"

"Yes, mama, you go ahead, and I'll bring you a tray," Krissy answered.

She swallowed the lump in her throat as she watched Taylor bow ridiculously low to her mom, like any real-life Prince Charming would. He offered Patricia his arm and walked slowly next to her while regaling her with local gossip that he'd gleaned from Clary, the Devlin boys' housekeeper.

Why did he have to be so sweet? The jerk. He didn't realize what it did to her when he did sweet things like that. *Or did he?* He turned his head, meeting her eyes for a brief second before helping her mother down the hall to her bedroom. The heat in his gaze was certainly new.

What had changed? Was he developing feelings for her? *No.* She wouldn't allow herself to think like that. *That way lies madness.* It would be detrimental to her entire well-being if she started believing Taylor harbored any feelings for her at all. Even if those feelings were only of lust.

"So, what brings you here Taylor? And don't feed

me any bull about wanting to see me!" Patricia's voice travelled down the hall to her daughter's ears.

Krissy cringed. *Oh boy, there goes mom again.* Patricia was sharp as a tac, if not weak due to chemo and radiation therapy. She imagined her eyeing Taylor with her best mom look until Krissy was sure he'd be ready to squirm right out the door! But he surprised her. *Again.*

"Actually, I was hoping to steal Krissy for a little while."

"I'm not working today," Krissy called to him automatically.

"You are not planning to drag her back to the office on her first week off in forever, are you Taylor?"

"No, actually, I was going to ask her to take a ride with me. I have some errands to run for Marcus and Leya, wedding stuff, and I could use a hand."

"Oh, well, it's not a date, but I think that would be okay. Won't it, dear?"

Krissy entered her mother's bedroom with her tea and pastry on a tray. She'd included some juice and a throat lozenge for her to suck on. It'd been feeling raw these last few days and Krissy wanted her to be comfortable.

"I don't know," she began.

"Come on, Dimples. Take a ride with me?"

"For Leya and Marcus?"

"Yep. I'm supposed to meet them in twenty minutes."

With her mother watching expectantly Krissy had no choice. She'd be suspicious if she flat out refused to go somewhere with her longtime boss and friend.

"Fine, but I'll take my car," she replied.

Imagine her surprise when after they'd said their goodbyes to her mother, Taylor got into her car and buckled himself in the passenger seat. *What was going on?*

"Okay," she said slowly, "Where are we going?"

"The bakery first," he smiled.

"But your car?"

"I'll get it later, come on, we'll be late."

Marcus and Leya were indeed waiting for Taylor at bear Claw Bakery. *Along with Nate. What the heck?*

"Uh, Taylor? What's going on?"

They walked into the store together and Krissy felt as if everyone was watching her. Nate smiled easily in her direction.

She noted nothing more than a friendly interest, but Taylor seemed to resent it. *Too bad for him. Possessive jerk.*

"Coffee?" Taylor asked.

"Sure," she said and watched him walk to the counter to speak to Marie. Of course, she was all smiles for the youngest Devlin, but that was Taylor for you.

The man was a natural charmer. A born flirt. Though he tended to be honest and fair with his conquests. *At least that was what she'd heard over the years.* Not that it was any of her business.

She shook her head and walked over to where everyone was grouped together, supposedly waiting for them.

"Hi Nate! Marcus, Leya," she nodded and sat down next to the man she'd met at The Thirsty Dog.

The same guy who Taylor beat the crap out of. Not that Nate didn't give as good as he got, though both Bear Shifters were healed by now. Krissy smiled, but hadn't gotten the chance to ask what was going on as Daniel strolled in a few seconds later.

The broody Bear sat on Krissy's other side, leaving Taylor to glower at her from across the table as he set her latte down in front of her.

She shrugged and took a sip. She had no idea what was going on, but Taylor had no claim on her. His behavior was certainly puzzling.

"Okay folks, as you know, Leya and I are getting

married," Marcus began and nodded as they clapped and cheered at the announcement.

"I'd like her to experience a real Barvale Clan welcome and to do that I was thinking," Marcus' dark eyes glittered with mischief as the boys and Krissy caught on to what he was hinting at.

"Bonfire!" Daniel, Krissy, and Taylor all yelled at the same time and laughed as the newcomers to town looked on skeptically!

"No really, Leya, it's tradition," Krissy began, "You see, Clan members since practically the beginning of Barvale, celebrate most special occasions on Lake Ursa with a real live clam bake and bonfire!"

"Followed by a little *Shifting* and *skinny dipping*," Taylor added the last bit in a stage whisper.

"Really?" Leya looked excited and Krissy couldn't help but giggle.

"Really! It's so much fun!"

"Where's the lake?" Nate asked.

"It's about a mile or so behind the Den," Daniel answered rubbing his short beard.

Krissy sympathized with him. Last time they'd had a bonfire, it was for Daniel's engagement. He turned his head as if to hide his reaction.

"Great," said Marcus before he went into plans

for the celebration. He wanted it to happen the following Friday.

After a few more coffees and some more talk, Krissy finally got the nerve to ask the question she'd been dying to know.

"Look, I apologize if this is out of line, but uh, Nate? What are you doing here?"

"You didn't tell her?" Nate's eyebrows shot up as he spoke to a suddenly, beet-red Taylor.

"Uh, slipped my mind?"

"Ah, well, if you don't mind," Marcus explained kissing Leya's knuckles before he spoke, "Let me introduce you officially to Nate Cordoza, *our brother.*"

Krissy got over her shock relatively quickly. The coloring was different, except for Marcus who had the same dark hair and eyes, but lighter skin.

Still, she could see the resemblance. Nate had the stockier build of the oldest Devlin, along with some of his mother's features no doubt, but that square jaw and straight nose were exactly like his brothers.

Wow. Another Devlin. Just what the world needs. There was no awkwardness between them, which was kind of nice. After all, she did sort of tongue-kiss the guy a few days ago. Even if it was for all of two seconds before Taylor slugged him.

"So, do you do any modeling," Nate asked Krissy as the others were still planning the bonfire.

"Who me?" Krissy asked incredulously.

She'd heard of men who asked women questions like that as some kind of cheesy pick up line, but he seemed to genuinely want to know.

"Um, no," she said and laughed modestly.

"Would you consider it?"

"*What?*"

"What?"

She turned her head realizing Taylor had been listening in. The jerk had asked the question at the same time as she did. *Humph.*

She frowned at him and turned her attention back to Nate who seemed to be watching the byplay with amusement.

"No creepiness implied, bro. I'm a graphic designer. I work for Grave Enterprises," he began.

"Oh! I know them, they put out *WolfMoon*! I used to play when I was younger," Leya exclaimed from across the table.

"Really?" Marcus smiled down at his mate and kissed her head.

"Yeah! I was a nerd. It started as just Were-wolves, I had the best little she-Wolf, but then they added other creatures on later. That's when it got really cool! My last avatar was this really awesome Witch who was also a Weretiger!" she laughed.

"Actually," Nate blushed a deep red as he spoke, "I'm kind of the reason that happened. When I was a kid, I found the online world of *WolfMoon* comforting, you know," he nodded at the other Shifters, "but I was pissed they didn't offer other avatars, you know, *like Bears*, so I wrote to the owner."

"Randall Graves?" asked Marcus.

"Yeah, you know him?"

"I've done business with him. For the bakery."

"Anyway, he invited me to create some avatars for *WolfMoon* and I did. I've been working for him ever since."

"What's that got to do with Krissy?" asked Taylor.

"Um, excuse you, but I think I can handle myself," she bristled.

"Yeah, easy buddy," Leya joined in, and fist bumped Krissy in a show of support. *Go girl power!*

"Of course you can, I just wanted to know where Nate here was going with this is all," Taylor looked to his brothers for support, but they just raised their hands as if to say, *you dug your own grave boy.*

"*Uh huh.* Anyway, Nate, what exactly are you asking me?"

"Well, uh," he looked from Taylor's glower to Krissy's own passive expression, "I am currently working on a project to design more female avatars for *WolfMoon* and I believe you'd be perfect."

Krissy ignored the low rumble coming from across the table and kept her eyes focused on Nate. She was flattered by his offer.

Not entirely sure what it entailed, but there was no way in hell Taylor Devlin was going to sit there and growl at her like she was some cub waiting for him to tell her what to do.

"Well, I am flattered. You know what, I'd love to, Nate. Thank you."

"How exciting!" Leya exclaimed then went on to aske Nate a dozen questions about what Krissy would have to do. Krissy didn't hear one word.

Taylor's green eyes glowed gold with his Bear. They raked her from head to toe and remained glued to her as she tried to remain calm in her seat. He was acting so possessive of her lately. *Could really mislead a girl.*

"I, uh, have to get going," she said and stood up promising to call Leya later that night.

She exhaled as she slid into the driver's seat of her car, then jumped as Taylor opened the passenger door and got in.

"What are you doing?"

"My car is at your house," he explained.

Of course it was. Why else would he get in the car with you? They drove in companionable silence for the few minutes it took her to get home.

"Krissy? Before I go, uh, will you be coming back to work soon?"

"You mean, I'm not fired?"

"Of course not! You're invaluable! I, uh, we, couldn't do without you," he scratched his head and looked decidedly uncomfortable.

"Okay then," she smiled sadly, "I'll be back to work Monday. I'm going to take the rest of the weekend if you don't mind."

"Of course not. I, uh, noticed it was that time, uh-" he looked pale and a little embarrassed and Krissy laughed.

"You saw my tampons? Is that what you're trying to say?"

"Um, if you need anything, I'd be happy to go get it for you-"

"I am fine, Taylor. I've done this before," she rolled her eyes. It was sweet, but unnecessary. And this was Taylor. *He'd never worried about this before, so why now?*

"Yeah, of course. Sorry. Look, I, uh, wanted to apologize you know, for-"

"For beating up your long-lost brother while I was having a drink with him?" She supplied.

"No, for behaving like an outrageous asshole when I should have just told you how beautiful you looked that night," he admitted.

Well, damn, Krissy sat speechless as he leaned across the seat and dropped a lingering kiss on her cheek.

"Have a good weekend, Dimples."

The weekend crawled by, but Krissy was feeling delightfully refreshed as she slid back into her routine. She sighed as she answered emails and returned phone calls. Surprisingly, Taylor had filled in for her beautifully.

He even watered her plants and tidied her desk. And she couldn't be sure if he simply left it there or got it for her, but there was a package of her favorite peppermint gum next to her keyboard and a new box of tissues. *Hmm.*

Bear Claw Bakery really was her home away from home. She'd noticed the looks she'd received from the bakers and the staff in the storefront when she'd arrived earlier that day.

Her hair was back to being curly, but the platinum tips still looked cute, especially hanging down her back in a low ponytail. She wore an old pair of jeans.

However, instead of her usual flannel top, Krissy wore a low-cut tank top that stopped right above her belly button. The dark pink color showed off her tanned skin and clung to her curves in a way that made her feel decidedly feminine.

Her jeans were soft and well worn. They hung low on her hips and hugged her ass in all the right places. She realized for the first time that morning that sure, she was a bigger girl, but she looked damn good.

She was tired of hiding because society exploited skinny women as the norm and made curvy women feel inadequate. Krissy was done with all of that negativity. She felt good about herself. *And it was going up to eighty damned degrees that afternoon.*

Spring in New Jersey was a fickle season. Cold nights and mornings, hot afternoons, and occasionally monsoon like rains. Still, she loved her home state.

Humming while she worked, she managed to clean up the mess Taylor had made of her files within two hours. Satisfied with her progress, she decided on a quick break. An impressive businessman and Keeper he may be, but organized he was not.

Her stomach rumbled. *Whoa!* It was almost time to go home. She looked at her phone and smiled. Luisa was due back from medical school any day now. It would be nice to have her younger sister home again.

Even though she would be starting her residency at St. Francis Hospital almost immediately. Still, at least she'd be living home again. Krissy called it a day, shutting down her computer and leaving the office. It was the first time she'd done so before the storefront closed in ages!

"Just the woman I wanted to see!"

Nate Cordoza ambled into the bakery with the swagger of a man in very high spirits. Krissy couldn't help but return his infectious smile. He was quickly becoming one of her favorite people. *In a strictly platonic way.*

"What's up, Nate?"

"I've got the best idea! Look, are you off now?"

"Actually, I was just on my way home a bit early today, but I was going to grab a *cream claw* and a cup of coffee first. Would you like one?"

"Uh, yeah, sure! I'll grab us a table, I want to show you something," he gestured to his tablet and

Krissy nodded before heading over to pour them both some fresh brewed coffee.

Bear Claw Bakery prided itself on the fact that a fresh pot was brewed every thirty minutes regardless of the time. They preferred to make small batches during off hours, while during their peak times they filled huge thermal jugs that lined the counter with no less than four varieties for their customers.

Using only fair trade and organic ingredients, *Bear Claw Bakery* strived to achieve the best tastes at reasonable prices. Most normals loved the stuff, but it was really the supernatural world that kept them in the black.

Because of their extremely astute senses, Shifters preferred all things natural, non-GMO, and organic. Chemical preservatives and iffy manufacturing of foods in modern society were a real turn off to *Weres* or Shifters who were more in tune with their animal-istic natures.

Krissy inhaled the rich, fragrant brew as she grabbed a couple of cream claws out of the display case. She added a few napkins to her pile then joined Nate at the table. His dark eyes nearly popped out of his head when he saw the enormous pastry, she placed in front of him.

"What is *that*, woman?"

"*That* is our exclusive *cream claw*. We take the delicate flaky traditional bear claw, with all the almond filling and the little shaved bits of almonds and coarse sugar on top, then we slice that baby right in half, like a sandwich, and we pipe in our homemade vanilla bean pastry cream, then we add a drizzle of locally sourced honey and, *voila*, cream claw!"

"That's it! Woman, you are marrying me!"

Nate was gazing at the pastry with pure adoration while Krissy laughed out loud. Neither one of them noticed the angry glare of the big blonde man who'd just walked in.

"*Shuddup*," she laughed, and play swatted his hand away when he went to grab her fingers with his mock proposal.

"I mean it, Krissy, this is amazing!"

"Alright, now will you please tell me what it is you wanted?" Krissy bit onto the pastry and moaned with delight. It really was that good.

"Yes," Nate said with a mouth full of cream claw, "Mmm. This is awesome! Anyway, it's about my designs. I have a great idea."

"Oh, yeah?"

"Yeah! Come home with me? We'll have dinner and I can show you what I need you to do."

"Okay, but I'm going to go home and shower first," she continued.

"No need, you look great. Besides *this* is the look I need to get down!"

"What? *Sweaty after work mess* is the look you need?" She laughed.

Nate joined her at first, then broke into an explanation on how the avatar he was creating with her in mind was an Ursine warrior. He needed to draw her in various states of exertion.

"So, you do want me sweaty?"

"My favorite look on a beautiful woman," he winked.

It was Nate's turn to laugh. They continued their playful banter until a huge noise erupted from behind where Krissy and Nate were sitting. They turned to spot Taylor standing just a few feet away. The Bear Shifter was shaking in his fury. The chair he'd been holding onto cracked beneath his grip.

His emerald eyes glowed with his beast and Krissy knew his Bear was close. *Oh crap. Now what?* She only hoped he wasn't going to freak out the way he did at the bar. Thank goodness they were the only customers. Suddenly, he took off like a rocket to the back of the bakery.

"Um, excuse me, Nate. Look, I'll meet you at the Den in a little while, okay?"

"Sure," Nate said and gave her a sad little smile.

It took her a few minutes to locate Taylor, but the wind carried his fresh cut grass scent to her nostrils. She inhaled and followed his path. A trail of ripped clothes littered the woods and she gathered them into a pile.

He must have really been riled up to have torn through his clothing. That was unlike Taylor. Usually calm and sophisticated. He never Changed into his Bear on the fly like that. Krissy was completely baffled. Since when did he go off in a snit?

"Taylor? Taylor!"

She called out his name. He'd definitely come this way. She brushed aside a few branches and inhaled the musky scent of his Bear. *Why was he hiding from her?*

"Taylor? Look, I don't know what's gotten into you, but, well, I have to go," conflicted she turned away. *Should she follow him?*

No. She told Nate she'd go model for him, and she planned on keeping her word. Taylor was a big boy. If he wanted to talk to her, he could find her. She frowned as she headed back to her office to gather her things.

A few minutes later Taylor exhaled slowly and walked out of the woods. His Change was swift as usual, but it left him panting. *What the fucking fuck? Hiding from her. That was your big answer to my new brother asking her out?*

He couldn't believe his Bear! Why the hell would the animal cower like that? He could take Nate! He knew he could.

Our mate doesn't need more jealousy. He paused as he listened to his beast. The Bear was right. *Fuck.* He tugged on his shirt and replayed the events that sent him scurrying into the woods like a fucking cub.

He hadn't meant to eavesdrop, but he couldn't help it. He was a freaking Bear! At first, he thought Nate had proposed to her, then he mentioned wanting her sweaty, and Taylor almost lost his hold on his Bear right there in the bakery! Thank the gods, it was near closing and there weren't any customers.

He knew he needed space, so he'd jogged through the back of the store to his favorite spot in the woods. After tearing through his clothing, he took off. *And she followed him.* His sweet, beautiful Dimples had come running after him. His Bear had wanted to roar with happiness, but he held it in. And he just watched.

She used her ursine senses to sniff out the trail he'd used. Damn, she came oh-so-close to seeing him, but he held himself still behind the den of a red fox, using the animal's odor to mask his presence.

She looked good enough to eat. Her pink tank top clung to her curves and her jeans dipped low to reveal that sexy little pair of dimples on her lower back. He'd nicknamed her years ago for the sweet little dimple on the side of her lips, but he was thrilled to learn that wasn't her only one.

Seeing those two little indents damn near killed him. He wanted to run his hands over them, test their depth. Trace them with his mouth. *Fuck.* Taylor growled and rubbed a hand over his face.

And he wanted to tear the eyes out of everyone else who'd seen them. *My Dimples!* What the hell was happening to him? He'd never been the type to have serious ideas about a girl or woman.

Hell, even in high school he'd never dated one girl. He had multiple girlfriends at a time. Transparent in all his relationships, he'd never made a secret of his man-whoring ways.

Shifters hated lying. Seeing as how they could usually sniff out a lie, they were discouraged practically from infancy from lying. Taylor never lied to a woman he dated or slept with. He even encouraged them to see other people.

Jealousy had never been a problem for him before. And yet, the last few times he'd seen Krissy talking with Nate, *talking*, mind you, *to his brother for crying out loud*, he'd wanted to commit murder.

Ever since the night at the bar, flashes of her piercing hazel eyes and her voluptuous body haunted him day and night. She had him literally on his knees! He was ready and willing to beg her for just a taste! *Fuck. I am so royally screwed.*

His Bear roared in his head and Taylor grimaced. *Okay.* So he didn't actually feel screwed. Truth was, he felt kind of good about it. Settled. Right on the inside.

She was the one then. *His fated mate.* He was finally ready to accept it.

Unfortunately for him, she fucking hated his guts at the moment. Only had friendship to offer him and probably wouldn't believe a word out of his mouth if he tried to tell her how he felt.

Fucking fuck.

"It's just this way," Krissy led Nate down the trail behind the Den to Lake Ursa.

They took a blanket, a couple of pizzas, and a six pack of cold beer with them. A sort of impromptu picnic.

"There are a few of these cabins dotting the shore. All of it belongs to the Devlin's. The entire property is more than fifteen miles of forest, lake included," Krissy announced as Nate opened the thin blanket for them to sit on.

The sun was still visible, and it was warm enough. Being Shifters, they usually ran a little hotter than normals.

"So, tell me more about this avatar you're

creating after me," she grinned and helped herself to a slice of pizza. *Sausage with hot cherry peppers. Yum.*

"Well, look, I mean it's not the *Mona Lisa*. I make avatars for gamers, you know," Nate shrugged and took a swig from the bottle of craft IPA he'd brought for them. It was obvious to her that he was uncomfortable talking about himself.

"You know, I happened to spend a few hours last night logged on to *WolfMoon* and I noticed dozens of avatars created by *N. Cordoza.*"

"You didn't," he sat there, mouth open with a bite of pizza inside and she laughed.

"Yes, I did. Whatever you want to call it, Nate, you are an artist."

His ears deepened in color to a dark red. *Awe, shucks.* The big, bad Bear Shifter was blushing at her mild praise! Imagine that!

"Uh, thanks. Your character is a female ursine warrior. There's been a demand for more female roles, and I've been slowly building their available character log. Of course, players can customize their avatars with thing like specialized weapons, clothing, hair and eye color," he mumbled and looked around, not quite meeting her eyes.

She smiled again, totally at ease with Nate. If

only her Bear sat up and took notice with him like she did with his annoying half-brother. *Oh, Taylor.*

Krissy was pretty much resigned to the fact that she and Taylor were a non-item. This newfound tendency to freak out on her was only because she'd developed a tentative friendship with Nate. She was positive he had no real or lasting interest. After all, she'd been around for years and he'd never noticed her before.

The party. Her inner sow insisted, but Krissy shut the thought down. The office party had been a fluke. *A total one-off.* If she really thought about it, she'd initiated that disastrous kiss. Lucky for her, he'd chalked it up to too much alcohol and never mentioned it again.

She'd be mortified if Taylor knew how she really felt. Krissy mastered the art of hiding her feelings pretty early in life. This was no different. She turned back to the conversation and realized she'd missed something.

"I'm sorry?"

"I asked if it would be okay to draw you now?"

"Oh, um, sure. How do you want me?"

"Um, can you stand up over there, near the water, and, uh, I need you to strip down to your underwear," his ears were red again.

Nudity was usually no biggie for Shifters. Clearly, Nate thought otherwise. She shrugged and stood up unzipping her pants as she went. She had no problem with her body, not really anyway. *It is what it is*, she thought to herself.

She was tall and big as, well, *as a Bear*. She smiled at her own self-deprecating joke as she pushed her jeans past her hips and down her legs. Krissy was glad she'd taken the time that morning to shave. That was the one thing about being a female Shifter she'd always hated.

Hairiness was not sexy on women. Especially women who lived by a damn lake! After a brief trial with laser hair removal, she realized whatever made Shifters excellent healers, also carried over to hair follicles. *Ugh.*

So, daily shaving would have to be it for now. Although, she had heard of a new salon in Maccon City that was supposedly opening soon. It was owned by *the Morrigan* herself! *Hmm.*

White Witches weren't common in the area, but if her friends from the Macconwood Pack trusted the woman, Krissy was certainly going to give her a try once she opened her doors. She tucked away the info for later.

Nate cleared his throat and looked her over with

an artist's eye and appreciation before he bent to his sketchpad. She inhaled and thanked the gods again for her good taste in underwear. Nothing fancy, mind you, just a plain pink t-shirt bra and matching bikini cut panties. *But still.*

"So, I'm gonna use some charcoals first, then I'll move on to ink, and eventually, to my tablet," he explained as his hand moved furiously across the pad.

"So, do I do anything?"

"Um, not yet, you're fine for now."

He didn't talk while he drew. The quiet would probably bother some, but not Krissy. She rarely got moments of peace. This was almost like being alone, so quiet and serene.

She stood near the water for a while then stretched and sat down with Nate's approval. He asked her to change position a few times to sketch her from the back.

"Okay, I need some points of reference for movement. Would you mind?"

"Um, no. So like running? Lifting?"

"Yeah, and uh, if you wouldn't mind, shifting?"

Krissy considered for a moment. She must have realized when he'd first asked about her posing for his ursine warrior that she'd have to Shift.

Werebears and other *weres* did it all the time in front of one another. It simply wasn't considered good manners to watch, and he was asking to do just that.

"I know it's not customary, but it's for art, I swear Krissy," his Texas drawl seemed to come out more when he was embarrassed.

"No, uh, I get it, okay just give me a second," Krissy inhaled.

Was she really going to strip down in front of Nate? He was practically a stranger. And yet, she felt completely at ease with him. He was funny and honest. Her nose would have sniffed out if he was a liar.

She liked him. That was true, but there hadn't been anything sexual between them since that night at the bar. Even that was more playful than heated, she realized. Nate was sort of comfortable to be around. Friendly even. *Almost brotherly.*

"Okay, I'll do it," Krissy announced to Nate's obvious pleasure.

"Great! Whenever you're ready."

Without any qualms, Krissy stripped down to her skin. The warm spring air still held a bite of crispness with the setting sun and she shivered in delight. It felt good to be outside. She spent so much time in the office, she sometimes forgot how much she enjoyed being in nature's loving arms.

She closed her eyes against any embarrassment she might have otherwise felt. Nakedness aside, she felt her other half brush against her mind with a gentle reaffirming touch.

This was her sow, *her inner self*, her Bear she was communing with now. Her Bear was strong, fierce, and beautiful. She recognized the inner peace her sow felt and longed to feel that way in her human skin. But something was missing, always just out of reach.

She forced her mind back to the present. Scents, familiar and new, invaded her nostrils. The sandy shore, the lake, the forest, and Nate. His presence was almost disturbing, but she acknowledged him for what he was. An observer. A friend.

He was a Bear like her. *Strong, trustworthy*, she told her sow. Her animal recognized his intentions as friendly, though she scoffed at the idea of allowing a man who was not her mate to watch her Change.

It's for art, she told her stubborn animal. The trust and connection between woman and Bear had always been strong. Her sow soon agreed to perform accordingly.

With a deep exhale, Krissy fell into that special place where both halves of her soul existed harmoniously together. Shifter magic wasn't something readily recognized in the supernatural world with Witches and Warlocks taking all the fame, but what else could it be?

That special plane of her existence that allowed her body to Shift from woman to Bear in a matter of seconds was the very essence of magic in her mind.

Shifters were more than just animalistic nature and brute strength. Her power pulsed within her very veins as her bones broke and reknitted themselves and skin stretched to accommodate her Bear.

It felt so good to let her sow out. Like a long stretch after an exhausting drive. She felt no pain with her Change. Not since she was a child. A low grumble rose up from her belly and she snapped her jaws.

Whipping her ursine head towards Nate, she preened to find him engrossed in studying her. His human fingers flew over paper as he sketched and sketched. She wondered what it was he captured there in his book.

Her Black Bear was large, though smaller than Shifter males. She had thick, dark fur that lightened to a warm brown on her muzzle and underbelly.

Huge four-inch claws tipped her paws and she flexed them proudly for Nate.

Not wanting to simply stand and pose, she did what Bears do. Krissy turned her body with the keen agility of her animal despite its size and waded into the cold lake water.

Nate laughed in delight as he continued to draw her. Feeling good, as she did, Krissy stepped out of the lake and ambled closer to where he sat. She shook out her fur to his mock anger and wails. Chuffing laughter as only a Bear could make sounded from her chest.

"Krissy! No, you'll get my drawings wet!"

She stopped her playful activity and looked towards the tree line. Her supernaturally keen sense of hearing picked up on something, or rather, someone coming up on them. The slow, almost silent steps of a predator made the fur on her back rise, Nate stilled next to her, his eyes glowed with his Bear.

A loud snort reached her ears, the animal announcing his arrival. A second later, an enormous Black Bear with white-gold fur stood less than twenty feet away from them, rising from the tree line like a ghost in the night.

The beast huffed, baring his teeth at Nate who'd

placed himself between Krissy and the animal. She was so not having that. He still wore his skin while she was in her fur. Besides, Krissy had nothing to fear. She recognized the man who belonged to that blonde fur.

Beautiful, she thought as she watched his beast hulk towards them, fur glowing white gold in the rising moonlight. An eight-hundred-pound Spirit Bear, rare and stunning to look at, she didn't understand what he was doing there.

She stilled all movement, her enhanced vision taking in his aggressive stance as he reared back. Taylor stood up on his hind legs and loosed a massive roar in Nate's direction. Her Bear preened with his action, while her human half scoffed.

What the hell was he doing? He's come for you, her Bear preened with the knowledge. Krissy's human half, however, was not ready to admit any such thing. Tension filled the air, Krissy stepped in front of Nate, shielding him with her body.

Unblinking she watched displeasure cross his face and the Bear reared back once more. He charged towards them, until he was hovering over Nate, who'd dropped his gaze and remained stock still.

Taylor opened his dripping jaws; a rumbling growl filled the air. *That's it!* Incensed, she huffed at him. His green gaze fell on her, eyes glowing in the darkness.

There was no reason for this! She moved in front of Nate again and pushed Taylor back with her snout. She almost had to threaten her Bear to get her to move, since the dumb animal was completely thrilled with his moronic show of aggression.

"Krissy, get back," at Nate's words Taylor looked at him once more and roared. Spittle flew through the air and Nate stepped back.

She'd had enough. Krissy pulled on that special Shifter magic that allowed her to swap fur for skin and started her Change. Panting and dripping sweat she gasped as both Bear and man remained caught in their tentative stand-off.

"Nate, go, now," she breathed and placed herself between him and the animal. She knew instinctively he would never harm her.

"You sure?" At her nod he backed up, slowly.

"Taylor, man, listen I was just sketching her, like we talked about," Nate moved slowly holding his tablet and his sketchpad in one hand and raising the other one in surrender.

He looked at her with a questioning glance, she nodded, and he retreated. Still refraining from looking Taylor in the eye as he did so. *Smart man.*

The huge blonde-Black Bear reared back and roared again, pounding his foot against the packed dirt angrily. Tension rolled off him in waves, again causing excitement to grow in Krissy's sow. *Good mate. He fights for us.*

NO! Krissy was not about to let Taylor challenge his newly found brother over a complete misunderstanding. She pushed her small human hands against him, and his sharp green eyes met hers.

All traces of anger fled as he gazed at her. A noise from the path caused him to refocus on where Nate had gone, and the Bear growled deep in his chest.

Enough of this nonsense. She didn't want any more confusion. Nate was a friend. But even if he wasn't, Taylor had no business interfering! She didn't belong to him! *Yes, we do.*

She vaguely took note of Nate's retreating form. Good. She didn't want him getting involved in this. It was well past time for her to take this thing by the horns.

"Taylor! Skin! Now!" she growled through human teeth.

It wasn't long before they both stood facing each other. He breathed deeply with the force of his Shift, the sounds of Nate's trek back to the Den echoing in the silence surrounding them.

Krissy was unsure of what to do next. They both stood staring until Nate called out to them. Of course, he knew they would hear his message with their Shifter senses.

"You both got some stuff to work out, I'm heading back to the Den. Yell if you need help."

Traitor! She wanted to scream after him, but she was caught in Taylor's emerald green stare. His eyes raked over her body like a lovers' hands. Heavy lidded, chest heaving he looked his fill until she squirmed under his gaze.

"Oh, Dimples you are beautiful," he growled.

Sure, they'd been on Clan runs together, but Krissy had always stayed close to her little sister. They were the only two in their family, and the Barvale Clan was not large by any means. Maybe seventy-five Shifters attended runs at a time, still enough to keep them apart.

Taylor had always been surrounded by friends and his brothers. He'd never sought out her company other than for things work related. But now, he looked at her like she was a feast and he a starving man.

"I need," he growled, tongue licking his lips as he stepped closer.

Heat pooled in her stomach and moisture slicked

between her thighs. Her body readying itself for her man. *Our mate.*

"You smell so good, sweet," he sighed.

His six-foot plus frame swayed closer to her, but she was frozen in place. His voice deep with his Bear, yet it sprung from him like a gentle breeze in the night.

Shaking her head, she exhaled, bracing herself against the temptation that was Taylor. Her heart squeezed in her chest. Her body, however, trembled with anticipation.

She was suddenly aware that she was completely nude in front of Taylor! *Eeek!* Self-consciousness reared its ugly head and she desperately wanted to cover up.

Krissy was a Bear Shifter. She was tall and big. Ample curves covered her near six-foot frame. Images of Taylor's girlfriends from over the years flashed through her mind. They were mostly petite and thin. Beachy looking waifs with big hair and flat stomachs. The complete opposite of Krissy. Her hands raised to cover herself, but she forced them down.

No. She was not going to go down that road. Krissy straightened her shoulders, eyes wide as he looked his fill. There was no denying her curves now.

Years of hiding behind shapeless flannels and jeans gone in an instant.

"Please," he moved closer, enveloping her in his fresh-cut grass scent.

"So beautiful, so mine," he murmured.

Krissy gasped in surprise. Her eyes dropped to the evidence of his attraction and warmth kindled once again in her belly. All self-consciousness left as he reached for her.

Slowly, as if he was afraid, she'd run, he raised his big hands. *Like a cowboy with a skittish mare.* The image popped into her mind as Taylor took his time invading her space.

Heat from his body tickled her damp skin. Arousal darkened his eyes. The heady scent filled her nostrils and her mouth watered in response. *Gods, he is so beautiful.* His naked body outlined in the silver moonlight brought a bone deep craving to her heart.

He was perfection, as if sculpted from the finest stone to her every desire. Whipcord lean and yet covered in thick ropes of muscles that most Shifter men seemed to share. But not overly so.

Not beefy, like his brothers, Taylor's stomach was flat, ripped with muscles. She counted eight but could have went further. Her eyes zoomed in on his hard length and he hissed in a breath.

He was so big. Everywhere. *Mine. Mate.* She wanted to devour him from head to toe. Awareness sparked and desire welled between them. *Still a golden god*, she mused as he leaned forward and breathed in her scent.

He wasn't the type to spend hours in a gym, and his shape screamed natural as opposed to sculpted. Taylor had no such leisure time. Often looked at as the easy-going Devlin brother, she knew just how hard he worked for the Bakery and the Clan.

It was simply easier to tell herself he was a shallow playboy, than to admit that Taylor Devlin was a real man of substance who simply didn't see her as mate material. Pain lanced her heart, but she pushed it away.

This might be her one opportunity, and right then, she made a decision. Krissy would have this experience. Even if it was only for one night. She'd cling to it wholeheartedly for the rest of her life.

"Need to touch you," he growled, lips grazing her neck.

She shuddered involuntarily as his fingers grazed up and down her ribcage to the undersides of her breasts, lighting fires in their wake. She arched into his touch, forcing his fingers to brush harder against her sensitized skin.

Longing to press herself fully against his body, Krissy tried to steady her breathing. He would be warm, she knew. Shifters had higher core temperatures than normals. *He was hot alright.* So hot, he could burn her up with one embrace. Right then, she wouldn't have minded at all.

Caught in the erotic game of looking and barely touching, Krissy moaned. Desire flooded her veins. The scent of their combined arousal painting the night air.

Did he smell her need? Hear her heart pounding heavily in her chest? It felt loud as thunder in her mind.

"Smell so good, Dimples, look so fucking good, bet you're gonna feel better," he growled and closed the distance fully between them.

The two of them groaned as his smooth skin slid right up against hers. He hissed as his hard shaft rested on her soft belly. He dropped his head, nostrils flaring and eyes blazing with lust. Krissy was lost in them. In him.

"I've been wanting to do this for a very, very long time," his whispered growl sent shivers down her spine.

Then they were colliding. No finesse, just raw need as he smashed his lips to hers. The kiss an explosion of feeling rather than the chaste meeting of lips she'd experienced in the past.

There was joy and happiness in that kiss, but also bone-deep need and desire. She never felt anything like it. Tongues warred, teeth scraped, lips clung, and through it all he repeated her name like a mantra. *Her name, not Dimples,* she smiled against his mouth.

"*Krissy,*" he moaned, sliding his hands down her back, over the curve of her ass, squeezing her.

"*Krissy,*" again he said it as he dominated their kiss, growling with the force of his desire.

"Yes," she moaned back, tilting her head to give him access to her neck and throat.

"*Krissy, sweet Krissy,*" he breathed her name, tasting her as he stroked and teased her, mimicking what their bodies were going to do soon.

They stumbled to the ground together grinding and moaning against one another. She didn't want to think. Only feel. No pesky *what about tomorrows* to mar this sweet interlude. *Even if it was the only one, she would ever have with him.*

Sex wasn't an easy thing for Krissy. She preferred sex with emotion, so it had been a while for her. Her body knew what to do, it responded instinctually to his sensual assault.

It was her heart that stuttered in her chest. She tried to soothe it, to lock it up inside, but it was a losing battle. *Mate.*

She loved Taylor. Always had. *Always will.* She hushed her frantic mind and allowed herself to fell back into the rhythm of their lovemaking with gusto.

"Feels good," she whimpered as he ran his hands up her leg and parted her thighs.

"Krissy," he moaned her name, licking at the valley between her breasts before falling on one hardened nub and then the other.

Her body responded, tightening and swelling, moisture pooling in her cleft. She arched her back, forcing her breast more fully into his mouth and reveling at the pleasure that shot through her. His erection pressed hard against her belly, she wanted him lower, deeper, filling her.

Taylor groaned around her nipple, sliding his fingers along her wet pussy. He played her like a master, sucking on her tongue before continuing his journey down her body. Drawing out moans and sighs with the slightest of touches.

Restless and needy, she ran her hands down his back, tracing and touching every inch of him she could reach. His chest rumbled under her caresses and she felt empowered. She continued her journey, running her fingers along the muscled curve of his ass, kneading the hard flesh and swallowing his moan.

"So beautiful, baby, I'm gonna make you feel so good," he groaned and pulled back.

Using his tongue and teeth, he nipped and licked a trail from her breasts down to her navel. He delved his tongue into her bellybutton and tasted the soft skin there, kissing and breathing her in at the same time.

Her eyes opened, thousands of stars dotted the sky, but she didn't see a single one of them as he slid further down her body, hands clamped onto her hips like vices. She whispered things, desperate for his touch. Drowning in her need, Krissy's legs parted, cradling him in the apex of her thighs

"*Gods, yesss,*" she moaned as his body slid down, shoulders parting her legs further.

Taylor pushed on her thighs and spread her legs wider. His hot breath warmed her exposed flesh as he parted her moist lips with unsteady hands.

"So pink and wet for me, aren't you, baby," he didn't wait for a reply. He leaned forward, his long tongue delving into her tight cleft.

Taylor groaned as he withdrew and slid his tongue

into her channel again and again. Growling deep with pleasure, his thumb found her clit and he circled, circled, circled the tiny nub until Krissy moaned aloud.

She hissed against the pressure of his tongue and the vibrations coming from his chest all the way up to his mouth. Rocking her hips against his face, determined to chase her pleasure, she groaned when Taylor grasped her hips and held her firmly.

Such sweet torture! Her head whipped from side to side as he flicked his clever tongue over her tight bundle of nerves. Her clit pulsed, needy and wanting.

"You taste so good, baby. This cream is all for me, isn't it? I'm gonna fill you now, stretch you," he growled.

Hands fisted in his blonde hair she choked back a scream as he filled her with both his fingers and tongue. Working in and out of her tight channel, wringing out every inch of pleasure.

Her entire body wound tight as a bow. Taylor grunted and doubled his efforts. Lifting her hips with ease, he pulled her up to his face, sucking on her clit as she rode his hand.

"Taylor!" she cried out, hips working in time with his clever hands and his tongue.

Krissy rocked against his sweet invasion. Loving the feel of his fingers as he stretched her, and yet wishing for more. Wanting his cock to fill her. Visions of him taking her with his shaft filled her head.

"Fuck yeah, baby, I want you just as much, but you gotta come for me first," he growled.

He lapped at her clit with long sweeps of his tongue. Whispering encouragingly and fucking her on his hand, he groaned as he swallowed her arousal.

Head thrown back, her pussy squeezed his fingers as he thrust them in and out of her sheath. She moaned his name, all sensation now. Uncaring of how loud she was or where they were.

She gripped his head with her thighs and tore at his hair with her hands. Ecstasy was right on the precipice; she could taste it.

Taylor growled once more against her clit sending waves of pleasure shooting through her. And then, it was hers. She moaned his name long and hard as her pussy clenched and her muscles spasmed. Pure bliss flowed through her.

"Taylor," she breathed as he murmured praises and kissed his way from her thighs to her mouth.

She grabbed him by the nape of his neck and tasted her salty sweet musk on his lips.

The frantic need to mate him didn't lessen with her orgasm. If anything, it grew more intense. Krissy found his hard length with her hands as he crawled up her body. She positioned him at her entrance and turned them both till he was on his back.

"Are you sure?" The question surprised her, but there was no turning back from this night. Not for her.

"Yes, need you," she slid her hands between them, measuring his thickness and length.

"Fuck, yes, need you too," he groaned as she slowly impaled herself on his cock.

ELEVEN

He knew the second he felt her tight channel clench around his cock he'd never have another. She was it for him. His entire world. *Mate. Mine.*

Holy fuck. Gods. Yesss! Taylor wanted to shout it to the world, he was finally fucking Krissy Sposa. His *Dimples.* Outside on the ground, surrounded by nature. And he wouldn't stop until she came all over his fucking cock. And he was pretty sure he wasn't stopping then either.

His Bear had been an obnoxious fuck these past few months. Anxious and upset all fucking weeklong since that night at *The Thirsty Dog.* And he finally understood why.

He'd decided to Change tonight and have a run

through the woods after that disaster at the bakery. He'd hid from her. *Like a fucking cub.* After that he'd retreated to the Den, finished some Keeper business, then Shifted.

He'd just about gone apeshit when he'd scented her on the air. His beast demanded he follow the trail, wouldn't take no for an answer. Then he did lose his shit when he saw her there. Krissy in all her naked glory, standing in the dark with her blonde tipped curls basking in the moonlight like some kind of gorgeous forest nymph.

A vision right out of his fantasies. *His top-secret dirty fantasies involving the delectable woman he was currently balls deep inside of.* Of course, his illusion was shattered when he fucking spied Nate. All soft visions dissipated pretty fucking quickly then, replaced by pure molten rage.

Motherfucker was sitting there smiling at Krissy! While she was fucking naked! His Bear had reacted without consent from his human half, but looking back, Taylor wholeheartedly agreed with the beast's reaction. No one should see Dimples naked! *No one but him, that is.*

He savored the taste of her on his lips as his fingers roved her body, gripping her hips. She was so fucking beautiful. Fierce and glorious, like the Amazons of old.

She rode him like a goddess. Her lips were parted, hair flying around her shoulders, breasts heaving in her exertion. Her name sounded from his lips and he grew harder inside her. *Perfection. She is perfect, Mate. Mine.*

Unable to be still under her ministrations, he thrust upwards, meeting her pace. The scent of their coupling threatened to overwhelm him. Her sweet jasmine fragrance mingled with his own musk, creating something new, something theirs. He loved it. Wanted to bottle it. *Grrr.*

Keeping in time with her sharp movements, he reveled in the heady evidence of her arousal. Her slick pussy squeezed him so fucking good.

"Tight, you're so tight, baby, s'good," he groaned.

The lewd sounds of skin slapping against skin was like a fucking symphony to his ears. He sat up, mouth catching and feasting greedily on one plump breast.

He couldn't get enough, he wanted to stamp himself all over her. His hands were everywhere, grasping and caressing, kneading her soft flesh.

He wanted to take control to throw her on the

ground and fuck her into oblivion, but the ground was hard under his bare ass despite the thin blanket she and Nate had brought with them. *Fucking Nate.*

He shook his head. He'd been enjoying getting to know his new half-brother, but he still didn't want the fucker near his mate. And Krissy was *his.*

Gods help him. He couldn't get enough of her. She filled his senses as he filled her body. The pulsing heat of her weeping pussy squeezed his shaft until he was blind to anything other than her.

His gums ached and fingertips itched. His Bear pushed him, drove him to seal their *matebond,* which pulsed unfinished between them.

Not yet. He wanted her desperately. Needed to bond with her, but first he needed to touch every inch of her. Her feet, her knees, her legs, her sumptuous ass. Krissy moaned and scratched at his shoulders, her movements turning jerky.

"Stay with me, baby, together," Taylor growled and sat up straighter, taking control.

"Yes," she moaned.

He gripped her hips and lifted and plunged, fucking her on his cock. He continued with one hand and held her face in his other one. Fingers stroking her cheek and throat, eyes locked on his. *Fucking gods, I'm a goner.*

She was so fucking gorgeous like this. Breathless and sexy as hell, hair floating around her shoulders, a sheen of perspiration glowing over her silky skin. His body ached with the need to come, but not yet. *Not yet.*

"Taylor," she moaned his name and it was music to his fucking ears.

He wanted to memorize every sweet inch of her luscious body, record every sound she made in the heat of their lovemaking. He might fuck her, but it was lovemaking too. Couldn't be anything else but with his sweet Dimples.

She arched up, chasing her pleasure, using his body. He encouraged her, wanted her to take from him, but he wanted something in return as well.

He reached up and tangled his fingers in her hair, pulling her to his mouth and stamping his lips to hers. He kissed her so thoroughly she stuttered in her pace. Lips locked they both moaned in the sudden stillness of their bodies, but not for long.

"So good, baby. Oh gods, yes," he groaned and flexed his hips hard, meeting her downward thrusts readily.

Taylor gripped her tapered waist and felt her thick thighs squeezing him as she found her rhythm once again. *Oh fuck, he was gonna cum soon.* But he would see to her pleasure first. *Hell fucking yes.*

"Ready for one more, baby? Come on, give it to me, Krissy, come all over my cock," he growled into her neck, licking the sensitive spot he was dying to sink his teeth into.

Her channel tightened in response. He sucked in air, trying to breathe as pleasure threatened to choke him. She squeezed and milked him as inch by inch he filled her sweet pussy.

"Taylor, I want," Krissy moaned and ground her clit into his pelvis, and Taylor grunted, lifting her easily.

He stood up, using his strength and gravity to give her more of what she needed. Her legs wrapped around his waist and hands gripped his shoulders. Eyes lit with surprise he continued to stretch and fill her, repeating the movement as she slid up and down his hard shaft.

"I'm here, baby, I'm gonna give you what you need," he felt his Bear rise and almost halted, but her sweet moans threw him off balance.

Taylor fought against the pain in his gums that preceded his fangs and pushed down on the beast who was riding him hard. *Patience.*

He wanted to mark her more than anything, but

they hadn't discussed it. *Maybe during round two*, he reasoned with his beast.

"Taylor," she raked her nails down his back. The pain intensifying his pleasure and he growled harshly in his throat.

Taylor couldn't get enough. He pounded into her, knowing she could take it. He wanted to drown out everything but her. *Thrust, grind, thrust, grind.*

His pounding rhythm was met with her rocking hips until his balls were snuggled up against her ass as he pushed deeper, deeper inside of her.

"More, Taylor, give me more," she growled and met him with her eyes. Gold with her Bear, Krissy reached around him and squeezed his ass grinding her pelvis and tilting to swallow him deeper.

Her breasts crushed against his chest. There wasn't room for air between them, nothing but him and her. Their bodies slick with their juices, rocking one another into oblivion. And still he wanted more.

He wanted this. He wanted her. Forever. He licked and sucked on her neck, scraping his teeth over her throbbing pulse. He reared back, lifted her up and slammed her down on his cock one more time, and a tidal wave of passion consumed them both.

Krissy cried out, her channel squeezing him as

she crested. A roaring sound filled his ears and he realized it was him. His orgasm shot through him like a lightning bolt. He pulsed against her heat, filling her with his cum.

He opened his mouth wide, almost unaware of what he was about to do. But deep down he knew. *Claim. Mine. Mate.*

Krissy turned away at the last second.

"No," she whispered.

Pain lanced his heart, but he focused on his breathing. *Why? She knew they were mates. Maybe she changed her mind? But that was impossible, wasn't it?*

His Bear wanted to rip him a new asshole for fucking this up, but the man needed to think. If only he hadn't blown his brains out of his cock a second ago.

No, she'd said no. No. His Bear roared his anguish in his mind's eye, but the man soothed the beast with the evidence of their coupling. *She carries our scent, soon she will bear our mark. Patience.*

They laid together on the thin sheet in a mass of sweaty limbs and tangled hair afterwards. Taylor wasn't a virgin, not even close. But damn if he hadn't felt like one. Touching her was like being reborn. How had he doubted for a second that this woman was meant for him?

As their breathing calmed, Taylor didn't stop to think as he rolled to his feet with her in his arms once again. There was a cabin a few feet away. Shower, talk, and maybe some food. After he loved her again, hard and good.

He wasn't sure what was going on in that amazing brain of hers, but the longer she kept silent, the more he worried. Fuck that.

Krissy was his. He just needed to convince her.

CHAPTER
TWELVE

"Taylor! Put me down, I'm too heavy!" Startled from her post-coital bliss, Krissy struggled, but Taylor held on strong.

"Unless you want us both to crash down onto this pebbled walkway, you'll keep still, Dimples," he growled into her ear.

Holy shit! We had sex. Taylor and I did the deed. OMG! Despite her inner excitement, Krissy clamped her mouth shut as Taylor carried her up the pebbled walkway to the first line of cabins that dotted the shore of Lake Ursa.

She needed to think. To regroup. But he was so close and so damn tempting. *And ours. Bite him.* Her Bear simply wouldn't give up on that. *Shh!*

Okay. So, they'd had sex. No biggie, right? She wasn't a virgin. He wasn't either. *No shit.* And they could avoid all awkwardness if she just went home now and forgot this ever happened. *Yes! Good plan!*

Except, how could she forget this happened? *One night, Krissy. That is all this is.* She exhaled and kept her head trained down on her abdomen. She felt Taylor's eyes on her but couldn't meet his.

"I won't know what's going on inside that pretty little head of yours unless you talk to me, Dimples," Taylor coaxed as he sat her down on the cold tiled counter inside the bathroom of the first cabin they'd come upon.

She yelped at the chill and he sent her an apologetic smile before turning around to draw a bath. She'd been so wrapped up in her thoughts she hadn't noticed where he was taking them let alone considered what was going to happen next.

Hmm. A bath. Made sense, she supposed. She slid off the counter and grabbed some fluffy white towels off the shelf and placed them on the mat. He stepped into the tub then turned to her and offered his hand. She took a moment to bask in his naked glory before sinking down in the bubbles facing him.

"Taylor," she'd started to talk but he was sliding

his legs along hers and pulling her closer so that she straddled his lap.

She moaned at the sensations of skin against skin. How could she want him again so soon? *We will always want him. Ours. Mate.* She leaned back, ready to slide off his lap lest she demand he have sex with her again. Heat burned her cheeks, but she was unable to move.

Taylor's thick cock hardened between their wet bodies. It pulsed against her belly as he held her firmly around her back. *Gods*, he was gorgeous. His deep green eyes raked lazily over her exposed breasts and face and she giggled when he leaned forward and pressed his cold nose to her neck.

"Now, tell me why you pulled away from me, Dimples," he asked the question and she swore sadness and pain lanced through his eyes.

Her Bear roared in her head. Displeased that she'd injured their mate. Krissy bit her lip. She didn't want to explain, didn't want to break this fragile spell. *Dammit.*

"Because," she said and tried once again to squirm off his lap, but he wouldn't let her.

"Because isn't an answer and I want you right here, Dimples, nothing between us. Just you and me," he announced.

"Because you don't mean it!" she growled and splashed him.

"The hell I don't" he grinned despite having a face full of bubbles.

Still, he wouldn't release his hold on her. Knowing how much soap stung, Krissy relented and wiped his face with one of the washcloths he'd laid on the side of the tub for them.

"Thank you, *mate*," he growled, his cock throbbing between them.

"What did you call me?" Krissy whispered the words to his chest before lifting her stinging eyes up to his face.

"I called you *mate*, Krissy Sposa, because that is what you are. *My fated mate.* You knew it too. All these years, you knew you were the one for me, didn't you, Dimples?" awe laced his voice as he gazed at her adoringly.

She gulped, not realizing he'd released his vice-like grip on her until his hands came up and wiped the tears she hadn't realized were falling. Emotion threatened to choke her.

"Don't cry, baby, I couldn't stand it if I made you cry. Please? Look, I know I'm no prize, but I swear to the depths of my soul that I will spend every day trying to make up for the asshole I've been the past few years. Just give me a chance, please, Dimples," his forehead pressed against hers as he whispered his plea.

Krissy couldn't believe her ears. This big, beautiful man called her mate? But no, it couldn't be. It was just the afterglow of good sex. Okay, *great sex.* But still, it was only sex for him! She'd be a fool to believe otherwise.

"Taylor, you're not thinking straight. This is just because someone else showed an interest in me. You're just feeling territorial cause I work for you, you know?"

"No. That's not it-"

"Come on! You never looked at me before that night at the bar!"

"I looked at you, Dimples, I just couldn't see. That night at the bar might have woken me up, and I am ashamed of that and I will pay for it every fucking day, Krissy. *But that is not it.* We are made for each other. *Mates,*" he touched his lips to hers with that word still on them and she swore she felt tingles shoot down her spine.

She turned away before she found herself believing him. There was still more to say.

"Taylor, I won't always be that girl with her hair done, and make-up on, who some guy wants to flirt with at a bar. I won't always wear tight jeans and a frilly top. Sometimes, I like baggy! I like sweats and flannels and my hair frizzes in the rain!"

"Baby, what are you talking about?"

"Look, I won't ever be one of those perfect petite little waifs you like to date! I won't, Taylor, I am just me! I love you, but I won't change for you!" She yelled, not realizing what she'd admitted until the last second.

"I thought for sure I'd have to steal those words from your sweet lips," he growled and kissed her hard and quick.

"What-"

"Thank the gods above, baby. I love you too, Dimples, so fucking much-"

"No, you're confused-"

"I mean it, *Krissy Sposa*. For the past few months I've tried to deny it. Ever since that party."

"When I made an ass of myself-"

"No. Never that, baby. You were brave and honest. I ran like a fucking coward and I am sorry. But I swear to the gods, I love every strand of curly hair on your precious head, every plaid shirt you own, every single fucking thing about you. I love it all. I wouldn't want to change a fucking thing. Stay the way you are. Exactly how you are."

"Taylor, please, don't-"

"I. Love. You. Krissy, I love you so fucking much," he captured her lips with his and kissed her. He kept right on kissing her, murmuring his love, until she softened in his arms.

Was she ready to do this? To trust her heart and believe in him? She opened her eyes and watched his expression as he kissed her. *Oh my.* This was Taylor. Her Taylor. And he loved her. She felt the truth of it down to her toes. *Mine.*

"I want to make love to you again, baby. Can I? Fuck you and cum in you, claim you with my bite right now. My mate. *Mine,*" his growl rumbled through his chest. His Bear was right there with him, shining in in his eyes and beating in his heart.

Taylor was *theirs* just as much as she was his. She ached for him with a soul deep longing that she'd never expected him to feel. But there it was. In his eyes, in his kiss, and the way he loved her. *Fated mates.* Yes.

"I will thank the Fates and the gods and whoever else is responsible for creating you, my perfect woman, just for me every day of my life. I just need your answer. *Please. Please say yes, Dimples, I need you,*" he begged as he kissed her.

Krissy's head was spinning. Her body

demanded she open to him, take him inside. *Mate him. Bite him. Take his claiming mark.* The warm water did nothing to soothe her as anticipation danced along her veins. His delicious mouth was teasing hers, his hard cock throbbing against her stomach even as her pussy wept, readying itself for his entry.

"Will you be with me? Accept my mark?" Taylor's words reached her ears as he nibbled along her neck.

She licked her lips and took her bottom one between her teeth. He opened his gorgeous green eyes and stared at her. She felt beautiful under his gaze.

He looked at her, waiting like a man on death row for some hint of reprieve. Then finally, she smiled, and it was like the sun coming out after a storm. His nostrils flared and he gripped her in his arms.

"Yes," she murmured wrapping her arms around his neck, "mate me. Claim me, Taylor. Here. *Now.*"

"*Mine,*" he growled, unable to keep his Bear back. He reached for her. Water slapped over the sides of the tub, but he didn't seem to give a damn.

Her sexy sweet mate was finally there and desperate to claim her. She wasn't going to waste another minute doubting him. Her Bear knew, she knew, he was theirs. *Since we were kids*, she smiled.

"We need a bed. I'm going to do this right this time," Taylor stood up with her in his arms and wrapped a large towel around them both.

"I thought you did okay the first time."

"*Okay*, huh? Well, this time we're gonna see stars," he growled and nipped her playfully.

She locked her legs around his waist, and he groaned as her heat pressed against his stomach. She felt his dick throb against her ass as he cupped her globes and carried her to the bedroom.

Preparations for Marcus' and Leya's upcoming engagement bonfire meant all the cabins had been cleaned and made ready for the event. Thank the gods or there wouldn't be any sheets for them to lay on.

He placed her on the bed, kneeling before her open thighs and gazing at her. She stared back at the ocean of golden flesh that was spread out before her. She couldn't wait to dive in and explore him. But her mate seemed to have other things on his mind.

"So beautiful," her sensuous mate parted his lips and ran his tongue over the tops of her feet. *Yes. Okay. Start there.*

He dipped his head and he continued kissing and

tasting every inch of her. Behind her knees, inside her thighs, one chaste kiss over her pussy lips that left her breathless, a lick across her soft stomach, nibbles across her breast, and finally a long lick up her neck before capturing her lips.

There was nothing like kissing Taylor. She sunk into the sweet pleasure that was his mouth as she relinquished control to his command. He licked her lips, her teeth, and twirled around her tongue.

"I am falling more and more in love with you every second, baby," he breathed in between swipes of his glorious tongue.

"S'perfect. Love you. S'good, mate," the words left her mouth before she could analyze them.

"You're mine, *mate*," he nipped her lip and mock growled as she giggled in reply.

Laughter turned to moans as their exchange became more heated. Laughter and joy had its place in every relationship, but Krissy was in love. And, more, she was loved in return. *Holy cow!*

"I need you. Want you, only you, sweet mate," he acknowledged their growing bond with every touch, every whisper. She felt his reciprocation of her love with each second that passed.

It was scary and heady, owning the tremendous feeling that was theirs to share. He must have known because he told her, again and again. Taylor carefully explored her body, slowly, taking his time, and talking to her all the while.

He whispered his love as he kissed her breasts and caught her nipples between his teeth. He moaned it breathily as he licked her pussy, swallowing her arousal like the sweetest cream. He roared it loudly as he finally thrust into her tight heat.

Keeping pace, he crushed his body against her welcoming one. Embracing her warmth, reveling in her passion that burned brighter than any star visible that night. *For him, only for him.*

Her Bear roared inside of her, she wanted him to claim her now. As if sensing the beast's impatience, he leaned down and captured her lips, sliding his tongue into her mouth. Using the same sweeping motion that his cock used to fuck her sweet pussy.

SHE WRAPPED her long legs around his waist, swallowing his growl as she squeezed him between her thighs. His large hands grasped her hips, anchoring her to him. *Yes.* Her entire body seemed to scream this word.

Her fangs descended as he pumped inside of her,

the Bear wanting to claim her man. She whimpered and moaned as he pulled her closer, the heat in his echoing her need.

Taylor rolled his hips, swiveling into her just right, touching her deep, so deep. She hissed and snapped her teeth, desperate to sink them into his flesh. He pushed harder, faster, rubbing his pubic bone against her sensitive clit. His dick throbbed inside of her tight channel. She felt her walls squeezing him as her orgasm hovered just out of reach.

"Love you, mate. *Mine.*" Taylor growled and with one final pulsing flex, raised his head and struck, biting down on her exposed throat.

A growl formed in her chest and she reciprocated. Her teeth sliced through the skin over his shoulder as they pushed and rocked against each other. She held onto his big body as her pussy clamped down on his cock. She sucked on the wound, mimicking his movements as his seed burst inside of her.

They were one in that moment, one body, one love. The ferocity of their lovemaking was nothing compared to the ecstasy inside of her as their mate-bond settled inside and over them.

Krissy groaned, her channel still squeezing and

milking him as she sucked and pulled his essence into her mouth. Her mate's blood slid down her throat sealing their bond and anchoring them together in a way she hadn't known was possible.

Her neck stung, but her mate licked and laved at the wound. Closing it with his Shifter's powers, and she did the same to him. The pain gone, only pleasure remained.

"Did you feel that?" Wonder tinged his voice and he nuzzled her neck, his cock still buried inside of her.

"Mmm," she wasn't quite capable of words yet. It was as if everything clicked into place. They were together. In each other's arms and hearts. *Forever.*

"I love you, Taylor," she whispered into his throat.

"I love you, *mate.*"

EPILOGUE

The fire crackled from the huge bonfire on the shore. Taylor watched his mate as she instructed a few of the younger Clan members to move the several long tables they'd gathered into neat rows.

A food truck was just backing into the lane and she waved at the driver. Her voice carried over to him as she ordered a few more young bears to empty the delivery into the waiting coolers, but not to mix them up with the drink coolers where cases of beer and wine, along with nonalcoholic beverages were currently chilling for the soon-to-arrive guests.

Huge kettles were set up over mini fires where they'd boil countless clams, shrimp, mussels, and lobsters to feast on. Potatoes and corn would also be part of the mix followed by an assortment of *Bear Claw Bakery* desserts for the occasion.

Krissy had their bakers design *his* and *hers* honey buns and bear claws. They were absolutely adorable with the boy version decorated with black fondant bow ties and the female version with pink and white frosting bouquets.

"Hey, Dimples," he scooted behind her and nuzzled her neck eliciting a moan from his sweet mate. She was so lush and responsive. *And his. Grrr.*

"Hi," she said and turned around to kiss his lips.

"Finally, you two took long enough," a voice said.

Taylor laughed as Krissy turned and gasped. Smiling she ran and hugged her little sister. Picking her up and twirling her around while kissing her cheek.

"Luisa! You made it! I am so happy! Did you see mom?"

"Of course I made it.! Like I would miss our Alpha's engagement bonfire! Yes, I saw mom first, she said to tell you she is feeling so much better! Now, I got this. You go take a break," Luisa Sposa rolled her dark brown eyes at her big sister.

Shorter than Krissy, she had honey blonde hair cut in a short, practical bob. Her no nonsense attitude and photographic memory made her an excellent student, and someday soon, would help her to be an excellent doctor. She grabbed Krissy's list of things to do and shooed her away, ignoring her searching hands.

"I said, I got this, sis."

"Yeah, come on, take a walk with me," Taylor held her hand and tugged her away from where Luisa was now harassing a number of young Bears about how they were setting the tables. Bonfires were utensil free events after all.

"Hey, you guys have a minute?" *Ugh. Stopped again. What the fuck was with his asshat cockblocking brother anyway?* Taylor stopped and narrowed his eyes at Nate. Fucking guy was forever popping up when he was trying to get some alone time with his mate. Still, he was growing fond of him. *Reluctantly.*

"I wanted to show you what I, uh, made for Leya and Marcus," Nate paused and grinned at the way Taylor's hand came around Krissy's shoulders possessively.

"Easy, bro. I know the deal, anyway look," in one hand, he held a framed picture and, in the other, a metal display stand.

"What do you think?"

He turned the canvas around, and Taylor was speechless. Krissy gasped and covered her mouth.

The picture was like something out of a fairy tale, a huge black bear stood on four legs in the middle of a dense forest. The Bear was big and regal with dark fur and even darker eyes.

Behind him stood a woman dressed in white with long flowing blonde curls and big blue eyes, her expression one of contentment and joy. It was obvious the woman was modeled after Leya, with her luscious curves and porcelain face.

The Bear was her protector, but more too. Her hand was open towards him and he waited for her, guarding her, but there was something else to their relationship. Something Nate had managed to capture with each stroke of his brush on canvas.

Love. The painting exuded love. Krissy's eyes pricked with tears and Taylor frowned.

"What the fuck, man, you made my mate cry!"

"Uh, Krissy? You don't like it?"

"Taylor! Hush. No, Nate, it's amazing. They are going to just love it. Look, I'm going on a break, just ask my sister, Luisa, where you should set it up. I'd say by the desserts but see what she thinks. She's just over there."

Nate nodded and turned. His eyes remained locked on the spot where Krissy's sister stood looking over her to-do list. Taylor watched as his eyes widened and he lifted his face to sniff the air. Taylor squeezed Krissy's waist and drew her along with him.

He couldn't help but wonder about his mate's little sister and his new brother. Nate was a fine artist, but Luisa was just starting her internship. She was hardly going to welcome his interest.

All thoughts of her sister and Nate fled his mind as his mate's scent washed over him. With a growl in his throat, he lifted her off the ground and jogged the rest of the way towards the cabin where they'd claimed each other just a week ago.

"What? Taylor! I thought you wanted to talk, not break for a quickie!" Krissy giggled though he knew she thrilled at the proof of his insatiable appetite for her.

He couldn't understand why it was so hard for to accept at first the fact that he wanted her all the time. *Cause he did.* But he didn't question it, he just showed her. He loved touching her, even if it was just holding her hand. *And then there was kissing.*

Nothing could compare to his sweet mate's lips whenever he tasted them. She was so responsive, so soft and open in her desire. He'd expected shyness, but not his Dimples. She was all woman. Aggressive when it suited her, she could be submissive as well.

Her moods ranged as much as her sexual appetites and he strove to satisfy each and every need.

He was made to do just that. To be her everything as she was to him. He'd been searching the journals for tales of fated mates and he'd been pleasantly surprised. Thought to be mere fairy tales, the stories he read proved they were rare, and yet, very, very real.

Not that he needed a journal to tell him that. He knew it in his heart. He and Krissy were fated mates. *Mine,* his Bear huffed. Hunger surged through him. He'd always want her. Always.

"First off, Dimples, a quickie, would never do. I need time to love you properly. Second, I do want to talk. *Here. Now.*" He punctuated his last two words with a kiss each.

Loving the way her mossy hazel eyes grew heavy lidded with her own desire he nipped her lower lip and took the globes of her ass in his hands, pressing his hard length against her.

"Mmm, I thought you wanted to talk?"

"Yeah, talk," he growled and nibbled her ear. Suddenly he walked her backwards to the far wall, kissing and caressing as they went. He reached for something on the dresser next to her.

"Taylor?" She whined as he broke their kiss and slid to his knees.

"Krissy, in the past I have been totally and utterly blind when it comes to you," he began trying to remember his practiced words, but failing in her presence. Especially with her delectable pussy so close to his face.

Fuck it, he just had to speak from the heart.

"Taylor, I told you it's in the past," she murmured and ran her hands through his hair, trying and not succeeding to pull him gently to his feet.

"Yes. It is in the past. I just can't believe how blessed we are, to have found one another. We are truly fated mates, and I know that makes us more than married in the Shifter world, but we live in both worlds-"

"Taylor, what are you saying?" She gasped as he revealed the small blue box in his hands.

"I've already asked your mom and she is totally on board. I just need to ask you-"

"Ask me? *Oh my gods*, Taylor!" She covered her mouth, eyes glistening.

"Krissy Sposa, my sweet and perfect mate, the one person in the world designed especially for me, I am asking you to be my bride. What do you say? Will you marry me, Dimples?"

She launched herself at him and it was all he could do to stand up fast enough to catch her. Their lips met and crashed against one another. He held onto her with one hand on her gorgeous ass and the other pushing her hair back from her face as he lovingly feasted on his mate's mouth. *Mine. Grrr.*

"Is that a yes?"

"Oh, yeah. That's a yes," she breathed and kissed him again.

She slid her feet down till she was standing as he placed the emerald solitaire on her finger. He kissed her knuckles when he was done, grinning broadly and admiring his handiwork.

"I can't believe it," she sighed and snuggled into him.

"Believe it, Dimples. *You. Are. Mine.* And I am never letting go," he kissed her again.

The end.

BEARLY TAMED

BEARLY TAMED

A BEAR CLAW TALE #3

For my husband! Mine! Grrr. 😉
del mare alla stella, C.D. Gorri

C.D. GORRI

Bearly TAMED

A BEAR CLAW TALE 3

BLURB

He's a Clan Enforcer who's sworn off women. She's human female looking for protection. Will fate bring the two of them together?

Lacey Esmerelda Alain can't help being beautiful. She was born with a face that is both a blessing and a curse. When her jealous ex-boyfriend turns into a monster before her eyes, she looks for help in a bakery of all places!

Daniel Devlin is the head Enforcer for the Barvale Clan. He is also one of the owners of Bear Claw Bakery Inc.

Daniel hasn't even thought about the opposite sex since his fiancée left him standing at the altar. That is, until he meets *her*. The stunning beauty makes his Bear stand up and growl, but he forces himself to ignore her.

Resolved to spending his life alone, he is prepared to devote himself to his duties, family, and Clan, but unforeseeable circumstances send her rushing into his arms.

Afraid and injured, Lacey comes to Bear Claw Bakery looking for help after her psycho ex-boyfriend revealed himself to be a dangerous Shifter. Crazed with jealousy the man threatens to kill Lacey, but Daniel's protective instincts kick in.

Can he keep things professional, or will his Bear demand he claim the beauty for his own?

A MESSAGE FROM TAYLOR, ONE OF THE DEVLIN BROTHERS...

Hi There, Clan-mates,

My brother Marcus and his mate, Leya, are off on their honeymoon!

I am pleased to announce that our father will be staying at the Den for the next few weeks to fill in with any issues that may arise. I am doubly excited to have him here as we welcome our newest clan member and our brother, Nate Cordoza.

Of course, Krissy and I will be available as well, should anyone have any questions that need to be addressed. The next Clan gathering will be on the night of the full moon as we will have some visiting Wolves from Arizona in the area and have been asked by the Shifter Council to host a run.

Bear Claw Bakery is going strong! Our newest

promotional plan to cater events and host a line of food trucks is going marvelously well. Especially on campuses across the nation. Some of our give-back money has been used to open a Pre-School with specially trained teachers in the know, and a new County Park and improved park right here in Barvale!

This is a reminder folks, that Daniel, our Clan Enforcer is not at your beck and call! He is a serious guy with a serious position. I don't know why or how the high school cheer squad got his cell number, but please if you have a child on the squad tell her to delete it. The man is busy protecting your Clan, so please, do not waste his time.

Lastly, with Marcus gone for a few weeks I know folks are bound to get antsy, but I assure you it is business as usual in Barvale.

Thank you!

-Taylor Devlin, Barvale Clan Keeper and co-owner of Bear Claw Bakery Inc.

PROLOGUE

"Where is she?" His voice spiked in his anger, like a childish whine that made her cringe and wish she could just shrink into the shadows.

Lacey held her breath, listening as he kicked and stomped. His outrage almost tangible in the cold night air. She ducked deeper behind the dumpster praying the dark alley would be enough to shield her from his eyes.

A rat scurried over her feet, and she stifled her scream. Rats had nothing on the monster that stalked her. The crushed pizza box at her stocking clad feet was crawling with bugs. She'd lost her shoes somehow when she'd run from him. Tearing the sheer material that had covered her toes in the process.

God, she hated her feet. They were huge. A whopping size ten. But that was the average size for many runway models. She learned that years ago when she'd first moved to New York City, the place where she thought all her dreams would come true. The clash of garbage cans being thrown tore her from her thoughts. The nightmare of the evening's events rushing back in like clouds in a thunderstorm.

Oh God, please help me, she prayed as she shivered in the torn remnants of the silk dress she'd been modeling for an up and coming new designer. His stuff was edgy and fun without being ridiculous like so many of the designs she wore. She wondered if she'd have to pay for the ruined sample. *Shit. Probably cost ten-grand.* Still, she'd happily hand over all her savings if it meant she'd survive the night. The pain in her face had dulled to a slow throb, reminding her of the damage she'd yet to see.

"*Esme, Eeeeesssmeeeee,*" he called out in a sing-song voice, a sick parody of the way he'd serenated her months before. She was such a fool! She thought all the attention he paid her was flattering at first, sweet even.

"ESME!" His outraged scream shook her to her core.

This was not the Tim she knew. The one she'd thought harmless. Lacey pressed her hand to her mouth to stifle the sobs racking her thin frame. She winced at the sting of pressure from her fingers over her split lip.

Cold flakes stuck to her eyelashes and she blinked rapidly. *When did it start snowing?* Sometime since she escaped the wrath of the man who claimed to love her. *Her boyfriend,* he'd called himself though she never agreed to that relationship status. Still, she could have been firmer in the beginning she supposed. *But how was I to know he was a monster?*

It was strangely quiet in the alley. Beautiful even with the play of shadows and light from the falling snow and the one streetlamp shining on the corner. She almost snorted aloud. Only an idiot like her would think such a dirty place was beautiful, especially with the enraged man throwing things around and screaming her name.

"ESME!," he bellowed, "I'll find you, precious, don't you worry your pretty little head. Filthy fucking whore!" He yelled and spit. Using her professional name that most in the modeling world called her by, despite her asking him to call her Lacey.

She was not *Esme*. Esme was made-up. Someone she invented a long time ago to cope with the burden of having a face most of the world envied. *Not anymore,* she thought and found it didn't upset her as much as it should. *Must be shock.*

Esmerelda was her middle name and she'd adopted a shortened version as her professional name. Esme had been a supermodel once upon a time. Gracing the cover of many magazines the world over. It was work to her, but to some, it was a lot more.

To Tim Shaw, her status was everything. Tim always called her Esme. At the moment, he was raging and screaming the name as he flipped over boxes and flung trash bags and cans in his rage. One landed with a loud bang a little too close to her hiding spot. She flattened herself back into the brick wall, praying her blonde hair didn't catch the dim light.

"Tim, man, we gotta go. The chick across the street is coming with her flashlight and she's got a phone in her hand. I think she's filming us, man. Come on! Put on these clothes, man, we'll get Esme later," Ricky, one of Tim's constant companions, attempted to reason with him, but Lacey knew he wouldn't give up that easily.

"Yeah, yeah. Whatever," she heard him slip on the clothing, but he wasn't through tormenting her just yet. She watched in horror as claws sprung forth from his hands. Thick and long the blackened nails were wicked looking and incredibly sharp. She knew that now; her hand went to the long scratch that still burned down one side of her face.

He scratched something into the side of the building, laughing maniacally as he shouted her name one last time. *Oh God, please help me*, she prayed again. She must be in shock, she thought again as the pain and anger faded. No more tears or hysterics. She just felt numb. Like everything that happened had happened to someone else.

"Honey, honey, you can come out now. I watched him. That creep and his buddies are long gone. Come on now, love," Lacey had been sitting there for God knew how long before she heard the woman's calming voice.

A bright light shone on her and she shied away from it. Her face throbbed and her jaw ached from how hard she'd been clenching her teeth.

"Oh my goodness, you're about halfway frozen, sweetie. Come on, my name is Amelia Grayson. I own *Skin Deep*, the boutique across the street. Now, I'm not gonna hurt you, come on out, let me see if I can help," her rounded face smiled down gently at Lacey.

She looked blankly at the woman. *Skin Deep*? Yes, she knew the place. A couture house for plus-sized women that Lacey greatly admired. Being a model, she was almost six-feet tall herself and had to have most of her clothing custom made.

At almost thirty, her figure had lost that waifishness of her youth that had made her so famous. That and her love of pastry cream with strawberries had left her with rounded hips and full breasts that were not exactly popular amongst the magazines these days.

Still, she'd found runway work for some minor houses and new designers. She was also about to feature in an art show by a very chic, local photographer, Parker Fiore. She was so grateful for the opportunity. Nearly broke and almost past the age where models could get work, Lacey had been more than willing to pose for the photographer.

How would she pay off the rest of the bills her mother had left? Lacey wondered if Mr. Fiore would still be interested in her now that Timothy had savaged her. She was sure to have a mark or two on her perfect face.

She realized she'd been staring at the hand

extended by Ms. Grayson for quite some time before pulling her thoughts together. She took the hand, grateful for the help as her legs and back seemed frozen in her huddled position.

"S-sorry," she said, her voice sounded raspier than normal. Probably from when Tim had grabbed her by the throat and squeezed before he-

She shuddered at the memory. Tim had been such a nice-looking man. Charismatic and handsome with his thick brown hair and matching eyes. He'd been the perfect gentlemen for months.

She was perfectly fine being friends with him, but he wanted more than she could give. Then he'd started with the whole jealousy thing. Angry and nasty to her when she had runway assignments. He criticized the clothing she wore and commented loudly when she was working with male models, designers, and photographers. She'd tried to be patient.

She was used to some degree of jealousy from others. Heck, it had happened any time she'd had a relationship. Friends, boyfriends, even her own mother had been envious of her daughter's beauty.

It's not my fault, I was born with this face and can't do anything about it, she'd often cried hating herself for not being able to keep any friends. It was lonely growing up. She didn't go to regular school because her schedule hadn't allowed it. Esme was a star by the time she was fourteen years old.

Her mother had controlled her career and managed her accounts. After her death, Lacey learned she was broke. Her mother had taken on enormous debts in her name leaving her with the balance. And she was utterly alone.

She had no choice but to work. Her face had been celebrated far and wide at the height of her career. Lacey had just turned twenty-nine, but she still garnered a lot of attention despite being "too old to model". *Gotta love the fashion world.*

She met Tim Shaw at a show. He was interested as many men had been, but he was sweet and kind. *Or so she thought.* Things changed when he started pressuring her for a commitment. She liked Tim, but she was not in love with him.

Lacey had watched what a loveless marriage could do to a person in her own mother. There was no way she'd end up like that. Stuck with a man and child she didn't care about.

So, she'd calmly explained to him that though he'd been fun to hang around with, she didn't feel that way about him. She told him it was better if they could just be friends. She had no idea what her words would instigate. Couldn't believe it now.

"You think you're breaking up with me? You fucking cock tease! You're supposed to be mine!" He raged.

"Tim, please, I am sorry, but I just don't feel that way about you," she tried again.

"It's that fucking Parker Fiore isn't it? You are fucking him! I knew it! Dirty fucking whore!"

"Tim, no! That's not it," Lacey backed away from his anger, but he caught her with one hand around her throat.

Before she could speak or try to defend herself, he used his fists on her. The first strike split her lip. The second knocked her to the floor. She was still in a daze when his yells turned to loud animalistic snarls. His friends were in the background just watching. Ignoring her pleas for help.

And then something out of a horror movie occurred. Tim's skin stretched and the sound of muscles popping and bones breaking ensued. Growls and snarls erupted from his throat as spit and saliva ran down his fur covered skin. When it was over, a huge brown Wolf stood over her. Tim was a real live Werewolf!

Horrified, Lacey bolted. She knew she couldn't outrun him for long, so she ducked down an alley and hid behind the piled-up trash hoping the stink would mask her human odor. Wolves had a superb sense of smell. Something her hours watching Animal Planet had taught her.

The rest of the night was history. Or it would be. *Please God, let me forget this ever happened.*

"There you are, love. Here put this on," Amelia Grayson draped a bolt of soft gray fabric over Lacey's shoulders and she almost collapsed against her.

"I've got you," she helped Lacey stand and walk forward. Shit. She must have lost her shoes.

"One step at a time," Amelia said, her arm felt solid and strong beneath Lacey's trembling hand.

"Th-thank you," Lacey said. She stopped walking when she reached the wall where Tim had stood earlier. Looked like he did scratch something into the surface with his horrible claws. The message made Lacey fall to the ground on her knees.

You're a dead woman. The sentence was ripped into the brick with deep, harsh gouges. Lacey trembled at the sight.

"Oh, shoot, I should have stood on your other side. Damn that stupid Wolf, scaring you like that. Come on now, upsy-daisy," Amelia practically lifted Lacey off the ground and frog marched her across the street to her boutique.

Lacey barely registered Amelia's words until she

was right in the middle of the woman's apartment that sat over her boutique. Her husband stayed in the other room, to give them privacy and for that, Lacey was grateful. She didn't want to be around men just yet.

"Now, is there someone you can call or somewhere you can go tonight? That Werewolf won't stop, you know."

"Um, so yeah, he was a Werewolf then?" She gasped after she uttered the last word. Kind blue eyes met hers and Amelia nodded.

"Honey, there are many things out there that would shock a normal like you. But not all of us are scary," in that moment something flicked across Amelia's purple eyes and Lacey's mouth dropped.

"There, there I won't hurt you, dear. Now, about where you can go?"

"Um, I, I think I can go to my cousin, she lives in Barvale, in New Jersey," Lacey said.

For some reason, the thought of her cousin's sleepy little hometown made her feel calm inside. Actually, it wasn't the town per se, but the image of a certain stone-faced man she'd met a few times while there last summer.

Daniel Devlin was a co-owner of the Bear Claw Bakery, and he was also one of the most confounding men she'd ever met. He had clear, light blue eyes like a December sky and short, thick hair the color of honey. His body was like that of a professional athlete. Tim had muscles, but Daniel had muscles on his muscles.

He was, in a word, gorgeous. And Lacey had wanted him the second she laid eyes on him at *The Thirsty Dog*, a popular bar in South Jersey. For once she didn't mind having a face people stared at, hoping to catch the handsome stranger's eye. Imagine her surprise when he'd glared at her for half the night and ignored her the other half.

The man seemed to hate her on sight. Stupid of her to think of him now. Lacey couldn't help her attraction, but she certainly tried to hide it the best she could for the rest of her visit. It was difficult in a town that size, and she had run into him. *Frequently.*

He'd even accused her of following him around when she'd stopped at Bear Claw Bakery for some pastries for her aunt and uncle.

"Look, I realize most men must bow down at your feet just to get you to talk to them, but I'm not most men. I'm not interested. Period." Lacey thought she'd die of embarrassment. She took the box a sympathetic cashier handed her and left the store without her change. The memory was one she'd like to forget. It

certainly didn't explain why she should feel so strongly about going there, *to him*, after Tim had knocked her around.

"Honey, Barvale is perfect! You will never guess, but I had a client recently, a bride, who married the Alpha of the Barvale Clan only a few days ago! I bet I can call them for help!"

"Well, I'm not really from there, but my cousin is-"

"Never you mind, these guys are the best and they have an Enforcer who would rip that pissant little Wolf apart of he even tried to get near you."

"I don't know why I even thought of Barvale, I mean I like the town, but me and Margot never have really gotten along-"

"Margot is your cousin?"

"Yeah. I, uh, have a complicated relationship with my family. You see her mom was my mother's sister. They had a sibling rivalry thing and I guess my mom always bragged about my career. I don't want to impose-"

"No worries, hon. Your family are all *normals*, so they can't know about us anyway. The people I have in mind to protect you are good people. Not all supernaturals are like that Wolf. Most of us are just trying to get by."

"I guess so. Um, it's just still a bit of a shock, I guess," she tried to smile, but this time the tears came.

"Oh, shush, come on let me make the call. You need to go somewhere tonight, hon. Somewhere that is the complete opposite of this hellbent city."

"Okay, I guess so. Thank you so much for your kindness," Lacey replied, surprised and happy to have found some help in a stranger. *A supernatural stranger.*

She barely heard Amelia as she dialed the phone and spoke in hushed whispers to someone on the receiving end. She was leaving the city tonight.

The town where she'd lived since, she began her modeling career, at the tender age of thirteen, had offered many opportunities, but never felt like home. It was her mother who'd wanted the fame and fortune. She had pushed her towards it when she was barely finished with grammar school.

"What else can you do with your height and that fine porcelain skin? Thank God you inherited my nose, nothing we can do about those lips. They really are perverse; they are so full!"

Her mother was always saying things like that when she was growing up. Lacey had learned to accept the compliments and ignore the rest at an early age. No one would believe she was starved for affection of any kind. Not with her looks.

Pale golden hair, emerald green eyes, ivory skin, with high cheekbones and perfectly symmetrical features. Her lips were very full, but she secretly liked them that way. *To hell with her mother.*

Lacey cringed and bit her lip at the sudden meanness of her thoughts. *Sorry mom.* Two years she'd been gone, and Lacey still apologized whenever she thought badly of her coldhearted parent.

Six months ago, she'd never have believed that Timothy Shaw would have turned into a Wolf right before her eyes because of some misguided jealous rage. Lacey excused herself to use the bathroom while she waited for the person Amelia had called to come and take her to Barvale.

She didn't know why she felt so strongly about going to the town, but she trusted her instincts. If only she'd done that when Tim had first asked her out. *Stop it,* she was not going to blame herself for this. Lacey had the right to expect people to behave reasonably and to treat her with common courtesy and respect.

Tim was an animal and not just because he could Change into a Wolf. He'd been rude, jealous, and inconsiderate at the best of times. *No*, this was not her fault.

Lacey gasped when she saw her reflection. Her already large lips were swollen from the punch to the mouth she'd received, one of her eyes was swollen and the skin around it was a dark purple, and there was a thin scratch that ran along her hairline on the right side of her face.

Photographers and fashion editors had called her face perfection for so long she wondered what they would think of her now. She could hardly bring herself to care as she ran the shower and began scrubbing the blood off her hair and skin.

Amelia had given her a long-sleeved nightgown and thick socks to pull on, having nothing else that would fit her tall, slender frame. She was grateful to be clean and dry. Another long glance in the mirror and she could not look away. Tears stained her cheeks, burning the thin scratches along her cheek and her swollen, split lip, but she couldn't stem the flow.

"Lacey dear, he's here," a gentle knock sounded against the bathroom door and Lacey as surprised to realize she'd been in there for over an hour.

She shook herself out of her stupor and opened the door to the bathroom. Angry blue eyes met hers as she stepped into the living room. *Familiar* blue eyes.

"Lacey," he growled her name as recognition registered across his face. But it was too late for her to respond, exhaustion and surprise had her fainting dead away. But before she could hit the ground, strong arms swept her up against a thick, muscled chest. She could have sworn someone whispered against her temple.

"I've got you, Lacey. You're safe now."

ONE

Daniel dropped the bar holding almost two thousand pounds of specially designed metal plates onto the thick rubber mats that lined his personal gym. Deadlifting was one of his favorite workouts.

The intoxicating burn of muscle as he heaved the impossible amount of weight, weight no normal could ever conceive of bearing, off the ground was addictive. His Black Bear roared in his mind's eye. The enormous beast was dark brown with golden fur along his head and streaks down his back as opposed to the true black coloring his normal kind were known for.

His younger brother Taylor was a true Spirit Bear

with golden colored fur, whereas Marcus was a true Black Bear in coloring and temperament.

Taylor, the tea drinking fucker, was bugging him lately about the way he flew off the handle at nothing. Well what did he know about it? He'd finally claimed his mate, their general manager, Krissy Sposa, and his Bear was all fucking happy.

In fact, the couple was now engaged and planning their nuptials with glee. Taylor, the lucky prick, was always griping about something Daniel did. But he didn't need to answer to him. He was the Clan Enforcer. Plus, he could still kick his little brother's ass any day of the week. *Hell yeah, I can. Grrr.*

His oldest brother, Marcus, was also the Clan's Alpha. He was mated and married to a bubbly blonde who made just about every Bear in the Clan feel at home with her genuine kind heart and soft smiles. All the brothers liked her, even Nate.

It had been a year since their father had retired from the position of Alpha. The old man wanted to travel in his golden years, or some shit like that. Daniel couldn't really understand anyone wanting to leave Barvale, and he could give a rat's ass why his father decided to go. He freely admitted to being on his mother's side of that doomed relationship, but with mom gone, he was at peace with it.

He sincerely loved his hometown. Loved the family business. Bear Claw Bakery was now a household name. The Devlin brothers had worked hard and long to make it so. They were certified billionaires nowadays. *Who knew normals would crave coffee and sugar to that level?*

Daniel wasn't complaining. In fact, it was pretty fucking cool knowing you could have anything you wanted whenever you wanted it. Well, not *anything*. Bitterness crept into his heart as he thought about the hole his ex-fiancée had left there. *Fuck it.* His Bear growled in his mind's eye and he prepared for his next lift, shaking out his hands and bending his knees.

It was three years ago, but that day would be forever etched into his brain. *His wedding day.* Or what would have been if the woman he'd chosen hadn't left him for someone else. Someone *normal*.

He'd been crazy about Melinda. From the first time he'd seen her with the kindergarten class she'd taught. They'd been on a tour at the bakery to see how things worked when he'd spied the petite brunette. *Should've run the other way,* growled his Bear.

He hated to admit the beast was right. His ursine counterpart had not been a fan of Melinda's from the very start. Daniel had to force the animal to accept even the idea of mating the woman. *Waste of time. Not ours.*

What could he say? His mother had just died, and his father was acting strange and restless. Daniel knew his parents were not fated mates, but he felt her loss keenly. As the middle child, he'd always been close to his mother. She was a wonderful person and she loved her sons.

He'd been desperate to start his own family. To fill the void and find someone to love and cherish. He thought that person was Melinda. The night before the wedding, he went to her place. He'd decided to share the secret of his Bear with her before they spoke their vows. Granted, he probably should have told her much sooner, but he'd always held back.

She'd been calm at the time. Had asked him politely to give her space when he would've stayed to make love to her. She even cited the whole bad luck thing. The next day, she just didn't show up.

He'd waited all day. Finally, he received a message from her. Melinda wrote that she was leaving him, and she did not want him to follow her. She had no idea what he was when she accepted his proposal, and she wanted no part of living with "an animal".

Not very surprising, she'd kept the four-carat marquis cut diamond he'd given her, that she picked out. She also cashed in the honeymoon tickets, emptied the joint bank account he'd set up for them, and left town never to be heard from again.

He supposed that was best. Daniel didn't know if he could take the constant reminder of her rejection had she stayed in Barvale. He bent and lifted the heavy bar again. Puffing out a breath and pressing his hips forward into the bar he corrected his stance.

Fuck me, he thought as he felt the burn rip through his thigh muscles and glutes. He was pushing the limit at a full ton, but he was determined. An Enforcer had to be.

The Barvale Clan was a peaceful bunch generally speaking, but they had their moments. He was responsible for breaking up fights before they became feuds. He also looked out for the security of the Den, it was the equivalent of a Pack House, but for Bear Shifters. Clan was sort of like family. Many of his clanmates visited the Den or the small cabins behind it that dotted the shore of Lake Ursa throughout the year.

Daniel was the head Enforcer, along with a small group of trusted Bears, including the newest edition to the family, his half-brother Nate Cordoza, he kept the homes of the Barvale Clan, and the wooded areas surrounding them, protected.

That paired with his duties to Bear Claw Bakery kept Daniel pretty much occupied. He needed all the work he could get, otherwise he might lose the tenuous grip he had on his Bear.

The animal had been tense and morose as of late. Taylor and Marcus both chucked it up to him mourning his fiancée, but Daniel knew better. His Bear had never loved Melinda. Hadn't wanted her from the very beginning.

Daniel was just too ashamed at the way he'd tried to force himself to marry someone not meant for him to admit it. He never told the truth to a single person. So, his brothers naturally assumed he was still lamenting his loss. *Fuck.*

He dropped the bar and stormed across the room to grab a water bottle. He knew from Marcus that a Bear sometimes went feral without a mate. *Fuck.* Daniel feared his time was coming. He had to somehow make it so that his work was enough to soothe the beast inside of him.

He was simply not meant for a mate. His parent's indifference had wounded him inside. While his brothers thought their family was ideal, he knew different. He'd seen and heard his mother cry in the silence of her room. Scented other women on his father's skin when he'd returned from one of his trips.

Ignatius Devlin was not a cruel man. On the contrary, he was kind and a loving father. His marriage had simply been arranged. He and his wife had come to an agreement and it had worked for them. *Mostly*.

When Marcus brought his mate back from a business vacation, Daniel had thought desperation must have pushed him to pursue the little normal. Then he'd seen his brother with Leya. The two of them were like halves of a whole.

So perfect together, it sometimes embarrassed him when he caught them looking into each other's eyes. Same could be said for his kid brother Taylor. The original *play-bear* had finally stopped fighting his fate and mated Krissy, their regional manager.

The she-Bear had been in love with Taylor for so long Daniel wanted to pummel his brother for being such a blind fool. What he wouldn't give for a woman, one woman, to look at him the way his brothers' mates looked at them!

He was jealous plain and simple. But not in an evil underhanded way. Daniel was happy for them. They deserved to find love. He just wished there had been someone for him as well. His Bear roared at the way he'd said that. As if there was no one meant for him.

Well, too bad, fucker. Daniel was a realist. He was meant to be alone. Always. Period. NO questions asked.

Of course, there was that one blonde who calmed his animal while making him stand at attention at the same time. The long-legged, impeccably beautiful female had been introduced to him through his brother's high school girlfriend when they'd been out celebrating Marcus' engagement.

Of course, Daniel had always hated the mean-girl cheerleader his brother had hung around with in his youth. Margot was a grade A bitch in his opinion. Surely, her gorgeous cousin was more of the same. *Grrr,* his Bear snarled at him and Daniel had to fight the pain the noise sent through him. *Fuck.*

Guess his Bear didn't like him having bad thoughts about the lovely Lacey Esmerelda Alain. Oh yeah. He knew her name. Looked up everything he could find about her after they'd met.

A top supermodel by the time she was fifteen years old, Esme, as she was called, was a knock-out. On a scale of one to ten she was a fucking twenty. But there was something else about her, something past the intangible beauty of her face. She had depth. And a kindness about her that made his Bear purr. *How fucking embarrassing!*

He cringed as he thought of their last meeting. Unable to take her nearness or the subtle scent of honeysuckle that clung to her porcelain skin, he'd flipped out on her. Basically, accused her of stalking him in front of the whole store.

He'd acted like a complete fucking jerk and then she was gone. Back to her big city life, he assumed. *Better for both of us.* But his Bear disagreed, the beast growled, and it was all Daniel could do to wrestle the animal down. Maybe he needed to do another set?

He was just about to add more weight to the bar when his cell chirped from across the room. He grabbed the smartphone and cringed, he fucking hated technology. Would rather spend his time outside checking point, but there was no getting away from it. Computers were already running the whole damn planet. The little box in his hand was just the beginning.

"Daniel here," he couldn't help the growl in his voice.

"Hello, is this Daniel Devlin? My name is Amelia Grayson, I have a Lacey Alain with me here, she'd been attacked and needs someone to come for her," the woman said.

"What?" Fear stopped his heart the second he heard *her* name through the connection.

"I said I have Lacey Alain here and she was attacked-"

"Send me your address and I'll be right there," Daniel dropped the phone and grabbed a towel. He wiped the sweat that clung to his brow and grabbed a clean t-shirt, slipping it over his head as he reached for his cell, wallet, and keys.

Someone hurt her. Someone who was about to fucking die. It was all he could do to stop the Change that burned his bones, but the Bear in him realized he couldn't drive the enormous reinforced SUV and since it was his fastest way of getting to her, he kept his human skin.

The drive normally took over ninety minutes, but he'd kept to the back roads most of the way and made it in fifty-five. Still too fucking long in his opinion.

He took the stairs three at a time, his long legs eating the distance like nothing until he stood outside the apartment door of the nice half-Fairy family that lived there. He recognized the address after he'd seen it in his GPS. His new sister-in-law had gotten her wedding gown made here. Really nice, couture stuff. Not that he knew couture from Walmart, but the females seemed to care. *Whatever.*

His Bear rumbled inside of him to get on with it. He needed to see her. Now. He raised his hand to the knocker, but before he could move the door opened. *Fairy magic,* he assumed. His knowledge of the Fae was minimal as they were secretive folk, best left out of Shifter affairs.

Still, this one was nice he recalled. Cheerful and jovial. Her purplish eyes were sad as they met his and he nodded as he walked into the room.

"Where is she?"

"Just cleaning up," her voice was like Christmas bells, reminding him that the season was almost upon them, "Daniel? Look, she has been through a lot tonight. A would-be suitor turned out to be a Werewolf with a jealous streak."

Daniel growled. Fucking Werewolves with their Alpha asshole tendencies. God knows he ran into enough of them at home what with Maccon City being so close to Barvale.

"What did he do?"

"She's bruised, but not broken. I believe she will heal with some time and care," she said.

"His name?"

"I didn't ask. But I believe he is affiliated with a smaller section of a Pack from upstate. The sooner the Wolves figure out this whole High Alpha thing, the better."

Daniel grunted. The Werewolves could keep their problems as far as he was concerned. The Bears had much easier ways of settling things. Step out of line and an Enforcer would come and make sure it didn't happen again. *Ever.*

"I'll just go get her for you," Amelia Grayson said and left him standing there.

Acutely aware of his size, he felt like a fucking giant in the tiny New York City walk up. Still, he should've taken a moment to prepare himself for what he was about to see.

The scent of honeysuckle tickled his nose, along with Ivory soap and water, then it hit him. The faint trace of blood behind all the others. *Her blood.* Daniel's bear roared his fury. *Someone hurt her. Protect. Then hunt.*

His blue eyes searched the hallway, stopping only when they met hers. *Oh God.* The woman who'd been haunting his dreams walked slowly into the room. But this wasn't a Lacey he was used to seeing.

This poor battered creature's head hung down, when she raised her face to meet his he sucked in a breath. Someone had beaten the hell out of this delicate flower. And he was going to make sure they'd pay. As soon as he got her back home to his Den. *Yes. Mine. Must protect.*

He ignored the Bear but couldn't stop her name from leaving his lips, "Lacey."

He stepped forward quickly, catching her as she fainted a few seconds after looking at him.

"Lacey! Is she okay?"

"She'll be fine, Daniel. You will see to it," smiled Amelia before walking him out to his car.

He cradled her small body to his chest. He loved the feel of her in his arms, but at the same time hating how fragile she seemed. *Fuck.* He needed time and space to clear his head, work through his emotions. But he didn't have that luxury. She needed help. And she needed it now.

He tucked her into the passenger seat and dropped a fleece blanket that he kept in the back around her prone form. She looked like an angel while she slept, despite the bruises.

"I've got you, Lacey. You're safe now," the words poured from his mouth without permission as did the kiss he dropped to her temple before closing the door gently.

Outside the car, snow continued to fall but he

didn't feel the cold. His Bear was agitated. *That was putting it mildly.* The beast was enraged, snarling in his mind's eye. He roared and bellowed, wreaking havoc with Daniel's inner sense of peace. *Fuck! What do you want?* But he knew what the Bear demanded. He felt it too.

The need to protect *her.* Lacey Alain. The beautiful woman he barely met a few months ago. The owner of the face that haunted his dreams. *No. Shit. It can't be. Not her.*

His Bear zeroed in on him, the animal was pissed at him for those negative thoughts. *Oh fuck.* The Bear growled and stomped on the metaphorical ground inside his mind's eye. *Pissed and more.*

One word reverberated through Daniel's brain after the Bear had finished telling him to fuck off. One word that threatened everything he thought he knew for sure. *Like his denying the pull he felt towards Lacey.* It was the only fucking word that mattered to any Shifter worth his salt.

Mine.

The sky was white outside the tan and green print curtains that covered the far window. *Such masculine colors,* she thought as she snuggled deeper into the matching comforter. The bed was soft and fluffy. So much better than the one she usually slept on. And it smelled fabulous. *Mmm.*

Gosh, she was sleepy. And her head hurt. Not to mention her lip. Lacey felt as if she'd been hit by a garbage truck. Wait. She had been hit, but not by a truck. *Oh damn.* She bolted upright in a strange bed as the previous night's events came flooding back.

"Ouch," she groaned as she touched the sore flesh of her bottom lip.

The sound of heavy footsteps thudded in the hall

before the door swung open revealing the very large, very naked torso of a man. Not just any man. But Daniel Devlin. *Oh my God, it was him last night.*

With her memories of being attacked by Tim, she recalled being rescued by a woman. *Amelia Grayson.* The name came back to her. She was a kind woman, with a family of her own and an amazing couture shop for plus-sized women. She'd told Lacey about Shifters and *supernaturals* in general, and she'd offered help.

"Is everything okay?" Daniel asked from the door, his blue eyes darted around the room checking for some kind of intrusion.

Suddenly, she felt foolish. Heat flushed across her face as she fiddled with the bedspread and mumbled her apologies. *Dang it. Why does he have to see me like this?* She'd thought about the serious, quiet man for so long only to have him come and rescue her from a *monster.* She shuddered thinking about Tim and his rageful outburst.

"Hey, easy now," he walked in slowly, hands raised as if he was afraid, she'd flee, "don't be sorry. I imagine you have some questions," he said.

"Um, yeah I do, but can I shower first?"

"Of course."

"Thank you. I hate to be so much trouble, but do

you have a clean change of clothes I could borrow?" She couldn't meet his eyes.

Shame washed over her, and she felt tears prick her eyes. Maybe that was why she hadn't noticed him coming completely across the large room. Daniel squatted down next to the bed, bringing himself to eye level with her.

His presence was almost overwhelming. *So big, so strong.* She waited for nerves or fear to wash over her, but it didn't come. Instead, she felt herself leaning towards him.

He had thick blonde hair several shades darker than her own pale gold locks. It was cut shorter the last time she saw him, but she found she liked it this length. The natural waves flopped over his forehead, making him appear boyish and charming.

His deep-set blue eyes were clear and bright under a jutting brow. Damn, she was staring. And judging by his calm, amused expression, she'd been caught. Lacey stiffened. Her embarrassment increased. *Dammit.* She was unsure of what to do or say.

"I know you must be having a lot of feelings right now, Lacey," Daniel's voice was deep, soothing, "but you did nothing to feel ashamed of. I realize that we only met a few times, and I wasn't very kind to you before. I want you to know I am very sorry for my previous behavior." He seemed genuinely abashed. His eyes flashed downwards, and she sort of missed that direct stare of his.

"Oh no! I mean, it's okay. You have nothing to apologize for. You just didn't like me," she shrugged.

"That's not exactly true," he muttered and rubbed the back of his neck.

"Um, so," she really needed to change the subject, "you are a, a *Shifter* then?"

"Yes, but I'm nothing like the piece of garbage that did this to you," his eyes went all intense on her again, and she shivered in response, "look, get dressed and I'll feed you, then we can talk, okay?"

Her stomach chose to grumble right at that moment. *Yikes!* Lacey saw his knowing smile before she even had time to be embarrassed. *Again that is.*

"Clary, our housekeeper, will make you anything you want," he grinned, making it all seem so normal. As if she woke up every day in his bed. *I wish.*

"Eggs sound good. I usually skip breakfast," she replied.

"Why would you do a thing like that?"

"Modeling hours are hell, and, well, eating is not exactly encouraged."

His responding grumble had her eyes darting

back to his. He sounded animalistic. *Well, duh, he is a Bear.* But whatever fear or nerves she expected to feel simply weren't present. Not with him.

"Uh, sorry, it's none of my business," he grumbled.

"I appreciate it really," she felt bad for having upset him.

"Alright, there is a private bathroom right through that door. I put some fresh clothes inside earlier. My sister-in-law gave me permission to raid her room for anything you might need, but I felt strange doing that. So, uh, I sort of ran to the store this morning for some personal, *uh*, things I thought you'd need," his face was beet red by then, and she couldn't look away. This serious man was embarrassed? *Oh my.*

"Thank you for everything, Daniel, I don't know how I will pay you back," she started.

"Don't even kid about that. You don't need to pay me to take care of you, Lacey. It's my privilege."

That serious expression was back on his face. His blue eyes glittered, maybe even glowed, but she couldn't be sure. Lacey didn't know why, but the knowledge that he was caring for her warmed her inside. *Don't get used to this,* she cautioned herself.

"Anyway, don't worry. We can talk about it all

later. The things I picked up should do for now, that is until you are ready to go out yourself, then I'll take you shopping anywhere you want."

"Oh, that's okay. I'm sure I can just get what I need from my apartment," she began, stopping when she noted the regret and anger that flashed across his face.

"What is it?"

"Lacey, I don't know how to explain-"

"Please just tell me what happened," she held her breath not knowing what to expect.

Lacey could tell by the array of emotions crossing his handsome face that something bad had happened. Well, something other than her being attacked by a real Werewolf, that is. Whatever it was, she could handle it. *She always has.*

"I'm not really good at this. I mean, I am the Clan Enforcer. I'm supposed to handle things like this, but I never had to tell a woman, er," he grimaced as he spoke and she couldn't help but think it endearing, the way he tripped over his words.

"It's alright, you're not responsible for what happened, just tell me. After all, I just had my face pummeled by a man who turned into a giant dog, what could be worse?"

His returning frown was not comforting in the

least. *Oh no.* Lacey tensed. It had something to do with Tim, she was sure of it. *What did that monster do now?*

"Lacey, um, I sent some of my men, other Bear Shifters from our clan who work under me, you follow?" At her nod he continued, "Okay. So, I sent some of my men to guard your place and to investigate any sign of the man who attacked you. When they arrived at your apartment, it was too late. A fire destroyed the whole building. We suspect arson."

"Oh my God! Was anyone hurt?"

"No people were injured, but a young girl did lose her cat."

"Precious? She belonged to a little girl named Ashley. I'm so sorry for her," she couldn't stem the flow of tears then.

"There was nothing you could do, Lacey."

"But maybe if I would have just-"

"Would have just what? Given that asshole what he wanted? Hell no. You did right."

"Yeah, right. Look at me."

"I am looking at you and I see a brave, strong woman who is more concerned with her neighbor's cat than she is for the loss of all her personal possessions."

"They're just things," she shrugged.

"Still, a lot of people would be grieving over their stuff. Pictures, television, clothes. I assume you had some pretty expensive things. Cause you're a model and all."

"My career had it's hay day a decade ago. Now I'm lucky to get runway jobs and even those are few and far between."

"But you were just in an ad?"

"Yeah. That money went to pay some outstanding debts my mom left me with."

"I'm sorry, I didn't know-"

"It's okay, we weren't close," she turned her head away from the pity in his eyes, she didn't need that, didn't want it.

"Don't worry about me, Daniel. I will get by. I have another job lined up, though it will depend on how my face heals I guess," he blurred in her vision as she wiped the annoying tears that insisted on falling. She would not feel sorry for herself!

"Hey, there's no rush, Lacey. You can worry about all that later," he caressed her fingers and she was surprised to see he was still holding them in his big hands.

"No, it's okay. Really. A friend of a friend knows a photographer who's interested in me for a photoshoot. I'll have to call him," she moved to stand up, but Daniel held her hand firm.

"Take it one day at a time, no one is rushing you. Rest now, get up when you feel like it," he coaxed.

"Um, thank you, Daniel, I-"

"There's no need. What you need now is a long, hot shower. Take your time, afterwards we'll talk, okay? I'll be right outside this door if you need me," he walked out of the room at her nod, leaving her alone.

Lacey exhaled and stood up on shaky legs. She'd been working late last night, trying on some samples to appease a rather whiny designer that she was right for the job. She'd just been about to take a snack break when Tim had showed up.

Damn. She should have never gone outside to meet him. Had no idea the crazy Wolf would kidnap her and try to force himself on her. Thank God, he'd been easily distracted by his jealousy. The bastard had been furious to think she wanted someone else.

After showering and dressing in the cute lavender panties and a stretchy sports bra he'd bought her, she donned the new pair of yoga pants he'd gotten but grimaced at the shirt. It was short sleeved, and she felt a little self-conscious with the bruises on her arm.

Lacey walked out of the bathroom and opened the closet. She grabbed an oversized purple sweatshirt and hoped to hell it was okay if she borrowed it. It didn't look like a woman's and in fact was about three sizes too big for her.

Still, it was soft and comfortable. *Perfect.* She inhaled the fabric and her entire body seemed to tingle as she caught a whiff of that pine tree fresh scent that always seemed to cling to *him. So, this is Daniel's shirt.*

She didn't take him for a purple guy, but clearly, he liked the color. A smile touched her lips and she winced at the way it pulled on the newly formed scab there. Just a reminder of why she was in Daniel Devlin' house to begin with. *Shit.*

"You look better, um, *nice*," he grumbled and stood to pull out a chair at the large breakfast nook. A tall, well-rounded woman with a stern expression swatted Daniel with a hand towel, before rushing over to Lacey.

"Hello, you poor, poor dear," she gave Lacey a quick hug and she noted the woman smelled like flour and herbs, it was a pleasant, calming odor that made her think this was what a home should smell like.

The kitchen was neat as a pin too. Warm, earthy

colors made it feel accessible. The mixture of high-end appliances and regular every day plates decorated with ceramic roosters made it feel lived in. *Nice.* Not at all like the apartments she'd lived in as a kid.

Those were always littered with empty bottles of alcohol and takeout containers from her mother and her friends. She'd never had any peace until she bought them each their own condos. *And mom managed to take that from me too in the end.*

THREE

"**I**'m Clary," the housekeeper's voice interrupted her daydreaming and she was glad for it.

No use going down that road anymore. Her mom was dead now and the money was gone. The end. Lacey would figure it out. She had no other choice. She turned her attention to the kind-looking woman.

"I've been keeping house for the Devlin family for a long time. Know these boys better than they know themselves, so if you have any problems you let me know and it'll be burnt toast and runny eggs for a month!"

"Oh come on, Clary, you know we'd never

mistreat a guest!" Taylor, the youngest Devlin, walked in with a familiar looking woman on his arm.

"Oh hush you! Good morning, Krissy. How do you put up with this mate of yours anyway?"

"Morning Clary! And he has his uses," the woman beamed at him. Lacey noted with some bemusement that they seemed perfect together. The tall handsome blonde with his curly headed woman.

She laughed out loud when he wrapped his arms around Clary and dipped her back for a loud kiss on the cheek.

"Taylor! Put me back on my feet! Krissy, tell this man of yours, I'm gonna deck him if he drops me!"

"Taylor, stop!"

"I'm sorry Krissy, but I love this woman," he kissed the older woman again and was rewarded with a slap to his head. Lacey had to bite back a grin at the whole scene while Daniel sat quietly.

"Don't let him goad you, Clary. We just came by to drop off the nuts and dried fruit you had me order to the store," Krissy said.

"Great! Set that stuff down over there. Oh, and you," she addressed Lacey, "sit down now, dear, and tell me how you'd like your eggs."

Clary's kind eyes smiled at her and Lacey found

herself responding. She'd been nervous at the amount of people who'd suddenly filled the spacious kitchen nook. Not just people, *shifters*, she guessed correctly.

Oddly enough it didn't upset her like she would've thought. She knew Taylor through her cousin, had met him before. He'd reclaimed his woman and smiled at Lacey with a sympathetic expression on his face.

He was movie star handsome, she supposed, but he did nothing for her. Not that it would've mattered judging from the possessive arm he had around the curvy woman next to him.

"You've met my fiancée? This is Krissy," he nodded, and the woman held out her hand.

"Nice to see you again. We sort of met a few months ago," Lacey said and took the proffered hand.

"Yes, I remember. I hope the other guy looks worse," she said, acknowledging the elephant in the room.

"He will," replied Daniel with a growl.

All the eyebrows in the room reached for the ceiling at that quietly uttered sentiment. Including Lacey's.

"So, the news I'd heard about you is true then, Taylor? You two are engaged?"

"Yes, we are," he smiled.

"Congratulations!"

So, the infamous playboy was really engaged! Lacey could not be happier for him. The bright and cheerful Krissy Sposa was wonderful from what she could see. *Poor Margot. Not.*

Lacey immediately liked Krissy and wished them both all the best. He'd always been very nice when she'd seen him last year. Though he was a little distracted the night they were introduced. It didn't matter. She suspected Margot only did that to earn some sort of brownie points with him.

Heaven knew she'd been paraded around often enough by people wanting to capitalize on her mediocre fame. She considered Margot a bit mean, but ultimately harmless. Taylor was too good for her cousin in a lot of ways. He was respectful and charming, so unlike most of the guys who often came on to Lacey.

"What are you making with all these goodies, you gorgeous thing you?" Taylor turned to where Clary was unwrapping the goods, they'd brought her.

"Clary? It wouldn't be some of that famous Christmas *stollen* by any chance would it? Tell me this is the year you give us the recipe for the store, please, my love?"

"Taylor Devlin you will get that recipe when you pry it out of my cold dead hands and not a second before! Now out with you! I've got people to feed," Clary grumbled, but Lacey could see the hint of a smile on her lined face. Clearly, she was pleased by the youngest Devlin's constant flattery.

"Okay, enough Taylor, leave Clary be. Is that the time? We've got to go! Bye Daniel! And Lacey? If you ever want to chat or need a little bit of girl time you give me a shout, okay?" Krissy called out as the happy couple left.

Lacey smiled as much as her bruised lip would allow and waved. Daniel just sat there silently pretending to read his newspaper, but she knew he was watching her every move. She could almost feel his eyes on her. Like she was breakable.

She wished he was looking at her for a different reason. *Stop it, Lacey,* she scolded herself. With her face and body, not to mention her pride, bruised, the last thing she needed was to pine after a man who wanted nothing to do with her.

"Well, how do you want your eggs cooked?"

"Oh, poached please," she replied automatically.

"Poached? You got it. How about toast?" Clary said.

"None for me, thank you."

Daniel frowned at her and she wondered what she'd said wrong. Then she guessed it. He probably thought she was vain and silly, trying to watch her weight. It wasn't that. Not really. Just force of habit she supposed.

"Actually, Clary, if it isn't too much trouble, do you think I could have my eggs scrambled with a little bit of milk and a slice of rye toast?"

"Sure, sweetie," Clary smiled and went back to the stove.

"Hmm," Daniel rumbled, but she could tell he was pleased.

"What?"

"I'm surprised is all."

"Why? Because I'm a model? Look Daniel, I have always had to watch my figure, but I like food. Besides, I won't be working now for a while if at all depending on how these heal," she spoke to the table as opposed to him. Not wanting to see the condemnation in his blue eyes.

"You'll heal alright. And for the record, you should never deprive yourself of a single thing you want. You're perfect," his voice was low, blue eyes capturing hers forcing her to meet his gaze.

She felt deliciously trapped in that constant stare of his. Heat seeped into her bones, pooling low in her belly at the almost overwhelming intensity that met her across the table.

Intense. That was one hell of an accurate description of Daniel Devlin. But before she could react, Clary set a plate in front of her piled with delicious smelling food. Lacey's stomach growled and she looked up to see Daniel grin before he dropped his eyes to his own plate. He'd waited for her to eat. That was interesting.

After breakfast, Daniel asked her to come to his office. She did, not sure what she expected. A conference call with the Barvale Clan Alpha, who was away on his extended honeymoon, was definitely a surprise.

"Ms. Alain, I am sorry about what's happened to you. I want you to know I've reached out to the local High Alpha and he's sending a team to track down this rogue," the Alpha Bear Shifter had a strong bearing, a straightforward expression on his face that commanded the respect and attention of everyone in the room. *Wow*, she thought, wondering how powerful he must appear in person.

"Um, do I call you Alpha or Mr. Devlin-" she started nervously, crossing and uncrossing her ankles as she stared at the image of Marcus Devlin on the screen of the laptop that sat on Daniel's desk.

"Call me Marcus, please. Should I call you Ms. Alain or Esme?" He spoke in a friendly, pleasant voice that belied his authority. It was deep and gravelly, some would say sexy, but it did nothing for her. *Not like a certain blue-eyed Bear.*

"Okay, um, *Marcus*. Please call me Lacey, no one outside of work calls me Esme. Well, except for Tim. That's his name, the guy who did this," she pointed to her face, and noticed the way the Alpha's eyes seemed to glow at her recitation of the last night's occurrences.

She explained how she'd been working. A late-night dress sizing for a picky designer she was working for. Tim had texted her to meet him in the lobby of the building for a second. She figured he'd just stopped by to say hi.

He did that now and then. Sometimes with gifts that she would politely refuse. Apparently, that just egged him on. Still, she had no idea what he was, or that he would stoop to such a level. She shuddered involuntarily as she recalled the pain that had exploded in her face at his first punch. But that was nothing compared to the fear of seeing him Change in front of her eyes.

"So, I take it you had no idea about Shifters before that?" She shook her head at the question. *Of course not.*

"I see. So, his full name is Timothy Shaw, he's a Wolf Shifter, and he has two male friends with him who are probably Shifters as well?" He asked, and she nodded.

"And you two were dating?"

"Sort of. Well, *no*, not really," she stopped when a rumble sounded next to her. One look at Daniel and she knew he was upset.

"I'm sorry, should I continue?"

"Of course. Daniel, stop your growling."

"Are you sure?" She addressed Daniel this time, and only continued after he nodded.

"He'd been dropping by runway shows and sending things to my apartment for months. Flowers and fruit baskets, that sort of thing. I ran into him at parties and events where I was networking, but I never went anywhere alone with him. Still, he seemed to think all that meant we were an item. He'd told several people I was his girlfriend. I only found that out yesterday, before he came to see me. In fact, it was why I went to meet him, to let him down gently."

"And what did he do then?"

"Last night he told me he wanted to make it official. When I explained that he was mistaken about our relationship he, well, he just exploded. I'd never seen violence like that," she shuddered and the sound of something cracking brought her attention up.

Daniel was sitting next to her; she didn't notice anything amiss. *But still.* She could have sworn she'd heard something break.

"Continue, please, Lacey," Marcus spoke to her, but his eyes were on his brother.

"I don't remember much, just the alleyway and the snow. I was cold. My dress was torn. Um, then Mrs. Grayson came. She took me in. She wanted to know if I had somewhere that I could go to," Lacey was surprised at how distant she seemed from the events. As if explaining it had somehow removed her from what had happened. It wasn't like she'd been physically attacked on a regular basis, but even she knew it could have been so much worse. Lucky for her Tim had been out of his mind and not focused on hurting her.

"And you thought of Barvale?"

"Yes."

"Okay. That's good. Anything else you'd like to add?"

"Um, my neighbors. Was all their stuff destroyed as well?"

"It seems the source of the fire was your apartment. There was other damage, for sure, but not as badly as your apartment."

"So, I was the target," she nodded and stared at the floor blankly. The men were speaking, but she wasn't listening. For the first time since she'd known about the fire, it hit her.

She had *nothing*. Strangely enough, it was rather freeing. She had no close family left. Nothing to tie her to the past. Just her face. But she could remake herself now. Choose the jobs she took. Yes, she still had debts, but she could work. *She hoped.*

"Lacey?"

"Huh?" She looked up to see Daniel at her feet, his hand on her shoulder. She must have zoned out for a few minutes.

"Marcus, do you have everything you need to reach out to Rafe?"

"Yeah, I'll handle it. You just watch over her."

"I got this," he said and inclined his head before closing the window on the laptop.

"Now what?" Lacey asked and ran a hand over her face. She winced as she made contact with the still fresh bruises.

"Here, let me look at that. I have a salve; it's made by a White Witch who is friendly to our Clan. This should speed up healing, though I can't make any promises about scars," he frowned as he reached into his desk drawer and pulled out a small glass jar.

"Thanks. It's no big deal, I suppose. Though I will probably have to think about work sooner or later," she stiffened when he leaned in and brushed her hair back over her shoulder. He smelled so good.

"Why do you need to work so soon? Surely, you can take a few months to yourself, to heal and rest," his voice was low, and she tried to listen for any judgement in it, but maybe he thought she had a fortune somewhere. She snorted.

"We're not all billionaires, Mr. Devlin," she hissed as the salve made contact with the scratches that bastard left along her hairline.

"Yeah, but, I mean, you're a supermodel, aren't you?"

"You checked me out? Well then, you must have seen my financial reports."

Pleasure at the thought of him looking into her made her smile despite the pain of her split lip. Daniel brought salve to it immediately soothing the wounded flesh. The slow brush of his fingers made her tremble despite her trying to hold still.

"Of course, I did. I need to know everything about you. Um, so I can protect you," he grumbled, dropping his hand all too quickly.

"Well, then you should know I was telling the truth before, *Mr. Devlin*," she figured she'd try for a bit of professionalism. Anything to stop the ache that was growing inside of her.

"I tried to explain before, but maybe I was unclear. My mother cleaned me out. Completely. My father and I are estranged. Before she died, my mother took out a reverse mortgage on my condo as well as several other small loans forging my name as a cosigner. My savings are gone. I've lost my condo, and I still have about a hundred thousand dollars in outstanding loans to repay. And now I don't even have a home. So, yes, I need to worry about work, but don't worry that I'm looking at you with dollar signs. I always pay my own way," she raised her head proudly, bruises or not she knew who she was. She would get back on her feet and repay all the kindness the Devlin's had afforded her. No matter what.

"I'm so sorry," he began, running a large hand through his thick blonde hair. *Why did he have to be so damn handsome?*

"Your own mother did that to you?" He frowned as if he couldn't comprehend such a thing. Lacey just shrugged. She wasn't there to disillusion him. These were simply the facts of her life up to date.

"Are you surprised? My mother didn't even want me. She was determined to make me pay for being born and she found a way the second I sprouted breasts. I'd been a tall, gangly thing before that, but with my height, my good skin, and carriage, she'd decided I could model and support her by the time I was twelve."

"Lacey, I'm sorry if I misjudged-"

"It's alright," she stood up, away from him and his tantalizing scent. She felt embarrassed and unsure. What kind of person lusted after someone a day after they were beaten up?

He was just so much man. She couldn't help but want to be near him. She closed her eyes on a wave of embarrassment. An avid reader, she'd dabbled in the paranormal genre and Shifters were said to have superior senses. He could probably tell she wanted him. *Oh God!* Lacey might die if he knew how she felt. She turned away and moved across the room, desperate for some distance.

"Lacey," he tried again.

"Daniel, I appreciate you helping me. And I know next to nothing about your world, except for what I've gleaned from novels. And how entirely accurate those things are I have no idea. But what I mean to say is, it's not all that surprising that you know nothing about my world."

"You'd be surprised about how accurate books like that are," he laughed and ran that same hand over his face now. Her fingers itched to move closer to him and follow the path with her own fingertips. Imagine being able to touch him whenever she wanted. Just thinking about it made her want to swoon.

"Um, I'd like to go lay down now."

She walked past him moving towards the door but stopped dead in her tracks. She noted the crumpled blanket and pillow on the sofa in his office. Had he slept there last night?

Lacey turned to face him as realization dawned. She'd displaced him in his own house. Heat spread across her face as she pointed to the couch and made to confront him.

She stopped suddenly as their eyes met. The big man looked so lost right then. His eyes followed her, but he remained immobile.

"You slept here?"

He nodded.

"You put me in your room?"

Another nod. This one followed by an expulsion of breath like he was embarrassed.

"Why?"

A shrug was the only answer she received.

"Shouldn't I find a spare room?"

"No! Um, that is, please. I would like you to stay there."

"Why?"

"My Bear wants you there."

"Oh. Okay," she replied.

Wide-eyed and unsure of herself she walked back to the bedroom. To *his* bedroom. Lacey might not know much about the Shifter world, but it had to mean something that he wanted her in his room.

Hope sprouted in her chest, swelling slightly as she closed her eyes and breathed in the piney scent of his pillow. She was tired and achy, but she was not afraid. Talking about Tim and her mom had opened old wounds, but the more she'd revealed the less burdened she'd felt.

Marcus didn't seem to judge her, he only wanted information to help protect her and hunt the rogue Wolf down. Even better, Daniel seemed to want to keep her near. He was the Clan enforcer, so maybe she shouldn't read anything into it, but it was sweet to dream. She'd allow herself that much for now.

Daniel, she thought and closed her eyes.

FOUR

*F*uck. *Fuck.* *FUCK.* Daniel grunted as he ambled through the woods behind the Den. Night had fallen early, as it was known to do in the winter months.

The cold of December had settled in and white puffs of air flowed from his Bear's maw as he stalked through the trees. His heavy paws crunched the snow laden ground, but he hardly noticed the chill.

After a quiet dinner earlier that evening, Daniel had waited for Lacey to make an appearance so that he could talk to her some more. Hell, he wouldn't have minded just being near her. Just seeing her would have been enough.

Only, she didn't join them for dinner. She'd opted for a tray in her room instead. *His room.* It was his room that she ate and slept in. That was just about the only thing in this fucked up situation that was calming his Bear at the moment.

He had to stop himself from breaking the door down about ten times that evening alone. He couldn't help it. *Sick fuck that he was.* His Bear snarled into the night, agitated that he was moving farther away from the Den. *From her.*

She's there to heal, he scolded the beast. Still, all he wanted was to be close to her. To get a whiff of her sweet honeysuckle scent from its source. To look at her beautiful face. To kiss every inch of her perfect body. *Oh fuck.*

He scored a huge oak with his massive claws before moving on to another. Needing to vent his frustrations, this seemed as good a way as any. God knows, he couldn't just break down her door and ravish her in the middle of the Clan Den!

What the fuck are you thinking? He wasn't exactly the ravishing type. That was Taylor's department. Or had been before Krissy caught the play-bear once and for all. His Bear snorted at the pair of them, recalling the night his baby bro finally gave in to what everyone else had always known. Taylor and Krissy were fated mates.

The man they now knew was their half-brother,

Nate, had come to town, looking for his family, the Devlin's as it were. He'd met Krissy at *The Thirsty Dog* and through a little harmless flirting. And one rather interesting body shot, Taylor was finally forced to confront his feelings for the she-Bear.

Took fucking long enough, Daniel thought. Not that he should talk. It had been years since he'd been stood up on his wedding day. Everyone thought he still mourned the loss of Melinda. Truth was, he'd dodged a fucking bullet there. Seeing two of his brothers with their fated mates made him realize he'd been settling for so much less than he deserved with the schoolteacher.

That night at the bar, seeing Taylor struggle with his feelings had really woken him up to the fact that Melinda was right to have left him. Yes, she was money hungry and a damned flirt, but he never loved her. She knew it too. Ironically, that was also the night he'd first met Lacey.

Seeing her in the dim light of the bar had sparked interest in his Bear like never before. What a sight she was, tall and slim with her long blonde hair hanging down her back. She was elegant perfection, like a fairy in the twinkling lights.

After that night, he'd seen her around town. She'd even come to the Bakery a time or two. Unable to stop his unwanted attraction, Daniel took his frustrations out on her. Like a fucking jerk, he'd confronted her, warning her off pursuing him when she'd never even made a move towards him.

Now he'd give anything to see her look at him the way she used to. With more than a little curiosity, and maybe a bit of heat. *Fuck. I am an ass.* To his shame, he'd been the one thinking about her for months, but too damn cowardly to follow up on it. Now she was here, but it wasn't the right time.

How could he pursue her when she was just hurt by some fucking Shifter with a death wish? It was all Daniel could do not to hunt down the fucker and gut him. He wanted to. Badly. But his Bear wouldn't allow him to leave her.

He made sure to double check all the security cameras and alarms before he went out tonight. *Draco Fortis* was the best in the business, but he had to make sure everything was up and running before he could leave her.

Besides that, he made sure that both Nate and his father were home. Nate had promised to listen for their guest. To be available if she needed him. That should have made Daniel feel better. But it didn't. Not at first. However, after he issued a warning to his newly found brother, he'd felt contented that no lines would be crossed.

"You go near her and you're dead."

"Chill bro. I'm all good," Nate said, hands raised and no small amount of amusement sparkling in his dark green eyes.

The fucking guy was alright, he guessed. Even more interesting to Daniel was the way his dad had reacted to seeing his other son for the first time. It was tears and bear hugs all round on that night.

"I didn't know, I am sorry I missed so much," Iggy Devlin had said.

Daniel wasn't much for public displays of affection. Had no use for them. *At all.* But he'd been moved by his dad's tears. Still, he wondered what his mother would have felt about Nate. Not being fated mates, his parents' understanding was, *well*, it was complicated.

His own feelings were much less so. His Bear wanted Lacey. The animal believed she was his fated mate. At least, Daniel thought so considering the beast growled the word *mine* anytime she was near. *Fuck.*

If he were being honest, he'd admit his human side wanted her just as fucking much. He just had so much baggage. *Not good enough for a mate.* Besides all that, she was a model. Breathtakingly gorgeous. Physical perfection in the eyes of millions. Could he stand all that attention on his mate? *Fuck.*

She was hurt now, but her bruises would heal. The deepest scratch, the one most likely to leave a scar if at all, was mostly covered by her hairline. She would work again. *As she should be allowed to do,* he warned the asshole alpha male part of his brain.

He wasn't always a Neanderthal. There was just something about her. He wanted to stake his claim. Mark her for the whole fucking world to see. *Mine. Grrr.*

He could just picture her now with that thick, glorious mane of blonde hair spread across his pillow. *Fuck. GRRR.* His Bear growled long and hard at the thought. *What the fuck are we doing in the woods? Go back. Claim her. Mine.*

Daniel fought the Bear. Pushed back his desires to claim the tiny normal who was sleeping in his room. He pushed his animal to tread farther away. The Bear was pissed, but he went. *Grrr.*

Snow continued to crunch beneath his paws along with fallen leaves and twigs. December in New Jersey was generally mild, more so than February, but it did snow on occasion.

He liked the winter. The cold wind and fresh

scent of ice and snow in the woods was like a cleansing of all the things that tarnished the past. He breathed deep, chuffing against the cold air. Watching the steam rise from his nostrils.

Daniel was a big fucking Bear. He outweighed even Marcus, who as Alpha, was as big as they came. He prided himself on his strength. Training and pushing himself to be the best. It was like an addiction with him.

An addiction that was slowly being replaced by his feelings for a certain willowy blonde. *Shit.* Her curious response to him was driving him mad. She seemed okay, at ease even. Despite everything she'd been through. *She is brave,* his Bear pushed the thought at him.

Not what he was expecting given her rough intro to the Shifter world. Hell, he expected her to scream her bloody head off and demand to go to the cops. But she didn't. Nope. She seemed to want to stay near him. His Bear roared. *Of course. She knows we can protect her. Mate.*

A noise to the left had him turning and Daniel growled a warning before his brother stepped out into his line of sight. Nate often wore a hat and jacket over his jeans. *Fucking lightweight.* But what did he expect? The half-Grizzly half-Black Bear had been raised in the hot ass fuck part of Texas. So, it made sense he'd tracked Daniel down in his fur.

"What the fuck bro? I thought you were staying to watch Lacey," Daniel growled into his brother's mind.

The discovery that they could communicate tele-pathically when both Shifted was a fucking relief to all of them who didn't know if it would work since Nate was technically half-Grizzly. The shaggy brown Bear snorted and scratched his back on the bark of a large walnut tree.

"Dude, Iggy's home. She's fine. Came out of the bedroom a while ago looking for you."

Daniel didn't know how to answer that. He stared at his brother's huge Bear and wondered for a brief second if it was possible the Grizzly-Black Bear outweighed him.

"Damn fucking straight, bro. You're a kick ass Black Bear, but I got you beat weight-wise."

"I can still kick your fucking ass."

"Maybe. But why would you stay around here trying when you got something better waiting at home?"

"Fuck you. She's not mine."

"No? Then you won't mind if I-"

Nate didn't even get to finish the sentence before Daniel's Bear had him pinned to the forest floor.

Saliva dripped from his bared fangs as he almost went crazy on his brother's ass.

"Easy bro, I was just fucking with you. Come on, get off me."

"Don't. Joke. About. Her. Ever."

"Okay, okay. Damn you really need to lighten up."

"Grrr."

"Okay, but she said she was gonna go out for a bit. She wanted to take a walk-"

"What?"

Before Nate could finish the sentence, Daniel was running full speed for the Den. What was she thinking? Going for a walk? It was well past midnight! The woman didn't even know her way around out here for fuck's sake.

Fear gripped his heart. Worry made him run faster than he ever had. *Because of her. She's ours.* The need to protect sent his Bear into overdrive. *Shit*, the animal was dangerously near to being out of control by the time he slowed his gait down.

Daniel had almost reached the Den when he caught her scent on the breeze. Honeysuckle and a hint of tea tree oil from the salve he'd used on her face earlier. His Bear grumbled, glad to have scented his mate. *Touching her skin had been a type of heaven,* he was sure of it.

He had to fight with everything inside of him at the time to not lean in and capture her swollen lip with his. He'd so desperately wanted to kiss the woman. *Fuck.* Thinking about it was bound to drive him crazy with lust.

Even his Bear wanted him to find her and *get it on. Yep.* It was a certainty. Daniel was going out of his mind. Fucking Bear was acting crazy. He attacked Nate for just making a comment about talking to her for fuck's sake.

He was acting like a fucking savage. But that was exactly how he was starting to feel about her. Savage and untamed. *Fuck.* Her scent was getting stronger and he picked up his pace.

His footsteps were purposely loud as he stalked her through the path. Lacey was still wearing his purple sweatshirt, but she also had a blanket wrapped around her shoulders and too large boots on her feet. *Shit. I forgot to get her shoes.*

Her pale skin glowed in the moonlight and the bruises did nothing to take away from her innate beauty. She truly was a work of art. Stunning. Almost mind-numbingly beautiful. More so than any other creature he'd ever seen. Still, she was so much more than her face.

He watched in stunned silence as she tilted her

head back. Her hair cascaded down to her hips in a curtain of gold that he was dying to bury his face in. She smiled, wide-eyed like a child as snowflakes started falling from the sky. Girlish giggles escaped her lips as she twirled in a dance that was both silly and intoxicating to behold.

She looked happy for a moment. Innocent and young. Not the tired woman who'd been pushed around by that fucking soon-to-be-dead asshole. *Magnificent. Mine.* His bear's thoughts pushed into his own and he chuffed loudly, wanting her to see him.

Startled by the sound, Lacey turned her head. Shock and fear crossed her face for one brief moment at seeing his large animal. It tainted her sweet scent, making it turn sour for the barest of seconds. He paused. *Shit.* Naturally she'd be scared of him. He moved to back away but stopped when she stepped towards him.

"Daniel?" Her soft question reached his sensitive ears like a caress to his skin. Lacey smiled then. The brilliance of it nearly blinding him as he stood stock still and watched his brave little normal cross the path to stand directly in front of him. *She is my mate.* He finally admitted it to himself.

"You're beautiful," she murmured and raised her

delicate hand to his snout. Unafraid she moved closer to the almost-thousand-pound Bear. Daniel didn't move a muscle, waiting as she brought her fingers up and touched his head, then his cheek.

He grumbled in pleasure and that noise seemed to embolden her to run her hands further along his neck and shoulders. She ruffled his fur, seeming to savor the thickness of it. He was a proud Bear. Happy his mate seemed to take pleasure in touching him in this form. *Yes.*

"Such a big, strong Bear. So beautiful," she murmured smiling and brushing his fur with her fingertips.

Grrr, his Bear rumbled happily as she stroked him. Daniel was truly a goner. A feeling of pure bliss rolled through him at the fact that his mate was freely accepting him in this shape. She was willingly touching him, marking him with her scent, whether she knew it or not. How he longed to carry that scent with him always. *Mine.*

Unable to hold back any longer, Daniel trembled as the familiar hum of magic settled over him. Changing fur for skin in the blink of an eye, he reached out with his human arms and caught Lacey before she could stumble. *Mine,* his Bear growled.

"Oh," she gasped. A reddish blush tinging her cheeks as she looked at him. *All of him.*

Like most Shifters, Daniel was naked when he switched back to his human form. The fact that she was staring at him like a thirsty man stared at water was very pleasing, indeed. He knew his body was good to look at. Well-muscled and fit, he was attractive to most normals. Not that he cared about any of them. *Just her. Only her.*

"Lacey," he growled her name, pulling her closer until she was flush against him.

He bent his head, unable to resist the need to get closer to her. Nuzzling her cold nose with his, he listened to the sound of her heartbeat. It raced inside of her chest as he pulled her into his embrace. *So, this wasn't one-sided?* The scent of her arousal reached his nostrils and he hardened in response. *She wants me too.* That was good to know.

"Daniel," she whispered his name like it was a secret. One that she'd said before, only now he was there to hear it.

Mine.

His Bear rumbled in pleasure as her hands came to rest on his shoulders. He reached out slowly, using one of his large hands to cup her cheek. He tilted her face, waiting for her emerald eyes to meet his before he closed the distance between them.

The second her lips touched his it was like the entire universe stopped. The snow, the stars, the forest around them, *everything* disappeared. Their kiss was the only thing that existed. *The only thing that mattered.*

Her lips ghosted over his at first, soft and feathery light. A whisper of a touch. But it wasn't enough. Could never be enough with her. Daniel increased the pressure, sliding his mouth over hers, coaxing her with soft, lazy strokes until she opened for him, like a flower blossoming under the sunlight.

She tasted sweet and fiery like the warm honey and cinnamon scones he preferred. *Delicious*, he thought as his tongue slipped inside the hot, wet cavern of her mouth. He drank from her lips like she was a life-giving fountain. *Maybe she was at that.* His Bear surged inside of him as he felt his heart race. *Mine.*

Sparks passed between them, a special kind of magical exchange that he'd never felt before. He swallowed her gasp, loving the feel of her mouth as she pressed her lips and tongue fearlessly to his.

Surprise caused him to falter, but she didn't stop. She was aggressive, taking her pleasure and giving him more than he could have imagined. He loved the bite of her nails on his shoulders, the feel of her teeth as she nibbled his lower lip. *Fuck.* He didn't think it was possible, but his cock grew even harder. *Slowly,* he told himself, unwilling to break the magic that was unfolding between them by rushing things.

Her soft breasts flattened against his chest as he tightened his hold on her. Both arms now wrapped around her slight frame. She was tall, which was good, but he stood roughly six-inches taller still. *Amazing.* She fit perfectly in his arms, her hold on him tight. She was stronger than he'd thought. More toned than he'd realized. He groaned as he deepened the kiss. Hungry to discover more about her.

Desire flared between them as the pace of their kiss increased. She moaned and he drew back, worried he'd hurt her. But all worries vanished as she chased his lips with her own. *Passionate. Tempting.*

His hands roamed over her body possessively. Raking over her shoulders and back, combing through her soft hair, all the way down to her tight, luscious ass. *Damn.* She was sexy as hell. And she was his. *Mine.* He hauled her up in his arms, and she yelped. That brought his head up when nothing else would've. *Fuck.*

What the fuck was he doing? Mauling her outside like a damned animal. *You are an animal.* He breathed heavily as he slowly allowed her to slide back down his body. Daniel kissed her lips once more, her cheeks, her eyelids, anything he could reach as he ran his hands soothingly over her body. A body he was desperate to see and taste. *Fuck.*

"Lacey," he growled her name, unable to keep his Bear from his voice.

"Wow," she whispered, leaning her forehead against his chin.

"I, I'm sorry," he began, not sure how she was going to react to what had just happened. She was a normal after all. He had to proceed slowly.

"No, please," her green eyes met his and he saw pain in them. *Fuck.* What did he do wrong?

"Did I hurt you?" He gently lifted her face and she pulled back, still with that wounded look in her eyes.

"No, of course not. But you don't need to pity me either."

What? Daniel had no fucking idea what had just happened. One second, he was exploring every centimeter of his mate's sexy mouth. Thinking he'd gone too far, he slowed down his assault, not wanting to overwhelm her delicate sensibilities. So, how the fuck did he get from being one second away from plowing into her on the snow-covered ground, to here? *Fuck.*

"Pity? What the hell are you talking about?"

"Forget it," Lacey moved around him. Taking her warmth, her scent, her taste, *everything*, with her.

Fuck. By the time he moved, she was already heading back to the house. Daniel wasn't a stupid Bear, but right then he felt like it. Naked, confused, and still hard as hell, he called her name.

"Lacey!" He ran after her, finally finding his feet. He caught up just as she stood at the back door to the Den.

Her long blonde hair blew in the wind, as she moved to turn around, but just then the back door opened. Ignatius Devlin, Daniel's father, stood there with his bushy gray eyebrows raised as he stared at his naked son and their red-faced guest.

"Danny? Ms. Alain? Everything alright here?"

"Um, yes, Mr. Devlin, everything is fine. Good night," Lacey didn't meet either man's eyes before she scurried into the house.

Fuck. Daniel stared at her, willing her to look at him, but she didn't. He'd fucked up somehow and he had no idea how to fix it. Head down, he felt the wall of misunderstandings and insecurities rising between them.

Shit. Daniel was stuck. He couldn't just run after her and kiss the doubt from her eyes the way he wanted to. Not in front of his dad.

"Fuck," Daniel growled.

"Uh, son, you may want to put on some clothes before you catch frostbite out there. Then why don't you step inside the living room for a little chat with the old man."

Ignatius Devlin was technically an old man. Older than he looked at any rate. Shifters aged differently than normal. They had longer lifespans too. As a perk, if they mated a normal, their lifespans increased too.

Still, Daniel had never thought of his father as the typical "old man" type the way normals did. The guy was built like a fucking brick house at six-foot four-inches tall. He was still robust and muscular despite his thick gray hair and short-cropped beard. Daniel shrugged into the sweats he'd left in the mudroom before Shifting.

He followed the familiar smell of his father's pipe and the tumbler of whiskey he knew would be sitting by the man's chair. The Den was usually well-stocked with Marcus' favorite blend of artisan whiskey, *Clover Bite*, but on the rare occasion their sire visited them since retiring almost ten months ago, they hadn't had the need to fill his supply of Mason Lane's only gold label bottle.

Love Bite was in high demand and short supply. The smooth, supple flavor and rich texture of the coveted whiskey made it a favorite amongst supernaturals the world over.

Mason Lane had gifted a case to the Alpha of the Barvale Clan, Daniel's father at the time, in thanks for supplying Bear Claw Bakery goods to his son's entire school one year during the holiday season. A gift that was most welcome in the Den, though his dad had taken to hiding the last remaining bottles. Daniel snickered.

It was a tradition they still held. Delivering individually wrapped cookies to all the students at local elementary schools from Thanksgiving through New Year's. His soon-to-be sister-in-law, Krissy, took care of all the arrangements.

Usually, he'd forego the offered beverage, but he nodded his assent and was grateful for the liquid as it burned its way down his throat. *Fuck.* He'd kissed Lacey. Tasted her sweet lips and held her in his arms. And then she'd run away from him. He realized he'd fucked up in some way. She thought he pitied her, though he had no idea how she'd arrived at that conclusion.

"So," his father began.

"So," Daniel echoed.

"You want to tell me why you were trying to dive down the throat of that very vulnerable, very human girl you're supposed to be protecting?"

Shit. This was not the conversation he wanted to have right now.

"Look Dad. *Oh fuck*, look, it's complicated."

"Yeah, I get that son. Especially when you still haven't gotten over Melinda and what she did to you. I don't want you taking out past hurts on this woman, she's fragile, the last thing she needs is for you to play with her emotions. She's not Melinda-"

"I know she's not Melinda! And who the hell are you to try and talk to me about relationships? In case you haven't noticed, your other *son* is here now. I know all about your views on *mating*, and if you ask me, Nate is some damn strong proof of your fucking morals, so don't preach to me-"

"Daniel, as your Dad I can forgive your anger, but as your Alpha-" His father's silver eyes glowed with his Bear, but Daniel didn't care.

How dare this man try and tell him how to take care of his mate! Dear old Dad was the one who broke his mother's heart with their loveless marriage and his affairs. Daniel was nothing like him. He made a mistake with Melinda out of desperation and loneliness. It was different with Lacey, this time his Bear was completely on board.

"You're not the Alpha, Dad. Marcus is. Now if you will excuse me, I'm gonna go hit the gym and try to forget we ever had this little talk."

Neither one of the two Bears noticed the woman listening in the hallway with wide eyes and her hand over her mouth. She shuffled quietly back into the bedroom and shut the door.

The next morning Lacey woke early. She felt much better. Patting her eye and lip as she strolled into the bathroom, she wondered if the salve Daniel had used on her contained more magic potion-y stuff than he'd thought.

When she finally caught herself in the mirror she stopped, staring at herself in awe. Her black eye had lightened considerably to a pale yellowish color. Almost fully healed. The long scratches Tim had left on her face were way, *way* smaller. Some almost completely faded away.

"Huh," she thought as she looked herself over. Not her top form, for sure, but better. Much better. She smiled.

Last night Daniel had kissed her, and it was more than she could have ever imagined. At almost thirty years old, Lacey was hardly a virgin, but damn if she hadn't felt like one when she was in his arms. Her entire body had lit up like a Christmas tree.

She sighed as she showered and dressed, mulling over the whole scene. Had she overreacted? Maybe. But she wasn't sure whether or not he was simply reacting. She was used to being sought after.

The men in her past had sometimes treated her as nothing more than a prize to be won. But the truth was, Daniel didn't seem overly affected by her fame. A billionaire, if the tabloids were to be believed, in his own right, he was probably used to rubbing elbows with high society. Beautiful women probably pursued him like Black Friday shoppers at Walmart! The image made her giggle.

Not that women would be after him for his money alone. You just had to look at him to know it was much more than that. He had a certain charisma. An animal magnetism that made him irresistible. *But why would he want her?* The question was vexing to say the least.

Braiding her long, damp hair took about ten minutes. After she was finished, she pulled on another one of Daniel's sweatshirts. This one was a dark green with the *Bear Claw Bakery* logo on the front. It was as big as the one from yesterday and fell to her knees.

Not that she cared about the color or the size of the shirt. *Nope*, she chose it because it smelled like him the most. She smiled and sniffed the shirt. His scent was imbedded in the fabric.

After their kiss last night, and the weirdness after, she sort-of needed the comfort. *Foolish girl.* Oh well, she could rationalize her idiotic behavior later. It wasn't every day a gorgeous mountain-sized Bear Shifter kissed the heck out of her.

But what a kiss! Holy hell. One second, she was standing with her hands on an enormous Black Bear with thick, golden fur on his head and neck, and the next, she was wrapped around a huge, gloriously naked man. *Daniel.* She'd known it was him from the start. Somehow, she'd recognized him in his Bear form.

As if some deep, dark secret part of her soul had immediately known him. She wasn't the least bit afraid of him like that. That same secret part of her, assured Lacey that he would never hurt her. And he hadn't. *Not until he pulled away from her.*

Ugh. Why were men so confusing? Sure, he'd told her he wasn't interested in her before, but ever since the Tim incident, he'd been acting sort of protective. Possessive even. He'd given up his time, his room, and had driven all the way to the city to get her. He would not hear of her going to a hotel.

Maybe she was a fool to think he returned her interest, but that kiss was special to her. It had warmed her on the inside like no other kiss she'd ever experienced. Not that there had been that many to compare it to. Despite what the tabloids claimed, she was a model, not a prostitute.

Lacey, you're just a face. Nothing more. Her mother's words came back to torment her as she looked in the mirror. Lacey frowned hard at her reflection. She might have been just a face once upon a time, but not anymore. At least, not right now. *You've definitely seen better days.* But still, he'd kissed her anyway. Bruises and all.

Pent up energy buzzed through her as she yanked on socks and a pair of boots that actually fit her. Another gift from Daniel, she surmised as much when she spied the delivery box sitting outside the bedroom door.

Well, she was all dressed now, and ready to do something. After laying around for the past few days, she was starting to feel like a loafer. Used to working long, hard hours, Lacey wanted to make herself useful.

The scent of fresh brewed coffee tickled her nose as she headed out to the kitchen, which seemed to be the main meeting area at the Den. Made sense. Bear Shifters weren't exactly small. She suspected they ate quite a lot to keep up their superior physiques.

From someone who'd spent a lot of time around what some considered the most beautiful people in the world, Lacey had to admit those models and jocks had nothing on the Barvale Clan men. *Holy Bear Shifters!* She was surrounded by gorgeous male specimens day and night. Even Mr. Devlin, the *dad*, was a total hottie. But none of them had anything on Daniel. He was perfect in her eyes.

From his soulful, sky blue gaze, to his dark, ash blonde locks he was ridiculously handsome. His features were chiseled as if from stone. Five o'clock shadow often covered his square jaw, but never hid his full, soft lips. *Oh boy, don't think about his lips.*

Then there was his body. *Sigh.* Lacey never thought of herself as the type to go with overly muscular guys, but Daniel definitely changed her mind about that. It wasn't because he looked like some kind of Mr. Universe body-builder man. *No way. Yuck.* He wasn't that veiny, oiled up, fake gym muscle guy.

Daniel was in a league of his own. He was definitely ripped. Enormous even. But it was a natural kind of musculature that was as mouth-watering as he was beautiful.

Thickly built with heavy ropes of muscle cording his entire frame, Daniel took her breath away. She'd freely ogled every inch of his naked body the night before as they stood together in the cold December air.

He'd made her feel small and safe when he was in his fur, and even more so when he'd Changed back to man and wrapped his two strong arms around her. Those were two things she'd never felt in her entire life. Being a tall woman was not easy. Before she modeled, she was often teased for her gangly appearance.

But she didn't feel gangly next to him. Couldn't help but be turned on just by being close to the man. She couldn't stop it if she'd tried, and why would she try? It felt so damned good.

Whenever he was near, she felt like some kind of mystical, magnetic pull to be near him. It made her want to leap into his arms. *Like a moth to a flame.* Heat burned her cheeks as she thought of her behavior. *Ugh.* She'd probably embarrassed them both with the way she threw herself at him. Nothing to do now, but push forward, she supposed.

"Good morning. Want some breakfast?" Clary interrupted her thoughts and greeted her with a warm smile.

"No, thank you. I thought I could maybe help you out in the kitchen today?" Lacey returned her smile and gestured to the wide clean space that was the Den's kitchen.

"You want to help me? But you'll get all dirty," the housekeeper protested.

"That's alright, I wash up just fine," she grinned.

"Well, I do have a ton to do with Christmas coming and all, so I hope you're serious," Clary laughed and handed her an apron.

"As a heart attack," Lacey winked at the older woman playfully and wrapped the apron around her waist.

The sun still hadn't risen yet and there was a bite to the air, but she felt alive like she never had before. After a few lessons from Clary, she quickly got the gist of what the woman wanted from her. Today, she was preparing the dried fruits and nuts that would go into her special German *stollen.*

Clary was serious about keeping the bulk of the

recipe hidden from prying eyes and ears, so she only gave Lacey bits and pieces of what she needed done. Apparently, this was a multi-step job that took several days of prep work. Lacey found it fascinating and absorbed everything the housekeeper said like a sponge.

"Now, don't you go telling the boys any of my special tricks, you hear?" She scolded as Lacey carefully measured brandy, sugar, and half a dozen different spices into a large pot on the stove.

"They could threaten me, yell, even beat me, but I swear I'd never tell," she answered with a giggle in her voice.

"Oh, honey," the housekeeper turned to her seriously, "You know the boys aren't like that. *Daniel* is not like that. He would never hurt you."

Suddenly, Lacey felt hunted. She touched her face self-consciously and blinked back the tears that came to her eyes. Still, she knew Clary was right. Daniel would never hurt her. Even if he didn't want her. So, she nodded her head.

"I know that, Clary. Tim was a monster. You, the Devlin's, I mean, you've really been great. I would never be so ungrateful-"

"Oh, hush, I know you're a good girl, but you know *what* we are. That dumb Wolf outed us in the most horrible way to a little thing like you. Now that you know about *Shifters*, that we exist, I hope you won't let that taint the way you see us," the woman nibbled her lip.

"Never! Clary, I'm not traumatized by Tim's actions, just a little bruised. I swear."

"You sure, hon? Daniel can come off a bit quiet and strong, but as the Clan Enforcer he has to be. It's a complicated job."

"Clary, *Shifters* are just people, and like people, they come in all shapes and sizes, though I guess you are all pretty big. Daniel too," she laughed and was relieved when Clary did as well.

"You sure about that now, hon? I mean you're right; we are just people."

"Tim was a monster, and I mean that in spite of his Wolf, not because of. *He* was the jerk. *You* are good people. *The Devlin's* are amazing. And I am very grateful that you all are helping me through this."

"*'Atta girl*. You know, he's been hurt before."

"He?" Lacey feigned ignorance as she chopped the dried fruit into small bits.

"*Danny boy*," the older woman said knowingly.

"Oh?"

"Yes. He was engaged. To a *normal*, that's what Shifters call human folk," she continued, "anyway, his mother had just passed, and he was the closest to her. Desperate to have a family, he proposed to the first woman he saw. She was hell on his pride. Loved his money, loved men, *any willing* man, and left him high and dry at the altar."

"Poor Daniel," Lacey said, her heart hurting for him.

"Well, I say he dodged a bullet. Anyway, it looks like you know what you're doing, now. Would you be alright if I ran out to the market for some more fresh oranges and lemons?"

"Yes, of course," Lacey nodded, her mind going a mile a minute with what she'd just learned. Maybe that was why he'd been so gruff when they'd first met?

She continued stirring the steaming pot of fruit in front of her. Careful to keep the temperature low, her attention was on the sweet-smelling concoction as her mind mulled over the conversation she'd just had with Clary. She meant what she'd said about knowing the difference between Tim and Shifters in general, she realized with a smile.

Lacey knew that he was the anomaly, the piece that didn't fit, the *monster*. Tim's behavior called him out as a jerk long before she saw him turn into a Wolf. He'd been jealous, controlling, whiny and demanding. She was not to blame for his actions and she certainly was not about to blame anyone else for them either. Then there was the other thing she'd learned.

So, he's gun shy. Maybe he was just using her to build himself back up. The thought was troubling. Kissing Daniel was beyond exciting, but she didn't want to make something out of nothing if all he felt was pity or some physical itch.

No, her heart couldn't take it. She made up her mind then and there. She would not play the lovesick fool here. *No.* She'd take a few days to heal, because, let's face it, she couldn't model like that. Then, she'd see about getting back in touch with some of her contacts.

There is always work, she thought. She still had her mother's enormous debt to pay off. And she needed a place to live. *Damn.* She'd almost forgotten about that. Best to just take things one day at a time.

Lacey sighed and settled in. She was grateful for the kitchen duty, not having much opportunity to do so in the past. She found she liked cooking. The actions of chopping, measuring, bringing the pot to a boil, then down to a simmer were soothing. She even liked filling the mason jars with the heated fruit, washing the pan, then doing it all over again.

She added the next batch of ingredients to boil then simmer while humming along with the carols in the background. It was fulfilling work, calming and reassuring in ways she hadn't felt in a long while.

The scents that hung in the air were sweet and spicy. Rich and homey. *Like Christmas in a jar,* she thought and wondered if it were possible to fall in love with a smell. An image of Daniel flitted through her head and she ducked her face down and inhaled the sweatshirt she wore.

His pine, fresh air scent was there, making her feel as if she was still in his arms. She breathed it in deep, allowing his fragrance to rollover her palate. *Sigh.* She had it bad alright.

Shaking her head, Lacey wondered how long this schoolgirl crush of hers would persist. She was a grown woman! *That's it.* She would not cave the next time she saw him. *Act disinterested, that's all. Uh huh. Like it was so easy.* She just had to go about her daily activities and ignore her increasing attraction to the man.

Surveying the work ahead of her, that wouldn't be hard. Just how many batches of Christmas *stollen* was Clary planning on making anyway? One of the two huge kitchen islands in the space was entirely covered in orderly rows of sugar, nuts, dried fruits, spices, and a few different liqueurs.

Clary had given her clear instructions on what Lacey was to do while she went to the market. Along with a warning from the older woman that forbade her from writing anything down. A huge canning pot and several more glass mason jars sat on one side of the stove. So far, she had three jars full.

I think I like this, Lacey grinned. She had eagerly absorbed the information and went about proving to the housekeeper that she could follow orders. She still couldn't believe that after only two hours of working with her, the older Bear Shifter had left her in charge! *How about that?*

She continued humming to herself as she stirred the large pot, setting the flame a notch lower. It was currently full of pitted dried cherries, half a bottle of brandy, the zests of three oranges and lemons, and four cups of raw sugar. Not to mention a bouquet of secret spices and herbs that Clary had already prepped. She'd prewrapped them in little cheesecloth pouches prior to Lacey arriving in the kitchen. *Dang it.*

The marvelous scents coming from the pot filled the large, state of the art kitchen. The aroma was positively heavenly. Cinnamon, anise, cloves, and all spice were some of the spices she'd identified. But the rest were a mystery.

Lacey sighed contentedly as she moved about picking up this and that and tidying things. She wondered if she'd still be there come Christmas to try the *stollen*. Her heart squeezed as she imagined she'd be gone by then. After all, she couldn't just move in!

Distracted by the task at hand and her wandering thoughts, she didn't notice the large man standing in the entryway with his mouth hanging open. She definitely couldn't imagine what he was thinking at the picture she made working in the kitchen with the sun just coming up, the soft rays shining through the frosted windows.

*H*oly *shit.* Daniel couldn't breathe. Beams of sunlight caught her hair and lit up like a halo of gold around her angelic face as she slid across the floor as smoothly as a knife through hot butter. She moved with grace and feeling, as if the chores she performed meant something to her. Maybe they did.

Hell, all he knew was that she looked irresistible as she moved about the Den's kitchen, his childhood home. His Bear chuffed happily at the thought. *Mine.* Fucking possessive prick that he was, he felt himself harden at the sight. She looked good in his space. *Would look better at our cabin,* the Bear grumbled.

Maybe, he agreed, but tried not to picture her in the cabin he'd built for himself over the past three years. *Started the day after Melinda had walked out on him.* Best fucking day of his life, as far as the Bear was concerned. The man agreed.

Lacey still hadn't noticed him. Considering himself lucky, he took the time to study her. The bruises were getting better, he noted. His Bear hated the reminder she'd been hurt, he wanted badly to avenge his mate. Daniel calmed the beast, telling him to just *look* at her.

Nothing would ever hurt her again. He'd see to it. Besides, he couldn't think of anything that could take away from her real beauty. The beauty that was inside of her.

Just think, a former supermodel was cooking and cleaning, walking around barefoot in his old sweatshirt. Her long hair was hanging down her back in a loose braid. She wore no make-up on her porcelain skin, nothing to hide the yellowish hued bruises that marked her skin.

She wore them proudly. Her back straight. Unashamed. *Like a warrior.* Yes, he wanted to kill the bastard who put them there, but he didn't want her to feel ashamed or like she had to hide them.

She was perfect as she was. A real woman. Flesh and blood. Enchanting as she was genuine. Not at all what he'd imagined she would be. What did he know of models anyway? Perhaps he'd judged her unfairly in the past.

Known the world over as a billionaire, he'd had his fair share of run-ins with the rich and famous. He loathed that kind of society. Felt much more at home in Barvale, with his Clan. That was one of the bonuses of being so damned rich. People thought he and his brothers were simply eccentric.

Damn, she looked great in his sweatshirt. He felt himself go rigid at the thought of his clothing covering her exquisite figure. He wanted to rip it off her. *Fuck.* He was jealous of his own fucking sweatshirt.

Then again, maybe that wasn't as crazy as it sounded. The lucky fabric got to touch and enfold every inch of her silky skin. He wanted to be the one embracing her body, providing warmth and shelter. *Fuck*, he had it bad.

She hummed off key, but completely un-self-conscious. Some corny love song with a Christmas-y theme. He knew the words to it but couldn't name the ditty to save his life.

Daniel smiled as he continued his perusal of her. Tendrils of hair had fallen from her braid, framing her lovely face and he itched to brush them back. He wouldn't want her any other way, he realized.

Not true. He'd take her any way she came. In diamonds and silk, like the last advertisement he'd seen of her on the internet that morning, or in yoga pants and his old shirt. She was fucking gorgeous either way.

Mine, growled his Bear. The growl in his chest reverberated loudly in the room until she turned to face him, and her emerald eyes shot to his. *Oh shit.*

"Morning," she said in a soft voice that caressed his eardrums like a lover's hands.

"Where's Clary?" He asked.

"She left a little while ago. Went to the market. Did you want breakfast? How about your father and brother?" Her words were hurried, as if she was embarrassed. *Couldn't have that.*

"No, I just dropped them off at the bakery. Brought back some rolls," he placed the large paper bag he'd been holding on the table, not taking his eyes off her.

The fact that they were alone in the big house seemed to scream at him from across the room. His Bear pushed at him. The beast wanted what he already considered his. He wanted *her.* The big Black Bear demanded Daniel get his head out of his ass and claim the tall woman with the honeysuckle scent.

"Lacey," he began.

"Um, do you think I could get another cell phone today? I sort of lost mine during the whole *thing*, that and everything else in the fire, I guess. Um, I think I need one now, more than ever. I have to get back to work so I can find a place to stay, I mean, I can't just live here. Anyway, there are people I need to contact, contracts I have to honor," she spoke quickly. Her sentences running into one another.

His chest pounded. *Fuck.* He'd been so thoughtless. Of course, she'd be feeling lost. And now it was as if everything was just catching up to her. Like the reality of her situation closing in. But she didn't have all the facts yet. She had no idea she was his. And he had no intention of letting her leave.

"I'm so sorry, Lacey, that was thoughtless of me. Yes, of course we can go get you a new cell phone," he ignored the pang of jealousy that shot through him thinking of who it was she wanted to call. He told his Bear to shut the fuck up, the woman had a life before him after all.

"The mall will be open at ten. Is that okay?"

"That's in half an hour," she fiddled with the heat on the stove. Turning it off, she set a timer for thirty minutes. Just as he imagined Clary had instructed her.

"What are you doing in here?"

"Just helping Clary," she shrugged as if it were no big deal, but he knew better.

The older woman was a Bear in the kitchen, pun intended. The Devlin's long-time, trusted house-keeper never allowed anyone to meddle with her recipes. Especially her Christmas *stollen.*

"It's quite the honor, you know. Being allowed to help Clary. She doesn't let anyone in her kitchen. Not even us, and we're professional bakers," he joked, and she smiled brightly at him. *Look at her smile, she's eating up attention like a flower does sunlight. I'll see to it she has as much attention as she needs,* he thought.

He found himself moving closer to her. She radiated light and heat and he wanted it. Insatiable beast that he was, he wanted her warmth all for himself. Shrugging out of his jacket, he let it drop to the floor as he ate up the distance between them.

Daniel inhaled as he brought his large hand up to caress her bruised cheek. *Fuck.* He closed his eyes, trying to tame the Bear that so wanted to strip her of her clothing and take her sweet body right then and there.

"Beautiful," he growled softly, cupping her cheek. He was unable to stop his Bear from making himself known. Lacey dropped her eyes, some of her light going out at his words, and he stilled. *Fuck. What did he do wrong?*

"Not anymore," she said, and he tilted her chin up, forcing her to meet his eyes.

"You couldn't be anything but beautiful, Lacey. And I don't mean because of this perfect face or your gorgeous body. I mean because of this. You're most beautiful right here, sweetheart," he traced his fingers down her cheek, to her collar bone, then further down to where her heart was pounding furiously in her chest.

His large hand rested there, and he felt the predator in him preen as the muscle raced beneath his palm. She wanted him. He could scent it in her heady musk, feel it in the way her pulse raced. *Yes. Mine.*

"Look, Daniel, about that kiss last night. I'm not an idiot. I know it didn't mean anything to you, not with the way you feel about me and women in general," she stepped back, and he allowed his hand to drop, but still, he followed her.

He simply couldn't let her move away from him. Not even if his life depended on it. Then he realized she was talking, but her words weren't making any sense. At least, not to his lust addled mind. The urge to mate was too strong for reason.

She smelled too fucking good, looked too sweet. He wanted her. *Wait? What did she just say?* The bulge in his pants was making it difficult for his actual brain to do any work.

"What are you talking about?" He cocked his head to the side and focused on her face.

"I don't want your pity. I don't need you feeling guilty over what happened. I get that some things are purely physical. I'm a model, or I was, but anyway, you don't have to worry. I'm not going to read anything into it. It was just a kiss-"

"Lacey-"

"And I'm sorry your father gave you a hard time afterwards-"

"Wait. You heard that?"

"I wasn't eavesdropping," she said quickly, her emerald eyes darting up to his and he missed the fire he'd seen in them moments ago.

"I just wanted a glass of milk and the two of you weren't exactly quiet. I know about your ex-fiancée, and I'm sorry that happened to you, but I won't be a stand-in," she shrugged and swallowed nervously.

Daniel followed the movement. Was it wrong he wanted to trace her throat with his lips and tongue? Maybe. *Fuck. I want her so badly.* But it was more than simple desire. He needed her like he needed air.

His Bear agreed with a deep rumble that started in his chest. Lacey was quickly becoming necessary to him. And he had no idea how he was going to explain it.

"Daniel?" She was looking at him questioningly and he had to wonder if he'd missed something else, she said.

Fuck, did she mention *Melinda*? His Bear snarled thinking of the other woman. She was not his. No. *Lacey is mine*. Well, she would be. He knew they had some ways to go for her to trust him. Especially, after what she'd heard about him and his fucked up past relationship. *Shit*.

He wished for the millionth time he'd never asked Melinda to marry him. But it was in the past. It didn't matter. Nothing mattered at that moment. Nothing, except the woman in front of him. He stalked her deeper into the room. Time to show her he meant business.

"What are you doing?" Emerald green eyes flashed up at him and he growled in response.

Mine.

"Showing you my ex means shit to me. I haven't thought about her in months."

"But everyone says-"

"Fuck what everyone says. I couldn't care any

less about her than I already do. You are all I think about."

"Daniel, you don't have to say that-"

"You had your turn to talk, sweetheart. Now I need you to listen. You have no idea how wrong you are thinking that kiss between us was nothing."

"But I only meant-"

"*Shhh, baby.* I'm going to show you just how much it means to me," Daniel reached out with his hands and took her by her indented waist.

Careful not to hurt his precious normal mate, he lifted her onto the granite countertop and wrapped his arms around her sleek body. *She weighs nothing at all*, he thought idly and made a note to see to it she always ate everything she wanted. She should never worry about her size or shape. *Perfect. Mine.*

He hesitated, giving her the chance to really see him, to recognize it was *him* touching her. She blinked those big, bright eyes up at him. Lust glazing the warm emerald depths.

Still, he moved slowly, not wanting her to feel forced. Daniel gave her one more moment to draw back, to slap him, to do something that would tell him she didn't want this. But then she did something amazing. *She stayed.*

He couldn't hold back any longer. Ducking his

head, he captured her lips with his. *Fuck. Yes.* He growled as her honeysuckle flavor burst on his tongue. Then she moaned and moved with him. Lips merged, tongues tangled, hips flexed.

Holy shit. The whole fucking world exploded with that one kiss. Daniel tilted her head back, deepening his possession. He needed to prolong the contact that would change his entire fucking life. *Mine.*

Her flavor was sharp and pleasing against his tongue. She was a complex mixture of everything he knew about her and so much more. All woman. *His woman.*

His Bear growled as Daniel stepped between her thighs and pulled her flush against his hard body. She sat on the counter with her long legs splayed around his impressive width. He was big, even for a Shifter.

Lacey was tall for a woman. Had to be in order to make it in the modeling industry. But even up on that counter, she was shorter than him. He liked that just fine. Liked her just fine. *Loved her?* He didn't want to think about that right then.

He lost himself to the kiss but managed to keep his Bear in check. It was touch and go for a minute or two. Especially when she responded so fully and eagerly to him. She opened for him like a ripened peach, bursting at the slightest of touches.

Her arms snug around his neck and waist. She was kissing him back for all she was worth. His cock hardened in his jeans, pressing against the constricting fabric, throbbing with need as he tried to get nearer to her heat.

Fuck. If they weren't in the kitchen, he'd have stripped her by now. His heart thudded wildly inside his chest as he did his best to kiss the hell out of her. Lacey needed to be kissed, to be thoroughly laved at and worshipped. By him. *Only him.*

Images of her naked beneath his lips and tongue made him growl. *Yes.* He could almost taste her. He grunted as she pressed herself closer to him, moaning softly as her tongue wrestled with his.

Lacey sighed his name as he nibbled her chin and neck, loving the way she sounded all breathy and dazed with desire. She willingly pressed into his touch. *So soft. So ripe.* Daniel wanted her with every fiber of his being. The need to claim her, to mark her with his bite filled him.

He licked that tender spot between her neck and shoulder, every inch of him aching with need. *Mine,* the Bear growled inside his mind's eye.

"Um, you all may want to stop that before Clary

comes inside. She's pulling in the driveway now, you know."

Daniel's Bear roared at the interruption. But the man was still in charge. He slowed their kiss. Bringing them both down carefully, he maintained eye contact with Lacey before he turned around to meet his brother. Subconsciously or not, *not*, he blocked her from view.

Her eyes were still dark with lust. She was still trying to catch her breath. *So soft, so beautiful.* No one else should see her like this. *Only me. Mine.*

Nate, his half-brother, was leaning against the doorjamb. His ever-present tablet and stylus gripped tightly in his hands as he fine-tuned whatever graphic design he was working on just then. *Good for him.* No really, it was very good for him. If he had been eyeing Daniel's mate in the heat of their shared passion, he'd be out cold right about now.

Hell, Daniel still wasn't sure he could keep his Bear in check at the moment. The Beast wanted to keep his mate away from other males at all cost. Primitive? *Yes.* Necessary? *Fuck yes.*

"Thanks. You can leave now," Daniel grunted and was thanked with a sharp poke in the back.

"Daniel," Lacey hissed from behind him. She was

trying to push herself off the counter, but he wasn't budging.

"Um, bro, I think your girl wants to get down," Nate smirked at him. Daniel loosed a long, slow growl in his brother's direction.

"Hey, don't shoot the messenger, man. Lacey, you know I was thinking, maybe you can model for me, you see I design characters-"

Daniel growled louder, bearing a fang in his direction. The younger man raised his eyebrows. Nate shrugged. Hands raised in surrender, he walked over to the side door and went to meet Clary to empty her car.

"Daniel!" Lacey hissed again and he finally relented and moved.

He turned her to face him despite her reddening cheeks and brushed his lips tenderly across hers. *So beautiful.*

"You're not modeling for my brother."

"But I need the work and if he's paying-"

"Lacey," he struggled to keep the Bear in check. He knew he was being a jerk, but he couldn't help it. His Bear would be overly possessive of her until he claimed her as his mate. *Fuck.* He'd have to explain, and he would, but not now. *Later.*

"Hey, you still wanna go to the mall?" He figured

he'd better change the subject before shit went south again.

"Yes, please. I need to stop at a *Universal Trust Bank* first," she began.

"Don't worry about it," he said and bit back his smile as she narrowed her eyes at him. She was so cute when she was all riled up.

"I do need to worry about it. I'm not a charity case, Daniel, I work for a living-"

"Hey, easy there, Lacey. I know you work hard, but in case you forgot, you don't have your wallet. No ID, no debit card, you won't be able to get a thing from the bank."

"Oh my God, you're right! I have to call the bank and cancel my credit cards!"

"It's already done."

"What?"

"The first night I went to get you, after I learned of the fire, I took care of everything. I figured you would need a few days to get back on your feet and I didn't want anyone messing with your accounts in the meanwhile."

"You did?" She asked, and he noted she still hadn't moved out of his embrace. A fact that thrilled him and his Bear.

"I am the Clan Enforcer. It's my job, and that of

the Bear Shifters who work for me, to keep the Clan safe."

"I'm not Clan," she said.

Her eyes went wide, and her pert mouth hung open at his answering growl. The Bear did not like that one bit. She was Clan, she was his. *Mine.*

"Bro, you have to stop growling at her, you do know that, right?" Nate walked back inside with a dozen grocery bags in his hands. He shook snowflakes off his head and smirked at the pair of them.

"Shut up, Nate," said Daniel, but he did cut off the growl. Lacey giggled. If Nate made her laugh, Daniel supposed he didn't have to pummel him. For now. Still, he was happy she seemed less tense.

"You ready?"

She nodded and he let go of her, missing her warmth immediately. He grabbed his keys off the rack and flipped his brother the bird before taking her hand.

"You need a coat," he stated and walked her over to the closet, frowning when he realized any of his were going to be way too big.

The thought of her wearing anyone else's coat made him want to roar. What was he supposed to do though? He couldn't let her freeze. *Fuck.*

"It's okay. I'll just wear this," she grabbed a freshly laundered throw blanket from the basket in the hall and folded it in half like a wrap.

He cocked his head as he watched her create a stylish wrap from a hand-crocheted afghan. *Wow.* It was almost as if she knew what was making him tense.

"See, I'm warm enough. Besides, I can pick up a coat there, but I insist on paying you back."

"Of course," he smiled widely.

He had no intention of allowing her to pay him back, but whatever made her happy. And he did want her to be happy, he realized with a shock.

It had been a long time since he cared about anyone's happiness. He liked the feeling. It made his Bear roar with pride. Without a doubt, this woman was his fated mate. He just needed to find the right time and place to tell her.

SEVEN

Christmas music swelled in the background of the parking lot outside the very crowded South Jersey mall. Lacey pulled the hat she'd grabbed from Daniel's SUV down on her head. She didn't want to be recognized she'd realized belatedly.

It was funny, she hadn't worried about how she looked the entire time she was at the Den. But she didn't want the kind of crowd she typically drew when she went out in public. Not now anyway.

She frowned as Daniel growled from his place next to her. The crowd was probably getting to the big guy. And they hadn't even gone inside yet. Well, it looked like that little bit of Shifter info gotten from her books seemed accurate.

She placed her hand inside of his and watched his reaction. The contact seemed to soothe him as they navigated through the lot to the large sliding doors. He squeezed her hand in his, keeping them firmly locked together as they walked side by side.

Not that she minded. In fact, she found herself fighting back a blush whenever he glanced down at her with those sinfully expressive blue eyes.

That steamy interlude in the kitchen had been a surprise to say the least. Not that she was shocked about the way she reacted to his overtures. Lacey was in serious lust, or well, *something* for the man. Had been for about a year now.

It was eye opening to recall how she'd responded to him. She'd wholeheartedly welcomed the big sexy Bear into her arms. *A Bear. She had the serious hots for a guy who turned into a Bear.* Nope, the irony of her situation wasn't lost on her.

She was only back in Barvale because a man who turned out to be a Wolf Shifter had gone batshit crazy on her. Now she had her very own Enforcer protecting her! Did she mention the way he kissed her back? It was obvious he desired her every bit as much as she wanted him. *Dayum!*

She could still feel Daniel against her lips. How could she not? He'd kissed the very breath out of her.

Everything she'd heard his father say the night before had flown right out of her head the second his lips came crashing down on hers.

The man was sex on legs. The stern expression he always wore belied the heat that lay just under the surface. She worried her lower lip, allowing him to gently tug her along to her service provider's kiosk that sat in the center of the first floor.

There was a bit of the line, but it was as if one of the men behind the counter knew them. A big, dark haired man nodded and signaled them to come over. She gaped as Daniel lead the way, ignoring the other customers and sat at the man's desk.

"Hello Enforc-, I mean, Mr. Devlin, what can I do for you today?" The younger man blushed furiously as he listened, then began typing her information into his computer.

"Okay, Ms. Alain, I have your information here. It says here that, *oh wow*, your Esme Alain? The *Esme*? Wow! You're like a world-famous supermodel!"

"Um, about that, I'm trying to lay low," Lacey nodded uncomfortably at the young man.

She felt a little embarrassed to be recognized in front of Daniel. He had never brought up her past fame, so she assumed he just didn't know or care.

"Wow! My sister is a huge fan!"

"Please, lower your voice," Lacey looked around, but no one else seemed to have heard him and she exhaled.

She could do without the sudden admiration of a crowd of strangers. A threatening growl sounded from beside her. From Daniel's throat actually. The young man blanched.

"Sorry, Mr. Devlin, sir. Um okay, let's see what we have here," the sales rep clacked away at the keyboard and frowned, "Es- um, I mean, *Ms. Alain* your account is, um, past due and I'm afraid you are too early for an upgrade. Looks like you never got the insurance plan either-"

"Oh, um, how much is a new phone then?"

"I am afraid the full price of the phone is $1,289. Then there is your balance of $327, and of course, the reconnection fee and tax," he paused and gulped as Daniel narrowed his eyes, another growl leaving his lips. He cut it off and handed the young man a platinum card.

"Add the premium plan and full insurance to her account. I want the newest model cell phone, fully loaded, and get her a damn case for the thing, *cub*," he growled.

"Daniel, no, I can't afford," she whispered, but his blue eyes met hers and she closed her mouth.

She knew she looked mulishly at him, but he just raised his eyebrows and proceeded to sign the credit card slip as if it was nothing. Probably was to him. *Well, fine then. Let him waste his damn money. I'll call and cancel everything later.*

"Um, what color phone case would you like?" The young man, whom she now realized must be a younger member of the Barvale Clan, asked.

"Uh, it really doesn't matter," she began.

"How about this one? It's the same shade of green as your eyes," he blushed as he spoke. Poor man almost jumped out of his skin when Daniel bared his teeth at him and snarled.

"That will be fine," she nodded at him as he ran off to the back room to set up her new phone.

"Daniel," she admonished the big Bear Shifter sitting next to her and was shocked to see him frown.

"Sorry, sweetheart. I just don't like him drooling all over you," his ears turned pink as he spoke, and she realized he was embarrassed. *He's jealous. OMG.*

"Daniel, he's just a boy," she started, only to see his eyes whip from the tall, well-muscled salesman to her again.

"He's man enough," he started.

"Not for me, Daniel. How could anyone compare with you?" She admitted the last without a thought.

Clearing her throat, she expected him to get embarrassed again, but was rewarded for her honesty with a smoldering look from Daniel. It was the kind of look that made her heart pound and her panties wet. *Oh my.*

"Ms. Alain? I went ahead and loaded your entire profile, complete with all your apps, contacts, and personal information onto your new phone. It will take another ten minutes or so to completely sync any updates, emails, and messages you may have received since misplacing your other phone. Um, I also installed the case for you," he smiled vacantly as he stared down at her completely disregarding the fact she had on no make-up and had a few still visible bruises on her face.

"Please let me know if you ever need anything," he said. He moved to shake her hand, but was cut off with an ever deeper growl from Daniel, "Um, I mean, let *us*, let *us* know if you need anything else," the young man jumped back when Daniel grabbed the bag with her new phone, along with his credit card, a little bit more forcefully than necessary from the young Bear.

Lacey thanked the young sales rep. She slid her

hand in the crook of Daniel's arm and accepted the phone from him. She walked quietly beside him as he led them to one of the many restaurants on the ground floor of the mall.

"Hungry?" She asked.

"Always. Bear, remember?" He smiled as they followed the waitress to an isolated booth in the back of the pub.

"I'm going to use the men's room. Will you be alright?" Daniel cocked his head and waited for an answer.

No one had ever done that before. Asked her if she was okay before they went and did something. *Hmm.* She wondered if she said no, would he just *hold it in? LOL.* He was truly a considerate man.

"I'll be fine. Want a drink?"

"Seltzer water, please. Be right back, sweetheart," he said and dropped a casual kiss on her lips as if it was something he always did.

Lacey sighed and touched her lips with her fingertips. Her whole world had changed over the course of a few days and she could hardly believe it. Sure, it had started with something truly terrible, but *this,* well, this was just wonderful.

The waitress came by, an older brunette with too much blush on, and asked her if they wanted drinks.

"Yes, two seltzer waters, please," she said.

She tapped her fingers on the table and waited for Daniel. Pulling out her sleek new phone as she did. It was the latest model, unlike her old phone that was a few years old at least. She didn't even want to look at the receipt. Not yet anyway.

She held her finger on the pad and entered her numeric passcode. The phone lit up and beeped and she realized she had over a hundred missed messages. She started flipping through them and stopped dead when she saw his name. *Tim Shaw.*

"Where are you? Fucking whore!"

"I'll find you, slut, and I'll make you wish you never ran!"

"You're mine, Esme."

"Gonna cut that pretty face to ribbons."

"Who are you with? Fucking some pretty boy, aren't you, slut!"

"You're nothing but a face and a pussy to fuck!"

"You've been very bad, Esme."

"Maybe I'll cut your boy toy up too."

"Gonna find you. Fuck you. Cut you. Slut."

She was shaking by the time Daniel came back. White-faced and no longer hungry, she jumped when he placed his hand on her shoulder.

"Lacey? I thought you might like these," he

handed her a box of chocolates from the stand outside.

She'd been eyeing them while they'd waited to be seated. She would have said thank you. If she weren't busy shaking with fear and anger. *Why won't he leave me alone?*

"What is it, sweetheart?" Daniel dropped the box on the table immediately and moved in next to her, gathering her in his arms.

"I was watching the restaurant, baby, I know no one came in or out from the mall. Did something happen?"

"Oh God, Daniel. He's just so vile and he's not gonna give up," she sobbed and that was when he noticed the cell phone. He took one look at the device and his features dropped.

Lacey watched the Bear within as he peeked out from behind Daniel's baby blue eyes. She didn't think she could handle an outburst, however well-intended. But once again, her Bear Shifter surprised her. He dropped his forehead to hers and kissed her lips tenderly.

"Fuck, Lacey, I'm sorry," he whispered against her mouth, kissing her sweetly and cupping her face in his large hands.

"I'm here, baby, I got you," Daniel murmured.

He was so big and strong. So very masculine. She'd seen his Bear, knew his inner strength was tremendous, and yet he'd only ever been gentle, protective, and supportive with her. Maybe that was his real strength. His tenderness.

She returned his kiss, desperate to maintain the contact with him. To make all the ugliness of Tim's words wash away in the tidal wave that was kissing Daniel.

If only she could curl up and fit inside his pocket, she'd never leave him. She sighed into his mouth surprised by her thoughts. *Yes, I'd keep him with me always. My Daniel,* she stilled at the phrase that whispered through her mind. *No, he's not mine. Not to keep.*

"I shouldn't have stayed at the kiosk so long, sweetheart, I'm so sorry. Come on, let's go," he dropped a hundred-dollar bill on the table and stood up. He leaned down and scooped her up in his big arms, leaving out the back door of the restaurant as if he owned the place. The workers just nodded and watched the two of them. Hell, for all she knew he did own the place. Bear Claw Bakery had many holdings.

But she didn't care about that. Only about him

and how good it felt to be in his strong, capable arms. She was glad he snuck her out the back.

It's like he knows what I am feeling or maybe he can read my mind. She snuggled into the safety of his warm chest, wishing for all she was worth that he really was hers to keep.

She had to stop this crazy infatuation before it got out of hand. Just *not yet.* She needed to hold onto him for a little while longer. *When he doesn't want me anymore, I'll leave, I swear,* she promised herself though she had no idea how she'd survive such a thing.

"Hold on, baby," his voice resonated within her and she trembled in his arms as he carried her through the parking lot to his SUV.

He placed her inside and snapped the seatbelt, pausing to drop another kiss on her lips before walking around to the driver's side. Lacey knew she couldn't have stomached the crowds after reading some of the things Tim had said.

Each text got more and more manic and threatening. He was graphic and disgusting, not to mention violent in his anger. *Sick man.*

What the hell happened to Tim Shaw anyway? He was just some nice man who complimented her after her shows. He'd been funny and sweet at first, but that soon changed. His attitude had totally altered from a friend to someone obsessed with owning her.

She'd done the best she could. Warding off his advances, then finally, telling him, quite firmly, that she had no romantic interest in him. She never led him on. That part was definitely a lie. She was no damned siren. Had never seduced a man in her life. Never wanted to. *Until now,* her thoughts turned to Daniel.

Maybe there *was* something wrong with her? She had one crazed Wolf stalking her and threatening her with harm, but all she could think of was this man next to her.

EIGHT

"You okay," Daniel asked from behind the wheel of his large SUV.

The vehicle was like him. Powerfully built but not ostentatious. He didn't need to beat his chest or yell to all what he was capable of. No, his strength was there for all to see, whether they acknowledged it or not. She supposed it was what made him a good Clan Enforcer, though she didn't know much about his job or what it meant to be a Shifter really.

"Lacey?" His softly uttered word shook her out of her reverie, and she moved closer to him across the seat.

An action that seemed to please him as he gathered her close and squeezed her shoulder with one arm. With the other he draped the afghan she'd worn earlier around her shaking frame and started the car.

"I'll turn the heat up," he began, but she stopped him.

"No, I'd rather just be next to you if that's okay. You're so warm," she could feel heat rush to her face. *You're warm? I sound like an imbecile.* But it was the truth. He seemed to be about five degrees hotter than she was at all times. Like her own personal furnace. *Yes, please.*

"It's a Shifter thing. We run a little hotter than *normals*, you know, humans, like you," he started the car and pulled out of the spot careful to look where he was going.

"Wow, that's really interesting. What else is different about you?" She couldn't help but ask.

"Well, I turn into a Bear," he grinned, and she laughed.

"Very funny, Daniel."

"I aim to please. But really, Shifters have various degrees of things that make them different from normals. I don't pretend to know about the others, but Bear Shifters have an average body temp of about 100 degrees. We're strong, dependable. We live by the rules of our Clan and our

Alpha. Blend in with society and take care of each other. That's what a Clan is really. Just a community."

"Wow. Sounds amazing."

"You're not afraid?"

"Of you?" She gasped astounded he would even ask such a question.

"Of Shifters. Now that you know about Bears and Wolves, there are others too, Lacey."

"Like what?"

"Dragons, Lions, Tigers, Hyenas, Witches, Demons, all manner of beasts and other supernaturals. They've been here as long as humankind. Maybe longer," he seemed to be watching her as he drove, gauging her reaction.

"I think it's incredible," she responded, "What? Did you think I'd run screaming?"

"Lacey, I just told you monsters are real. That reaction wouldn't be unwarranted," he turned the wheel and headed out onto the highway, but she stayed glued to his side. Safe and snug next to him.

"Daniel, from what I have seen you are a good man and Bear. Everyone else deserves to be judged according to how they behave. Tim is a monster. Not because he can turn into a Wolf, but because he doesn't have an ounce of humanity in him. He treats people, even his Wolf buddies, like dirt. Thinks people are possessions. You're nothing like him."

Daniel seemed to preen at that. He squeezed her shoulder and drove with one hand, a low, slow rumble sounding through his chest. How could he think she would put him and that Wolf in the same category? *No way.*

"Wanna get some drive thru, baby?"

"Yes, please," she nodded. Now that they were away from the mall, her stomach was grumbling.

"Okay, I know a great chicken place," he said.

"Mmm. Fried? I haven't had fried chicken in like twenty years," she smiled at his astounded look.

"Daniel, model remember?" she pointed to herself.

"Yeah, but what does that have to do with fried chicken?"

"Look, I was born with this face, so I don't pretend to have earned that, but everything else is a lot of work. When I am working, and that has been non-stop since I was a kid, I eat mostly vegetarian. Raw foods, steamed, or boiled. Nothing fried or fatty."

"That sucks!"

"I mean, I don't know. I guess I am healthy,

right? But I admit fried chicken and coleslaw sound yummy."

"Good. Cause I'm gonna feed you all the fried chicken and coleslaw you want tonight."

Lacey laughed at his serious expression. She rested her head on his chest while he drove, secure in his competence behind the wheel. Before she knew it, she was dozing off in her seat.

When she came to, it was to her being carried out of the car once again by Daniel. He seemed to love the feel of her in his arms, and she wasn't complaining. How often did a girl who stood almost six-feet tall get swept up in a man's arms? *Not very.*

His face was so much more thrilling up close. His blue eyes were glued to her, taking in every nuance of her expression. She felt her own face burning and could only imagine the blush staining her normally pale cheeks.

"This isn't the Den," she said and straightened in his embrace.

"No. I brought you to *my place,*" his gravely voice did funny things to her insides. Like he was kindling a small fire inside her with the promise of it turning into an inferno.

"I thought you lived there," she said breathily, surprised at the change in her voice. She'd never felt this way before. Anxious and nervous, craving him on a level that was new to her.

"I do sometimes, but I like my privacy. When I'm not working, I stay here."

Here was a beautiful two-story log cabin that sat on the shore of a huge lake. Several large windows looked over the land with equally sized wooden shutters. There was a huge, wrap-around porch, with oversized Adirondack chairs overlooking the lake. Both the shutters and the chairs were painted deep, forest green. She loved that color. Heck, she loved the house.

"It's so beautiful," she marveled.

"Yes," he said but was still looking at her, "Uh, I mean, thanks, I built it myself. The Clan has several small cabins dotting the lake shore, but this one is mine."

"Are the other cabins close?"

"Not really, we're a good half-mile from the nearest one," he grinned as he carried her over the threshold and the scents of food, *fried chicken maybe,* and burning wood floated to her nostrils.

"I came in and started a fire before taking you out of the car. The food is warming on the stove too," he ducked his head and she saw a blush spread over his cheeks.

"You can put me down now, Daniel."

"What if I don't want to."

Her eyes flashed at him, loving the feel of being in his muscular arms. He stepped a little bit further inside of the room. The décor was big, masculine like him. All dark greens and tans, but it was neat as a pin.

What would it be like? To stay here with him. The very thought thrilled her at the same time, it broke her heart. Yes, he was attracted, but he never said forever. *Don't borrow trouble. Live for today*, she told herself firmly.

"Hey, come back to me, baby," he said in her ear and she whipped her eyes back to his oh so close face.

"That's it," he growled out the words and let her down.

She slid against him. He was holding her so close. Allowing her to feel every hard edge and rip of his body. And boy, was he hard. Like everywhere. *Oh my.*

Lacey bit her lip. She felt heat pool in her belly and dampen her panties. Desire and need rose within her as he closed the door with one arm behind him never breaking contact. Anticipation was like a living breathing animal, and it had taken up residence right there in that room, in that inch of space that was still between them.

"Are we alone here?"

"Yes," his answer was thick with his Bear.

The flash of power in his eyes brought more moisture to pool between her legs. She licked her lips and Daniel followed the movement like the predator he was. Lacey loved that she could drive him to the edge of his control.

"Good," she said and pressed herself closer.

Daniel grunted as she tugged on his head, pulling him down to meet her willing lips. That was all it took. Her big Bear grabbed her by the waist and wrapped her in his steel embrace.

Melting their mouths together, they collided in a frenzy of passion. Clothing was moved aside, or just ripped off, in their need to get to each other.

"I'm starving for you," he growled against her mouth, cupping her face with one hand and claiming her with a searing kiss. She wholeheartedly agreed with the sentiment.

Lacey arched her back to get closer to him, opening her mouth and tangling her tongue with his. She ran her hands over the hard muscles of his stomach. Reveling in every flex and tremble of his flesh. She affected him alright. *Good.* Cause God knew, he affected her as well.

"Daniel," she moaned his name, inciting him even more.

His growl reverberated through the room as his hands dipped under her bra, tugging the confining material away from her heated flesh. He groaned as he gazed at her bare breasts. As if he was unable to decide what he wanted to do, touch or lick.

He made up his mind quickly, yanking her off the floor and bringing her freed breasts to eye level. Clad only in her now damp cotton panties, Lacey wrapped her legs around his waist. He cupped her ass, securing her to his body before dipping his head and suckling one hard nub into his mouth.

"Oh, yes," she moaned loudly as he gripped her tighter, flexing his hips and brushing his steel hard length across her core.

With every pull of his glorious mouth she felt a tug all the way down to her needy clit. Never had sex felt like this. Her entire body hummed with desire. She craved this one man's touch like she needed oxygen to live.

"Smell so good, baby, Need you, Lacey," his growl was deep and rumbled through his chest into her.

"Yes! More," she cried out as his lips sought and found her other breast.

He held her tighter, higher, suckling her nipples, one at a time. Each delicious tug sent more ripples of pleasure through her entire frame. On and on he kept up the rhythm, relentlessly until she cried out.

In a blur of movement, he whisked her down the hall and through an open door. She was suddenly pressed against a firm mattress, Daniel breathing unsteadily over her. Not because he was winded, no, she gathered the Bear Shifter could outrun a whole flock of New York marathoners should he feel the need.

This kind of breathing had to do with their lack of clothing and the acute desire growing between them. His blue eyes darkened to a sapphire color and she swore she saw his animal looking at her for a moment, triumph in his gaze. Just like that the Bear was gone, replaced by the man once more. *Maybe I imagined it.*

"Are you sure about this, Lacey? Once we start, I don't think I can stop," his voice went even deeper if possible and she shivered in response.

"Yes, I'm sure. Please, Daniel," she writhed beneath him, eager for his touch.

"Thank God," he growled.

His face had gained a rigid look, as if he were straining hard to control himself. *Oh no.* That wouldn't do. She reached up with her fingertips and traced the lines of his forehead, smoothing them out until he sighed and lowered his face. *Thank God,* she echoed his sentiment and met his lips with hers.

Daniel's tongue pushed past her lips with ease, sliding into the warm cavern of her mouth. She opened for him willingly, wanting more of him. As much as he would give her.

His growl was never ending, a low, deep rumble that made her sex pulse with need. His callused fingers stroked her neck and shoulders, leaving slivers of pleasure shooting through her entire body. Like he was branding her with his touch. And Lacey wanted more.

Sensing her need, he moved down, the sound of his skin brushing the bedspread was a muted sort of rustle, but it was nothing compared to the pounding of her heart. Daniel grabbed her hands and pushed them over her head aggressively. But she wasn't frightened. No, she wanted more.

He licked her neck and shoulder, paying particular attention to the place where they met, nipping the skin lightly before moving down to lave at her breasts. She was not overly large, but she had no time to be self-conscious as he tweaked her nipples and tugged on the sensitive flesh with his lips and teeth.

Lacey moaned and bucked while he nuzzled and nipped her sensitized skin, licking where he'd playfully bitten her until she was moaning is name.

"Want more, baby? Want it all?"

"Yes," she hissed and watched him. With a predatory smile on his handsome face, Daniel traced the lines of her body with eyes that glowed with his Bear.

Yes, she recognized the signs now. Was in awe of herself that she could make him so hot that his animal would make itself known. Daniel leaned back into a kneeling position.

He was deliciously naked. All hard lines and ripples, a smattering of golden hair on his chest and stomach where his muscles tapered off into a perfect V. Beneath the golden curls was his long, thick cock. Jutting out proudly, a pearl of precum leaked from his head and Lacey moaned with need. *Later,* she promised herself.

Shifters really were bigger than humans. Everywhere. He groaned and stroked his length, looking at her near naked body just lying there on display for him. *Damn.* That was so sexy, she writhed on the mattress. Watching and waiting.

He released his dick and pressed her thighs open, giving her a long hard look. Daniel ran his hands over her flat belly and down her smooth legs. Then he eased himself down, fitting his large shoulders between her splayed legs.

Close. So very close. Lacey whimpered and he grinned. *The tease.* He blew hot air on her panty covered sex and she whimpered. She wanted more. Needed so much more from him. Now.

"Daniel," she pleaded, flexing her hips until he came nearer to where she needed him.

"Please," she practically begged. And this time, he didn't tease or make her wait.

Her Bear was more than ready. With his teeth, he tore the cotton panties from her hips, revealing her near bare sex to his rapt gaze. As a model, she'd had her hair lasered off years ago. She worried he wouldn't like it, but all worries ceased when he stroked and parted her slick folds.

"So pink, so pretty, so mine," his voice was raspy with need or his Bear or both, she supposed.

She wanted to move, to bring him closer to her needy sex, but he held her still. Inhaling deeply, his chest rumbled, the natural instinct of his animal drawing forth an unpredictable reaction from her.

Lacey bit her lip as she felt moisture pooling, her pussy readying for him. The plump flesh of her nether lips throbbed, and she panted with need.

"Patience, baby. I got you, Mine," he growled and dipped his head down.

He took one long, unsteady inhale of her heady scent before snaking his tongue out to taste. Lacey moaned long and loud as he tasted her in one long swipe of his tongue from her forbidden hole to her too sensitive clit. He repeated the move once, then twice, before delving into her sex.

His inhumanly long tongue tasted her from the inside as her channel squeezed him like it would his cock. Any minute now. If he would just give her what she wanted.

He groaned as he fastened his lips onto her clit and exchanged his tongue for his hand. Thick fingers entered her moist heat and stroked, finding that secret place inside of her that made her scream his name.

"Don't stop, Daniel," she moaned, lost in sensation.

He seemed to be touching her everywhere. One handed was buried in her needy sex while the other caressed her breasts, tweaking the nipples and roaming over her flat stomach, to her rounded hips and ass.

Stars exploded behind her eyes as his lips latched onto her clit, fingers thrusting in and out of her slick heat faster, with more purpose.

"Come for me, sweet," he growled over her clit and sucked until she felt the edge of the world slip away.

Never had she ever felt anything like it. It just went on and on, wave after wave of pleasure, until suddenly she could breathe again.

In that moment, Daniel raised himself to his knees. His thick cock jutted out proudly as he gazed down at her face.

"Mine."

The single word hung in the air as he placed his cock at her entrance. Lacey's eyes flashed and her nostrils flared.

That word sounded pretty fucking good to her.

CHAPTER
NINE

"Lacey," Daniel groaned her name as he slowly pushed himself inside of her tight, welcoming heat.

Inch by inch he moved, at a torturously slow pace, until he was fully seated inside of her. This was completely out of his level of experience.

She was beyond anything he'd ever felt or imagined he could feel. *Perfection personified.* And it was not because of her exquisite looks. It was because she was made for him. Fated to be with only him. *Mine. Mate.*

The Bear pushed at him to claim the tiny female. Mark her as his own so no one could dare question where or with whom she belonged. *Not yet,* he cautioned.

The pleasure of being inside Lacey was almost too intense. Daniel flexed his hips, sinking deeper, stretching and possessing her. *Yes. Grrr.*

"Lacey," he sought her eyes, capturing the emerald green pools in his gaze. She blinked up at him, mouth open, she panted her pleasure. Her face aglow with their passion. *Beautiful.*

"That's it baby, look at me," he growled as he dipped his head, capturing her lips.

He was careful not to crush her with his weight. He just needed to feel every single inch of her delicious self, pressed as close as he could get her to him.

Daniel held himself still, giving her time to adjust to his impressive girth, but that did not stop him from sliding his legs against hers, pressing her soft breasts to his hard chest, kissing her lips until he felt her relax and welcome him. *Fuck. So good.*

He swirled his hips against the apex of her thighs. Spearing her slick heat with his cock, Daniel pumped, unable to wait any longer. *Retreat, thrust, swirl, grind.* He set the pace, slow and steadily increasing, reacting to the signals her body sent him.

"Oh God, yes," she moaned as he stroked that spot inside of her with his length. She locked her legs around his waist, cutting off his retreat. So he flexed and swirled, grinding his pubis against her sensitive bundle of nerves.

Her sex squeezed, clutching at his cock like a velvet vise. *Flex, swirl, grind.* He moved faster, lifting her by the ass and sinking deeper into her heat. *Fuck. So good.*

Her moans intensified. She was so beautiful. Her hair had somehow escaped its braid during their heated exchange. He reached out with one hand and touched the silken locks, spreading them like a golden halo across his pillow.

Fuck. She looked perfect there. Belonged there. To him. *Mine.* He couldn't think in complete sentences. He could only feel as he made love to Lacey. *More. Love. Mine.*

Her sex clenched and she moaned. She was close. Daniel growled. The Bear wanted to love her sweetly, but he was too desperate for her. He rose to his knees, lifted her legs onto his shoulders, and sank even deeper into her heat.

"There? Like that? So good, Lacey."

Daniel moved in and out of her sex, watching greedily for her every reaction. He found her sensitive clit with his thumb, stroking the tiny nub in time with his thrusts. His cock stretched her, his thumb stroked, building pressure, moving faster and harder until they both couldn't take it.

"Daniel," she yelled with her head thrown back. She was right on the cusp of her first release and he wanted to make sure she was with him every step of the way.

His cock throbbed inside her intense heat. He was like a bomb of ecstasy just about ready to go off. Every retreat and flex of his hips sent more shock-waves of pleasure throughout his body, straight to his balls. But he needed her there with him. *All the way.*

"Look at me, baby," he demanded.

She did. Her dark emerald eyes flew open, as her movements became jerky and her back arched. Over-whelming sensation built up inside of him, the Bear pushing to get out.

"Oh God, almost," she yelled.

"Gonna take you there, baby," he promised.

And he meant it. *Fuck yeah.* Her cream coated his passage, making each stroke that much more perfect. *Swivel, grind, thrust, repeat.* Her pussy pulsed around him. In time with the same word whispered in his brain over and over. *Mine. Mine. MINE.*

"Daniel!" She moaned his name long and hard as

he swirled his hips, ground his pubic bone onto her sensitive clit, and pushed her right over the edge.

The muscles of her inner walls clenched down on his cock, squeezing him, calling for his cum. Daniel couldn't hold back if he tried. His balls tensed and he came right there with her. His seed exploded into her womb as he released her legs.

He leaned down and caging her body in with his. Their hands locked together, he ground himself harder into her, bringing forth a second, even stronger release from his beautiful mate. *Grrr.*

Over and over, Lacey called his name, gasping for air as her channel continued to milk him for all he was worth. This was ecstasy, pure unadulterated bliss.

Coming inside his mate was like nothing he'd ever had before. She was heaven and home, and she was his. Only his. *Mine.*

His teeth lengthened, the Bear pushing for him to mark her, claim her as his own. But he hadn't asked her yet. He needed to. Needed her permission before bonding to her permanently.

"Lacey," he breathed as he slowed his movements. His dick still pulsed inside her.

She reached for him with her tiny hands, ghosting kisses over his lips. Moments later he slowly eased himself from her, careful not to cause her discomfort. He was big, even for a Shifter, and his mate was small and delicate.

He tucked her into his side and kissed her temple, glorying in the love they'd just shared. *Has to be love*, he thought as she settled her hand over his heart and dropped a sweet kiss on his chest.

"You hungry?" he asked after what felt like an eternity later. The Bear in him demanded he take care of her. Feed her. Provide for her. *Love her.*

"I could eat," she smiled as she looked up at him. A slow pink blush crept across her cheeks and he grinned. He loved the fact that she could look so innocent and beautiful and still be a wildcat between the sheets with him.

"Okay. Come on," he stood up and noted she still lay in the bed with a sheet over her body. Daniel cocked his head to the side.

"Don't tell me you're bashful now, baby," he smiled at her shy giggle.

"Now, baby, I have seen," he stopped and dropped a kiss on her lips, "tasted," another kiss, "touched," *kiss, kiss,* "and loved every single inch of your body. You never have to be shy with me," he smiled warmly.

"I know, but I guess I am, a little bashful that is,"

she shrugged, and he could scent her embarrassment.

"Okay, baby," he smiled and walked to his dresser where he grabbed one of his plain white t-shirts and gently put it on her.

"Better?"

"Much," she smiled and kissed him on the lips. Her tongue snuck out of her mouth and he welcomed it, greedy for all of her.

"If we do much more of this, we won't eat," he growled and nipped her lip.

"Feed me," she said and gasped when he lifted her off the bed, princess style, and carried her to the living room sofa. What his woman wanted, she got. And right now, she wanted feeding.

Daniel was used to nudity and didn't mind being undressed. Especially not in front of his mate. He made a plate piled high with the fried chicken he'd bought earlier, corn on the cob, coleslaw, and some fries. He'd kept the food warm on the stove for them.

He walked into the living room to see her sitting in the middle of the couch watching him and his heart swelled in his chest. *Mine.*

Yes, he was a possessive bastard, but God, he'd love her. *Yes. I love her already.* He felt it all the way to his soul. His Bear watched in approval as he made sure to bring enough food for the two of them.

I will be a good mate, he told himself. Doubt, that ugly son of a bitch was trying its damnedest to wiggle its way into his mind. *Melinda left you. She didn't think you were good enough. What if Lacey doesn't think so either? Can you really survive another woman dumping your sorry ass?*

Fuck. He tried to shake himself free of those thoughts, but they were there now, and they wouldn't go away. Not without some convincing.

Okay, so pros as to why she'd want him. Daniel was a wealthy man, not that she seemed to care about money, still it was good to have. He had family, and she seemed to like his brothers. He was a fierce protector, a good Enforcer and a strong Bear. He'd make sure she felt safe and taken care of, always.

Yes, he'd make a good mate. He'd love her and take care of her in every way. *And he meant every possible way.* Confidence restored he carried the plate inside.

"Here," he said and handed her the mountain of food while he sat down next to her. Using the side of the couch as a back rest, he settled her between his legs and took the plate from her fingers, grinning at her wide eyes.

"How many people are we feeding in here?" She asked.

"Open," he said, ignoring her comment. He smiled and slipped a piece of crispy chicken into her mouth.

"Mmm," she closed her eyes with a look of pure bliss as she chewed.

"Damn woman, I never saw anyone react to fried chicken like that!" *Could he be jealous of food?*

"That's because I haven't had anything like this in years," Lacey laughed and reciprocated, feeding him a drumstick and licking the crumbs from his mouth.

He found himself laughing between bites of food and kisses from his mate. They talked and joked, fed each other bite for bite. It was fun. Their relationship was real, not just sex and frenzied mating, he realized, and his heart thudded in his chest.

"This is so good," she laughed and chewed a fry as she fed him a bite from a crispy chicken leg.

"Mm hm," he agreed, but he meant them as opposed to the food.

Daniel caught her hand with his before she could pull it away. He licked her fingertips one by one, noting the heated glaze that settled over her emerald eyes.

His nostrils flared, picking up the increased scent of honeysuckle and Lacey's arousal in the air. *Claim her.* The Bear pushed at him, and he fought for control. Sometimes the animal was just so strong. He often feared he'd go rogue without a mate. He was barely tamed as it was. But now, he found her. His one true mate. *Finally.*

"Lacey, he growled as she turned around fully, dropping the plate onto the coffee table, and straddled his hips. She'd donned a t-shirt but was still bare underneath. Her moist sex slid against his cock. *Grrr.*

"Daniel," she gasped as their lips met.

He opened for her, thrusting his tongue into her willing mouth. He liked her like this, as the aggressor. She was fierce and proud and beautiful. His Bear was angry about the bruises on her face, but she was getting better. Almost fully healed. Not that they mattered. He only saw her.

"I want you," she said against his lips and he groaned.

"I'm yours, Lacey."

"Really?"

"Yes."

She met his gaze and sat back, forcing his cock to snuggle against her crack. *Fuck.* She was gonna kill him. Holding his stare she lifted his shirt off of her body, revealing every inch of her porcelain flesh to his hungry eyes. And Daniel was hungry. For her. *Mine.*

"So fucking beautiful," he said, but didn't move. *Not yet.* This was her show. He wanted her to feel safe and comfortable to do anything she wanted to him.

"You're beautiful," she countered, and he smirked. *Him? Beautiful?*

"I don't know if I qualify-"

"Are you kidding me? Just look at you, every sculpted inch of you is a fantasy come to life, but you're so much more Daniel. And I want all of you," she moaned and lifted herself, her tiny hands gripping his shoulders with everything she had.

He groaned as her silky, wet lips kissed the tip of his dick. Her eyes flashed emerald fire at him as she came down hard, taking every inch of his steel length inside of her. *Fuck.* He lost himself to the pleasure and feel of his glorious mate's tight sheath wrapped around him. A perfect fit, like she was made for this. For him.

Yes. Her pussy squeezed and fluttered. So fucking

good. The scents of honeysuckle and his mate's sex teased his nostrils. She rose up till he was almost all the way out of her, then swallowed him back down inch by inch with her sopping wet heat.

"Mine," he growled, as she lifted her breasts to his face. He couldn't resist snaking out his tongue and licking one then the other. Light, whispery strokes that made Lacey moan and grip his head.

"More," she pleaded, and he complied, taking one tight bud into his mouth and suckling her long and hard.

Her pussy clenched in response, sending spikes of pleasure racing through his blood down to his balls. *Fuck.* He felt ready to explode inside of her, but he had to hold off. Needed her to come first.

"Daniel," she moaned his name and he loved it. Loved the sounds she made as she lifted her body up only to slam back down against him.

The sounds of their lovemaking filled the room. Their combined scent, a sweet and heady musk permeated the air. It was fucking perfect. At least he thought so. His Bear agreed.

Daniel growled and groaned as Lacey rode him. He flexed his hips to meet her downward thrusts. marveling in each sensation she caused within him. *Pleasure, love, bliss, permanence, ecstasy, possession, fulfillment.* Every stroke along his cock was like a pull straight down to his balls, begging for his release.

Her cream scented the air, covered his shaft, making the passage so fucking good and slick he never wanted her to stop. He wrapped his muscled arms around her, pressing her against his chest as she ground herself down, riding his dick like a fucking champion. *Lacey. Mine.*

"You're killing me," he said and loved the smile she flashed at him.

Breasts bouncing, hair floating wildly behind her, she was a fucking vision. And she felt so damn good! Her inner walls sheathed him like a fucking glove. *She was made for me*, his Bear growled. He loved seeing her like this. Loved feeling every breath and twitch of her body.

Bold and sexy as hell, his mate scratched her nails down his chest. She licked and sucked at his neck, marking him with her scent. Hell, she even bit him, which had his Bear roaring.

"Daniel!" She moaned his name as her channel started to squeeze. Her movements grew jerky, her body arched. Daniel growled in response as he felt her pleasure start to take over.

"Lacey! Fuck, baby, that's it. Want you so damn

bad. Need to make you mine," his voice deepened with his Bear.

"Yes," she answered. Her pussy quivered, moisture pooling around his cock. *Fuck, yes.* She liked his words, liked what he was saying. That was a good sign.

"No, look at me, baby. I need you to understand. I want you to be mine. I'm asking you for *forever*," he growled the words, unable to keep the Bear at bay.

Lacey's eyes flashed. She pumped herself harder onto his cock, her pussy stroking every one of his nerve endings. *Lighting him up like a match to gasoline.*

"Yes, oh yes," she replied.

"You have to mean it. I can't undo it once it is done, baby."

"Yes. Daniel, I want to be yours, please. *I need you to make me yours.*"

"*Fuck,*" he moaned as she ground herself down on him, "Yes?"

"Yes. My answer is *yes*," she grabbed his face and nodded.

Her eyes were wide with pleasure and something else. Something warm and inviting. *Could it be?* His heart thudded. *Maybe.* He wanted to ask but didn't want to. *Not yet. That could come later.* He needed to make her his first.

"Do you know what you're saying? What you're agreeing to?"

"You want to claim me, bite me, give me your mark. Yes, Daniel. I am saying yes."

At that moment the Bear took over. Standing up with his dick still throbbing inside his mate, Daniel moved carefully, flipping Lacey over the side of the couch onto her knees. She was still hovering on the brink of her orgasm and he meant to give her one she'd never forget. *Fuck yes.*

His. She was all his. Daniel loosed a long slow growl. He was going to brand every fucking inch of her with his scent. Her sexy as sin hourglass frame called to him, ass pushed out, begging him to fill her, and he did. In one hard thrust, he was balls deep inside her. His Bear roared, anxious to finally be claiming this woman as his own.

Her slick pussy gripped him, made to fit him like a fucking glove. He stroked her walls, loving the feel of her. She moaned his name, still riding the wave of pleasure from her near orgasm. Daniel was determined to make her see the fucking heavens this time!

"Come for me, baby, then I'll make you mine," he

growled into her ear, caging her from behind as he thrust deeper and deeper into her wet heat.

He felt his teeth lengthen in his mouth, his Bear ready to strike, to claim his woman. *Mine. Forever.* She moaned in response. Breaths increased. Heart pumping. Almost, but not quite ready.

Daniel grunted as he reached between them and found her nub. He flicked her clit, rubbed and pinched the tiny nub. He reveled in the sounds of her responding moans, took pride in the shiver of her flesh as he loved her good and hard. Sex with his mate was unlike anything he'd ever felt.

Her inner walls tightened, squeezing his thick shaft with unbelievable intensity. *Fuck yes.* She was feeling the first waves of passion, and he was right there with her. Every step of the way. He wasn't gonna stop until it was a full-on explosion for the both of them.

The Bear wanted to dominate her, to show her he was capable of taking care of her in every way. Especially this way. The man wanted to be gentle. It was a toss-up who won, but his mate sure as hell wasn't complaining. *Thank fuck for that.*

"Daniel," she moaned as her sex clamped down hard. He almost lost it then.

The sounds of their skin slapping together, their

moans and breaths, all of it, was a symphony to his ears. *Deep, deep, deep.* He stroked her inside. Not stopping as she called out his name over and over again, her orgasm taking hold.

Moving her hair off to one shoulder, Daniel shuddered as he viewed the beautiful patch of skin that would bear his mark. *Mine. Forever.*

He told himself over and over again that she was a normal, he had to remain in control, to not hurt her. *Never hurt*, his Bear answered his worries.

Then it was all he could do to keep his head on straight. Lacey leaned her head all the way to the side, bearing herself for him as she pushed her sweet ass back hard against his cock. *Fuck. Mine*, his Bear roared. Daniel struggled for control. His gums ached and claws stretched through his fingers. *Mine.*

"Daniel, make me yours," she moaned.

"Mine," he growled and bent his head.

His canines sliced through her ivory flesh like a hot knife slices through butter. The second her blood filled his mouth, his seed exploded into her channel.

A white-hot explosion of ecstasy raced through his blood as he filled and tasted his mate. Her sweet as honey blood flowed down his throat as he laid claim to his fated one. *Mine*, the Bear roared.

He suckled her neck, drinking her down and

marking her perfect skin. He licked the wounds closed, still growling with his Bear at his possession of her. Her pussy gripped him one last time, determined to take every last drop of cum into her womb. As it should be. *Yes. Mine. Mate.*

Their passion rose so fucking high he thought he'd die from it in those moments. *Never like that before.* The fiery bliss of their completion washed over him in waves as passion slowed to mutual satisfaction. She was so fucking perfect. *His mate.*

Beast sated, he turned her and pulled her into his embrace, allowing the warm glow of the matebond to settle over them both.

"Mine," he growled.

TEN

Lacey snuggled closer to Daniel in the huge bed of his cabin by Lake Ursa. She couldn't believe what had happened over the last twelve hours.

They made love. Multiple times. *Sigh.* Then, Daniel bit her. Well, he *claimed* her. Lacey smiled as the warm tendrils of their *matebond* flowed over her. Protectiveness, affection, desire, caring, tenderness, and strength pulsed between them.

What of love? She knew the answer for her. Felt it in her heart. She loved the man. Could only have ever given herself like that in love. He hadn't said anything about love, but he must care for her. *Yes.* She knew he did.

It was like she could feel him, inside her. The

strength of his Bear was somehow connected to her. She didn't know much about it, only what she'd learned in one of her chats with Clary about Shifters and mating.

The older woman was careful to tell her about biting and marking one's mate. She'd told her their legends of *fated mates*. Such beautiful stories of men and women destined by the universe to be together forever.

Like a fairytale. If only she was that to Daniel. But she wasn't going to complain. She'd settle for him choosing her. It was enough. *Would have to be.* After all, she'd wanted him since she'd first seen him at *The Thirsty Dog* last year with her cousin. *Oh my God,* she hadn't even thought of Margot since she'd been here. She supposed she'd have to visit her aunt and uncle and cousins at some point. *Crap.*

Was it silly for her to be making plans? *No, right? I mean he marked me. We're a couple now.* Still, doubts butted in on her peace of mind and Lacey frowned thoughtfully. He made no mention about living together or anything. And she didn't want pity. *Crap.*

A buzzing noise sounded to the left and she moved, careful not to jostle Daniel. The man was sleeping. *Like a Bear.* She snorted at her lame joke and stood up, looking for the source of the noise.

Underneath their discarded pile of clothes, Lacey found her new cell phone. *Shit.* There was a new message from an unknown number. Shivers racked her body as she read the venomous words. The same threats and promised violence were right there in the text. *Tim.*

Daniel must have had his number blocked, but that wouldn't stop him. She could've told Daniel that if he'd asked. She closed her eyes and counted to ten before reading what he'd sent.

"Hello Slut, Did you enjoy fucking yogi last night? To think I could have had you first, but don't worry, I'll fuck his claim right off of you, whore. You have ten minutes to come out and meet me or I'm coming in."

Lacey stifled her gasp. He was there. Tim was there! No. He had to be bluffing. This was Bear territory. The phone buzzed again.

"Your Bear should think about shades if he's going to fuck you in the living room. I'm gonna rip his fucking bite mark right off your skin, clean you up real good, you fucking slut. Don't try waking him. I'll see you. I've got a gun aimed right at his big head. Eight minutes now. Then I am shooting first and coming in for you. Guns and claws blazing."

Oh God, no. Lacey wanted to scream. She wanted

to run to Daniel to wake him up. The tiny red dot that marked his forehead stopped her.

Tim was insane. There was no question there. But he was also an expert marksman. She recalled him showing her pictures of his various awards one time or other. He'd always been a braggard. *Shit.* She should have seen this coming. Should have told Daniel how relentless and crazy Tim was. It was too late now.

She might not be a Bear or a Wolf, but she could protect her man. She would give herself up for Daniel's safety. It was the only choice she had. *Yes, I would happily die for him.* She fought against tears at this damn twist of fate. It was so unfair that she should finally have a chance at love, only to lose it so soon.

She locked down as her cell started to buzz again and realized she had yet to move. *Damn.* She would kill for another minute with him. Wiping her eyes, she read the hated text.

"Tick tock, Esme. You coming or do I kill him?"

Decision made, she grabbed her things and moved to the living room. She pulled on her pants and Daniel's sweatshirt. Tears rolled down her cheeks as she breathed in his scent from the soft, faded material.

No. She wanted to yell, to scream, to rage against Tim and his fucking mania. But she couldn't allow him to hurt Daniel. She simply would not permit that.

Because I love him. More than my own life. Her heart swelled with the knowledge. Last night had been the most intensely pleasurable night of her life, but it had been so much more than sex. She'd felt as if their souls had joined.

The inexplicable bond that they'd created had made her feel like she had a home for the first time in all her life. Lacey bit back the sob that threatened to rack her body. *Oh Daniel. I'm sorry I never said it to you, but I hope you know it in your heart, I love you.*

She opened the front door as quietly as she could and went to meet her fate. Sadness gave way to anger as she spied the monster that threatened her and all she held dear. The man responsible for taking away her one shot at true happiness.

"Well, at least you can follow orders, slut," Tim sneered in her direction. His rifle still aimed at the large window that looked right into Daniel's bedroom. *That is so not happening.*

Ignoring the swirling snowflakes and the otherwise pristine beauty of the woods and lake surrounding them, Lacey focused on the madman who was holding her lover hostage. She needed to get that gun pointed away from Daniel.

"I'm here Tim. Isn't this what you wanted?" She pointed at herself and raised her eyebrows.

"Shut up, slut. You'll talk when I tell you to," the face she once thought pleasant turned to her with an animalistic snarl.

"Why did you call me out if you're not even going to look at your prize?"

"You fucking whore! You were perfect! MINE! Beautiful and untouched! Now you're just another slut!"

"I hate to break it to you, but I was never yours," she answered firmly. She hoped to make him focus on her, to give Daniel time to wake up. To get out of the line of fire.

"Shut up! Fucking cock tease! Your fucking Bear can't give you what I can! You'll be begging for me in the end!"

"I'm here now, Tim. Why don't you put the gun down and show me what I'm missing?" She taunted.

He turned then, a large, feral smile on his face. He was alone. Surprising really, since he never went anywhere alone.

"Afraid I'll kill lover boy? I don't need a gun for that," he growled deep and long.

Lacey flinched as her mind flashed back to the other night. God, was it just a few days ago? His claws popped out one at a time, his face lengthened, taking on the shape of his Wolf more and more with each passing second. Her eyes went wide. *Distract him,* her brain screamed at her.

"Where are your friends, Tim?" She thought if she could ask questions, maybe he'd retain his human form.

"Those pussies wouldn't go against the Alpha, but I'm stronger."

"Yeah, you're strong. So strong, Tim. Let's just go, leave here and you can do what you want," she needed him to leave here. To make sure Daniel was safe.

"Not until I kill the Bear. I'm stronger than him, Esme."

"No! You said you'd leave him alone if I came out," she cried out.

"You need to be punished, Esme. You'll see him die, but first," he roared and lunged for her, grabbing her hair in his fist.

A furious bellow sounded from behind her and Lacey turned to see Daniel in his Bear form charging through the snow to where they were standing. Tim snarled and threw her to the ground. He lunged for his rifle, but she sat up and grabbed him around the legs.

Daniel bellowed again, still running towards the struggling couple. Lacey screamed as Tim kicked her off his legs. She stood up just as he raised the barrel at her Bear.

With a loud yell, Lacey threw herself into Tim's side, hoping he would drop the weapon. But she wasn't strong enough. He still managed to get off a shot. The sound of Daniel's furious roar made her sink to her knees.

He was hurt. *No!* She tried to lunge for Tim, but he knocked her back, preparing to aim for her mate once more. Daniel was still thirty feet away. Too far to make it in time.

Lacey reached on the floor for something, anything to help her. Her fist closed over a rock and she brought it up, hurling the stone at Tim's head. It was getting harder to breathe, but she fought for air. Watching as the Wolf Shifter turned on her, snarling as he struggled to keep his shape.

"You little bitch!" he shouted and swung his fist at her, catching her on the temple.

Lacey fell back against the snow-covered ground. The sky was so pretty. A clear blue. *Like Daniel's eyes.* Her heart squeezed. She wished she'd had the chance to tell him that she loved him and that she'd have given anything to be his fated mate.

Still, she was grateful for the time they had. He was such a wonderful lover. And he'd definitely wanted her. She was sure of that.

Tim raised his rifle and aimed it at her. *At least he wasn't aiming it at Daniel anymore.* The movement was all the distraction her Bear needed. She watched through heavy lidded eyes as with an earth-shattering roar, the golden-headed Black Bear closed his huge jaws over Tim's wrist.

A sound blasted to her left and Lacey felt a heavy thud as she fought to stave off the darkness as long as she could. But there was nothing she could do about it. Resigned, she closed her eyes to the sound of Daniel's bear growling and Tim wailing in pain. *At least Daniel would be okay.* The darkness took her after that.

Lacey moaned as she woke. Her head throbbed in time with whatever was making that horrible banging noise. She tried to sit up, but a heavy hand pushed her gently back down against the bed. She struggled against the blanket, frightened for a minute before she blinked and opened her eyes.

"Easy, now. Sit up slowly, baby," Daniel spoke

softly, brushing her hair back and helping her to sit up.

"What's that noise?"

"Oh, my dad and my brothers are, uh, cleaning up the mess outside."

"Mess?" She asked, eyes going wide when she realized what he meant.

Daniel smiled softly and placed a pillow behind her head and dropped a soft kiss on her lips. Lacey sighed and felt herself tremble as she looked up at him.

Tears welled in her eyes as she brought her hands up to cup his handsome face. She wasn't bothered by the thought of whatever violence had occurred after she'd blacked out. He'd protected her after she failed to protect him.

"Daniel, I'm so sorry-"

"Shh, baby," he ground his teeth and closed his eyes.

His thick blonde eyebrows furrowing as he kissed her palm. He sucked in a deep breath as his lips touched her skin. Lacey felt her smile wobble as she spied the white bandage across his shoulder. It was visible in the gray tank top he wore.

"Daniel, you got hurt?" Her voice sounded

hoarse to her ears and he immediately handed her a glass of water.

"Here, sweetheart, drink this," he whispered as the cool liquid slid down her throat.

She sighed in relief as the water soothed and refreshed her. He handed her two ibuprofen tablets and she took those as well. Grateful for his care.

"You're okay now," he said as the reality of everything that had happened sunk in and threatened to break her.

"Oh God, Daniel, what happened to Tim? Are you okay?"

"You'll never hear from him again," he said, and his eyes went hard for a moment.

"I'm so sorry, Daniel."

"Hey now, easy. You have nothing to be sorry for," he slid in next to her and cradled her in his arms as she wrapped hers around his neck. They were in his cabin still, she noted. Pleased that he brought her there. it felt right. *Felt like theirs.*

"I'd never forgive myself if something happened to you," she murmured against his neck. There was no stopping the tears now. He was here, and she was safe, in his arms.

"I'm fine, baby. This is just a scratch."

"Oh God," she sobbed.

"I'm a Bear, I'll be good as new in a day, I swear it. But why didn't you wake me, baby?"

"He had his rifle trained on you. I saw the red light on your forehead," she shrugged. Too many emotions were crowding in on her and she felt overwhelmed.

"I got you, love," he said and held her/ he rubbed her back in smooth slow circles, "Thought I lost you, Lacey. Couldn't live without you."

"Oh Daniel," she slid up his body, careful of his wound and wrapped herself around him, sobbing into his neck. His arms, like steel bands, circled her waist and squeezed.

"Alright you two, that's enough of that now," said Clary as she bustled into the room with a folding table. Nate followed holding a tray with two bowls of chicken soup.

"Clary! Nate!"

"Well, of course, I'm here! Now, I'm gonna make sure you're back on your feet in no time, here's some good chicken soup for you both," the woman announced, while Nate opened the table and set the tray down on it.

"Hey Lacey, Daniel," he nodded but didn't look at either of them. *Smart Bear.* She elbowed Daniel when his Bear started to rumble at his presence.

"Well," Clary said looking at Daniel expectantly, "Get up and feed your mate! Haven't I taught you anything?"

"She can eat after Luisa has a look at her," Krissy, Taylor's mate, said from the doorway.

"Luisa's here?" Nate asked, but was largely ignored by the room. Daniel grunted and Lacey bit her lip nervously.

"Don't worry, baby, I'm not leaving. Luisa is Krissy's sister, she's a doctor," he held her hand and sat up, making sure she was covered by the blanket just as a serious faced woman with short blonde hair entered the room.

"Lacey, this is my sister, *Dr. Sposa*," Krissy grinned as she said it and the younger woman rolled her eyes.

"Hi Lacey, how are you feeling?" Luisa looked at everyone in the room, eyebrows raised, "You all mind clearing out and leaving me with my patient?"

No one moved until Daniel let out a little roar. Lacey just grinned. He was so protective of her! She loved it, though she realized she'd need to keep a lid on that. Didn't want him getting all cocky now, did she?

After chatting with doctor, Lacey allowed her to take some vitals and blood samples. She tried to ignore the tension between Nate and the pretty young doctor, but it was difficult. She wondered if maybe there wasn't something more going on there than meets the eye.

"Want anything else, baby," Daniel asked as he and Lacey ate the reheated soup Clary had made them.

"No, this is good," she smiled. And it was. Sure she wanted to talk with him, but she was so tired.

"Christmas Eve is coming soon, should we get a tree?"

Lacey was surprised by the normalcy of the question.

"Will I be here then?"

Daniel stopped in his tracks and looked at her, his blue eyes glowing with his bear.

"Mine," he growled possessively, and she felt heat flood her belly. *But was she really his?*

It was time for some answers.

ELEVEN

"Lacey, we need to talk," he began after he'd returned from the kitchen and his Neanderthal display.

"Is everyone still here?"

"No, uh, they took off. Marcus and Leya called after you though. They are coming home tomorrow and want to stop by if you are up for it."

"Sure. Did your dad leave too? He didn't have much to say," she remarked thinking it odd that the gray-haired man smiled and kissed her on the head before leaving though he hadn't said a word to her.

"Yeah," Daniel ducked his head.

"Look, I want you to know, I had a talk with him. Told him about where you stand with me," he flushed as he spoke and Lacey bit her lip. This sounded serious.

"And where do I stand?"

"Lacey," he looked at her with a confused expression, "you're my mate. I claimed you."

"I know, I was there, but I still don't know what it all means exactly," she shrugged, not yet fully clear about what any of it meant to him.

"I forget you're a normal sometimes," his raspy voice sounded good to her ears. He settled next to her in bed, his face hovering above hers as he traced her ear with his finger. He moved on to her eyebrows and her nose, lips next, and throat, down to the mark he'd left on her skin.

Shivers pulsated through her body, little flashes of lightning at his touch. Lacey licked her lips. She was antsy and nervous. She hadn't been allowed to leave the bed all day except to bathe.

Every Bear in the house had been overprotective. Bringing her things and keeping her company when Daniel was forced to leave to check the safeties and the perimeter of the Barvale Clan land.

It was troubling that the Wolf Shifter had been able to sneak up on them and he never wanted to be caught like that again. She'd understood really. And she put up with everybody's pampering. It was actually quite lovely, even if she didn't want to admit it.

"Lacey," his voice brought her back to the present, "Claiming you with my bite is the way I show the entre Shifter world that you belong to me. Now, I know you're a normal, and it sounds boorish, but I swear to you it is a good thing."

"I never said that, but it's like you think you own me or something now?"

"No. Not at all. Let me finish, baby. It's not ownership, it's just an announcement. Like normal wear wedding bands to announce they belong to each other."

"So, you belong to me too? Even though I didn't bite you?"

"Well, to be truthful now, I recall some biting and scratching on your end, baby," he growled and nipped her earlobe. Lacey flushed. *Yes, she did do that, didn't she?*

"So, are we like engaged?"

"More than that. We're together, good as married in the Shifter world."

"Oh," she said and tried not to frown. All her dreams of wedding bells and a long white dress crumbled with his words. She loved him and she was happy. *But every little girl dreams of having a big white wedding someday.*

"Now, it's true that I was engaged once. I'd rushed into something with someone who was utterly wrong for me. It was a mistake, and I never thought I would say this, but I thank God she left me. She wasn't the one."

"She wasn't?"

"How can *you* ask that of all people?" he tucked her hair behind her ear and nuzzled her nose with his. *God*, she loved it when he did that.

"Daniel?"

"Yeah, baby?"

"Clary told me a little about mates and fated mates, and I was wondering-" She paused and swallowed. Certain she was about to make a fool of herself.

"Wondering what?"

"Is it, *that is*, are we?"

"Lacey," he growled and kissed her lips, "don't you feel it too? This bond between us, my God, don't you know why I woke up like that and raced outside to you? Because I felt it in here," he tapped her chest over her heart, "I felt you saying goodbye and I couldn't stand it," his voice cracked, and she stared wide eyed as he went on.

"I tore out of my bed, out the front door, and saw him hit you and turn his gun on you and I lost it. For the first time in my life I was so fucking happy my Bear was so fucking untamed. It was all I could do to stop myself from ripping him to shreds," he growled.

"You killed him?" Her eyes went wide.

"Almost. I sure as fuck wanted to," he growled, but cut it off as he looked at her.

"My brothers stopped me. He's in custody now, shipped off to the High Alpha. He's like the boss of the bosses of Wolf Shifter society."

"Oh. I guess that's good then. Look, Daniel, I'm so sorry I put you through that. I just wanted to save you," tears snaked down her face, but she made no move to hide them.

"No, I am the one who is sorry. I should have done a better job protecting you, little one."

"Oh hush, you've done nothing but protect me."

"I can't help it, baby, the Bear is possessive, protective. Wants you so bad. All the damn time."

"Daniel," she gasped as happiness surged through her. She felt his love pulsing through the matebond they shared and reciprocated the feeling tenfold.

"I love you," she sighed.

"I love you too. I know I claimed you, but I want

to marry you as well, Lacey, will you?" he growled and snagged her close in a tight hug.

"Will you marry me?" He repeated the question and she realized she'd yet to answer.

"Yes! Yes, I will."

"You're finally mine, my sweet Lacey, and I'm yours."

"Yes. You're mine," she agreed, liking the feel of the possessive word on her lips. She may not be a Bear, but she loved just as hard as one. She crushed her lips against his.

"Are you sure about this," he asked as he slowly tugged away her clothing.

"I've never wanted anything more," she moaned, loving the feel of his mouth on hers.

They'd had fast and passionate, but with all that had happened between them, tonight they both wanted something different. She needed something else from him. Reassurance maybe. That he was there, unharmed.

A slow intensity grew between them as Daniel nestled between her thighs. Wanting to feel him everywhere, she ran her legs up and down the back of his calves and his thick muscled thighs. Her feet brushed his, as her hands travelled down to grip his powerfully built ass and hips.

Lacey bit back a moan at the immense pressure she felt as he pushed, slowly into her heat.

"Okay?" he asked, hissing a breath as he seated himself to the hilt inside of her.

"Yeah," she nodded capturing her lips with his.

"Love you," he moaned and began moving. Slow, long, languorous strokes that she felt all the way to her toes.

Pleasure and heat blossomed, their *matebond* making it all the more poignant. He whispered encouragingly as he licked her neck and kissed her flesh, tasting her, marking her. She knew now that the more their scents mingled, the happier his Bear was.

She was more than fine with that. Lacey moaned his name as he increased the pressure. Hips jerking, she rose up to meet his thrusts, marveling at the slow roll of his hips. *Damn*, he was incredible.

"Baby, gonna roll you on your side," he moaned and positioned her so that they faced each other. One leg wrapped around his waist as he gripped the other with one hand.

Slowly, carefully, he pumped. Lacey cried out, nails raking his back as he plunged in and out of her slick, wet sex with increasing urgency. Joy filled her as Daniel worked her body into a frenzy.

"Love you, baby," he said as he pushed her from one peak to another until she thought she'd die of it.

"Daniel," she moaned, her back arching, breath gasping.

"Now, baby," he ground her against him, nipping her neck in the same spot where he'd claimed her the night before.

White hot sparks exploded behind her eyelids as she cried his name. On and on it went, a rising tide of ecstasy that throbbed and tore at her heart. She felt his love fill her, soothe her and she knew he was right. They were fated mates.

Mine. Forever.

EPILOGUE

P arker Fiore snapped his camera and looked briefly at the huge man standing behind his shoulder. He supposed he could forgive him for being protective of his new wife.

Esme Alain, or Lacey, as she insisted on being called, was probably the most beautiful model he'd ever worked with. She'd called him up after some accident had left her with a slight scar along her hairline, explaining that she wouldn't be able to fulfill their contract.

He'd insisted on seeing her immediately and when he did, he could've kissed her! Not that he tried it. Not with that huge Bear of a man grumbling behind her.

The scar gave her depth. It was so slight, but the knowledge of it, he'd explained, made her real. And here he was seven months later, doing a full pregnancy shoot starring the newly married supermodel, Esme!

"Yes, darling, now if you could turn to the left. That's it," Parker instructed as he snapped off some more shots.

He'd wanted her nude for the shoot, but her husband was rather convincing when he'd suggested she wear a bolt of green silk to bring out her eyes. Damn the man for being right. The material was fabulous against her ivory skin. Strategically placed to hide her *assets*, he was still able to showcase her perfectly round belly.

"Finished yet, Fiore?" Daniel Devlin grumbled.

"One more minute, please," Parker found he could be gracious to the man. Especially since he'd bought the gallery that housed his work and was funding this little exhibit.

"Now. My wife needs to rest," the large man moved right into the shoot and wrapped his wife in the silk material before lifting her up in his arms.

Certain no one was looking, he snapped off a few images of the gorgeous couple. Later, he'd label the pictures a *study in love* certain that he had never seen and never would a more in love couple in his entire career.

Later that evening...

"Daniel! The baby!" Lacey grinned as her husband came bolting into the room.

"What is it time? It's too early!" He yelled as he dropped the platter of fruit, he'd been making her to snack on, on the smooth wood floor.

The AC was blasting, as was the enormous flat-screen television he'd gotten her for their first Christmas after learning she liked to have one in the bedroom. Not that it got much use. So many better things to do in this room, she thought with a smile.

Still, despite all the noise, she had no problem hearing her Bear roar. He was so damned cute when he came running in with an apron thrown around his waist.

He took his roles as mate, husband, and expectant father very seriously. She loved him fiercely for it. Especially when he was being overprotective like he was now.

"No, not that," she laughed and grabbed his hand placing it on the huge swell of their child, "Feel that? He's kicking!"

Daniel smiled. His eyes wide as he felt the proof of his love for his mate. Pure joy pulsed between the two of them as their love filled the room.

"Isn't it wonderful?" She said, a small tear escaping her emerald eyes.

"You're wonderful," he answered, and the truth of his statement shone in his blue eyes.

"I'm also kinda hungry," she began with her bottom lip between her teeth. The little Bear growing inside of her was a bottomless pit.

"Well, I dropped the fruit, unfortunately, but Clary did drop off a special batch of *stollen*," Daniel began and smiled widely at Lacey's wide eyes.

"She did? But she only makes it for Christmas!"

"Not when she's got a new mama to feed," Daniel grinned and kissed her on the lips, rubbing her stomach in tiny, gentle circles with his large, capable hands.

"I love you, Daniel. So much. Thank you for giving me this, for giving me you, a home, a family," she sighed into his arms as he embraced her gently.

"I should be thanking you, baby. You've given me everything I've ever wanted and so much more. I love you."

Her stomach grumbled and the couple laughed.

"Yes, baby, I'm gonna feed your mama. Give her everything she needs."

"I just need you," Lacey opened her arms and kissed her mate. Reveling in the way they fit perfectly together. *Mine. Ours.*

The end.

BEARLY MATED

BEARLY MATED

A BEAR CLAW TALE #4

To the dreamers...don't stop.
del mare alla stella, C.D. Gorri

USA TODAY BESTSELLING AUTHOR
C.D. GORRI
Bearly
MATED
A BEAR CLAW TALE 4
A BEAR CLAW TALE

BLURB

He's an artist, she's a doctor, can their worlds mix long enough for them to be mated?

Nate Cordoza is just discovering his family of half-brothers and his absentee father when he runs across the one being he never thought he'd find, his mate.

Luisa Sposa has no time for men! The young doctor is too busy with her new job at the Barvale Urgent Care Clinic to worry about a relationship.

Fate steps in when the two of them are thrown together as part of a destination wedding party. A little bit of magic and a whole lot of tequila later, the two Shifters wake up mated!

Will Luisa open her heart to Nate, or will she end up barely mated?

A MESSAGE FROM DANIEL, ONE OF THE DEVLIN BROTHERS...

Hello Clan members,

You know me as the head Clan Enforcer, but my name is Daniel Devlin.

First, on behalf of my brother and his new mate and wife, Krissy, we'd like to thank all of you for your well wishes for the newlyweds. We also wanted to say thanks for the two dozen of you who managed to fly down to Cozumel for their destination wedding.

The resort on the Playa del Carmen was simply beautiful and the tequila was plentiful! Anyone with any photos or video clips of the celebration that evening is encouraged to send those images to Taylor and Krissy for their approval before posting to the Barvale Clan website forum. Use your best judgement. Thanks.

I am also pleased to announce that my mate and I

are settling into life after the arrival of our sweet cub. Again your well wishes and baby gifts are all very appreciated. Lacey and Mia send their love.

As head Enforcer, it is my pleasure to inform you that my brother, Nate Cordoza, has been officially inducted into the Barvale Clan. Not only that, but he has volunteered to teach his substantial skills in combat and surveillance to our new recruits. You met them at our last Clan gathering. Bowie Atiqtalaaq has joined us from Alaska along with his cousins, the Nanouk triplets, Locke, Tonic, and Bolder.

The four Polar Bear Shifters are a welcome addition to our New Jersey Clan, bringing with them some much appreciated muscle and enthusiasm. As we all saw during our run with the Arizona Wolves, these four Bears were more than handy at controlling the crowd!

Now, what I am about to tell you is troubling news, but do not panic. Our friends of the Macconwood Pack have notified us of some recent trouble with a group of rogue Hunter Vampires. In case you are not familiar with the term, these are creatures no longer in touch with their humanity. They are dangerous and non-discriminating in whom they hunt. If you see them do not engage. Call the Clan emergency hotline for help. Our new Enforcers will be responsible for the security of our Clan under my order.

Any questions you may have can be directed to our Clan Keeper, my brother Taylor. You can reach him directly on his new cell number, 663-386-2327 (That's ONE-DUM-BEAR). He's available to you at any time.

As usual, you can typically find us at Bear Claw Bakery or supervising the ongoing additions to our new Bear Cub Park right here in Barvale! Special thanks to our Falk Clan neighbors, the creators of Draco Fortis, for the donation of some pretty awesome security tech for the park.

Marcus, our Alpha, is back in residence with his mate at the Den, should you need him and Ignatius, retired Alpha is home as well.

Also, I am pleased to announce our very own official Clan doctor! You can meet her at our new Barvale Urgent Care Clinic, secret hours for Clan members will be held on Tuesdays, Thursdays, and Fridays 4pm-2am. It is my pleasure to introduce our very own, Dr. Luisa Sposa.

Also, please note, cubs experiencing their first Change are welcome to contact her to discuss anything they are experiencing. That's all for now.

Thank you,

Daniel Devlin, Barvale Clan Enforcer and co-owner of Bear Claw Bakery Inc.

PROLOGUE

"What the fuck, Daniel?" Marcus roared with his copy of the Barvale Clan newsletter in his hand.

It was still early morning, but the Alpha had been up for hours. Morning sickness, not his, but his mate's, was a constant companion and it was wearing thin on his nerves.

"What did I do?" Daniel asked trying hard not to gaze adoringly at his mate and cub who were sitting over at the old scarred table in the Den's kitchen.

"You gave out that ridiculous fucking phone number you got me? For fuck's sake, Danny," Taylor grumbled.

"What? I told you I didn't want to write the damn thing!" Daniel replied angrily.

"Hey all, what's with all the ruckus?" Nate entered the Den's kitchen to see Clary, the Devlin boys' housekeeper and fellow Bear Shifter, humming to herself as she stirred a large pot of what smelled like the beginnings of a savory clam chowder. The woman was a damn fine cook if he did say so himself. Usually, he loved a good chowder, but he was preoccupied as he had been for days now.

Leya, Krissy, and Lacey, the three most important women in the lives of his powerful and sometimes grumpy as fuck brothers, were sitting around the large kitchen table, *oohing* and *aahing* over the new addition to their family. Little Mia, his adorable baby niece, was doing something marvelous like gurgling or blinking with her wide bright eyes, while his three half-brothers were facing off in the middle of it all.

"Guys?" He tried again. The growing tension made his Bear want to burst free of his skin and that would not be a good thing with the way he was feeling just then.

"Did you see this?" Taylor demanded tossing his cell phone at Nate, who easily snatched it out of the air. Shifter reflexes and all.

It was only a few days after Taylor's and Krissy's destination wedding and as he skimmed the newsletter, Nate tried not to grin. Yup. Daniel had put his foot in it this time. Giving out a newly married man's cell phone number was kinda insensitive. Especially since he'd assigned the cell phones to the immediate members of the family as Head Enforcer.

"You know Daniel made sure his cell number spelled out *one-dum-bear*, right?" Leya asked from her chair, her ever-growing belly was pushed up against the wood and Nate wondered if it bothered her for a second. Not that he stared long, he didn't want to piss Marcus off. Taylor frowned at his sister-in-law and Nate wondered if the man really wanted to leave his mate a widow so soon?

"Yes, love, we knew that. You need anything?"

"No thank you, I'm fine," she smiled radiantly with that special glow pregnant women seemed to have.

Marcus smiled down at his mate with a look of love so strong Nate felt himself blushing. Damn what he wouldn't give to be able to express himself so freely. *Luisa,* he thought and turned to see Marcus drop a solid punch right on Taylor's arm, probably for daring to frown at his beloved mate. *Sensitive much? Fuck yeah.*

"Ow! What? You know he's the fucking jackass here!" Taylor threw a kitchen towel at Daniel who ignored it as he bent over his precious daughter to tickle her tummy.

The baby was just learning to sit up on her own and even Nate had to admit, she was pretty darn amazing. *Cubs. My cubs. Mate. Now.* His half-grizzly half-Black Bear grumbled from inside of him and he turned his back on his brothers antics for a moment to get himself under control.

Shit. He'd hoped to have this crap all handled by now, but she was avoiding him. *Luisa,* the bear growled her name again. He felt his Shift coming on strong. *Fuck.*

He ran out of the house, hitting the woods before he could burst out of his clothes. *Again.* Shit was happening pretty damn frequently since he'd been back from Mexico.

"Nate?"

"Bro?"

"You alright?"

He ignored his brothers' calls and kept running, needing to put space between them before he confessed his sins to them all. Krissy was gonna be pissed. That was a given. But what the hell was he supposed to do?

Finding his half-brothers had been a real experience as far as he was concerned. *Hell.* Who knew the Devlin's would welcome his sorry ass with open arms? His own little Texas Clan didn't even want him. After the death of his mother, he had no reason to stay in that shitty little town full of bigoted Shifters who hated him for being a half breed.

Well, fuck them, he thought, as he always did when that small Clan he'd grown up in invaded his mind. The letter he'd discovered from his father, Ignatius Devlin, to his mother had brought him here and he hadn't regretted it since.

Sure, it was awkward at times, but he'd made peace with the old man. Iggy, he couldn't bring himself to call him dad, had never known about Nate. Not until he'd come to Barvale and gotten summoned to the Den by Marcus after accidentally hitting on Taylor's mate.

He hadn't known the curvy Bear Shifter, now Taylor's wife, was taken. Her scent had been mildly attractive, and she was good to look at. Of course, now he knew why he'd taken an instant liking to the she-Bear. It was all because of *her*.

Luisa Sposa. The new doctor in town was shorter than her sister Krissy. Sexier too, in Nate's eyes. The she-Bear had chin length blonde hair and stunningly large eyes the color of ground espresso beans. She had full breasts and an indented waist that flared out to rounded hips made to tempt any man to sin.

She looked like a 1950's pin-up girl, all curves and legs in a petite package. *A body heaven made for sin.* And she was all his. Nate's fated mate or she would be if she just accepted it already. *Fuck me.*

He opened his large jaws and let out a mighty roar. The beast angry and wanting his mate. *Mine.* His angry tread tore up the grass as he sank his claws into the moist earth. He'd run all the way from the Den, but the Bear was still angry.

He needed an outlet for all his frustrations, but nothing would work. *He needed her.* Rejection stung and the pain of their separation burned through him. *Worthless*, he thought, and his Bear growled deep and low.

His animal did not like it when Nate blamed himself for his mate's skittishness. He urged the man to be patient but firm. To show her he was hers. *Claim.*

Nate paused his huge furry body for a second as he got near the shore of Lake Ursa. His Bear stood up on his back legs and watched the still water as his human mind wandered back to just the week before.

Seven days, ten hours, and forty-three minutes earlier...

Mexico was hot. Like really fucking warm. Especially to a half-Grizzly half-Black Bear. The plans were made, security set, and Nate Cordoza had nothing else to do. So, he changed into a pair of swim trunks immediately upon arrival.

He'd opted for a dip in the ocean while the others chose to get ready for the party. He didn't understand the fuss. Shower, shave, put on clothes, what was it that took others so fucking long?

Here he was for Krissy and Taylor's destination wedding. *Whatever the fuck that was.* He didn't really know. Apparently, it was a trend nowadays. To a Texas boy, a trip to Mexico meant hopping in his truck and taking a weekend to drive down to the Gulf.

To his New Jersey brethren, it was more like a week-long party at an exclusive resort that began with a trip in the Bear Claw Bakery private jet. *Fuckers sold a lot of pastry*, he thought fondly.

Shit. He wasn't poor. Not exactly. But Nate wasn't a billionaire. He'd worked his way through college earning his degrees in Fine Arts and Graphic Design online. It had been touch and go as money wasn't the easiest to come by in his youth, but he'd done it. Sure, his mother had helped, but he'd paid her back before the end. Thinking of her still made his hearts squeeze in his chest. She was the only person in the world who ever truly loved him.

After graduating, he then put his considerable skills to use for Grave Industries. Nate was the sole creator of several one-of-a-kind illustrations for the online roleplaying game, *WolfMoon*, that launched the Werewolf owned company into stardom.

He'd even gotten Krissy, his soon to be sister-in-law, to pose for him before she'd officially mated Taylor, his half-brother. *Good thing too.*

No mated Shifter was going to let an unmated male near his woman. Especially not naked as she'd been in order for him to capture her during her Shift. She was a wonderful girl. Real in a way many weren't in this cyberage of instant gratification and self-importance. Taylor was a lucky Bear.

Nate smiled at the waiters and hotel staff as he jogged down to the sand. Pools were alright, but he preferred natural swimming holes like lakes. He just loved the sea. His Bear was sensitive to artificial things, so chlorine filters were out, but saltwater was just fine with him. The sun shone down on his dark head as he tossed his t-shirt onto what he thought was an empty lounge chair.

"Hey!" the voice seemed to reach out and stroke

his beast, the Bear inside him taking notice immediately.

"Shit. Sorry, honey, I didn't see you over the back there," he grinned as he walked around to the front of the lounge chair to get a better view of the owner of that familiar voice. *Luisa Sposa.*

The scent of the ocean had momentarily kept her sweet vanilla mint fragrance from reaching his nostrils, but now that he knew she was there it immediately invaded his senses. Warm and bright, just like her it stirred his Bear and other things. *Fuck,* he just hoped his trunks were big enough. *Grrr.*

As usual, his Bear was standing up and taking stock of her presence. The same way the beast did whenever she was anywhere near. *Mine.* Nate smiled and played off the intensity with which his Bear prodded the ground of the metaphysical plane of reality where he resided when Nate walked the Earth on two feet.

He'd done a pretty good job keeping his distance from the petite she-Bear. It hadn't been easy. Not when he knew what he knew about her. A whole year of wanting and waiting since he'd first seen the small beauty.

"Yeah, yeah, I am aware that I'm short," she

replied and crinkled her pert nose before standing up in front of him.

The top of her head barely reached his shoulder and it was damned near impossible to stop himself from reaching out and gathering her in his arms. *Mine.* Still, he resisted. He knew she needed time.

"Not short, honey, you're *petite.* Petite and perfect," he countered with his best smile on his face in an attempt to seem friendly and not so overwhelming.

Though, truth be told, his Bear wanted him to just toss her over his shoulder and drag her away to some cave where he could spend the next few days claiming her and marking her over and over again.

"Same difference, cowboy," she snorted the last word as if it was funny and sashayed past him in her teeny tiny, hot pink bikini.

Nate growled at seeing all that sumptuous skin on display. Silky and smooth. Her lush curves were highlighted by the sun. The valley between her ample breasts on display as was the curve of her ass in those barely there bottoms.

Shit. His cock grew hard just glimpsing her sweet form. There was no denying that Luisa had a killer body. He could just picture her wrapped around him. *Grrr.* Probably a bad idea in his yellow swim shorts, he huffed out a breath and followed her towards the surf. He needed to cool down fast.

Those tiny pink triangles did nothing to cover her. She was temptation and promise personified. His gaze was rivetted to her as she walked away on those long legs. *Yup*, despite her short stature, those babies were about a mile long and led up to full hips, a gorgeous peach of an ass, then finally, to her small, softly indented waist.

Fuck. If he could see all that hotness, it meant others could too. His head whipped right and left glaring at the other beach goers who were gawking at her as if they had any right. Shifters were notoriously possessive over there mates. *But she's not ours yet*, he reminded the Bear.

Grrr. Mine. Shit. Nate counted to ten and closed his eyes. He tried to put a leash on his beast, to stop the animal from becoming enraged. Sure, the animal inside him had recognized her as his fated mate a year ago, but he hadn't exactly approached her about the fact that she was his one and only just yet.

He wasn't a coward, but Luisa was a *doctor* and a precious she-Bear. There weren't many female Shifters out there to be claimed these days. Where he was from, they were often saved and used as bargaining tools for trading with other Clans.

Fucked up and ancient, yes, but that's the way it was. The Barvale Clan was different, that was true, but he couldn't help but think he wasn't good enough. She deserved so much more than he had to offer. *No. We are meant to be. Perfect. Destiny. Mates,* the Bear argued, and Nate couldn't fault him for that. The Bear wanted his mate. *Now.*

The whole concept of fated mates was something of a fairytale to Nate. Though lately it seemed the universe had chosen to grant that special blessing to all Shifters once more, if his contacts through his work for *WolfMoon* were to be believed.

Perhaps it was because of dwindling numbers, or maybe it was the destruction of the old Werewolf curse, the curse of Natalis, that had affected all of the Shifter World, whether they knew it or not.

It didn't really matter to Nate. He just knew one thing was true above all else. The very prim and proper, maybe even a little uptight, Luisa Sposa was all his. *Mine.* And he'd been trying for months now just to get her to smile at him without being a pushy jerk.

He watched as she dove beneath the waves, holding his breath until he spotted her pretty little blonde head surfacing once again. Determined to ignore him as always, he noted with a frown. She seemed to purposefully swim towards a group of single young men wading in the surf.

He heard them greet her and her noncommittal response. The woman was a hard ass. He'd often admired her spunk and sass, but he was on edge. Especially with her splashing so close to those men. *Grrr.* He'd given her the space he thought she needed, perhaps he'd given her too much?

He frowned as one man, tall for a normal, swam up to her and reached out to take a small clump of seaweed out of her hair. He was all teeth, smiling at her as if he had a secret and couldn't wait to share. And she was eating it up! Nate had to pull out all the stops just then, holding on to his beast by the back of his neck while he watched the normal whisper something into her ear.

Whatever it was, she must not have liked it. Luisa's dark eyes narrowed, and Nate's Bear reacted. His animal surging forward, prickling along his skin, but before he could swim out to her, his fiery little honey reached out with one closed fist and socked the stunned normal right square in his jaw.

Prim and proper she might be some of the time, but the rest of the time his soon-to-be mate was a total badass. Pride and satisfaction flowed through him. She was perfect.

The normal held onto his no doubt aching jaw and looked as if he was about to say something back to her. Wisely, the fool noticed the tall, menacingly dark shadow that had fallen over him. He looked behind him to see Nate standing right next to where the guy paddled to stay afloat. In the five and half feet of water, Nate's extremely tall frame stood a good eighteen inches above the near clear liquid.

"You were saying?" Nate drawled.

"Uh, nothing. My apologies, if you'll just excuse me," he murmured and swam back towards his group. Nate followed him with his eyes, making sure he did indeed swim towards his buddies before turning back to Luisa.

"I had that," she said, treading water, "you don't have to recue me."

"I know that, honey girl, but I couldn't just stand there," he said in a low voice.

"Fine," she replied.

"Fine," he echoed unable to resist the urge to trace the line of her face from her pale blonde hairline, to her dark brown eyebrows, all the way to her plump pink lips. *Satin*, her skin felt like satin in the water against his fingertips.

"It is natural, in case you were wondering too,"

she muttered. He looked at her, cocked his head to the side waiting for an explanation.

"*My hair*. I'm a natural blonde but my eyebrows and lashes are dark," she shrugged as if that explained whatever question she'd imagined he'd asked. Then it hit him *Hell*.

He wanted to turn around and go after the *sonovabitch* who dared ask her such a thing! *Grrr*.

"Hey cowboy, I'm fine," she said with her small hand on his shoulder. The contact sent lightning strikes of awareness zipping through his body and he couldn't help but growl. *Mine*.

Her eyes widened, the chocolate depths swallowing him whole and he cursed the stupid fucking normal for talking such foulness to his woman. *Shit*. None of it mattered to him. Hair color, eye color, height, weight. Nate didn't care if her eyebrows were blonde, brown, or purple. She was beautiful. Perfect. *Mine*.

"Luisa," he began. For a moment it looked as if she was softening to him. Her head tilted back, both hands resting on his broad shoulders and he slowly pulled her closer in the water, holding her afloat.

His eyes glittered at her as she swallowed nervously. He didn't want her nervous. *No*. He wanted her blind with passion and deep in lust like he was. *Fuck.* It was more though. So much more than a physical itch he needed to scratch.

It was his heart she held in his hands whether she knew it or not. Suddenly she pushed off him and he would've stumbled if not for the water. His she-Bear packed a powerful punch indeed.

"Save it, cowboy. I've got to go. Bridesmaid duties and all," she said quickly and headed for shore.

Damn. He just watched as she got out of the water and walked with her back straight to gather her towel and wrap it around her luscious curves. Then she just walked away from him. Never looking back. Not even once.

Sassy little thing. His Bear wanted her even more for it. Not only was she gorgeous and smart, but she was strong-willed as well. A real hellion. *She will make a good mate*, the animal grumbled in his mind's eye.

A wolf whistle sounded from that same throng of *normals*, and Nate growled loudly in their direction. His beast enjoyed the way they yelped and swam for the shore. *Fucking better run. She's mine.*

Nate snorted and dove once more under the surf. Maybe he could clear his head if he swam hard enough or long enough. But the truth was, the water wasn't deep enough for him to drown out the burning desire that roared to life every time he looked at her. She was everything to him. His heart and soul cried out for her, but she refused to acknowledge it, to accept him. Pain radiated through him at her rejection.

And seven days, ten hours, and forty-five minutes after that day in Mexico, he still couldn't forget her. Mine.

"Hey Nate, why'd you run off?" Daniel's Bear communicated with his through their Clan bond. The strange intrusion was oddly welcomed. At the very least, it shook him out of his painful memories.

"Yeah, bro, what's up," asked Taylor, still in his human form.

Nate grumbled and pounded the earth with his front claws. He didn't want to talk about it. Didn't know how to admit what he'd done. Daniel head-butted him from behind, hardly moving him.

The slightly smaller, yet strong as fuck Black Bear was obviously trying to get him to open up. But Nate wasn't ready.

The ground shook as another Bear joined them. This Black Bear was large, thick, and brawnier than all of them, with darker fur and huge fangs that he bared for all three of his brothers.

"Yes, Marcus, you're the Alpha," said Taylor and yet, despite his sarcasm, he averted his eyes in reverence to his oldest brother's position.

Continuing to use his mind link, Nate faced his three half-brothers. He wasn't sure what to do. His old Clan had different rules, practically none when it came to women's rights. Instinctively, he knew the Barvale Clan was different, even though he was still unaware of the particulars.

"Okay," he said, manning up and facing his brothers, "I have something to tell you about me and Luisa."

"Luisa?" asked Taylor. It seemed that even the mention of his sister-in-law set him on guard.

"Yes. I, uh, we're mated. She and I."

"What?" Taylor roared.

"Oh fuck, man, Krissy's gonna be pissed," snorted Daniel.

"Nate," said Marcus, silencing the others, "please, explain."

"Look, I've known she was the one, my fated mate since your engagement party, Marcus-"

"That was a year ago," he said and if Bear's could frown, his was. *Deeply.*

"Yes. I know that. I've been trying to give her time, space," he said and paced again.

"Go on," growled his Alpha.

"At the wedding, Luisa had been drinking some shots of tequila-"

"Like sixteen shots of that hard, clear stuff," snorted Daniel again and Nate just growled at the man. Fucking dick couldn't give him a break.

"Okay, she'd been drinking a fuck load of shots of tequila. We'd had words earlier, flirting if you will, and she was, I don't know, feeling good I guess and one thing led to another-" he'd Changed back to his human form before he knew it, unable to talk about her, about what he'd done, as his Bear. Hell, the beast saw nothing wrong with it, but the man knew better.

He needed to be human, to speak with his voice instead of his mind. Little did he know he should've kept his fur. The sound of his brother moving met his ears too late after his rushed Change back to human.

"Fuck," he grunted as he stumbled. Pain exploded behind his right temple and he bared his teeth ready to retaliate before he got his bearings.

"You dick! That's my wife's little sister!"

"Easy, easy," Daniel switched skins and was now standing between Nate and Taylor with both hands raised. The Enforcer ready to take both of them apart should the need arise.

"Enough," roared Marcus. The fact that three of the brothers were standing in the summer heat, dicks swinging in the wind, seemed to matter very little to all of them. Shifters were pretty much used to nudity.

"Look, no disrespect to Luisa, but I am assuming you two had sex? She was a consenting adult?" Nate growled, eyes smartly averted, but answered his Alpha's question with a quick nod.

"So, what is the issue?" Marcus continued.

"I marked her."

Fists flew at the statement. A few well aimed kicks too. Nate would have been able to hold his own had he not already been feeling like shit as a result of being apart from his mate over the past week. The thud of his body hitting the ground beneath his two brothers' combined weight echoed loudly throughout the woods. As was their Alpha's bellowed commands following the free for all that had begun at his announcement.

"Get off him, you idiots," Marcus held his head as the three younger Bears stood up slowly. Blood trickled from Taylor's nose where Nate had elbowed him, and Daniel was wheezing, trying to catch his breath.

"Guess that sympathy weight thing is real?" remarked Taylor who got another elbow, this one from Daniel, right in his gut.

"Oof!" Taylor groaned and sank to his knees, while Nate high-fived Daniel.

"Right," Daniel said and nodded.

Nate hadn't noticed really, but he supposed the older Bear had gained a few pounds during his wife's pregnancy. Not that he was unfit in any way. The guy was a brick fucking house as far as Nate was concerned.

"Okay, fuckheads, you ready to listen?" Marcus asked. They were Bears, not idiots, so the three younger men nodded.

"Good. Now, if you marked Luisa, may I ask why you're not living with her? Hell, how the fuck is your Bear not tearing you a new asshole for being apart from her?" His honest curiosity surprised Nate who wasn't sure he'd ever get used to an Alpha who was as caring and open as his older brother.

"Well," he hedged, not sure his brothers would believe him.

"Well *what*?"

"Yeah man, I'd fucking go nuts if I'd been separated from Lacey after we mated," Daniel added.

"Well, it's been hard alright," he grumbled and ran a hand through his thick hair.

"So?"

"So, she's been ignoring me."

"What?"

"Oh dude, you gotta be kidding me?"

"Wish I was, man. Truth is, I think she wants her career more than she wants a mate," he finally admitted out loud and the truth of it fell on him like a ton of bricks crushing his chest.

"How is your Bear not ripping you apart balls first?" asked Daniel, his voice incredulous.

"It's a near fucking thing," Nate growled.

"Okay, boys, we need a plan."

Nate looked at his three brothers and furrowed his eyebrows. The three men who looked a bit like him, who had grown up together, had readily taken him in with nothing more than a little instinct and a letter his mama had saved. Tears threatened to appear in his eyes, and he blinked hard against them because you know, he was a man after all and fuck that shit.

"What do you mean *a plan?*" He cleared his throat and asked.

"Well, little brother, I am talking about a fucking foolproof Bear Claw Bakery brotherhood plan," said Marcus.

"Hell yeah," said Daniel.

"Hell to the fucking yeah," echoed Taylor.

A loud rumble echoed from their left and all four boys looked to see a slightly graying, large Black Bear amble towards them. The four men tensed before Marcus broke out into a wide grin.

"Am I late?" The huge Bear spoke through their Clan link.

"Nope," Marcus answered.

"Good. Hello boys. Nate," he nodded his great ursine head at the new addition to this family.

"Let's get you properly mated, son," said Ignatius Devlin and all three of his half-brothers nodded their agreement.

Well, alright, thought Nate.

Luisa stretched her back as she headed for the pot of what was probably stale or burnt coffee in the doctor' lounge at this time of night.

The Barvale Urgent Care Clinic was a twenty-four-hour operation open to *normals* and *supernaturals*, but most of her patients tended to be from her Clan. The Bear Shifters of Barvale, New Jersey were a rowdy group made up of a couple of hundred Black Bear Shifters and the odd Kodiak, Grizzly, and Polar here and there. Transplants to the northeastern state, but welcome, nonetheless.

The Devlin brothers opened the Clinic for the community as part of their give back program, having made billions when they'd decided to go international with *Bear Claw Bakery*. Who knew the entire world would go nuts for some organic, non-GMO, honey glazed sweets?

Not that she could blame anyone. Those bear claws were damn good, and with Leya, the Alpha's mate, heading up their new marketing campaigns, she wouldn't be surprised to see their goods featured at the White House and the United Nations! As it was, she rummaged through the leftovers on the break table and was disappointed to find every single one of them gone! *Pooh!*

She cringed at the faux curse word but having to work with kids meant cleaning up her potty mouth. Krissy had laughed at her when she told her what she was trying to do, but she just glared at her older, happily mated sister. *No, I will not think about mates cause then I'll think about him and I have work to do!*

Back to the bakery. She'd almost gone nuts when a certain royal couple with a brand-new baby was seen with a specially shipped box of fresh strawberries and cream claws just the other day! Luisa sighed. Boy was that redheaded prince gorgeous! Okay, so she used to have quite a thing for naughty Prince Harry. Although lately her taste ran to tall, tanned, green eyed Bears.

Grrr. Her she-Bear raised herself up in that meta-physical plane of reality where she existed when Luisa wore her human skin. *Easy there*, she hushed her Bear. She knew why the animal was angry, but she didn't want to think about it.

Sixteen hours into her double shift, she still had a long way to go before she could get home and rest. *No rest. Get mate.* The she-Bear inside her was pissed as hell. *One week. You've denied us a full week. Want. Now.* Luisa closed her eyes and counted to ten.

It had been one week. Her Bear was correct about that. One week since her sister Krissy had finally married the man of her dreams, Taylor Devlin. One week since their private jet had touched down in the hot and tempestuous Cozumel, Mexico. One week since she'd been claimed by her mate.

"Shit, I mean, *pooh!*" She groaned, unconsciously rubbing that spot over her heart where he'd bitten down, slicing through her flesh like butter and staking his claim for the entire Shifter world to see. Shivers ran through her body at the light contact and she whimpered as her sex grew moist and pulsed with need.

"Excuse me, doctor?" Nurse Colby opened the door, poking his shaggy brown head in and stopping when he saw her. She quickly straightened, not wanting him or any other male to see her like that. *Just Nate.*

Colby was young and dedicated. A Clanmate who'd managed to rise out of the stigma of being a male nurse in the highly patriarchal society of Shifters. He came from a good hardworking family and claimed to love his chosen profession. Luisa knew him from high school. Colby Lee was a good man, a good Bear, and a damn good nurse. She nodded her head expectantly waiting for him to continue.

"Uh, we got, Clan problems," he murmured low enough so that any normal passing would not hear, but she had no trouble discerning his words. She ignored the slight flare of his nostrils and glittering of his eyes. Staring at him cool as any ice queen she nodded her head.

"Alright, Nurse Colby. Remember we're calling them Code Black for now?" He ducked his head, cheeks blazing pink. Clearly, he'd forgotten, but she'd let it slide. They'd only been open a few weeks and this was new to all of them.

Shifters were not known in regular society. Their survival depended on keeping themselves separate, a secret from *normals* or the human world. *Normals could be such monsters,* she cringed at the thought.

Of course, there were some who felt that Shifters and others should come out and live openly in society, but Luisa knew better. She'd gone to college and medical school. Saw what people did to things they didn't understand. *A hundred years of modern medicine and we are still glorified butchers*, she thought with a frown.

She shook her head away from the melancholic turn of thought. It wasn't anyone's fault that technology had simply not caught up yet with the medical world. Yes, there were amazing advances every day, but the really miraculous ones were kept somewhere in a lab under lock and key. *Doing no one any real good*, she thought again angrily.

"Doctor?" Colby interrupted her thoughts as she took a swig of the bitter black coffee in her mug. *Ugh. Must be a day old at least!*

"Yes, I'm coming," she sighed and followed the tall nurse down the clean corridor to exam room three.

The familiar scent of autumn sage and sun kissed skin assaulted her nostrils. Her heart sped up. What was he doing here? Then the coppery aroma of fresh spilled blood hit her, and she almost stumbled.

Nothing you haven't smelled a thousand times before, she reminded herself angrily. *And yet.*

Straightening her shoulders, Luisa stepped into the room. Her Bear roared at the sight that met her eyes.

Four enormous Bear Shifters crowded the table in the small area. All of them reeked of sweat, fur, and earth. Not bad smells, but out of place for her sterile clinic. Her curiosity would have to wait.

She pushed through the throng, ignoring them as she neared the table. Her sense of urgency growing with every second. Her Bear was nearly in a rage. She'd smelled her mate, and he was injured!

"Nate?" The question sprang from her lips as she took in his form. He was lying on the table with blood gushing from his head.

"Hey now, honey girl. There you are," he smiled, his Texas drawl thick with his nearly unconscious state.

"What the hell, I mean, *heck*, happened?" She blurted out the question as she checked his pupils and ordered tests.

"Well, you see Doc, it's complicated is what it is," Bowie stepped forward. She recognized him as one of four recent transplants from some far away Polar Bear Clan up in Alaska.

He was hugely tall and muscled, with a shock of white hair against his caramel colored skin. Ice blue eyes looked into hers, and she could sense his regret.

"Complicated? It looks like somebody hit him with a crowbar," she growled and struggled to take off his shirt. One of the other Polar Bears, a set of triplets if she recalled correctly, lifted him, while another stripped the cotton shirt off Nate's broad shoulders.

"That would be Locke. Though it wasn't a crowbar, it was a tire iron."

"What?!"

"We were training," he said as if that explained everything.

"Explain," she hissed as she poked his wound, "now!"

"Nate was training us, and well he told us to mount a surprise attack. He just maybe forgot to say when," the one called Tonic spoke next.

"Why so worried?" Nate smiled drowsily and she growled again.

"Do you four have any idea how difficult it is to give a grown Bear Shifter a concussion?" Luisa spoke through tight lips as she took in the four gargantuan Bears.

Polar Shifters were notoriously big, but these guys were damned near giants to the petite she-Bear. Not that she cared, her Black bear was furious that they'd hurt her mate. *Mate. Mine.*

NO! She told her Bear firmly. Now was not the time for another trip down *sinfully-delicious-sexy-times-lane*. Of course that was exactly where her mind went. *Holy hell.* One night of superb loving from her now unconscious half-Grizzly half-Black Bear mate and she was hooked.

You're a slut for the guy. Admit it already! She closed her eyes and counted to ten before calling for Colby to set up an IV with some fluids and vitamins. Not much more she could do for him. His Shifter healing abilities would kick in soon, for now it was just rest and fluids.

"Alright boys, he's going to have to stay here a few hours. Why don't you all go back and explain to Marcus what happened today," at the mention of their Clan Alpha the four Polar Bears looked every way but at her.

"Look, miss, um, I mean *Doctor*, we weren't *trying* to give him a concussion. We just didn't realize he meant that as a future lesson. We really don't want to do anything to jeopardize our joining you all officially," grumbled Bowie.

"Marcus isn't that kind of Alpha. He will understand, but he will also be missing his brother. So, I think you four have some explaining to do," she raised one eyebrow and nodded to the door.

"Right," said Bowie, rubbing the back of his neck and looking like he'd rather be doing anything else than confront their Clan leader.

"I'm sorry, Bowie," said Locke.

"Apologize to him, idiot, not me," he growled back.

"Enough, my patient needs rest. You four out," Luisa commanded and pointed to the door. *They look like four schoolboys who got caught skipping class*, she thought and shook her head. Truth was they were hardly more than a year younger than her, but they seemed so much younger.

"She's bossy for such a little thing," grumbled one of the triplets from outside the door and Luisa rolled her eyes.

"Shut up! She can hear you!"

"What? All I did was call her a little thing. She is little, except for those breasts-"

"I said shut up about her breasts!"

"Alright, can I mention her ass then?"

A thud followed the question and she had to wonder which one had smacked the speaker. Good thing too or she might've followed them into the hall and smacked him herself.

Shifters in general had highly developed libidos and Bears were no exception. Not even Polar Bears.

Dogs, all of them! She turned back to Nate and frowned already forgetting about the randy Shifters she'd just kicked out of her exam room.

All of her attention focused on the one man she'd been trying to avoid for a year now. *Not much use now is there? We're mated and yet not.* She frowned.

Nate looked so innocent in his sleep. She couldn't see those mossy green eyes of his. *Pity.* She loved those eyes. They'd light up like green lightning whenever he looked at her. She felt that electrical spark all the way to her toes every single time she caught him watching her.

His hair had grown long. The thick, dark locks met his shoulders in a gentle wave that most women would pay hundreds for but came naturally to him. Relaxed in his unconscious state, she was able to study his strong jaw and straight nose, those full lips that had brought her so much pleasure. There was no denying it. Nate Cordoza was handsome as the devil and sexy as hell too.

Luisa sighed and pulled the sheet up over him. He was nude except for his gray cotton boxer briefs. Even in his flaccid state the material stretched over his bulging sex. He was more than incredible in that department. Something she'd never forget that was for sure. Thick and long, slightly curved at that perfect angle to reach that special spot inside of her that only he'd been able to touch, bringing her to orgasm faster than any other man or toy had ever been capable of.

His thickly muscled chest, arms, and legs were bare. The smooth, tanned skin revealed for her perusal. *A medical necessity*, she told herself as she was beginning to feel like a voyeur. But it was the truth, she had to remove his clothing to evaluate his condition.

She scolded herself not to look at him lustfully while he was unconscious. She even repeated the mantra several times. *Firmly*. Thank goodness he had no other bruises on his person. Just the one rather large bump and scrape on the side of his head.

That Polar Bear Shifter, Locke, had whacked him right on the temple. Dangerous for *normals* and Shifters alike. She knew Nate had been taking on more Clan duties and was working under his brother, Daniel, as an Enforcer these days. Still, Luisa was shocked to find he was actually concussed. Locke must have really surprised him with that tire iron. *SMH*.

"You're going to be just fine. I'll be back soon,"

she whispered into his ear. Before she knew it, she was bending down to brush a kiss across the straight line of is mouth.

Her heart squeezed painfully as she stepped away. She had other patients to attend to. No matter how much she wanted to stay by his side, she'd perform her duties as expected. Luisa was a doctor first.

Stay, her Bear commanded. *No*, she told the animal firmly. She couldn't no matter how much her heart was breaking. It would send the wrong message. *I already told him I couldn't do this.*

Stepping out into the hallway, Luisa leaned her back against the wall, eyes closed. She'd learned a lot about anatomy and physiology during her years of schooling, but what did she know about matters of the heart?

Only that hearts could be broken. *Like Mom's.* Maybe it was unfair of her to make the comparison between her father and Nate, but she couldn't help it. Since she was a young cub, she knew she wanted to be a doctor. To heal sick people, Shifters and *normals* alike. People with little money and chronic illness. *Like her mother.*

The possibility of finding a mate had never entered her young mind. *Until now.* She wiped at the tears that flooded her eyes. Memories of what tran-spired a week ago came flooding into her brain making her heart squeeze painfully. She gasped and put her hand over her chest.

Oh Nate.

TWO

Cozumel, Mexico was a magical place.

At least, that had been Luisa's first impression. She was still a little shaken by her earlier interaction with a certain sexy half-Grizzly half-Black Bear Shifter. Just being near him sent her girly parts all a flutter. Still, she'd managed to leave the beach without him being any wiser to her real feelings.

Mine, the she-Bear inside of her voiced loudly. In fact, the sow made her opinion of the male known every single time Luisa thought of him. *Grrr.*

Nate Cordoza was new to the Clan and to the town of Barvale. It was recently uncovered that he was in fact the half-brother of her Alpha and his other brothers. Like the rest of the Devlin's, he was breathtakingly gorgeous, charming, and generally perfect.

But not for me. She told herself firmly for the umpteenth time. *Oh yes, he is. Mate,* insisted her Bear. She growled to herself as she donned the short pink silk wrap-around dress that Krissy had chosen for her as maid of honor.

Never a girly girl she'd scoffed at the pink confection but looking at herself now in the mirror she recognized her sister had chosen wisely with the help of Lacey. Daniel's former model wife was a wonder with clothes.

She was talking about starting her own line of children's fashion now that she'd had hers and Daniel's first cub. Luisa thought it was a marvelous idea. She had all that creativity, might as well do something with it.

Luisa on the other hand did not have a creative bone in her body. She was all science. Always had been. That was another reason she and Nate were totally wrong for each other. He was an artist for Pete's sake! She shook her head and put the tall man out of her mind concentrating on getting her hair to behave in the humid weather.

Her sister's upcoming nuptials were taking place in a midnight ceremony on the cool white sand under the pale moonlight. It was twenty minutes till they started, and Luisa was trembling with nerves. Of course, she was thrilled with her sister's choice and relieved that after a lifetime of duty and responsibility, her older sister was finally going to let her hair down.

"Almost ready?" Leya Devlin, the mate of their Alpha, Marcus, asked from the doorway to the suite where the wedding party was getting dressed.

"Be right there," Luisa said and frowned as she looked at the retreating woman. Heavily pregnant with her first cub, Luisa had almost insisted Leya stay home for the wedding, but the spunky normal wouldn't hear of it.

Luisa shrugged. It was her choice of course, but at least a doctor was nearby should she need it. That reminded her of yet another reason why she was fighting her attraction to Nate. She'd spent years of her life studying and preparing for the day she would finally be a doctor. And here it was!

She owed it to her sister and her mother to put her career before any personal happiness. From her experience, Shifters were notoriously chauvinistic. Always wanting their mates barefoot and pregnant. *No thanks.* Sure, she wanted a mate and cubs someday, but not yet.

Luisa had worked too hard to be told what to do by some overbearing man. Or worse, left, by some no good, double dealing Bear! She wouldn't let that happen to her. No way. She was going to help her Clan the best way she knew how, by using her skills as a doctor in their new Barvale Urgent Care Clinic. Being mated was simply not in the cards for her.

She frowned as she took in her reflection. Her hair was curling around her face, the soft dress caressing her curves. The sound of Krissy's exuberant laughter came floating in from the other room and Luisa smiled. Her sister truly deserved this chance to be happy, and she was ecstatic for her.

We could be happy too with our mate, her Bear spoke up, but Luisa shushed the beast. This was about Krissy, not her. Luisa was going to celebrate Krissy's happiness with her. She would finally pay her sister back for everything she'd ever sacrificed for the younger woman.

She was already working on it, putting money in an account till she had every last cent she owed Krissy for her tuition, not to mention the years she'd taken care of their mother and worked to put Luisa through medical school. Now, she could make it up to her older sister and she would by not being selfish and worrying about Nate on Krissy's big day.

Luisa walked with the rest of the wedding party to the small sectioned off area where the ceremony was going to take place. A small bonfire, a tradition in their Clan, was lit far enough away from the waves to ensure its survival. There were a couple dozen Clan members and friends attending the event. *A nice turnout for a destination wedding*, Luisa thought.

The musicians began playing and the soft sounds of their guitars washed over the crowd like a gentle wave. Luisa sighed. It was perfect. Pink and white blossoms decorated the gazebo. The moon was bright and full. The sky was clear of clouds. Stars twinkled and the waves seemed to accentuate the rhythm of the band.

Luisa was aware of everything. Mostly she was aware of *him*, but she studiously ignored the big green-eyed man standing with his brothers as she preceded the bride, along with the other brides-maids, down the center aisle. She took her position and gasped with joy as she watched her tall, curvy sister walk down the aisle on the arm of their Alpha.

Marcus was grinning as he handed a stunning Krissy, decked out in a form-fitting lace mermaid dress that clung to her shapely body, over to her mate. He winked in the direction of his own wife, who was part of the wedding party. Leya's belly was round with their cub. She still looked beautiful in her pale pink dress, especially when she smiled at Marcus. The affection between the two was palpable.

Luisa had to look away for a second. She smiled at the two bridesmaids with tears in her eyes. Leya and Lacey Devlin, were two of the luckiest mated women she knew. Both of them practically glowed with the proof of their husband's love and devotion. Lacey held baby Mia and cooed at the infant while the ceremony began.

Luisa gritted her teeth. *No cubs for a while yet*, she told her Bear after the animal let out a bellow of longing. She felt *his* eyes on her and turned to see Nate staring in her direction.

His intense gaze seemed to start a fire right in the center of her soul. She felt her panties moisten and nipples harden under his scrutiny. Almost twenty-feet of space and a dozen people separated them, but it was like they were the only two people there.

Luisa's pulse raced and her breathing increased, but no one seemed to notice. The rest of the crowd was watching Taylor and Krissy say their vows to one another. But not Luisa. *No*, ungrateful sister that she was, she was on the verge of a panic attack just imagining all the decadent things she wanted to do to Nate. *Grrr.*

Heat pooled low in her belly and her pulse raced. Images of all that tanned skin under her hands and mouth flashed through her mind, filling her with need. *Physical urges can be controlled,* she chided herself. Nate grinned and she scowled, furious at his cocky arrogance. As if he knew what she'd been thinking!

She turned her head back to the couple. Telling herself to ignore the commanding presence of Nate. It didn't matter that he looked tempting as hell in his ivory linen slacks and pale teal shirt that set off his golden tanned skin.

His hair was by far one of her favorite things about him. The way he wore the thick, longish locks tousled and hanging down to his shoulders had just the right amount of artist meets careless rocker that made her want to moan. The dark waves almost covered his eyes from her. But she didn't need to see them in order to feel them.

Those eyes were burning holes through her body. She felt them riveted to her face, her neck, her breasts, and belly. She knew he was watching her still. It had been that way ever since she'd literally run into him when they were celebrating their Alpha's engagement to his mate. The little normal had turned out to be quite a fierce Alpha mate and Luisa admired her greatly.

She'd recognized Nate then as *hers*, but she'd been denying it. *Denying him.* Luisa's Bear sniffed and pawed at the ground in her mind's eye. She wanted her Mate. The animal hungered for him.

She wanted to be claimed on some primal level. She craved his dominance and the exertion that would come from being taken by such a strong Shifter male like him. *Nate,* the she-Bear growled his name.

Traitor, she thought at the beast. Luisa had spent far too long studying and working to earn her degree to give it all up now. Just because she was horny! *No way.* She had a battery-operated friend in her suitcase for just this reason!

Her whole life and career were in front of her. She had so much left to accomplish. Why had the universe chosen now to send her a mate? And a fated mate at that! It had to be some sort of cruel joke. Some irony she couldn't comprehend despite her fancy degrees.

Miserable now, she shied away from thinking about him as she tossed flower petals and blew bubbles at the happy couple. Cheers erupted and she joined the throng.

Suddenly it hit her that Krissy had a husband now. Taylor would come first with her. *Not me, not anymore*, she thought and was startled by her own selfish meanderings. *You have a mate too*, her Bear reminded her, but she ignored her animal. Putting on a happy face for her sister, she joined the crowd even though she felt more alone now than ever before.

A tear fell from her eye as she suddenly thought of her mom. Patricia Sposa had suffered plenty during her too short life on this earth. Luisa and Krissy had watched their poor mother suffer for years at the hands of a husband who didn't truly love her.

Her father, or *sperm donor* as she thought of him, had used his normal wife to fit into society. After their marriage and the birth of both his daughters, Gianni Sposa had taken off like a shot, leaving his fragile wife with two small cubs to raise.

Another tear fell for the mother who had sacrificed so much for her two girls. She'd finally succumbed to the ovarian cancer that had plagued her nearly her entire adult life just six months earlier. Gratefully, Luisa had been home for it all. A doctor now, she was able to ease her mother's passing and take some of the burden from Krissy's shoulders.

Her death was the reason Krissy and Taylor had waited so long to say their vows. So much pain and grief and yet her mom always had warm words and smiles for her two daughters. *I miss you, Mom*, she thought sadly.

"Hey, I did it," Krissy laughed and walked into Luisa's embrace, gasping when the younger woman squeezed her hard.

"What's up, Lu?"

"I'm so happy for you Krissy," she said and kissed her sister's cheek.

"Me too. I can't stop thinking about Mom," Krissy's watery smile triggered her own tearful response and the two women embraced again tightly.

"She'd be so proud of you," she murmured, and Luisa nodded.

"You too, Krissy. Mom loved Taylor," she wiped her eyes and laughed as the man himself came walking over.

"Hey now, no crying on our big day," he squeezed his wife's hand and pulled her into his arms.

"I got you, Dimples," he whispered and kissed Krissy's full lips.

Again, Luisa found herself looking away from a couple so much in love it hurt to see it. She'd just watched Krissy stand before the man she'd loved nearly all her life with a radiant smile gracing her face as she promised to be his for always.

Taylor had returned the sentiment, proclaiming his love and dedication to her in front of the most important members of the Barvale Clan. It had been both beautiful and deeply moving.

Luisa couldn't be prouder or happier for either one of them. Her foolish eyes roamed back to the man who was standing just behind his half-brothers as they toasted Taylor and Krissy with some special label tequila, they'd purchased for the occasion on account of it being Krissy's favorite drink.

Nate Cordoza was a mystery to her. A Devlin and yet not a Devlin. What did she really know about him? Besides him being a super hottie who'd gotten her pink bits tingling from just looking at her. *For Pete's sake.*

Okay. *Yes,* she sensed he was honorable and trustworthy. But he was something else, completely different and out of her element. An artist for one thing, where she was a scientist. *Mate*, her Bear insisted.

"Drink up!" Krissy handed out shots and slices of lime while Luisa simply allowed herself to be dragged along with the crowd. The music was riotous, the light of the bonfire low as the throng celebrated the wedding.

Okay, maybe he is our Mate, she agreed after another shot of the strong, clear liquor. Krissy had insisted she keep up and drink with her and, everyone knew the bride got what she wanted on her wedding day. It was a universal law, Luisa was sure.

Still, as she watched the handsome semi-stranger hold a beer bottle to his full sensuous lips she wanted to moan. He was so handsome. *So very fine*. But she wasn't ready for the type of commitment he would want.

Luisa was scared to death he'd want more than she could give. *What if he can't live with my choice? My career? It's better to stay away then, right?*

Still, there was a secret place inside of her that *wished*. Okay, *maybe a not so secret place*, whispered the naughtier part of her brain that was slowly waking up under the influence of the alcohol she was readily consuming.

Nope, if she were being honest, it was more than the place between her legs that wished for him. More than the throbbing, moistened cleft that was clenching on air, desperate to be claimed by him.

Every time he was near it got worse. Her entire body was readying her for the invasion that was inevitable. Her body could take it, she was sure. But it was the place inside her heart that she was worried about. That secret place where she knew she could lose herself entirely to him. She shivered at the thought.

What would become of her if Nate, this gorgeous, larger than life man, completely took control of all of her desires? Who would she be if he could steer her life with a crook of his long fingers? As if she was a ship, just a vessel with him at the rudder telling her which way to go. Luisa's eyes narrowed.

No way. She wouldn't allow herself to be taken over by Nate. Even if the universe had declared him her mate. That didn't mean she had to go along with the universe's plans! *Heck*, it seemed to her the universe was being a bit of a bully!

She snorted as she thought the words. Tipping back her sixth or was it seventh shot, she sucked on the lime and grinned wickedly.

"I have plans of my own, you know," she announced to the bartender who smiled and poured another shot.

"*Si, senorita!*" He agreed.

Damn straight she did! *I am going to be the best doctor EVAH!* Luisa was going to help her Clan by offering care and aid to young Bears during their first Change! And she was planning an entire series of classes specific to Shifters. Imagine a new age where expectant mothers of Shifters could learn how to carry and care for their young and prepare for the birthing process. Fortunately for her, the age of chauvinism was coming to an end.

With more female Shifters stepping up and entering the professional world they truly had a chance to make a difference. She knew they were rare and precious, but women were made for more than breeding! She bit her lip, excited to implement her ideas among her Clan. She'd been thinking about it forever and could finally do it in her new position. It meant the world to her.

Having been born to a *normal* mother who knew very little about what having cubs meant, Luisa understood that what she was offering was unique and very much needed. She would be able to help the new generation of Bear Shifters that would someday lead the Barvale Clan from the moment of their conception!

The universe was just going to have to shut up about Nate Cordoza. She was not mating him. *Period. The end. Bye-bye!* What the hell was up with that anyway? Sure, her girly parts were literally drooling for the man, but that was just too bad! Nothing *Mr. Vroom-Vroom* at home couldn't fix!

Firmly decided that she wasn't about to stay home, *barefoot and pregnant*, just because the universe threw her fated mate at her now of all times, Luisa straightened her shoulders. *Whoa! Why is the room spinning?* It didn't matter, she was going to tell that big old sexy Bear exactly how she felt.

Well, as soon as I finish this shot!

THREE

After the speeches were made and the bar was nearly empty, Luisa finally remembered her new resolve to confront Nate. A few Clanmates were plucking away at their instruments and she rocked her hips and danced across the sand in her bare feet. Where did her sandals go anyway? Oh well. She had bigger fish, or bears, to fry! She moved with new determination around the bonfire to where she'd last seen him.

A few Bears asked her to dance as she made her way and she might've been sidetracked a bit. Luisa loved music and dancing, not that she was any good at it. That natural rhythm that most Shifters had seemed to pass right over her, but she gave it her all. Breathless and laughing, she gently pulled out of the man's arms she'd been dancing with and stopped right in front of the man she'd been meaning to set straight, Nate Cordoza.

His green eyes glittered down at her and he bared his teeth at the young Bear who she'd just been dancing with. The man scurried away. Frightened no doubt by the possessive gleam in Nate's eyes. It should have pissed her off, but it didn't. In fact, it seemed to warm her from the inside out. *Mine*, growled her Bear.

She gulped, need and hunger rising within her as she took in his large tanned body evident through the gap of his now unbuttoned shirt. Holy hell the man had a physique to die for! She should know. Being a doctor made her somewhat of an expert, didn't it?

His usually easy green eyes focused on her every move as she leaned closer to him. Nate was looking at her like a starving man stared at an all you can eat buffet, all but licking his lips as he stared.

"Hey there, honey girl, 'bout time you came 'round my way," his cocky grin had her frowning through the alcoholic haze that fogged her brain.

"I came t-to tell you something," she wobbled a little and he reached out and gripped her by the waist.

Luisa closed her eyes against the onslaught of tingles that zipped through her blood at the mostly chaste contact. His fingers squeezed tightly, but not uncomfortably and he dipped his head, inhaling her scent. His eyes glowed as his Bear joined their exchange and Luisa felt hers rise in response.

Awareness flared to life starting deep in her belly and moving throughout her entire body. She sucked in a deep breath. His woodsy autumn sage scent filled her nostrils. Heady and spicy, her Bear growled deeply, savoring his natural fragrance.

What was she doing again? Telling Nate to back off. *Why would she want to do that?* Because...uh, just because-

"I knew you'd come to me, I just had to be patient. Didn't I, honey?" He breathed the word against her temple, his full lips pressing soft kisses to her hair and cheek.

Luisa leaned into him, loving the feel of his big, strong body. He was barely touching her. Hands still at her waist, mouth brushing baby soft kisses against her skin. But still, she couldn't catch her breath. *Not why you came here. Have to tell him.*

"Nate, I-"

"Yes?" He asked, slowly travelling down her face

to her neck and collar bone, pressing butterfly soft kisses there before looking up to meet her gaze.

She wanted to look away, to fight being trapped in his emerald gaze, but she had no will left. She was powerless to fight her attraction and her growing need. Maybe it was the tequila or maybe the moonlight? *Shit.* Maybe it was just him.

"I-" she gasped as he pressed one long kiss against her lips, slowly dipping his tongue inside the warm cavern of her mouth. Eyes open, he watched her. Saw the reactions she couldn't suppress plain on her face. Luisa's Bear roared in her mind's eye as Nate lifted his mouth from hers and held her face in his hands.

"You. Are. Mine." Each word ended on a meeting of lips and Luisa had no rebuttal for the sentiment. Every single inch of her burned for him. She was his as much as he was hers. In her heart, that was the only truth she needed.

Tossing caution to the wind, she placed her hand on his chest. It was hard, like concrete or steel, but hot to the touch. *Very hot.* She smiled against his lips. Nate was here now, with her. They were both alive, together. She felt his heartbeat thunder along with hers as they pressed against each other for one long minute.

"Yes," she said looking at him through lust glazed eyes.

"Luisa," he breathed her name, his forehead resting on hers as he twirled a lock of her hair around one of his long fingers.

Hand in hand they walked towards the row of tiny cabanas where most of the Clan was staying. Before they reached the door to his room, he swept her off her feet and carried her to a dark corner where his lips crashed into hers.

It was as if the entire world stopped and shook at the same time. Her Bear roared and pawed the ground inside of her mind's eye. *Yes,* her entire body seemed to scream the word. The rightness of them coming together echoed through her and set her heart aflame. His fingers skimmed her curves, the slightest of touches making her want even more.

His hands were callused as if he spent a lot of time outdoors. *He might.* She knew he liked to draw outside, using pencils, charcoals, paints, and even just his tablet at times. At the moment, those talented fingers seemed to be everywhere. Running across her jawline, down her neck, over her large breasts to her soft belly, and down further to her knees. He parted her legs with his knee, his tongue still exploring her mouth as his hands slid underneath the clingy dress up her smooth thighs, to where she wanted him most.

It was getting harder and harder to breathe as he continued the physical onslaught that was just this side of overwhelming to her tequila addled senses. *More*, her Bear roared. She agreed with the sentiment. She wanted more of him. *All of him. Now. Mine.*

"Honey mine," Nate murmured as he nipped her ear lobe. That tiny mark of dominance sent a shudder of pleasure spiking through her veins and she clung to him.

"Nate, inside now," she demanded, and he complied. Making a noise somewhere between a moan and a growl, he lifted her up, Cinderella-style in his arms. He suckled her neck as he carried her the rest of the way to his own private cabana.

Nate opened the door with a quick punch of numbers on the pad over the doorknob. He slammed it shut with his foot, capturing her mouth once again as she attempted to slide down his formidable length.

Luisa trembled as he stamped himself on her with his kiss. Her raging desire grew with each swipe of his talented tongue. Licking, sucking, nibbling, he didn't let up. Not for one second. *Thank God.*

She hardly knew where one kiss ended, and

another began. His rough hands kneaded the plump flesh of her ass, tearing her dress off with a few quick movements. Cool air met her moist skin and she shivered deliciously as he went about removing his own clothing.

"Fuck, honey, you're so beautiful," his voice was deep and husky, sending shivers through her as she stood before him in a pair of skimpy pink lace panties and a matching strapless bra.

Luisa mewled as he pulled her into his body and pressed his mouth to hers once again. She found pleasure and sweet oblivion in his expert kisses. All her worries faded away with each passing moment. She had one goal now. *Nate. Mine.*

The room was spinning, but whether that was from the tequila or Nate she couldn't say. *Never like this.* She hardly felt it as he dropped her onto the soft cover that draped the extra-firm mattress. Her senses were almost totally overwhelmed with all things Nate.

The Bear inside of her grumbled approvingly as he dominated her, pressing her into the mattress with his incredible bulk. She felt his rock-hard length at the apex of her thighs, and she looked down. When had he removed the rest of their clothes? Didn't matter. He was magnificent.

His hands were rough against her skin, but tender, oh so tender. They felt good. His eyes were heated, wild, almost as if he wasn't quite in control. She liked that. *A lot.* The Bear inside him peeked out, causing his dark green eyes to glow in the darkness of the room.

Luisa was blind, deaf, and dumb to everything but him. Every touch, every kiss, was perfection. The universe sure knew what it was doing, she admitted as he dipped his head and captured one plump nipple in his mouth.

Eyes wide, he watched her every reaction as he bit the taut nub and placed his engorged cock at her slick entrance. Lifting up he looked into her eyes solemnly as he thrust his hips, entering her slick heat in one swift motion while keeping their gazes locked.

"That's good, honey. You feel so fucking good," he growled the words as he pushed deeper inside of her wet heat. Using every inch of his body he pressed himself against her drawing out a long, slow moan from her lips.

He was magnificent. She wiggled to get closer, sliding her hands up and down his muscled back, pulling him closer. Chest heaving, he pressed her knees out farther and she welcomed the bite of pain, needing to get closer to him.

Nate opened her up, wide and good, using his thumb to circle her swollen clit as he swiveled and pumped his thick cock into her tight channel. She loved the warm hard feel of him touching her deep, deep inside.

"Nate," Luisa said his name as she writhed beneath him.

Embracing the crush of his weight as his hair roughened chest pressed into her sensitized nipples, she raked her nails down his back drawing a low growl from his lips. Pleasure zapped along her nerve endings like lightning and she squeezed him tighter, noting the flare in his glittering green eyes.

"More," she moaned.

"Yes," he growled the words into her neck, "Mine."

She nodded her agreement. It was the only answer she could give him. Together they moved as one, towards the same goal. There it hung just out of reach. The ultimate glory. And she would have it. Tonight. Now. With him. Only him. *Swivel, swivel, thrust, thrust, swirl, swirl. And repeat.* On and on they continued, grasping and clenching, pushing each other further and further until she was mindless beneath him.

Nate and the exquisite pleasure of his touch were the only things that existed for her in their fevered embrace. Not rushed though, never that. He was undeniably thorough as he touched, licked, fucked, and worshipped her entire body.

She cried out as her channel clenched around his shaft, the beginnings of her orgasm making her grow taut as she found her release. In that exact moment, Luisa reveled in Nate's fangs as they sliced through the skin just above her left breast.

Yes! Mate! That wild part of her, unburdened by doubt cried out in happiness. Her Bear roared joyfully as the bonds of their matehood began to wrap around the two of them.

The she-Bear inside of her bellowed, demanding she reciprocate. And she did. Mindless to all but the animalistic need inside of her to claim her mate. To make her his. Luisa bit down on his shoulder, loving the feel of his cock as it pulsed deep within her. She swallowed mouthful after mouthful of his sweet life-force. Heat and desire flared to life once more.

He was breathing heavily. His chest pounded against hers with the strength of his heartbeat. Luisa's eyes flared. She watched as Nate groaned aloud, clinging to her body as she licked the wound closed. Never before had she seen a man so vulnerable. It was private and secret. A wondrous thing only mates shared.

His cock still pulsed within her and she felt her Bear rise. The animal was sated, pleased that his seed had bathed her womb, marking her from the inside out. She felt the magic of their matebond pulse around her. It was new and fragile, but it was real. It was there.

Luisa sighed and watched as his breathing began to return to normal. His mossy green eyes held hers in a stare so intense she couldn't break it if she tried. The entire world could be on fire, but she wouldn't know it. When she was with him, he was the only thing that existed.

He bent his head, eyes still open, and touched his lips to hers. This kiss was slow. A toe-curling monument to kissing. Delicious and warming, she readily opened her mouth for his tongue.

Sex was sex, but this was something else. Something she was unable to stop or slow down. Why would she want to? This claiming was an ancient and powerful rite and Luisa would own it. *At least for the while.*

They'd remained indoors the entire next day.

She'd finally managed to sneak away while he went out to scrounge up some food. She'd felt horrible about it, but she couldn't think when he was near. She'd needed some space. So, she'd left him a note.

It had been a cowardly move. She still felt ashamed. But he'd respected her wishes. Nate, ever the gentleman, had given her space. Almost an entire week's worth.

But he was here now, in her clinic, with a concussion. She walked down the hall to check on her other patients. She needed time. *You've had time,* her she-Bear growled. Her heart was beating her to death. Nate was so close. All she wanted to do was go to him.

But how could she remain who she was and do that?

FOUR

Nate woke up to the sounds of machines beeping and the smell of strong antiseptic soap burning his nostrils. He'd always had a sensitive nose, even for a Shifter.

"Fuck," he groaned as he tried to sit up. His head was fucking pounding. *Goddamn Polar Bears!* Those mountainous fucks from the North that had recently moved to Barvale did this to him! His Bear, that half-Grizzly half-Black Bear monster that lived inside of him, growled long and hard. The beast demanded he get his revenge.

"What are you doing? Stop that!"

Only that voice could make his beast stand still and take note. The fact it was tinged with a hint of annoyance made him want to grin, but he couldn't ignore the fact of how she'd left him in Cozumel. He couldn't deny she'd rejected his mating claim. But he also couldn't deny himself the pleasure of being near her, so he turned around.

His aggravated Bear immediately calmed just looking at his lovely little mate. Luisa, *or Dr. Sposa,* since they were in her clinic walked over to him from the doorway and placed her hand on his chest, shoving him back down on the bed. Damn she was strong. Even for a she-Bear.

Not that he minded. Still, he'd have preferred she'd do that to him in their own bed. The one he'd ordered specially for her the second he'd gotten home from Mexico. *Alone.*

In fact, he'd spent most of his free time the last week fixing their den. The cabin on the shore off Lake Ursa was one of the larger ones his half-brothers had owned. They'd wanted to give it to him as part of their Bear Claw Brotherhood plan to win his mate, but he insisted on paying for it at the current value of both the land and the house.

"Fine," Marcus had agreed and named the six-figure price. Nate hadn't even blinked. He wasn't quite in his brothers' category as billionaires, but he'd done alright over the years. Made some good investments and earned a pretty penny with his

graphic design artwork. Software and video gaming companies were always after him to work on their products.

Lately, however, he'd been a little preoccupied. For the past year or so, ever since he'd laid eyes on *her*. Moving to Barvale had been a hasty decision on his part after the death of his mother. Even after he'd met his brothers, he hadn't been sure it was the right thing. Then he'd seen Luisa, and all his doubts faded. *Mine.*

She was the most beautiful woman he'd ever laid eyes on. She was a tiny thing, though she probably preferred to be thought of in terms of her intellect. He couldn't help it though. She was sweet and sassy, and he stood more than a foot taller than her. Not that he minded the height difference. Not at all.

His woman was all woman with soft lush curves and milky smooth skin. Everything about her was made for him. She was the one. His fated mate designed by the universe to be his and his alone. The Bear rumbled remembering their one night together. The night they'd claimed each other.

Fuck. It had been perfect. Or at least he'd thought so. Sure, she'd been tipsy at first, but he'd figured she'd just needed a little Dutch courage to approach him. By the time they'd started with the heavy petting, her Shifter metabolism had burned through the alcohol. By then, they'd lit their own fire.

His pulse raced as she frowned and read his vitals. Feeling like a cub again, he had to hold himself still or he was gonna make a grab for her. *Then I'll really be in the doghouse. Time. My woman wants time. Away from me.* His bear bellowed a mournful sound and Luisa's eyes met his, as if she'd heard it.

"Getting up too soon can cause a setback-" she began.

"I miss you," he breathed the words interrupting her.

He inhaled her sweet vanilla mint fragrance, allowing it to flow through him soothing both man and beast. She made to step back, but he captured her wrist in his hand and held her there gently. *Shit.* He was fucking this up, but he couldn't help it. He needed to touch her.

"Nate, please, I'm at work. I can't talk about this here," she said not quite meeting his eyes.

"Where then?"

"I don't know."

"Come to my place tonight, please," he'd get on his fucking knees and beg if she wanted him to. Pride had no place in a mating. That's what his mama had told him.

"I don't know if that's a good idea, Nate. I asked you for some time," she held her stethoscope tightly in her hands and he knew she was struggling, but he needed his mate.

"It's been a week, honey. I need to see you," he couldn't disguise his Bear in his voice. The animal wanted her with him. She might as well face the truth.

Nate had heard stories in his youth of mated couples separating and the Shifters going mad from it. His own Bear had always been volatile, on the edge, and he'd hoped that finding his brothers and belonging to a good Clan would calm the animal.

Hopes of finding his true fated mate never entered his wildest dreams. But he had. Only she didn't want him. *Cause you're nothing but a half-breed freak, even for a Shifter.* He closed his eyes and fought back the taunts and doubts that plagued him his whole life. He didn't need to lose his grip on his Bear in front of her. *Not here. Not now.*

"You alright?" Concern made her brown eyes grow even darker and he warmed at the thought. His Bear rumbled, mollified that she was worried for him.

"Yeah, uh, little headache from that tap on my noggin is all," he tried to hide his reactions with a grin that he'd been told was sexy a time or two. *Maybe it would work on a reluctant mate?*

"A tap, huh? It was a tire iron, Nate. What were you doing with those four Polar Bears anyway?" She narrowed her eyes and took his pulse again.

"Training," he replied.

He'd been showing them some different methods of hand to hand combat he'd learned growing up with the Flint Bears Shifters. Grizzlies, all of them. *Nothing but a bunch of bigots.* They'd all but kicked him out because he was a mixed breed.

One benefit, *hell, the only benefit,* he'd gotten from that shitty little Clan he was from was his training. Those Bear Shifters in eastern Texas had their share of Native American ancestry and secrets had been passed on from generation to generation. Of course, he had to prove he was worthy of such teachings by beating the shit out of every Bear in the vicinity.

They'd taught him, begrudgingly, but still. He'd been eleven years old when the lessons started. Of course, his were always a little but rougher than those the other boys received. The way he saw it was it only made him better and stronger. Besides, he had a right to those secrets. They were the secrets of his people.

His mother had explained to him when he was a cub that his people had come from Spain to Mexico, but he also had a mix of Native American blood. Mainly Caddo and Apache. Combined with his Irish American father, Nate had a whole slew of history running through his veins. It explained the enormous monster inside of him at any rate.

"Training, huh, well you will need to take a few days off," Luisa's voice brought him back to the present.

"Will you come tonight?"

"I don't know if that's a good idea," she replied.

"Please."

"Okay," she said breathlessly. Awareness surged through his veins. Before he could stop himself, he'd pulled her into his embrace.

"What-what are you doing?"

"Luisa," he said her name, bent his head.

Their breath mingled as he closed in. Need and desire pulsed through him until he thought he would burst. Never had he wanted a woman like this. His raging arousal pulsed in his briefs and he wondered how long it would take to strip her and bury himself in her heat.

He stopped, gave her a second to step back, to make the decision herself. It was one second too much apparently. A knock on the door had her shoving out of his arms and turning her back just as Marcus and his very pregnant wife strode into the room followed by the four huge Polar Shifters.

"Dammit," Nate mumbled but turned to greet the Alpha couple with a grin and little wave. Thank God for the paper gown he had on or his sister-in-law would be seeing a whole new side of him.

"Nate! What did you do to him you brutes!" Leya teared up looking at his bruised face, but she did that often now that she was carrying the future of the Clan.

"Oh ma'am, we are so very sorry," Bowie began, but one growl from Marcus had him shutting up.

"Here, sit down, Mrs. Devlin," the one named Tonic pulled a chair from the wall and offered it to her with an approving nod from Marcus.

"So, doc, how is he doing?" Marcus asked.

"I'm fine. Ready to go in fact," Nate began.

"I wasn't talking to you. Besides, have you seen yourself? You've got a welt on the side of your head bigger than my hand," Marcus snorted, and Nate glared. Finding his older brother sure had seemed like a good idea at the time, but he wasn't so sure just then.

Before he could retort, his little mate was speaking again. She'd managed to regain her composure as she addressed Marcus. Still cute as a button, she exuded intellect and command in a way he found impressive and sexy as all get out.

He enjoyed seeing her like this, professional and in control. Hell, it turned him on knowing she was that damned good at her job. He knew it was the reason she was avoiding him, but for the life of him, he couldn't imagine why. He stopped thinking to focus on her strong voice.

"His vitals are good. He's strong and healthy, but I wouldn't recommend any more *training* for a week at least, especially not with those four," she gestured towards the four Polar Bears with a glare that had them bowing their heads. A few muttered *sorry's* were spoken, but she didn't acknowledge them.

"Alright, you're the doctor. You heard her, Nate, that means no more hammering either at all hours of the day and night," Marcus eyed him, and Nate shook his head.

"Hammering? I thought you were a graphic designer," she said, those near black eyes focused on him again.

"I am, it's nothing," he answered her and glared at his brother.

"Sure, Nate here is an artist, but he's taken up construction as a part-time gig," Marcus said with a wink.

"You should come see what he's done to the place, doc."

"Very subtle, dear," Leya smirked at her tall husband.

"Marcus," Nate growled.

"Um, sounds interesting," Luisa said noncommittedly.

"Maybe you should come see it. Maybe we can have a bite to eat too?" He asked cautiously.

"Um, maybe-"

"Oh!" Leya let out a pained gasp and all eyes flicked to her.

"Leya, what is it?" Marcus knelt at her side.

"I'm okay, a little cramp is all. I think the baby is kicking. Whew! It was a whopper of a kick too," she laughed and pressed Marcus' large hand to her abdomen.

"Love," he kissed her temple and rested his head on her shoulder.

It was eye opening and touching to see his powerful Alpha humbled by his tiny mate. Could

Nate be so honest and open with his emotions with Luisa? *Damn straight.* But it was Leya's trust in her mate that made their relationship work. Leya knew that Marcus loved her unconditionally and she never doubted him. He just had to make Luisa see him that way.

Nate noted that everyone looked away from the couple's private moment. Except for Luisa. Nate noted the wide-eyed look in her eyes as she watched the two mates. He could almost see the invisible wall going up between them. *So that was it*, he thought to himself.

Just something else he didn't know about her. But he wanted to. That was an irrefutable certainty. Whatever preconceived notions his little mate had about him were about to be destroyed! He promised himself he would find out whatever it was that was giving her cold feet and he'd do his best to remove the obstacle.

"Okay, everyone, my patient needs to rest before I can discharge him. Marcus, would you please bring Leya next door? I'd like to examine her since you're here. Is that alright, Leya?"

"Sure," the bubbly blonde readily agreed and allowed her husband to help her stand.

"You four can wait outside," she pointed at the

Polar Bear Shifters and they bowed their heads like cubs who'd just gotten a good scolding. Nate grinned. His mate was a fierce little thing. Protective too.

"They'll be good, honey. I mean, *Dr. Sposa*, honest," he winked at her and she turned her head, but not before he saw the pink blush spread across her cheeks.

Oh yeah. He needed this woman in his life permanently. Wanted her not only in his house and his bed, but with him for good. *Shit.* Shifter *matings* didn't always mean love, but he could already feel her there in his heart. *Mine.*

He stared unabashedly as she retreated from the room with Leya and Marcus. The Alpha looked after his wife with loving concern as she waddled into the corridor with her enormous load. She was awful big. Must be carrying a litter. And wasn't that a glorious thing?

Nate wouldn't mind babies. Hell, he'd spoil them rotten trying to be a good daddy like he'd never had. He'd love them, that was the honest truth, but he could wait. There was no rush now that he'd found Luisa. He'd wait for cubs until she was ready.

"So, uh, sorry about knocking you out there, boss," Locke spoke up, interrupting his thoughts.

Nate narrowed his eyes at the younger Bear. He was a fucking monster of a man. Almost seven-feet tall and composed of huge bronze muscles. He was the largest of the three Polar Bear Shifter triplets with jet black hair and piercing blue eyes.

Multiples in Shifters was exceedingly rare. A novelty for sure. Though they were not identical, it was obvious the Nanouk boys were related. They all had dark hair and were hugely muscled. They had odd names too. *Locke, Tonic, and Bolder.* Their cousin Bowie Atiqtalaaq was older than them by about three years.

Apparently, they were infamous in their small Alaska Clan for getting into trouble and were sent to Barvale to be put to good use. Nate genuinely liked the young men, though they had a lot of growing up to do.

"You four are gonna have to learn to listen to everything I say before you go running around half-cocked-" Nate began.

"He said sorry," Bolder frowned as if he didn't want to hear it, but Nate interrupted him.

"Sorry ain't gonna matter in a life and death situation, son. We've got a viable threat coming. You four know that. If we're gonna get ahead of this thing, you'll have to cooperate. So just what the hell were you thinking, comin' at me with a tire iron when my back was turned?" Nate's unintentional growl had all four Shifters baring their necks to him.

Despite their size, he was the more dominant Shifter in the room. His Bear was still pissed they'd laid him out and it was all he could do not to paw the ground and charge at one of them. Challenges, or fights to prove dominance, were rare in Barvale, a fact that had taken some getting used to after being raised in the Flint Clan. Still, it was a better way of life. *More civil at least.*

"You said that surprise attacks were useful-"

"In the field, son, not at me. And sure as fuck not after we'd finished sparring and I was heading home!"

"Sorry, uh, I'll make it up to you?" Locke said, but for some reason it sounded more like a question.

"Damn straight you will. All four of you are taking on extra patrols starting tonight," Nate glared at the men and all at once the grumbling stopped.

"Yes, sir," Tonic said, ever the soldier. As Nate understood it, their Clan back home worked closely with a group of honest to God Dhampirs.

The half-vampire Clan was dedicated to hunting down those Vampires who no longer had the will or self-control to live among *normals*. Hunter Vampires, as they were called, were more or less the most dangerous things on the planet. They killed without conscience and worse, they could sometimes be controlled by Dark Witches to execute their evil wishes.

The Polar Bear Shifters were here to train with the Barvale Clan, but also to teach them how to handle the Hunter Vamps as some had been seen in the area. Apparently, after the fall of a local Dark Witch Coven, a group of the creatures had gotten free. Not all had been rounded up in the aftermath, and these Polar Bears had more than enough experience to get the job done.

Of course, that was only half their story, as Nate understood it. These particular Polar Bear Shifters were also in trouble for some risky behavior back home. Due to their size and threat level, their Alpha was anxious to send them off and Marcus had readily made their home available to them.

The four young men had seemed shocked and surprised when they'd arrived. Nate could understand that. His old Clan hadn't been too keen on keeping him around either. Marcus had assigned him to take charge of the four monstrously strong Shifters and he had. Or, well, he tried to. The tire iron to the side of the head made him think he had more work cut out for him than he'd originally thought.

"Anything else, boss," Bolder asked.

"Yeah, run to the market and grab me everything I'll need for a romantic dinner for two."

"Uh, boss?" Nate rolled his eyes at Bowie's wide-eyed expression.

"It's not for *you*, idiots. It's for me and my mate," he began.

"You have a mate?" Locke asked.

"The doc," Tonic said elbowing his brother.

"Oh man, the good ones are always taken," Bolder nodded sagely.

"Oh for Pete's sake, get out of here," Bowie shoved his three cousins to the door and nodded at Nate, "We got this. Don't worry."

FIVE

Leya finished her rounds at around eleven o'clock that night. Her replacement, a young doctor named Adrianna Curry had just been hired to lighten her load. Though she was a normal, she'd been born to a Bear Shifter and was technically still Clan.

Luisa waved to the pretty dark-haired woman as she left. Her eyes went over the closed door of exam room three and she swallowed. *Coward.*

She'd managed to avoid going into Nate's room again for the rest of her shift. *What about dinner?* She shook her head, closing the buttons on the light denim shirt she'd changed into as she crept across the parking lot.

The soft wind was chilly even though it was

summertime. Never could tell what the weather would be like in her little Jersey town. She sighed and ran a hand through her short blonde hair, almost missing the long shadow that marred the concrete floor in front of her.

Startled she stopped in her tracks. Looking up she saw a tall, intimidating figure leaning against the lamppost that marked her parking space. Heat filled her stomach as she recognized the shape. *Nate.*

What was it about this man that made her want him from the second she laid eyes on his sleek, hard body and his exquisite face? *Fate.* Her mind hadn't conjured the word out of nowhere. It was her she-Bear that insisted he was hers. *Mine.*

"You were released hours ago," she said without greeting.

"Yes. But since you had a nurse do that, I thought I'd wait for you, so you didn't forget our dinner date," he spoke through tight lips and hooded eyes.

He was sexy as hell, bruised face and all. The doctor in her wanted to check his vitals one more time, the Bear wanted her to strip down and demand he take her, and the woman, well, she was stuck somewhere between wanting to do both. She was having difficulty with it though. The incredible sex they'd shared was one thing, but the caring for him that came with having found his one true mate was almost too much. She didn't know if she could handle the weight of that kind of feeling.

"I'm sorry, Nate, I'm really tired," Luisa tried to fight the barrage of emotions that threatened to crush her and unlocked the doors to her trusty little Camry.

"Of course you are, honey, that's why I thought you might appreciate a nice homecooked meal."

"You cook?"

"Matter of fact," he grinned, and she found herself responding.

Dinner did sound good. She'd snacked on a couple of granola bars during her shift but hadn't had a lot of time for anything more substantial. Food sounded good. Alone time with Nate, not so much. It was far too dangerous to be alone with him. But she couldn't seem to help herself.

"I guess I can follow you," she began, but he was already shaking his head.

"No good, doc, I had the boys drop me off."

"The boys being those young idiots who almost broke your skull apart?" She frowned and he laughed.

"They're not so bad. Just need to do some growing up is all."

"Hmm."

"You drive, I'll ride shotgun," he grinned and she damn near melted in a puddle at his feet.

Surprised that he didn't demand to drive she found herself agreeing with him. Most Shifter males would've taken her keys, but not him, she admitted to herself. He was a cut above. *Darn it.* If she wasn't careful, she was gonna wind up head over heels for him. *If she wasn't already.*

He shouldn't be this good looking. *It ought to be illegal,* she thought as she stopped at a light and tried her best to ignore the deep bass of his voice as he sang along to the classic rock station, she'd always kept her car radio tuned to.

"Baby, baby, got some good lovin' just for you," he sang in that sexy as sin voice of his and her knees turned to jelly. Thank God she was sitting. Still, she was so shook up by being near him she almost missed the turn off for Lake Ursa.

"Um, which way?" She asked when they came to a fork in the road.

"Left. The cabin on the right about a mile down the road," he'd leaned over her to point and she caught a whiff of that incredible autumn sage scent that seemed to cling to his skin.

She nodded and stepped on the gas. The car

seemed to hum with anticipation as she pulled into the graveled driveway of a large, two-story cabin that was clearly undergoing some renovation.

"This is yours?" She asked and whistled as she took in the huge wraparound porch and second floor deck that overlooked the lake that sat about a hundred yards away. It had to be twice the size of her childhood home where she still lived.

It was beautiful. A brand-new coat of natural finish gleamed over the authentic wood siding. Her sensitive nose picked up on the fact that he had indeed been updating this place.

"It's really coming along, Nate," she smiled.

"I've been making some changes here and there. Getting it just right," he murmured, and she swore his cheeks grew pink in the dim light of the car.

They stepped out and she enjoyed the crunch of the fresh gravel under her sneaker clad feet before following him up the stone pathway to the front door. Evening mist crawled above the ground covering he'd planted across the front yard and she felt like a princess in a fairytale climbing the steps of the mysterious prince's castle.

But Luisa Sposa was no princess. She was a doctor and Nate Cordoza was a graphic designer and an Enforcer. *A warrior not a prince.* The thick corded muscles that wrapped round his arms and legs were a testament to that fact.

Her she-Bear approved of his commanding physique almost as much as the woman in her lusted after it. *Dinner. It's just dinner.* She repeated the phrase to herself knowing that whatever this was, it would end with something far more satisfying than the pasta sauce she smelled simmering on the stove.

"You really do cook," she sounded surprised even to her own ears.

"Well, I can't take all the credit for this here," he nodded towards the kitchen and guided her inside with a hand on her back, "I have to admit I'm pretty damn good at grilling a steak and potato now and then, but Clary sent the sauce for the pasta over earlier and I set it to simmer while you were finishing up your rounds."

He rubbed the back of his neck when he talked. She wondered if he was embarrassed by all the effort he'd put into this dinner, or the fact he'd gotten help from Clary, the Devlin's trusted housekeeper.

Not that he had reason to be. It was incredibly thoughtful of him. For a curvy girl, Luisa couldn't boil water. Her dinners were mostly takeout or frozen meals from the supermarket. This was especially nice.

Luisa couldn't help but be touched. He was more thoughtful than she would've given him credit for and that was enough to stop her in her tracks. It would be easier to deny him, to deny *them*, if he just stayed the one-dimensional cave-Bear she'd imagined him to be.

The kind of mate who'd demand his woman stay home and cook and clean and make babies. The kind who would object to her chosen career. But he wasn't cooperating. *Darn Bear has to go and be all wonderful and stuff...Ugh!*

"Take a load off, honey, I'll bring you a plate."

She sat down at the enormous granite table that sat in the far corner of the large kitchen. Unlike most of the cabins that dotted the shore, this one had all modern appliances and was obviously recently redone. She approved of the clean lines and expensive materials that he'd chosen. Not that she was concerned with having the best, not by any means. It just looked neater and cleaner that way. She did love a clean kitchen.

Even the color palette was not unlike what she'd have done. Warm yellows and oranges looked well with the soft wood cabinets and chairs. The Granite was a mixture of browns with gold veins that accentuated the light dandelion colored walls.

It was a dream of a room. Comforting and inviting. *Just the kind of kitchen mom and Krissy always raved about.* She smiled thinking of her family. Mom was finally at peace. Krissy was married. Luisa was a doctor. *Holy cow!* When did she grow up?

It seemed to have happened suddenly. Like some sort of dream or nightmare when she thought about her mother's passing. She'd never really known her father. The bastard had abandoned them years ago, and she couldn't muster any desire to track him down. Not now anyway.

Krissy had been her rock. The one who'd take care of things when their mom was ill. And that had been far too often for a single mother with two Bear Shifter daughters. Still, she'd done her best.

Luisa's interest in a career in medicine stemmed from her mother's illness. Determined to fight cancer and all manner of disease she'd studied hard throughout her life as a student. Of course, that meant leaving the more mundane, everyday things to Krissy. Not that her older sister complained.

Now that she was back in Barvale, she'd moved into her childhood home. Sadness plagued her every time she stepped over the threshold. In fact, she'd been dragging her feet the last fifteen minutes of her shift, hating the idea of returning to the old house that held so many memories for her.

"Would you like some pepper or cheese on your pasta?" Nate asked, jogging her from her reverie.

"Please," she answered.

"Alrighty, then," his Texas accent was slight at times, but she still picked it up. It kind of tickled her senses, like that crazy good scent of his.

She smiled at the homey picture he made, dishing up some delicious smelling *fusilli* and serving her as if he'd done it a million times. He was at home in the kitchen, unlike herself. She was a certifiable mess when it came to cooking. Always been too busy studying to do anything like that. She frowned.

"What's wrong?" Nate cocked his head to the side as he placed the dish in front of her.

"I was just thinking," she began.

"Well now, that will get you into all kinds of trouble, honey girl."

"I don't cook."

There. She'd said it. Just left it lying there out in the open unlike the dirty little secret she'd been hiding for years. Female Shifters knew how to cook for their men.

"And?" One sleek eyebrow raised; Nate looked at her as if she'd lost her mind.

"What do you mean *and*? I don't cook, Nate. At all. I could burn water."

"Seeing as how Clary loves to cook in bulk, I imagine she'd be happy to feed you. But just in case this has anything to do with me and you and that big ol' elephant in the room otherwise known as our mating, well now, honey mine, I gotta say, I don't give a rat's ass if you cook. Got it?" He wouldn't let her look away. Not until she nodded while staring at the arrogant gleam in his glittery green eyes.

"Now try this," he grinned and held a fork full of *fusilli* coated in thick, red sauce to her mouth.

She accepted the bite, allowing him to feed her. It was sensual and sexy and made her stomach clench and her head spin. The spicy flavors burst on her tongue. Sausage, garlic, crushed red pepper, sea salt, ripe plum tomatoes, and olive oil.

It was fucking, *er, frigging* delicious. But not as good as what came next.

Heat flared in Nate's eyes with every bite he fed her. When she shook her head, he held his glass of red sangria to her lips, watching as she swallowed a good, long slip. Then he pulled his chair right against hers.

Sitting on it sideways, he opened his long legs and fit hers in between. She chewed the slice of fresh fruit he fed her from his wine glass. She moaned at the burst of citrus and sweet wine flooded her senses.

Luisa swallowed it down and licked her lips, her gaze never wavering from his. His face was serious as any hunter as he fed her another bite of fruit, and another until she pushed his fork away.

"I can't eat anymore," she whispered. The room was growing warm. Or was that just the wine? She swallowed and licked her lips again, aware of the way his predatory eyes followed the movement.

"Aren't you having anything?" She asked, only now realizing he'd fed her but not himself.

"Good idea," he answered.

Next thing she knew, Nate had closed in on her. One hand wrapped firmly, yet gently around the back of her neck while the other tilted her face up to his.

"I've been waiting a week for this," he growled as he claimed her lips.

This was no tender meeting of mouths, *no sir*. It was heat and passion. His work roughened hands felt good as they trailed along her arms and soft belly, touching her everywhere. She knew where they were going, where this was heading, but she was powerless to stop the force of sensations that threatened to overwhelm her.

He was so big, so powerful and she loved his easy strength as he stood up and lifted her swiftly into his arms. She'd never been one of those dainty little girls people liked to carry. Luisa was a Shifter. A curvy one. Strong as a, *well*, as a Bear. She also enjoyed food and didn't let modern day sensibilities dictate her appetite.

She loved her curves. Was at home in her short yet fluffy body. She had no doubt that Nate found it attractive. Especially if the way he was currently feeling her up said anything about his thoughts on the subject. He laid her down on his enormous bed and hovered over her just looking. *Must be custom made*, she thought idly as she bounced on the hard surface.

"You are so beautiful, honey," he murmured and caught her mouth again in a kiss that was soul shattering. Touching nothing but her face he devoured her lips as if he could not get enough. She knew she couldn't. *Oh Nate.*

The past year had been rough. Sure, she'd gotten that inkling that he was her mate when she'd met him, but she hardly knew what that meant. She'd been finishing her residency over at the nearby St. Francis Hospital and couldn't afford to follow her natural instinct.

Of course, knowing all that didn't mean her sow was okay with it. Oh no. Her she-Bear always seemed to be on edge. Then of course the biggest life-altering event in her life up until now had happened.

Her mother's illness had grown worse until she'd succumbed to it. Patricia Sposa deserved to rest in peace, but Luisa still missed her. Through it all, Krissy had been her rock. Her sister had always been more mother than sibling, but Luisa had been hit just as hard by their mother's death.

But Krissy wasn't the only one who'd walked with her through these times. Nate had been there too, she finally realized as his mouth made love to hers. Always in the background, still he'd been there. A solid, calming force, available whenever she'd needed him. And she had alternately ignored him or maintained her distance. *Until last week at the wedding.*

"Look at me, honey, stay right here with me," he spoke softly, and she obeyed the subtle command. She wanted this. Wanted him. So much.

In a flurry of motion their clothing was gone, she

felt him against her as he nuzzled her neck, down to her breast, brushing over the claiming mark he'd left on her body. Sensation sizzled through her, tightening her stomach, making her pussy weep for him.

"Nate," she cried out as his thick fingers stroked her slick entrance. So good, the burning press of his fingers stretching her sent tendrils of pleasure snaking through her body. *More.* She wanted more.

She ran her nails down his back and through his hair. Needing that tactile connection she didn't, *no*, she *couldn't* stop. Touching him wherever she could reach was of the utmost importance.

"Want you," she moaned as he licked a trail down her gently rounded belly to the soft blonde curls that shielded her sex from his eyes.

Nate growled deep in his throat as he pushed her legs further apart. His chest rumbled as he looked his fill, parting her folds and gaping at her exposed heat. Luisa grew even wetter under his stare.

Never before had she been so revealed to any man. Her she-Bear was strong and dominant in her own right. The beast hated the idea of submitting to anyone. *Except him. Mate.*

She watched his head dip and felt his mouth on her, insistent yet gentle. He licked and suckled her into oblivion. Seeming to savor every drop of her moisture, he caressed her with his lips and tongue, even using a fang to scrape against her sensitive nub. Luisa was still gasping with the force of her first orgasm when he flipped them over and lifted her onto his body.

He kissed her lips, and she tasted herself on him. The sweet musk should have been strange, but it was sexy and natural coming from him. She moaned and tangled her tongue with his, licking her way to his neck and shoulders, to the place that bore her mark.

She loved the shudder that racked his powerful body. Reveled in the power she had over him like this. Their mutual desire crested, and Nate's firm hands gripped her ass and hips as he lifted her and slammed her down hard on his thick shaft.

"Fuck, honey, so tight," he groaned.

His girth stretched her to the limit, filling her so good. She yelled his name and rode him like she was born to. That feeling of rightness reached all the way down to her bones as Luisa lifted back up and slammed herself down on his engorged sex.

His head was arched back, he gasped for air and grit his teeth as she took the reins. Luisa watched greedily as his movements became jerky, his plea-sure just out of reach.

"Not without you, honey," he growled as his thumb found her clit. She moaned low and hard as he stroked her sensitive nub in time with her shaky movements. Nate flashed his fangs as the Bear came out to play, but he managed to control the animal.

She cried out, explosive ecstasy crashing over her just as his own body went rigid. He pulled her to him, teeth slicing through her skin as he marked her once more, this time on her shoulder.

Their matebond pulsed around them, tightening and winding. *An unbreakable thing. Or was it.* Her father had married her mother, called her mate, then up and left.

She was too afraid to believe in *it*, in *him*. Too afraid he wouldn't accept her career or her life choices. It shattered her just thinking about it. Luisa felt that pain and fear all the way to her core.

CHAPTER
SIX

She left. *Again.* Nate punched a whole clean through his living room wall when he'd finally realized Luisa was gone the morning after they'd made love.

He thought for sure she was going to stay this time, acknowledge their mating as she hadn't done after the wedding, but no. *Fuck it all to hell*, he growled. He was wrong. *Again.*

What was he going to have to do to make her see? He frowned as he saw the hole in his sheetrock wall and cursed the extra work, he'd made for himself. *Shit.*

Well, there was no use delaying the inevitable. His headache was gone and any danger of him having a concussion was over. Despite the doctor's orders to stay off his feet, he ambled over to the garage and got some supplies.

He had the hole patched in under fifteen minutes and went on to take a look at the addition he'd been working on. Luisa didn't know it yet, but he'd bought this place with her in mind. Determined to make it *their* den. A place he could finally call home.

He opened a can of pale blue paint and went to work on the second coat. Krissy had assured him it was Luisa's favorite color. The blue would really pop once he had the white trim finished. It would be just fine for the tiny medical examination room he was adding onto the side of the garage for her.

Back in Flint, the Clan doc had something similar though not as modern. He figured Luisa would enjoy having someplace handy to care for her patients should they come a knockin' in the middle of the night as Shifters were known to do.

The medical table had already arrived along with several other top of the line machines he'd purchased for her. Once the paint dried, he'd polish the tile floor one more time, then he'd be able to move everything in. Next to the examination room was a large airy office space for her. Other than the basics, he'd left it empty, figuring she'd like to choose her furnishings.

The entire house was something of a testament to his feelings for her, but instead of showing her that last night he'd jumped her bones. *Idiot.* But it wasn't as if he could help it. Whenever he was within twenty feet of her the only thing his Bear could think of was sinking into her sweet heat. *Double shit.*

He needed to Change, to walk through the woods and commune with his inner animal. It was the only way he could ground the beast and satisfy the urge to simply grab her caveman style and hide her away until she accepted him. Not that that would work. *Would it?* Oh fuck it, he had enough for the day. After he put away the paint and supplies, he went to the woods behind the cabin.

His Shift breezed through him like a soft summer wind. One second he was a man, the next his enormous Grizzly Black Bear stood on four legs. Almost a thousand pounds of muscle and shaggy brown fur, Nate pawed the ground making the very earth shake before taking off into the dense trees behind his large, open backyard.

The Devlin family had built along the coast of Lake Ursa for generations. They owned the land and lake alike. Strange, but not unheard of. They cared for the land as if they were a bunch of environmentalists, he knew that for a fact. Pouring a good chunk of their money into keeping it safe and protected for the Clan.

What am I gonna do about Luisa? He pondered his sweet, curvy mate as he ambled through the blooming forest. Summer had brought with it countless sunny days and ample rain, turning the Garden State into a certifiable rain forest in his eyes.

He pressed his nose into the dirt taking a good whiff of the muddied path before his senses started to stir. Something was off. A scent in the air like rotted meat met his nostrils. Nate growled deep in his bearish chest.

He followed the scent all the way to a most unexpected place. The Barvale Urgent Care Clinic. *Grrr.* Without thinking of the consequences, he shifted back into human form and walked up the back steps quickly. He didn't want to have to explain why he was naked.

He ducked into a supply room and shrugged on some too tight scrubs before walking into a room with a plaque on the door that labelled it the doctors' lounge. He thought about how long it would take him to find her in this place with its clinically clean smells, but he needn't have worried. *There she was.*

His Luisa was curled into a ball on the couch sleeping soundly with the scent of old coffee wafting in the air around them. He walked to the pot and sniffed. Shuddering at the contents. He walked to the sink and dumped the contents, putting on a fresh pot before turning to her. She'd appreciate it when she woke up, he was sure. Besides his Bear approved of him caring for her like that. *Good mate.*

His eyes ate her up. He didn't want to disturb her as he knew she'd had a long shift yesterday and probably had the same today. He flicked his gaze over to the microwave and noted it was seven o'clock at night. Time must have gotten away from him between his renovations and walk through the woods.

As if she sensed him near, she turned her face towards where he stood. Sniffing the air deeply, she must have scented something she liked as a wide smile curled her pretty pink lips upward. Nate couldn't help himself, he eased down on his knees like a man possessed and brushed her soft blonde curls away from her face.

"Mmm, Nate?" she asked opening her chocolate brown eyes and smiling at him.

"Hey there, honey," he said and pressed his forehead to hers before dropping a quick kiss on her mouth.

He sat back on his heels enjoying the short time before realization dawned on her face. She sat up fast and almost fell off the couch before he grabbed her.

"What are you doing here?" She gasped and turned her face left and right. The soft lazy look in her pretty eyes turned quickly to shock then annoyance.

"I was, uh, walking in the woods and I tracked a stench I discovered all the way to this place. Wanted to check on you, make sure you were safe," he said and stood up, giving her the space she obviously needed no matter how much it cut him inside.

"You broke into the supply closet?" She said and looked at his scrubs.

"Sorry. Didn't think you'd appreciate me walking round here naked as the day I was born," he smirked at her blush and not for the first time counted himself blessed with such a gorgeous mate.

Luisa wiped the sleep from her eyes and stood up, not before frowning at his bare feet. She walked over to one of the tall lockers that lined the wall silently. Opened the door without even glancing in his direction, grabbing a new pair of men's slides and thrusting them out to him. *A perfect fit*, he thought, secretly pleased that she'd guessed correctly.

"Thank you, honey," he said and put them on.

"Sure. We keep a bunch of these on hand in case of emergencies," she was filling the air with ordinary words, but her eyes were saying something else. Something wary and hidden.

Nate wanted to pry those secrets from her, but he was a patient man. It would take patience to win a woman like Luisa and he had every intention of doing just that. Like Taylor said, though Nate didn't need to be told, she was totally fucking worth it, so he better slow the hell down. His brother didn't mince words.

Nate exhaled and broke their heated gaze. He nodded to the waistband of her scrubs where her cell phone was tucked.

"Can I use your phone? I need to call Daniel."

"Of course, um, I'm going to pour a cup of coffee, someone must have made a fresh pot," she replied and handed over her phone, "want some?"

He nodded his thanks and punched in the number, watching as she walked over to the large stainless-steel sink and splashed some water on her face. Her skin was like milk. Clear and smooth, pale and soft to the touch. He was crazy about it. Wanted to touch it, taste it. *Grrr.*

"Black," she said and handed him a steaming mug. He was happy she knew how he took it. She took a long sip of her own, *two creams one sugar*, and placed the mug on the counter.

"I, uh, should probably go do my rounds," she turned to him and faltered endearingly as he lifted the edge of his shirt to wipe his brow, revealing a patch of smooth dark skin. *She likes my abs. Good to know.* He smiled at her as he stored away that piece of information.

"I'll find you before I leave," he promised.

"You will?"

"Sure I will. To give you back your phone," he said with a forced casualness he didn't feel.

The Bear in him was roaring up a storm. Demanding he pick up his mate and love her long and hard till she wouldn't even think of running out on him again. *Fuck.* He turned his back on her, fighting his beast and the raging arousal he felt just by being near her.

She tested his self-control as nothing else ever had. Not even all the fighting he'd done growing up in a Clan where he was hated. Not even the time he saw his babysitter, a fine as hell girl-woman aptly named Shelly Hills, take off her t-shirt to show him her breasts after she'd lost a game of Uno when he was just twelve years old.

Keeping calm in both of those situations were a piece of fucking cake compared to being near his fated mate and not being able to touch her freely. Oh, he'd given in when she was asleep with that subtle brushing of her hair and chaste kiss. But that was nothing compare to the turbulent desire that flared to life whenever she was close by.

Get a fucking hold of yourself, you're not a cub anymore. The sound of a gruff voice on the line grabbed his attention and suddenly, Nate was all business. *Clan business.*

"Yeah, Daniel? It's Nate, I'm calling from Luisa's phone," he spoke into the cell phone, grinning when he heard his little niece let out a demanding wail.

She had her daddy wrapped tight around her chubby little finger. *As it should be*, he thought. Mia was one cutie pie of a cub. Destined to be a heart-breaker he was certain. He hoped she liked that soft, plush rocking-bear he'd sent over for her the other day.

She was a bit small for it, but soon she'd be able to use the thing. He specially designed it using her daddy's bear's coloring so the little one could have him near when the real thing was unavailable. As head Enforcer, Daniel was a busy man. Honest to a fault and bullheaded, he'd been a bit of a prick when Nate first met him. Who knew his surly brother would take to fatherhood like a duck to water?

Daniel's dedication to his mate and child surprised everyone, but not Nate. Not really. He might be new to the family, but he recognized the love his brother had for the lovely Lacey. Hell, he saw it in all three of the Devlin men when they looked at their mates.

Jealousy threatened to surge inside of him as he thought about the three devoted couples, but he shot it down fast as it sprung up. Nate was happy for them. Yes, he was a bit envious of the ready way all three women had accepted their mates, but that was only because his Luisa was cautious. He couldn't fault her for that.

She'd worked hard her whole life. Had a shitty father who'd abandoned his wife as her first example of marriage. Watched her sister Krissy pine for her mate for years before his idiot half-brother, Taylor, finally realized she was it for him. So, yeah, she had some reservations.

Nate understood that, but he was just a man. Okay, *a man and a Bear*, and he wanted her with him now. It was damned frustrating the way she kept sidestepping their mating. Still, he was not going to give up. *Hell no*, his Bear growled. *Soon*, he promised himself. He'd have his mate by his side soon.

"Did you mark the locations of the scent?" Daniel asked through the cell and Nate turned his attention to his brother, all business now.

He spoke in low hushed tones, aware of the fact that all of the staff at the Barvale Clinic were Shifters, mostly Clan. Still, the things he'd discovered in his walk through the woods were for Enforcers ears only.

"Yeah, I marked the trees for our men to find. Should be easy enough. There were remnants of chewed up animals drained of their blood, some scat, and a particularly grotesque amount of other bodily fluids surrounding this small, hidden cave about half a mile from the clinic's front door. It was deserted now though," Nate recounted the events preceding his arrival at the clinic.

"Good work. I'll call Bowie and get him over there right now. Oh, I'm also going to set up a meeting with someone who has expressed great interest in this new threat," Daniel returned quietly.

"Who might that be?"

"Later. You coming up to the Den?"

"Thought I'd wait for Luisa to finish up first, make sure she gets home alright."

"I see. Making any headway there, bro? How is our little operation going anyway? Did you show her the exam room?"

"Easy, nosy Nellie! It's early days yet."

"Fuck off, bro," Daniel laughed into the phone, "Look, I just want you to know I wish you good luck. Nothing in the world beats waking up to your mate every morning except maybe lying down with her every night," he chuckled.

Nate just grunted. He had the lying down part alright. It was the getting her to stick around till morning that he was struggling with. *FML.*

"Alright, bro, gotta go."

Luisa might need time to come around to the fact they were mates, but he was not about to risk her safety. Those Hunter Vamps were hanging in the area for some reason and they were too fucking close for comfort.

CHAPTER
SEVEN

Luisa stood under the spray of hot water with her eyes closed as she washed off the remnants of her shift. It had been a hard one. Twelve hours of countless runny noses, three broken arms, four sprains, a lawnmower accident, a nickel stuck in the nose of a hysterical toddler, and a pre-teen Clanmate who was just upon the first stages of his Change.

But none of that was the reason why she felt tense and out of sorts. *Oh no.* It was the near seven-foot-tall model gorgeous Bear who'd shadowed her around the last few hours of her shift. Of course, he'd ignored her when she said she didn't need him to stay.

Nate had showed up completely uninvited. *And naked.* She couldn't forget that. Well, he'd come in wearing scrubs he'd swiped from the supply closet, but that only meant he was naked when he'd arrived. *Too bad I missed it. Grrr.*

No. Bad Bear! Just thinking about his rock-hard body made her tingly in all her secret pink bits. *Sigh.* What could she say? She was a total slut for the man. Making love with him was like she took the best sex she'd ever fantasized about and gave it a good dose of super strong fucking steroids. *Yeah.* It was that good.

She was still aching from the way they'd gone at it in his house the other night. He'd kissed and licked and fucked, er *made love* like a god as far as she was concerned. This whole not cursing thing was really difficult for her. *Sigh.* But yeah, sometimes it was making love and sometimes it was down and dirty fucking, either way it was the most fabulous sex she had ever had. She'd loved it every single way they'd come together, and she couldn't wait for more.

Sneaking out while he slept was the hardest thing she'd ever done. But it was for her own sanity! Okay, so maybe she had to tell herself that over and over. But it was still true.

He was a guy. *A Shifter.* You know the type, the super macho, dominant, he-man, *me say you do* kind of guy. She had no doubt in her mind that he'd want to keep her chained to the bed or the stove depending on which one of his appetites ruled the day! There was no way she was up for that kind of lifestyle. *Hell to the no!*

But have you ever heard him say those things or act that way? Ugh. Her annoying she-Bear spoke up at the most inopportune times! Like when she was trying to convince herself she was better off ignoring her premature mating.

He waited for over a year to claim us. And you kind of instigated the whole thing. A whole year, Luisa. You scented him that day on Lake Ursa too and you knew he was ours then.

She stepped out of the shower and grabbed a nearby towel. Rubbing it roughly over her skin till she was huffing from the exertion.

It was true. She'd known from their first meeting who he was to her and, yes, she suspected he'd known it to. But he hadn't forced the issue then. Truth was, he hadn't forced it now either.

For all intents and purposes, Luisa was the insti-gator here. She'd come on to him at Krissy's and

Taylor's destination wedding. *Gulp. Just admit it.* She stood stock still as shivers went up and down her spine.

Here she was ranting over her uncontrollable desire for a man who'd been nothing but kind, passionate, tender, and patient with her. And, to top it off, she'd initiated the whole damn thing. *So, why don't you just enjoy it?*

"Maybe I can't enjoy it because he won't fit into any one category, I try to put him in!" She yelled at no one as she stomped over to her dresser and grabbed a thin nightgown. It was rather warm that evening and she was a fitful sleeper.

"Oh great! Now I'm talking to myself!" She stomped down the stairs into the kitchen and grabbed the counter with both hands. She counted to ten then exhaled.

The kitchen of her childhood home felt empty and sad all of a sudden. It still held fond memories of Krissy and her mother and the frequent tea parties they'd shared while she was growing up, but that part of her seemed so far away. Good memories for sure. To be cherished and saved and taken out every now and again to look over.

She missed her mother, though truth be told she was hardly around the last few years. College and medical school had taken up a lot of her time. Her mother had understood and encouraged her youngest daughter to go out and conquer the world. She was always so giving and understanding. *You were always there when I needed you, Mom.*

What advice would she have given her daughter now? Her mother never allowed the unfortunate circumstances of her health and marriage to make her bitter or resentful. She was no man hater. In fact, she'd often told her children stories about true love and her hope that they would both one day make good marriages.

She'd called her mom hopelessly old fashioned after such discussions. Only now did she realize what her mother was trying to do. She was trying to ensure her daughters saw the world with fresh eyes. Without the taint of their father's abandonment and that evil indiscriminating monster that was cancer. Her lower lip trembled as she filled the old tea pot up with water and placed it on the stove.

Her mother was gone now, to a better place. She understood that, but Luisa still missed her. And even though Krissy was only a fifteen-minute ride away, Luisa still felt alone in the empty house. *You don't have to be alone. You have a mate.* Inhale. Exhale. *Do I?*

"This is silly. You are being morose," she told

herself as she got out a ceramic pot and jar of loose tea leaves.

She wasn't a little girl anymore, but she still enjoyed a nightly cup of peppermint tea. *I wonder if he drinks tea.* She shook her head disgustedly. She was a grown ass woman now. A doctor! If she wanted to know something about him, she should just ask him.

She grabbed her cell phone and opened her contacts. He was right there under *Nate*. Exactly where she put him a year ago. After learning of his introduction to the Barvale Clan, she'd been kind of wary of her feelings for him.

After all, he had tried to pick up her sister at *The Thirsty Dog*. Of course, both had explained their rather chaste body shot had been a bit of fun that had gotten blown out of proportion by a suddenly very jealous Taylor Devlin.

If anything, Nate was the catalyst for her sister's present state of marital bliss. Maybe she should thank him. Of course, Krissy and Nate had been platonically friendly afterwards. He'd even asked Krissy to model for him for one of those avatar thingies he was always working on for Grave Enterprises.

That was weird. *Hmm.* Krissy had stripped down to her fur for him. Shifted so he could sketch her transformation from woman to Bear. But he'd never asked Luisa to model for him. Heat burned her cheeks and she stopped midway to the whistling kettle as realization struck. *OMG. I'm jealous of my own sister!*

Shame filled her and she shook her head, dropping her cell phone to the counter just as it began to ring. *Damn.* It was Nate. She clicked the little green icon before she could talk herself out of it.

"Hey there, honey," his Texas drawl made her smile as it had a hundred times before.

Good thing he wasn't there to see it. Last thing he needed was some encouragement. Especially when her own feelings were so jumbled.

"Hi," she replied. Was that breathy voice really how she sounded?

"I was just thinking about you," he continued.

"Oh yeah? Me too," she conceded.

"Really? Well, that is nice to hear."

"Are you outside?" The sounds of the evening breeze and chirping crickets met her sensitive ears.

"Yup. Walking back to my place from the Den. Had a meeting with the boys."

"About what?" She chatted with him about the meeting and all matter of little things, just liking the sound of his voice and the way he didn't rush her or put pressure on her about their mating.

"Made it back," he announced, and she recognized the sounds of his front door opening and closing.

"Did you?" She paused, realizing she didn't want the call to end, but she felt foolish prolonging it.

"You on in the morning tomorrow?"

"Not till three in the afternoon actually," she said and bit her lip. *Waiting.*

"How about I swing by and fix you breakfast before you go? Around ten alright?"

"Sure," she agreed quickly.

"Alright, I'll see you then, honey."

Luisa could practically here the smile in his voice and she found herself grinning back. He was so sweet like this.

"Um, Nate?"

"Yeah, honey?"

"Do you drink tea?"

"Tea?" She could hear the smile in his voice. It was infectious.

"Actually, I have been known to have a glass of

iced sweet tea now and then, but I also like a cup of Moroccan Mint once in a while."

"Good," she said, grateful once again he couldn't see her grinning like a damn fool just from hearing his voice.

A crash sounded from outside and she turned towards her back door. She frowned, distracted now by his voice and whatever was happening outside.

"Luisa? What was the noise?"

"Um, I don't know. Let me check," she began.

"No, honey, don't go outside. I'll be right there."

"Why? What's going on, Nate?"

"Just stay on the line. I'm texting Bowie and the others to swing by your place too."

More loud noises and the screech of a neighborhood cat made her blood chill. Luisa was no scared kid. She was a woman. *A Bear Shifter*. She moved to her back door.

"I'm just gonna take a peek," she said.

"Luisa, please, I'm almost there. Stay inside," his gruff command was followed by the squeal of tires on pavement.

"Don't tell me what to do. I'm not a child, Nate," she replied angrily. *Here it is*, she thought to herself, *his cave-bear attitude in full force*! But instead of feeling vindicated, she felt sad and hurt.

"Honey, it could be dangerous-"

"Yeah well, I'll see for myself," she clicked the cell phone off and shook her head.

Wasn't that just like a man? Trying to give her orders as if she would simply obey! Luisa growled. Even her Bear was annoyed. The noises seemed to stop so she opened her back door and stepped onto the wraparound porch in her bare feet and thin nightgown.

"Anyone there?" She called out and sniffed the air. *Ew!* The stench of rotten meat reached her nostrils and she had to fight not to gag. Some animal must have gotten her neighbor's garbage since she herself rarely ate at home, there wasn't much refuse to throw away.

The sound of heavy breathing brought her head around and Luisa gasped. She stood face to face with the most grotesque looking creature she'd ever seen. Her Bear roared in her mind's eye, but she stood frozen in the thing's black-eyed stare.

Long, needle-like teeth protruded from black lips and gray skin as the creature hissed at her. It was tall, thin, and held its clawed hands out aggressively. Black liquid oozed from its mouth.

"Back up," she ordered the thing, but it threw its head back and screeched into the air.

"*Eeeeeeeeeee*," the sound was worse than nails on a chalkboard and she covered her ears but didn't back up.

Every instinct was telling her to flee, but she remained frozen. Its bat-like face was covered in something wet, some kind of mucus and the sickly-sweet stench of rot and decay clung to its matted hair and emaciated shape.

"What are you?" She said aloud only to be answered with another deafening shriek.

The sound seemed to bring more of them. Three, if she guessed correctly. She couldn't make them out as they clung to the shadows, but she did hear one more take to the porch.

The first creature lunged for her, barely missing her exposed flesh with its claws and Luisa cursed the tiny nightgown she wore. She ducked quickly missing another swipe by the creature.

She might be an egghead, but she was a Bear too. She had quick reflexes and used every one of them right then. Another creature dove for her from behind and she soon realized retreating to the house was no longer an option.

She rolled off the porch onto the grass and took off to the woods. The things followed behind her. They were fast, but so was she. Her first concern was for her normal neighbors. Whatever these things were, they were not part of the normal world and needed to be kept hidden. *Why didn't I listen to Nate?*

She'd beat herself up about it later. Right then, she needed to stay alive. A creature landed in front of her with a thud and she stopped in her tracks. Panting for air she looked and realized she was surrounded.

"Luisa!" She heard Nate cry her name, but it was far away.

"You sure you want to do this?" She growled at her attackers.

"Fine then," she said and burst through her nightgown in a blur of fur and claws.

One creature got hold of her before her shift was complete and sliced through the skin of her left forearm. Luisa roared and swung her fully changed paw, knocking the thing back.

She did her best warding them off. Fighting three at a time was not easy on the she-Bear. They seemed to be coming from every direction. They were inexhaustible as they scratched and clawed at her.

The fight seemed to go on forever but in reality, must have only been a few minutes. Still, she was more than grateful to see her huge Grizzly Black Bear mate charging towards them.

He took on the leader, slicing with his claws and retreating to stand in front of where she'd slumped to the ground. The scent of her blood seemed to be driving the creatures wild. As a Shifter, she was aware of many supernatural beings, but these things were out of her purview. *Must be the Hunter Vampires Daniel mentioned in the Clan Newsletter,* now if only she'd read the whole thing. *Ow!* Her Bear roared as the scratch bled and pulsed beneath her fur.

She recalled what she could about the Clan newsletter and with a shock realized these were the creatures they'd been warned about. But they were nothing like she'd expected. Nothing of the human beings they once were remained in these beast-like creatures. And yet, they were not animals either.

They simply seemed *wrong* to her. An ungodly abomination. She shivered at the thought but was unable to do much more than that. The last attack had left her pretty winded.

Nate bellowed and pawed the ground threateningly. The Hunter Vamps were forming a semicircle around him. There now six of the things and Luisa trembled. They were sickly looking but much stronger than you'd think. Pain emanated from the wound causing her Bear to bellow and writhe on the ground.

Nate roared as the leader charged him. He stood on his hind legs, all thousand pounds of him and landed in the creature with a thud. As the rest of the Hunters charged her mate, Luisa thought she saw four large white blurs heading their way.

That was all she recalled before everything went black.

CHAPTER
EIGHT

"Luisa?" Nate's voice sounded panicked to his own ears, so he gritted his teeth and forced a calmness he didn't feel into his words.

"Can you hear me, honey?" Fear settled in his stomach and he swallowed back the bile that threatened to rise. He couldn't lose her now.

Nate sucked in a great big breath and removed the blood-soaked bandage on her forearm. The jagged wound had been raw and bleeding when he'd carried her back home. He noted with relief that the skin had already began knitting itself together. *Thank fuck for Shifter healing.*

Her skin was looking better now too, her pallor fading. She had more color than she did a half hour ago when he'd first scooped her blood splattered body up off the forest floor just a few yards from her house.

Dammit. I should have never left her alone. He cursed himself ten times a fool for not forcing the issue of their mating. Seeing her prone form lying there so still and silent was almost too much for him to handle. The Bear in him threatened to go apeshit as he looked at her so quiet and unmoving.

After he'd basically stomped the brains out of what appeared to be the leader of the clutch of Hunters, the other Enforcers fought off the rest of the Vamps. He'd quickly turned to tend his mate when the rest of them fled. His overprotective Bear had snarled and snapped at the four Polar Bears when they'd come too close to his wounded female.

Realizing these men were his allies and Clanmates he forced himself to Change. Luisa had turned back to her human form after losing consciousness. He hadn't allowed himself to focus too heavily on her nudity or the fact there were other unmated males able to see her. He wasn't a complete fucking jerk though it was a near thing. She was injured and needed attention.

After he'd settled her on the couch, he tended her wounds. And after he'd reassured himself that she was alright, he'd ordered the four males to contact Marcus and to act as sentries outside her tiny house.

"Mmm. Nate?" Her voice was breathy and soft as she called his name. It worried him to hear her so fragile.

"Hey, now, easy," he said as he helped her sit up.

"There were Hunter Vamps outside," she shook her head and he saw fear light her eyes. He didn't like that at all.

Gathering her up close, he eased down to the sofa while she clung to him. The thin sheet he wrapped around her body did nothing to hide her soft, sexy curves. *I am nothing but a fucking animal thinking about her body while she is scared and hurt.*

"I should have listened," she said, but he shook his head.

"No, honey, I should have explained better. Taken better care of you. I am so sorry," he smoothed her hair away from her lovely face.

"Sorry, love, so sorry. I'll do better, promise you, honey. I promise you, my love," he said and kissed her cheeks and her eyelids, her nose and her lips.

It was true, he realized with a start. He loved this woman. Her stubbornness and sass. Her incredible brain and dedication to her career. Not to mention her beautiful face and body, and the heart that went with it. Yes, he loved her. And he'd do anything to make sure she knew it. *Starting now.*

"Hey boss, the Alpha just pulled up," Bowie called from the doorway.

The Polar Bear Shifter was smart enough not to enter the room without permission. Good thing too, cause Nate's inner Bear was dangerously on edge. *Grrr.*

"Marcus is here?"

"Had to call him, honey. Daniel will be with him too."

"Luisa!" Both Nate and Luisa looked up to see Krissy Devlin charging into the room.

Nate tensed as his mate's big sister dropped to her knees and ran her hand over Luisa's brow and arm before pulling her into a tight hug. His mate sagged against her sister, but to his utter delight and surprise, she remained rooted to his lap.

"You okay?" Krissy asked and sat back on her feet. Her wide eyes shot from her sister to Nate and the tall she-Bear's eyebrows shot straight up.

"I'm fine, Krissy. Nate, uh, got here just in time," Luisa's voice was calm and reassuring for her sister's benefit he was certain. She'd been a mess a few seconds ago.

Not that he blamed her. Those Hunters were nasty pieces of shit as far as he was concerned. He was satisfied he'd killed one of the fuckers, though his animal wanted them all dead.

As long as they stayed the fuck away from his mate, he was fine. Hell, he was just trying to understand what this new development meant to their relationship. His Bear growled, but Nate shushed him.

Just because she was willing to sit on his lap in front of her sister didn't mean she was ready to call a preacher. He could wait. Would wait. As long as it took. *Grrr,* said his Bear. *Fuck you,* said Nate.

"Nate?"

"Yes, Krissy?"

"Um, why is my sister on your lap?"

"Well-" He started but Luisa interrupted him.

"What happened to the Vamps? Are they all dead?"

"Not all of them-" again he tried to speak but this time Krissy was screeching at him.

"What do you mean *no*? Those bastards tried to kill my sister and you let them live?"

"He had no choice, *bellissima*," a tall, svelte man dressed in all black entered the room as if he had every right.

His commanding presence had every creature in the house focused on him. He was beautiful. Well, prettier than any man Nate had ever seen. Not exactly a compliment in his book. Still, something was off about the guy.

The stranger had long dirty blonde hair, straight as a pin but styled in choppy waves like some kind of celebrity. He had an air of arrogance about him that was undeniable. His eyes were like liquid metal. A dark gray that bordered on black.

He made no move towards Nate or the two women who were in the room with him. He noted with a grunt that the robe he'd dressed Luisa in was covering most of her, but still. She was vulnerable. *Injured. Mate. Mine. Protect.* His Bear was chomping at the bit, demanding to be released, but he held on. *Barely.*

He eased Luisa off his lap and tried to tuck her behind him, but she seemed shocked by the man's presence. The stranger smiled at her and his Bear just about went nuts. Nate noted Bowie's silent approach and waited for the Polar Bear to sneak up and disable the cocky fuck. The man grinned wildly and sidestepped his attack, grabbing his wrist and slamming him into the wall as easily as if he was half his size.

"Fuck, let me go," Bowie growled, but the stranger simply tapped him on the top of his head and the Polar Bear Shifter slumped to the floor. *Shit.* This was no normal. Not a Shifter either. Nate inhaled. *Vampire.*

"Who the fuck are you and what are you doing here?" Nate growled at the dangerous stranger.

He'd had little interaction with bloodsuckers, but he knew enough about them to accept the fact that despite being bigger than the fucker, he was nowhere near as strong or as lethal. *Fucking shit.* He sure as hell didn't want one around his injured mate.

"My name is Baldassare di Capua, but you may call me Bal, young one," he smiled as he spoke revealing two needlelike fangs that set Nate's lip to curling as he sprang from the couch and landed in front of both women.

"Are you threatened?" The Vampire laughed, and Nate's entire body shook with rage.

"You won't be laughing for long, you *sonovabitch!*"

"Please my ursine friend, be at peace, I am not here to harm you," the stranger said, but Nate doubted his sincerity.

The sound of a car pulling up and the heavy thud of feet running towards them had everyone's eyes turning to the door. Except for the Vampire and Nate. They simply stared at each other like two prizefighters circling each other before one of them decided to throw down.

"Alright, what's going on?" Marcus bellowed as he strode in the room and took in the situation. He immediately extended his hand towards the Vampire and Nate growled louder.

"Hello, Bal. Made an entrance, did you?" the Alpha shook his head before turning to Nate.

"Easy brother, he's a friend," Marcus pushed a little Alpha power into his voice and Nate's Bear immediately stilled. Grateful for his Alpha's guidance.

"Krissy? Luisa? You ladies alright?" Marcus asked and at their nod he visibly relaxed.

"Taylor is in the car with Leya, she's having some back pain," he said and looked relieved as both women shot to their feet and headed towards the door.

The Vampire Bal wisely walked inside, leaving the doorway free and clear for the women to pass through. Nate stopped snarling and addressed his Alpha.

"Marcus, Luisa was attacked tonight, and I want to know why the fuck I wasn't allowed to hunt down and kill every last one of those fucking monsters," as he spoke that last word the Vampire hissed angrily, and his eyes shot to him.

"Because, cub, those *monsters* are beyond your comprehension!"

"Enough! Nate you will get your explanation and Bal, you are here as a guest, on Rafe Maccon's recommendation. Don't make me kick your undead ass out of my territory," Marcus snarled in his best Alpha voice.

"Technically I am not undead," the Vampire's immediate calm was eerie, but Nate followed suit by addressing Marcus alone.

"Whatever," Marcus said and nodded towards the small kitchen table.

"Look, I just want to know why the order to kill was revoked," Nate began.

"Because I once helped a Werewolf get his mind and his mate back, and the Macconwood Wolves owed me a favor in return. This is that favor," Bal shrugged one shoulder and Nate raised both his eyebrows.

"Isn't that a bit unusual?"

"Yes, well. I am old, Mr. Cordoza, and I have many friends. Iggy Devlin among them," he nodded at both men.

"You know my father?" Marcus seemed shocked by the revelation, but Nate just waited.

"Indeed. Now *mi amici*, I think it is time we get down to the issue," his voice was lightly accented, Nate noted the hints of the Vampire's Italian ancestry and wondered if he had to work to keep it going. Shifters accents tended to change in his experience.

He'd heard stories about Shifters moving from one place to another and adopting new speech patterns based on location due to their supernatural hearing. That natural bonus also allowed Shifters to become excellent musicians. *Was the same true for Vampires?* He wondered.

"I have located the Hunters nest, but they have not returned as of yet. They seem drawn to this place, to the delectable doctor in fact, not that I blame them. Her blood, *deliziosa*. She smells sweet and bright like a new dawn, I am sure you understand her appeal to us then," Bal said but was interrupted by Nate's snarl.

"You get one warning, bloodsucker. Just one," he growled.

"Ah, I see. She is *taken*. Well, *salut* my friend, that she-Bear is very lovely," Bal grinned widely, revealing his fangs and Nate felt his hackles rise.

"Okay, easy now," Marcus gripped his brother's shoulder, and Nate realized he was holding him down.

"Sorry," he said to Marcus.

"Bal? What is the plan now?"

"Well, my friends, I suggest we lay a trap. The Hunters won't be back tonight. Tomorrow, after sunset, they will most likely try again. The one you unfortunately killed was quite strong, if anything he was the leader of the clutch. If you are going to post guards you must be discreet, their sense of smell is triple that of a healthy Vampire," he said.

"What does that mean?"

"That means think of your own ursine noses and amplify it by a hundred. They have latched onto the she-Bear's scent. They will come for her."

"Over my dead body!" Nate roared.

"Probably, yes," the Vampire agreed, "but let us hope it doesn't come to that. The Hunters are strong, I wish to avoid their deaths. But if you are cornered do not hesitate," his voice was grim, but Nate suddenly felt a new respect for the man.

"Who are they to you?"

"My friends. My family. Strangers. It is hard to tell once they have crossed that line, but there is someone I owe my life to. It is for this person that I try to save these twice damned souls," Bal said with an edge of deep sorrow to his tone that made even Nate sympathize with the Vampire.

"We understand and, because of your friendship with the Macconwood Pack, we want to help. But you must also understand that Luisa is newly mated to Nate, he is going to be extremely protective of her-" Marcus began.

"You're damn fucking straight I am. Listen up, anything happens to her-"

"Understood, my new friend. Please, believe me when I say I will not risk her safety in place of any Hunters now that I understand the situation, I vow this to you," the Vampire nodded as he spoke his oath.

With their plan finalized, Nate bristled. He did not want to put Luisa in danger. Especially when she wouldn't take their mating to the next step.

But how could he protect her when she wouldn't recognize what they had?

Luisa woke alone in her bed. For a moment, she smiled happy with the world and everything in it as she inhaled that subtle autumn sage scent that clung to her skin. *Nate.* She smiled again. Her Bear was satisfied knowing she had a mate and reveling in his claim.

Then reality set in. She was mated and yet *not.* *My fault.* Pain lanced through her connection to her animal. The beast did not understand her human's reticence. She simply wanted her mate. *Now.* Especially after being attacked by Hunter Vamps the night before.

She-Bears were strong, but Vampire strength was something out of the ordinary even for supernaturals. Hunter Vamps were especially dangerous because they no longer bore any semblance to the human beings they once were. Any moral or ethical code they may have once lived by was long gone once they fell into madness.

Bal had explained the night before that the supernatural community still widely debated whether or not that fall was a choice. Immortal beings were tricky. Even those with the mere potential for immortality.

Imagine spending hundreds or thousands of years in a world where the average lifespan was gone in the blink of an eye. Luisa shivered just thinking about watching all her family and friends die. *Horrible.* No wonder they went mad. Her knowledge of Vampirism wasn't as extensive as she'd have liked, but she understood loneliness.

Growing up with a sick mom was difficult, but watching her older sister take every responsibility wasn't any easier. Luisa did her share, but she knew Krissy had sacrificed much of her youth in her effort to care for both Luisa and their mother.

Luisa paid her back by acing her way through college and medical school. Coming back to Barvale after a stint at St. Francis Hospital to work in the brand new Barvale Urgent Care Clinic was like a dream come true.

It was also the reason she'd been hitting the brakes on this thing between her and Nate. *This thing is our mating. Come on. Go get our mate.* Her Bear's mournful growl made Luisa frown. The animal within her had never been so forlorn. She sat up and strode to the bathroom, surprised when the scent of fresh brewed coffee met her nostrils.

Brushing her teeth quickly, she strode out to the kitchen and was shocked to see Nate standing at her stove. He wore a pair of low-slung jeans on his narrow rodeo rider hips and nothing else. Luisa bit her lip as her dark eyes traced every visible inch of him.

His sleek muscles were tanned and glistening in the summer sunlight that streamed in through the windows. He looked good enough to eat. Especially as he worked his magic at her stovetop. She sniffed and sighed. Pancakes. He was making homemade blueberry pancakes drizzled with honey and whipped butter. If she hadn't been in love with him before, she sure as hell was now.

Mossy green eyes caught hers as he turned with a tray in his hands. His smile lit up the room and she was breathless for the second time that morning.

"Morning, honey, I told you I would make you breakfast today. I was gonna surprise you and serve you in bed," he said and placed the tray down on the table before he reached for her.

Luisa went willingly, raising her lips to his only to be disappointed when he dropped a chaste kiss on her mouth. Still, he swallowed her in his embrace. She loved the feel of his warm, sun-kissed skin against hers.

It was nice waking up to him, she realized with a smile. Even though she was fairly certain he spent the night on the couch instead of in her bed. She frowned and bit her lip.

"Hungry?" he asked as he backed away from her and moved the food from the tray to the table.

"Yes, thanks. Did you make all this?" She took a bite and moaned as the flavors burst across her tongue. Was that lemon zest mixed in with the blueberries? *Pure heaven.*

"Sure did," he poured them coffee and fixed hers perfectly before he sat down to join her.

"Oh my God, Nate, this is really *really* good!"

"Thank you. My mama taught me how to cook when I was younger," he shrugged off her compliment and she was delighted to learn her mate was shy!

He stood and refilled his cup of coffee lazily before sitting back down at the table. The intimacy of it felt cozy and right to her. He laughed and smiled a lot. Teased and joked as he refilled a plate with thick bacon slices laced with his special blend of cayenne and brown sugar.

"This is like bacon crack," she moaned and bit into her third slice.

"I sure love to watch you eat, honey," he said.

Luisa swallowed her bite down and licked her lips. That deep growl in his voice matched the flash of light she saw in his green eyes, but still, he did not touch her. Nope. *Disappointed sigh.* Nate remained firmly in his seat.

She felt herself leaning towards him, desire pumping through her veins. What was it about this man? Even when he wasn't touching her, she wanted him like no other. *He's our mate*, her Bear answered readily.

"Nate," she said and moved closer to him.

She was very aware of the thin robe she wore. Knew that in the right light it was practically see-through. His eyes flashed as she placed both hands on his shoulders, pushing his chair back so she had room to scoot up on his lap.

His large hands came around to cup the rounded globes of her ass, keeping her firmly straddling his legs. Her secret place pulsed with need and she gave a little flex of her hips, rubbing against his jean covered staff. He was hard and ready, his breathing uneven as she ran her hands up and down his naked pecs.

"Luisa, what are you doing?"

"You know what I'm doing," she nuzzled his nose and brushed her lips across his. He tasted like coffee and brown sugar, with a hint of cayenne that left her lips tingling for more.

"Honey, this is dangerous," he nipped her lip and she couldn't agree more.

She reached down between them and unfastened his jeans. Holding him in her fist she gripped his hard length and squeezed, loving the hiss that escaped his lips and capturing it with her mouth. She kissed him without reserve. Tangling her tongue with his, savoring the strong spicy flavor that was all Nate.

His cock pulsed in her hand and she moaned. *Mine.* Her she-Bear growled the word into her mind, and she knew the animal inside of her was tired of being kept from her mate.

Luisa was going to fix all that. She was going to tell him she'd made up her mind. Right now. But first, she needed to taste him. *Yesss.* Her she-Bear hissed the word, approving of the way she took control of the situation.

Unused to being the sexual aggressor she found herself invariably turned on by this role reversal. Sliding down his body, she knelt on the floor at his feet. His green eyes glittered in the sunlit kitchen.

"Honey, you don't have to do this," he said and cocked his head to the side, running his tanned fingers through her messy blonde curls.

"I know that, but I want to. Need to taste you," she moaned and leaned forward. With the tip of her tongue she traced his engorged mushroomed head before taking it inside the warm cavern of her mouth. She licked the slit, tasting the salty drop of precum that greeted her lips. He was sweet and savory, everything she could ever need, and she wanted more.

"Damn, honey," he moaned and held her hair back from her face as she took him fully into her mouth.

Luisa had never been so turned on in her entire life. Taking her mate into her mouth she basked in the spiciness of his unique tang. He growled and his grip tightened as she took him *deep, deep, deeper* down her throat. Using her left hand she cupped his balls, stroking the sensitive skin and moaning as she continued to taste him.

"Honey, you gotta stop now," he said and tried pulling her up, but she was a Shifter too and determined to swallow down every last drop of her treat.

Faster and tighter she sucked on his bulbous head, pumping him from root to middle with one hand, while tracing the rest of him with the other. She was amazed by how much she was enjoying herself. Her nipples tightened to hard beads and her own sex tightened and clenched on air as she worked to bring her mate to fulfillment.

"Fuck, Luisa. I'm gonna come," he roared, throwing his head back as his cock jerked in her mouth.

She moaned long and hard as he spilled himself inside of her. Luisa took everything, swallowing all he had to give her. He moaned as his body went limp. Still she continued licking and sucking him until he was clean.

She leaned back on her heels, a satisfied smile on her mouth. She wondered if he understood her message. If he knew what this meant? She had no time to ask as his glittery eyes held hers.

"My turn," he growled and pulled her up from the floor. Sitting her on the counter he parted her robe, stilling her protest with a shake of his head. He cupped her breasts, tweaking the nipples as he ran his hands lovingly over every roll and curve. She was unashamed of her body, loved the way he obviously worshipped it.

"Nate," she protested. This had been for him. A way to demonstrate her love for her mate, but now the tables were turning, and she wasn't sure she could last.

"You had your breakfast honey, now I get mine," his head dipped, and she felt a tug on her panties.

Cool air washed over her throbbing sex, soon to be replaced by his warm tongue. Luisa bucked against him, banging her head on the cabinet, but she hardly felt it. She cried out in her passion. Her slick sex was more than ready for him. He slid two fingers inside as his mouth latched onto her swollen clit.

He was so good at this. So good at everything when it came to her body. Not to mention his skill at his work. Art was never something she excelled at, but she appreciated it. Appreciated him. *Especially when he was going down on her. Oh my gawd!*

She was not much into video games, but she'd seen his work. Had been curious about him from the get-go. Her mate was immensely talented. Had to be to work for Graves Enterprises. Randall Graves was a discerning businessman, a Werewolf who lived in the close town of Maccon City. He was a tech-genius and had a knack for making a success out of anything he touched.

No wonder he wanted her mate to work for him. Nate's artistic talents were incredible. The painting he did for Marcus and Leya was the most beautiful thing she'd ever seen. He managed to capture the love between the couple in the strokes of his brush as he'd portrayed Marcus in his Black bear and Leya as her beautiful self.

Don't get her started on the amazing renditions he'd made of her sister Krissy. The tall, Amazonian Bear Shifter looked regal and stunning as the newest she-Bear Avatar in the *WolfMoon* gaming world. He had an eye for beauty and the talent to go with it. *Wonder what he sees when he looks at me.*

Nate growled deep in his throat and it was all she could do to remember to breathe. The vibrations struck a chord inside of her like she'd never felt. She opened her eyes, watching his head move between her thighs as he brought her to heaven and back down again. Soothing, licking, tasting, kissing. He was simply amazing and all hers if she would only take him. *Mine.*

"Nate!" She called his name, bucking wildly as those expert fingers of his stroked that special spot inside of her that made her see stars behind her eyes.

Lick, suck, stroke, lick, suck, stroke. His mouth was like magic. She held onto the cabinet above her head as he continued his sexual onslaught with his mouth and hands. It was like he could read her mind, she thought with wonder as he added a third finger into her slick heat. With his talented tongue he tapped out a rhythm and she was mindless with it.

"Come for me, honey," he growled against her sex and that was all she needed. That show of dominance, the slight command had her falling apart against his mouth. Willingly submitting to his decree. *Hell yeah.*

As she sat panting on the counter, he took her face in his hands and kissed her lips, allowing her to taste herself on him. It was different from anything she had ever experienced and sexy as hell. His lips travelled to her ear and her neck. Finally, they closed over her breasts, sucking her nipples through the thin fabric of her gown.

She moaned and gripped him by the hair. Holding him to her breast and wrapping her legs around his waist. She wanted him inside of her. *Right fucking now.*

A knock at the back door brought Nate's head up and he growled intensely. Luisa buried her face in his neck, the passion they'd just shared and were about to share still held her in its thrall.

"Hey bro, you in there?" Daniel called and she heard the knob twist.

"Don't open that fucking door!" Nate yelled.

Luisa almost laughed as she saw the big man's shadow through the curtains. He'd raised both hands and was now sniffing the air. She could almost imagine his expression. She giggled against Nate's neck and he looked at her.

"Um, sorry to interrupt, bro, but I have to talk to you," Daniel tried again, but wisely did not move to open the door.

"Yeah, I get that. Give me a minute," Nate said in a calmer voice this time.

Luisa bit her lip, looking for all the world like a kid who'd gotten caught with her hand in the cookie jar and he laughed as he helped her down from the counter. He looked good when he laughed. Hell, he always looked good to her.

His Spanish ancestry was evident in his features especially in his straight nose and gorgeous caramel skin, but those mossy green eyes of his were all

Devlin. A throwback to his Celtic forefathers. He was, in a word, gorgeous.

She loved looking at him. *Hell*, she loved every single thing about him, she realized. Her heart thudded in her chest and she swallowed hard.

"You alright, honey?"

"More than alright, um, Nate-"

"Good, cause I don't want to rush you or confuse you," he tucked her hair back and held her face in his large, gentle hands. He pressed a soft kiss to her lips that made her toes curl.

"You've been very patient, Nate-"

"I don't mind, honey. I'll wait for you. I want you to know that, Luisa. As long as it takes."

"Nate-"

"Nate, come on, stop fucking around and open the door," Daniel growled and knocked again.

"One fucking minute," Nate replied and turned to the door.

"He's my brother and all, but I'll rip his head off if he sees you looking like that."

"Like what?"

"All soft and loved, honey. That look is for me alone," he dipped his head and kissed her again and the world seemed to stand still.

"Now, what do you say you go and get dressed for me, honey?"

"I will, but Nate-"

"That's my girl," he tweaked a curl and kissed her head, turning to the door to let his brother in.

He looked at her expectantly with his hand on the doorknob. She left the kitchen with a loud sigh. Luisa couldn't believe this. She was finally about to tell the insufferable man she wanted the mating to be real and he wouldn't let her get a word in. *Go figure.*

Well, one thing was certain. Luisa was finally ready to be mated for real!

CHAPTER
TEN

ate was still itching to drag his delectable mate into a corner and love her till she agreed to never leave his side, but fucking Daniel had interrupted them.

He'd planned on finishing what they started when he left, but of course the head Enforcer was followed by the four fucking stooges otherwise known as Bowie, Locke, Tonic, and Bolder. He rolled his eyes and pretended to listen to them while his mind was focused on the footsteps overhead.

She'd just gotten out of the shower. He could practically see her supple curves glistening with water droplets as she patted herself dry and readied herself for her workday. He could still taste her honey on his tongue.

That single sweet-as-honey vanilla mint flavor that could only be his Luisa was better than anything he'd ever had. *Ever.* She blew away the memories of every other woman he'd ever known. They were nothing compared to his mate. *My Luisa.* That smart, sassy, no-nonsense kinda woman who knew when to take and when to give in and out of the bedroom had him wrapped around her little finger. She was his every dream come to life.

Strong and sexy, a thing of pure beauty for sure on two legs as well as four. Seeing her in her fur was something he relished. She was the cutest Black Bear he'd ever laid eyes on with her soft fur haloing her chocolate dark eyes and rounded ears. Much smaller than his own shaggy-furred half-Grizzly half-Black Bear self, he couldn't help but wonder what their cubs would look like.

He knew it would be a while before she would settle down enough to want cubs, but a man could dream. Besides, he respected her hard work and dedication to her career and had every intention of supporting her choices.

Another thud from up the stairs and he could hardly keep his eyes off the ceiling. Was she putting on her shoes? Stepping into the tennis sneakers she preferred while working perhaps? Her tiny feet were absolutely adorable. *Hmm.* He'd neglected those toes. Maybe later he could give them the attention they deserved.

Of course he'd have to distribute that attention to other areas of her delectable body as well. For example, not many people looked beyond the obvious assets of a woman, but he was beginning to discover an unusual fondness for that tiny dimple to the left of her mouth.

Not to mention the tiny indent between her neck and shoulder. He sure enjoyed kissing her along there. Especially the way she moaned and clung to him when he was doing just that.

There was also the prettiest little freckle on her right hip. He'd seen it earlier when he was feasting on other things, but he had every intention of circling back to it before Daniel and his untimely interruption.

It seemed his childhood dream of having brothers and Clanmates who valued him was not all it was cracked up to be. The cock-blocking assholes had done it again! He growled in frustration. Another soft thud reached his sensitive ears and he could practically see her bent over tying those sneakers in his mind. *Grrr.*

Nate was hardly aware that he had moved

several steps closer to the staircase, *closer to her*, before Daniel called him back.

"Bro, you listening or what?"

"Yeah, I'm listening." He was listening. *Just not to Daniel.*

Besides, he knew the drill already and he didn't fucking like it any better now than he had last night. They'd discussed the matter until he was blue in the face, but he'd been outvoted. By Luisa herself. His damn courageous mate had volunteered to be bait! He growled and rubbed a hand across his face.

Luisa had fallen asleep in the living room after Krissy had finally convinced her to let him clean out her wound. Having an injured mate was almost too much for his Bear to handle. After he'd cleaned the already healing scratch, he'd picked her up and carried her to her bedroom.

He'd noted with a fond smile that his little mate slept in her childhood room as opposed to moving into her mother's old one. The old house was small, but comfortable. Paid off by Krissy's hard work as he understood it. He'd befriended the oldest Sposa sibling almost immediately. She was a sweet woman, especially now that she was married to his brother Taylor.

She'd done right by his mate and for that he

would be eternally grateful. *Yes.* It was a fine house. A little too close to other people to truly suit his tastes, but it was a house filled with love.

He still harbored a secret hope that she'd like his cabin as their permanent residence, but if she insisted, he would live here with her. Hell, he'd live anywhere just to be with her. Damn. He might as well cut off his balls and hand them to her. He chuckled and shook his head. *Fuck it.* She was his mate and he'd do anything to make her happy.

Though, he had to admit he'd prefer to live on the lake. The woods surrounding it were peaceful and he could Shift into his Bear any time he wanted to or just go out on the porch with his sketchpad to work without anyone bugging him.

He was almost finished putting together the little emergency medical room and office he'd built for her. Of course, she didn't know about it yet. How was he supposed to tell her when he couldn't get within five feet of her without wanting to strip her down and bury himself inside of her?

The mating urge was strong enough before he'd claimed the luscious she-Bear. Now that he'd had a taste of her, his beast was insatiable. She was all he thought about. First thing on his mind when he woke up, last thing on it when he went to bed.

"It's normal, you know," Daniel said as the four Polar Bears argued over who was taking which shift.

"What's that?" Nate feigned ignorance.

"The wanting. I wanted Lacey like mad when I first met her. After I touched her, *fuck*, it was a million times worse," Daniel looked at Nate with a big goofy grin on his face as he spoke of his mate, "Even after Mia, I still want her like crazy. All the time, bro. She's everything to me. They both are."

"So, how do you handle it? How do you keep from scaring her?" Nate really wanted to know. Luisa was skittish before they'd become intimate and he was doing his best to keep to her terms, but his Bear was getting restless. He wanted his mate.

"Fuck if I know," Daniel grinned, "Lacey says she wants me just as much. Guess I'm lucky that way. Now come on, we have a plan for keeping your mate guarded at all times during the day. Then when she gets home, and yes, she will have to drive herself. Don't worry, bro, we will intercept the Hunter Vamps," he said. Nate listened. Luisa's safety was of the utmost importance to him.

But something else was bothering him. What if Luisa didn't want him the way he wanted her? Was that why she'd been so reluctant to announce their mating and make it real? *Fuck*. After living his whole life on the fringes of a Clan who barely wanted him around, he'd finally found a place where he thought he belonged. But could he live with himself if he was unwanted again?

"Hey, you alright?"

He turned around at the sound of that familiar voice and his insides clenched. She was so beautiful. In a pair of light gray capris and a short-sleeved blouse with yellow flowers on it, she looked good enough to eat. *Again. Yes please.*

The concern in her dark brown eyes brought him up short. Maybe she cared more than he thought? He gave her a small smile and nodded at her. Best to play it cool. His passion that morning might have backed them up a few steps, and he didn't want to make it worse.

"You ready to go to work, honey?"

"Um, yeah. Let me grab my bag."

Nate watched her as she walked away. Her cute little heart-shaped ass was so damn sweet it could bring him to his knees. Especially when it was snug in those tight capris and wiggling this way and that as she walked away. *Damn.* He was hard again. He untucked his t-shirt and hoped it hid his sudden and yet semi-permanent condition when he was around his mate. *Grrr.*

"Yo, boss? Want me to drive the doc to work?" Locke's eyes seemed to also follow Luisa as she picked up her medical bag and the small wristlet that held her wallet and phone.

"Fuck off," Nate growled at the Polar Bear.

The man raised his hands in surrender, averted his eyes, and backed up to the kitchen, but not before letting a low whistle slide from his lips. Nate's fist shot out and caught the stupid Shifter in the jaw as he was about to inch out of the room. Before the huge man could react, Daniel was there pushing the male back.

"Give him a break, fellas, and don't ever disrespect a man's mate like that again," Daniel said through gritted teeth.

He ordered Bowie and Tonic to Shift and take to the woods. Warning them to stay downwind when they got to the clinic. They'd have to use extreme caution as Polar Bears were not exactly New Jersey natives. Nate rolled his eyes. With their luck the idiots would be seen by a group of hunters and they'd have everyone from Fish & Wildlife on their asses.

"I'm ready," Luisa said, and reentered the room oblivious to the tension. Nate nodded and opened the front door for her. At least he'd have a few minutes alone with her.

"I'm coming too," Daniel announced, and Nate sighed. *Or not*, he thought. Thwarted again.

The day dragged on or so it seemed to Nate. He'd been outed from the clinic by Luisa herself and that grated on his nerves.

"I can't work on patients with you breathing down my neck, Nate, go get a coffee or something," she'd growled the order at him when he objected to her examining a young unmated Bear's naked torso after he'd sustained an injury horsing around with his brothers.

It was nothing serious and Nate wondered why the young male had even bothered showing up. Then he saw the Bear's eyes sparkle as he watched Luisa bend over to retrieve some medical supplies from a low drawer. That's it. He was gonna burn those damned pants of hers later.

The little fucker! Nate couldn't help it. He felt his Bear rise to the surface and he snarled at the barely adult male. As if that wasn't bad enough, he almost leapt over the table to throttle the little shit when he gulped but still looked back at her again. *Grrr.* Not that he blamed the kid. She was fine as fuck.

"What is going on?" Luisa cried out as she

turned around to see him towering over the now trembling youth.

"He's only here so he can ogle you," Nate growled and looked out of the door to the line of patients outside in the waiting room.

Most of them were Clanmates. Almost all of them were young unmated males. *Fucking hell.* His Bear bellowed in his mind's eye. *Grrr.*

"Nate! Control yourself or you have to leave," she began, but he was too riled up to settle. He turned away, refusing to meet her angry eyes. Not trusting himself.

Mine, his Bear roared. The animal inside him was furious that his mate, *his mate who refused to acknowledge their mating,* was on some level choosing to be with these men over him! His beast saw these men as competition. The fact that their mating was only half-sealed was also driving the animal to want to challenge everyone who even looked at her.

"Are you crazy? These are patients, Nate! Besides I chose you, didn't I?" She whispered vehemently.

"Did you Luisa? Cause far as I can tell we're still livin' apart!" He slammed his hand against the wall and turned around. *Fuck.* He needed to get a grip. His skin was itching, fingertips tingling, jaw aching. The Bear wanted out. *Now.*

"Nate?"

He squeezed his eyes tightly. Embarrassment heated his cheeks. He hadn't lost his cool like this in years. When he was a teenager, he'd been unable to control his Shift. He'd needed his mother's help.

She'd been firm with her cub, but gentle as always. God, he missed his mother, but he was grateful for all she did. Still, he'd had no father around when growing up to teach him about control. *Shit.* That was another thing he had in common with Luisa. They'd both had lousy role models.

Iggy Devlin might be easier to get along with these days, but they'd been strangers for a long time. Nate had decided upon meeting the old man that he was going to forgive him for leaving his mother as it was an impossible situation.

His Grizzly Black Bear had seemed to settle a bit in Barvale. Lake Ursa was a prime spot for him to Shift almost daily without notice by *normals* or challenges by other Bears seeking to prove their dominance.

In fact, the Barvale Clan was unusual for a Shifter group. Marcus had claimed the seat of Alpha when his father gave it up, without quarrel or fight. He was strong, there was no doubt, and he had a good head on his shoulders, but the fact that he ruled without question was simply astonishing.

He was an Alpha whose devotion to his Clan showed in all the little ways he tried to make life better for everyone around him. Nate included. And yet, here he was, making an ass out of himself. He counted to ten, like his mama had told him, and fought back the Bear inside him.

Shit. He hadn't had an episode like this in years! And now here he was, acting like a cub again, in front of the woman that he loved! *Great way to win her over, asshat.* The Bear growled and pushed. Nate groaned with the effort it took to wrestle the animal back down. *Fuckin' shit!*

"Nate," he felt pressure on his bicep and realized she was touching him. That had to mean she wasn't as mad as he expected, right?

He opened his eyes and looked into her sinfully dark, chocolate brown eyes. The anger he expected wasn't there. In fact, she looked more concerned than upset.

"Excuse us for a second, Tim," she said to the young Bear who was avoiding eye contact with Nate at all costs. "Come in here. Please, Nate?"

Nate allowed her to pull him into what looked like a private bathroom away from all the prying eyes and supernaturally enhanced ears. She turned on the light, switched the overhead fan on, and locked the door.

"Luisa," he began. The need to grovel and fall to his knees begging for forgiveness was almost overpowering.

"Nate, I need to apologize to you-"

"No, honey, I'm the one who just acted like a complete idiot in there," he said wanting desperately to make that sad look in her eyes go away.

"Please let me finish," she tucked a stray curl behind her ear, and he followed the movement before settling his gaze back on her pretty little face.

"The truth is, I've been scared."

"Of me?" His brows furrowed.

"No. Well, yeah, actually," she looked down at her feet, but this was too important for misunderstandings. Nate used two fingers to gently lift her face to his.

"Honey talk to me," he whispered.

"I, I didn't want to find my mate so soon," her admission caused him to tense.

Pain lanced through his chest as if she'd struck him. Hell, he wished she would. Anything would be better than having his mate tell him she didn't want him.

"When I met you at the bonfire for Marcus and Leya, I felt this little zing that went straight through my body. I knew you were my fated mate even then. And I was scared to death."

"Honey, if I did or said anything to scare you, I am so sorry," he apologized.

"No, it's not that. You're wonderful, Nate. Every woman's dream. You're gorgeous, smart, talented, and you've done nothing but shower me with attention and patience."

"Then why all this? I'm sorry I snarled at the little guy in there and I'll apologize, Luisa, but please don't end this. Don't give up on us," the words rushed out of him as he tried to imagine a world without her.

He couldn't survive it. No way. He needed his mate. She was his reason for being. If she wanted more time, he'd give it to her. *Anything. Just don't leave me.*

He held his breath, waiting for her to speak, to show him just a hint of what she was feeling, but she remained silent. Her huge eyes grew luminous with unshed tears and he wanted to kick his own ass. He'd made her cry! *Fuckin' asshat!*

"Nate, I love you so much," she said and not half

a second later, Nate had himself two arms full of his sexy as hell little she-Bear.

"I love you too, *honey mine*, my own Luisa," he said between kisses and gropes.

Hope blossomed along with something else and Nate couldn't stop grinning even as he struggled to hold onto her as she pulled down first her pants than his own in the tight, little space.

Hot damn! His prim little doctor mate had jumped him in the bathroom at the clinic with a waiting room full of patients!

Luisa returned to the examination room to find it empty. She looked at her watch, cheeks burning. She'd been in the *bathroom* for twenty-three minutes.

Her clothes were hopelessly wrinkled, but the white coat she wore over them hid most of the damage. She licked her lips tasting the autumn sage flavor that imbued her mate's kiss. *Delicious.*

Her Bear was glowing within her and she knew the animal was practically preening in her satisfaction. Never an extrovert, Luisa had practically attacked Nate in the bathroom. *Okay. She did attack him.*

It was crazy. All the reasons she'd given herself for keeping him at bay had fled her mind the second he started talking as if she was leaving him. Fear had made her stand still as he'd talked on about her giving up on them and she just couldn't take it anymore.

She had to show him. *And boy, did she ever.* Making love while standing up in the close confines of the clean, but small doctors' bathroom at the clinic had been exhilarating. Though a little painful. And she didn't mean from the matching bite marks they'd given each other during the height of their passion.

She rubbed her hand over the symbol of his claim. This one sat high on her neck behind her left ear. Shifter healing abilities meant it was little more than a scab at the moment, by tomorrow it would be a slightly raised scar. A testament to her status as a mated female and a sign of Nate's love for her.

Her Bear grumbled happily inside her as she called the next patient into the room. A glance at the back door told her Nate had swapped places with one of the Polar Bear triplets. He'd needed to stretch his legs, or so he said.

"All I want to do is take you to bed," he whispered with his slight Texas drawl between kisses to her new bite mark, "And I plan to. Later. I'm gonna show you how a real Bear pleases his mate, again and again," he kissed

and licked her neck until she damn near came again from that alone.

Tonic, or was it Bolder, nodded his head at her a slight blush on his cheeks which told him they were probably not as quiet as they'd thought. *Oops.* He went back to scrolling through his phone. She doubted he was really looking at the screen, but he was operating under the pretense of being a patient.

She understood the reason for him being there, but she hated the whole situation. The Hunter Vamps were a deadly problem for not just the Clan, but the *normals* who lived in Barvale as well.

The doctor in her even accepted the fact the creatures couldn't just be killed, but her she-Bear demanded their blood. They'd injured her and attacked her mate. Oh yeah. She wanted them gone. *Grrr.*

The day passed quickly, and Luisa rolled her shoulders. Summer days sure were long. Even when you were working. *Ugh.*

Nate had returned a couple of times. Once with coffee and fresh honey glazed pastries from Bear Claw Bakery. *And she didn't think she could love him anymore.* The caffeine and sugar were the very things she'd needed to get her through the last batch of patients.

It seemed an entire group of Bear Scouts, *don't laugh*, had wandered into a patch of Poison Oak and then foolishly ran into a cave. Something inside bit one of the kids and he needed to be seen and treated immediately. The rest of them were okay except for a nasty case of the itches. *Normals and their kid's clubs. SMH.*

The Clinic catered to Shifters mostly, but the odd group of *normals* did come in from time to time. As Luisa irrigated the wound, she became concerned. The flesh was ragged and torn as if with a serrated blade, but that wasn't as troubling as the fact that the patient was missing about a pint of blood.

"What was it that bit you, Jimmy?" Luisa asked as the boy's foster father who'd been reluctantly called in sat in a chair nearby.

Apparently, the boy was the child of the man's late stepdaughter. Both the boy's mother and grandmother were gone, taken by the same hereditary heart disease that plagued the boy with chronic fatigue and less than average physical strength. He had no living relatives save the unkempt looking older man who reeked of beer and stale cigarettes.

"You almost done here?" Mr. Green's voice interrupted Luisa's train of thought and she glared at him with barely concealed hostility.

"Your son's condition is serious, Mr. Green. I had to call in an expert if you would please wait-"

"Hell, the boy ain't mine! Nothin' but a damn bother. If it wasn't for those checks I get from welfare he'd be out on his ear, wouldn't you boy?" He sneered and little Jimmy shuddered and closed his eyes.

"Wait outside, you're upsetting my patient!"

"Fine, I gotta take a leak anyhow, missy."

The rest of the troop had long since left and the sun was setting outside. Luisa went through the motions of slipping on sterile gloves and donning protective glasses, though truth be told nothing in this boys blood could hurt her. *Except for maybe some Vampiristic virus?*

"Shit, I mean *pooh*," she mumbled.

"Excuse me, ma'am, but did you just use a curse word?" The boy asked.

Luisa blushed under his wide-eyed stare. Little bugger was cute with his blue eyes and short brown hair. She'd have to watch her language even more if she was going to be a mom someday.

She'd never thought about having kids before, but now that she'd accepted Nate into her heart, she could almost hear their cubs laughter in the near future. *Sigh.* He was going to be a wonderful father.

"I'm sorry, buddy. Now just sit down," she began and looked up when the sound of someone coming in from the front door met her ears. Nate was here! *Thank goodness.*

"Luisa?" His mossy green eyes found hers as he came into the examination room to find a crying child without a caring parent in the room, and a worried mate.

"Nate! Um, so this is Jimmy. He's here with his foster dad who, uh, had to step outside," her eyes explained the rest to him, and he nodded his understanding, a silent plea for her to continue, "His Bear Scout troop brought him in."

Luisa explained the situation best she could with the tiny normal listening in. Jimmy listened and filled in the blanks when it came to what exactly had occurred.

"Nana signed me up for Bear Scouts before her heart whispers got badder," the little boy said. Luisa nodded and listened.

After talking briefly to Mr. Green she soon inferred what the boy had meant. His grandmother's "heart whispers" was in fact a serious murmur which was part of a genetic defect that plagued little Jimmy Nielson, *not Green*, and both his mother and grandmother.

He was often on medication and needed plenty of care. Care she was certain he wasn't getting from Mr. Green. A growl escaped her lips as she left the old man in the chairs reserved for waiting family. *The jerk.* She went back to listen to more of Jimmy's story.

"Mr. Bobby, our Scout leader, he's nice but he's not very good at woodsy stuff. He's a 'countant. I think that means he counts things. We walked into a bunch of leaves and they made us itch and some of the kids cried. I was brave so I kept walking up ahead to find the road."

"You did? All by yourself?" Luisa couldn't believe that an able-bodied adult had let this child wander off. Of course, *Mr. Bobby* had been covered in the worst of the hives of the bunch, so he was probably a little preoccupied at the time.

"Yeah except, I heard noises and I ran into a cave. That's where the *meanie* got me," his voice dropped to a whisper.

"Meanie?"

"Uh huh. He had black eyes and a smushed up face and he took my arm and he bit me! Biting is not allowed in Bear Scouts!" Jimmy said.

"You're right about that, buddy," Nate gave

Jimmy a pat on the head, but his eyes met Luisa's and she didn't like what she saw in them.

Fear. For the boy. She released a frustrated sigh as she walked out of the room in search of a snack for the child. Nate agreed to stay with him until she came back, his kind eyes and smile earned the child's trust instantly. *Luisa's too.* He was telling jokes when she walked back in with a glass of milk and a few sugar cookies someone had left in the break room.

"Okay, Jimmy, now you just sit tight and do what the pretty doctor here tells you to," Nate smiled at the boy and slid past Luisa, touching the small of her back in an intimate caress that made her heart flutter.

He was on the phone almost immediately with Marcus. She heard the steady, calm voice of her Alpha through the cell phone and smiled at Jimmy as he attempted to eat.

Her worry increased when he spit out the cookie and said it tasted bad. *Uh oh.* Nate appeared in the doorway his face solemn as he watched the boy try the milk with the same results. *Not good.* If she wasn't mistaken, a certain tall, blonde Vampire needed to be called immediately. As if he read her mind, Nate started the call.

Anger coursed through her at what she suspected. Jimmy had been bitten by a Hunter Vamp. Little was widely known about Vampirism as they tended to stay out of other supernatural affairs, but the stories had gotten one thing correct. Biting was key in turning someone. *Maybe now they could put an end to those nightmarish creatures.*

Minutes turned to hours before the cavalry arrived and it was all Luisa could do to placate Mr. Green and stop him from leaving the premises with Jimmy. The jerk really wanted to get home to his couch and TV.

"Look lady, I'm getting' hungry and my dog is expectin' his dinner," he started, and Nate sidled between her and the increasingly angry normal.

"Your dog? You haven't even asked if your son was hungry, Mr. Green, and you expect me to believe you're worried about a dog?" Nate growled.

"I told the girl he ain't my boy. Wife got custody of her grandson when her daughter died. Then she got sick too. Damn weak family and now this little shit gets himself bit-"

Before he could get another word out Nate had him hauled off the floor by his collar. Marcus arrived at that moment. Without his wife for the first time in memory and Luisa realized he must have argued long and hard before his stubborn good-hearted mate agreed to stay at home.

"Nate put the man down," Marcus ordered and Nate listened though she could see it was with a great amount of reluctance. Not that she blamed him. The guy was a total jerk.

Taylor and Daniel were with him, which also led her to the conclusion that they wrangled both Krissy and Lacey into staying behind as well, probably with the very pregnant Leya. Her eyes widened as Iggy Devlin, the old Alpha and father to the four men crowding her waiting room entered.

He was still powerfully built and had an edge to him despite the gray hair and wrinkles at the corners of his eyes. His natural dominance seemed to have muted in deference to his son's position as Alpha. That alone was a testament to his strength and generosity of spirit.

"Luisa," he inclined his head and she smiled at him, seeing for the first time the resemblance between him and Nate. It was there alright. She warmed inside as her eyes darted back to her mate.

The Devlins' were definitely as clever as they were powerful and good-looking! Of course, she preferred the newest addition to the family. A certain green-eyed Texan with his Spanish nose and panty-wetting smile.

She practically melted every time he flashed that grin at her. At the very least she should start bringing extra undies in her pocketbook. The little bathroom escapade had left her drawer-less as it were. Heat suffused her cheeks and she took a breath to calm herself.

The Shifters in the room would be able to pick up on her emotions. That was not something she wanted to discuss at the moment. More than one perfectly arched eyebrow raised in her direction and she cleared her throat. *Not now.* Not with everything that was going on.

She heard a commotion outside and started towards the door. Suddenly, Bal himself entered with one of the enormous Polar Bear Shifters slung over his shoulder.

"Does this belong to anyone?" He said in a bright, slightly accented voice.

"Ah, *bellissima*, we meet again," he tilted his head towards her. *Italian,* she thought and couldn't help but return his charming smile. The Vampire was movie star gorgeous, but he didn't make her heart speed inside her chest. Only one man did that.

"Get your damn eyes off my mate," growled Nate and he moved in front of Luisa, "and put *him* down."

"Of course," Bal shrugged as if he'd done nothing wrong.

He dropped Bowie unceremoniously on the linoleum floor and winced as the man's head made contact with the corner of the wall.

"Oops," the Vampire grinned unrepentantly.

She'd recognized the downed Polar Bear once she was able to see his face. He was breathing steadily, but his eyes remained closed. Her doctor instincts kicked in and she went about checking his pulse and looking for any obvious signs of injury.

"He seems fine though I don't know why he's unconscious."

"Ah, *dottore*, that would be my fault. You see he objected to my entering this fine *public* building, so I used certain methods of persuasion available to me, but in light of events I thought it better to bring him inside," he flashed a smile and Luisa shuddered slightly. Those needlelike teeth were on display lending a slightly lethal air to the otherwise friendly Vampire.

"Will he be alright?"

"Yes. He may have a headache, but it was unavoidable. Now, take me to see the boy," he moved forward, but Nate was there again, hand raised to stop his forward progress.

The other four Devlin's in the room watched the interaction, ready to step in if needed. This was a different Nate than the one she was used to. The jovial, sexy as hell, smiling Texas artist was gone, and the Enforcer took his place.

Luisa had to admit he looked pretty damn serious just then. The she-Bear inside of her approved wholeheartedly of his display of dominance and the way he sought to protect the boy. The woman didn't mind it either. *Grrr. Mine.*

"Hold up here a second. First, I need your word the he will be unharmed," his eyes narrowed.

"Marcus, are you going to instruct your brother to move out of my way or shall I remove him myself?"

"Think you can do that without help?" Nate drawled.

"Easy as pie, as you Americans say," Bal hissed.

"Okay there, boys, were on the same side," Marcus growled.

A whine coming from the examination room had everyone's head turning.

"Jimmy?" Luisa ran ahead. She heard the men

talking and following her, but her concern was for the injured boy.

"My tummy hurts," he cried, and she went to him.

"Move out of the way, please" Bal inserted himself between Luisa and the boy.

Instinct made her want to push the Vampire out of the way, but she was obviously dealing with something she couldn't quite comprehend. She watched with Nate standing right behind her as Bal looked directly into the boys eyes.

"*Ciao*, Jimmy," he said in his accented voice, "I want you to calm down now. *Calmati. Si.* Very good, I know it is hurting you, sleep now, it will soon be made right," and just like that the boy was asleep.

Bal extended one pale hand and lifted Jimmy's damaged arm, peeling the bandage back. His smooth face and beautifully chiseled features revealed no emotion as he bent his head and sniffed the wound. The only affectation that Luisa noted was the small frown beginning at his perfectly proportioned lips.

"He has been *bitten*," Bal announced.

"Who the hell are you people? What are you doin' in here? I told you we need to leave now, little boy is more trouble than he's worth," Mr. Green came stomping into the room and moved to grab the child. Before he could get to him, Bal smoothly intercepted the horrible normal.

"You are tired from your day. Why don't you take a nap?"

Everyone stood still and watched in awe as the man simply nodded and smiled at Bal like they were best buddies. He walked to a chair and sat down heavily. Seconds later, he was snoring.

"Who is that man in relation to the child?" Bal asked.

"His guardian. No blood relation," Luisa answered.

"Good. The child will need to be removed from his care. I will have a friend who is a social worker get on it immediately."

"Wait, what is happening to him?" Luisa asked.

"He has been *bitten*. Hunters do not normally turn others as their appetites are so uncontrolled."

"In other words, they usually kill their food," Nate murmured.

"Yes," Bal agreed.

"But I thought that was a myth? The whole biting thing," Luisa frowned.

"All myths have some basis in truth, do they not, *bella*? Vampires are one of the most secretive of people inhabiting this world. A *bite* is merely the first step into what it means to become Vampire. Unfortunately, it is irreversible, but it can be *managed*."

"Managed? He's just a boy! Not some kind of pest or problem!" She answered angrily.

"I apologize if my words offend you. What I mean to say is we will care for little Jimmy. See to his needs and help him adjust. Have no fear."

"Well, I don't know about you all, but I am a little afraid for that boy there," Nate replied and stepped to Bal.

"He's right," Marcus interjected, "We can't possibly be prepared for what the boy will need."

Luisa left the room. Her she-Bear grumbled inside of her, protective instincts she didn't even know she had, came charging forward.

"This was an unfortunate turn of events, but I swear it will be better for him. He will learn to control his thirst. He will be with others who understand him," Bal was speaking from inside the room, but she didn't want to hear it.

It irked her that this Vampire was calling the shots. Especially since he was the reason those Hunters hadn't been killed to begin with! Just who the hell does he think he is?

"He is the oldest, most powerful Vampire on the

continent. Bal has been a friend to the Barvale Clan ever since my ancestors settled here," Iggy Devlin stepped out of the shadows and took seat on the bottom step of the concrete staircase outside the clinic.

"Oh," Luisa said inadequately, "I'm just worried I guess."

"It is understandable. You and Nate have both been under a little bit of stress as I understand it," the blush staining his cheeks made him look younger, she realized what he was talking about and felt her own cheeks heating up. *He knows about our mating! They all do.*

"Oh, uh, Mr. Devlin-"

"Please, call me Iggy, all my daughters-in-law do. I figured you are as good as one since Nate there is inside arguing over why they should call off this thing tonight. He doesn't want anything to happen to *you*, my dear," he stated that as a fact, not something that was up for debate.

Warmth flowed through her just thinking of Nate inside the clinic, arguing for her safety. *Good mate. Fine protector.* Her she-Bear preened with the news and Luisa bit back a snort. *Not in front of his father.* She nodded and sighed, love for him filling every inch of her heart.

"Look, uh, I know I've been kind of hard on Nate, but that's all over now," she faced him with her shoulders squared and her head raised high.

Her old Alpha simply smiled. He opened the bottle of water he must've brought out with him and took a long sip. The night around them was quiet. Summertime could be fickle in the Garden State, but it was clear and dry. The moon was almost full, but not quite. She exhaled slowly and waited for him to speak.

Ignatius Devlin was never one to rush things. She recalled the times in her youth that he had offered guidance and shelter to the Sposa cubs. He'd been there for them after their own father had left town. She looked up to Mr. Dev-, er, *Iggy*. It was going to be strange to call him that, but she thought she'd manage just fine given time.

"*Matings*," he began, "even *fated* ones, are not easy things, Luisa. You did what you had to do. My relationship with Nate is still new, but I confess I love him as much as any of my other sons. You'll do fine by him, I know it," he rose from the stairs and walked away leaving Luisa with her thoughts.

She turned to the nearly empty parking lot and looked out at the copse of trees that sat behind it. It was quiet. Almost too quiet. She stilled. There was literally *no noise* coming from anywhere. She stepped forward, her own curiosity getting the better of her.

Before she could do more than scream, two thin, grayish arms tipped with curled claws reached out and grabbed her covering her mouth. The Hunter was so disgustingly happy with itself it tossed its bat-like face back and howled to the night sky.

"Eeeeeeeeeeeeee!"

"We'd need more than your assurances, Bal," Nate said.

"Like what?" answered the Vampire while he studied his nails.

"For one, Luisa gets to keep treating the boy. For another, we want access to whatever info you're hiding about what it takes to become whatever the fuck it is that you are!"

"You want to know what it takes to become one like me," growled the Vampire and for the first time Nate caught a glimpse of the terrifying being that lurked within the pale man who stood before him.

"Guys, maybe we could hold off on this pissing contest for a second and discuss tonight?" Daniel interrupted.

"Tonight is on," Marcus stated.

"Not if we can't guarantee her safety," Nate argued.

"Silence!" Bal roared and the four, no five, Shifters now that Bowie was awake looked at the Vampire as if he'd gone crazy.

"What the hell is going on in here?" Iggy Devlin, Nate's formerly estranged father stepped inside.

"Nothin' Dad," Taylor began, but Nate was distracted.

Iggy had followed Luisa out before, and here he was back inside. But where was she? At that moment, a loud screech sliced through the air.

"Eeeeeeeeeeeeeeeee!"

Nate didn't think, he just sprang into action. He could hear his brothers and the rest of them talking, but he didn't care what they were saying. He just needed to get to her.

"Luisa!" he growled as he leapt over the six steps to the concrete.

His enhanced vision allowed him to see the end of the empty lot where his mate was struggling with one of those butt ugly monsters. No! His Bear burst free from his skin.

Claws clacked on the pavement as he hauled ass over to where she struggled against two, no, three

Hunter Vamps. He heard the roars of his brothers behind him. A streak of white to his right told him at least one of the Polar Bear Shifters who'd been told to guard the woods had emerged just a smidge too late.

He watched Luisa's eyes go wide as she struggled against the grasping Vamp. One grabbed her head and pulled it back exposing her suntanned throat while the other lunged with his mouth wide. *No!*

Nate slammed full force into the one whose mouth hovered over his mate's vulnerable flesh. The force of impact sent the creature flying into the trunk of a nearby tree. It's head lolled to the side and he was certain he'd broken its neck. A fatal blow? Maybe. But he didn't give a fuck. No one was hurting his mate.

Several Hunter Vamps emerged from the trees, there was an entire clutch of the beings. Odd since they were not known to stay in groups. But since the Witches who'd originally bound them were destroyed, these Vamps had gone rogue, establishing their own hierarchy and agenda. Mainly to feed.

Soon, the others joined the melee. Bodies flew at each other in unchecked violence. The sounds of blows being exchanged rained down like a tsunami of savagery. He received one painful scratch down his right foreleg, but a short furry Bear pummeled the creature out of his path, and he realized Luisa had joined the fray.

Hell no. His new mission was to simply protect his mate, no matter how she tried to wiggle past him. Before he knew it, they'd rounded up all the Vamps with only one fatality. It seemed a broken neck and severed spinal cord was close enough to a decapitation to render the creature nil. The blood-sucking fiend had almost bitten his mate, he deserved it as far as Nate was concerned.

The Shift back to human was effortless, his Bear knew he needed to be a man to touch her and ensure she was in fact whole. He ran over to where Luisa stood a few feet behind him. Her dark eyes were wide with shock, not that he could blame her. She was a healer. Violence went against everything she stood for.

"Honey?" he whispered waiting for her to acknowledge him.

"Nate?" Her voice was low and soft, but strong. Relief washed over him.

He grabbed her by the waist and lifted her up in his arms. Happiness and love flowed through him. The onslaught threatening to crack his chest wide open as she returned his embrace with so much strength, she nearly strangled him. Hell, he was fine with that. As long as Luisa stayed in his arms, where she belonged, anything and everything was just fine by him.

"Nate, thank God you're okay," she said.

"Me? I was worried to death over you," he kissed her mouth and pressed his forehead against hers.

The Bear inside of him growling contentedly now that the fight was over, and his Luisa was safe.

"Damn, doc, I knew you were gorgeous," said Locke who'd ambled over with several gaping wounds and bruises before he passed out at her feet.

Good thing to, because Nate was about to knock the fucker out, but first he had to cover his mate. He grabbed her lab coat from the floor where she must have thrown it and quickly shoved it on her body.

She just smiled at him amusedly and let him dress her, understanding his need to shield her nudity from the eyes of others. After checking on the four Polar Bear Shifters who worked under him and his brothers and father, Nate finally turned to the Vampire who was currently scratching runes into the dirt surrounding the remaining Hunters who were tied up with some sort of enchanted silver chain far as Nate could tell.

"Hey, I just wanted-"

"One second," he pointed at Nate while still working on the spell he was casting around the group of snarling yet beaten Vamps.

"I don't want to miss a single rune and risk this lot breaking free while I wait for my assistants to arrive. There now, all done. How can I help you *Signore Cordoza?*" He turned to Nate with a bemused expression on his aristocratic face.

"Hell, call me Nate. I saw you in there. You fought hard against them, though I won't pretend to understand why you didn't just put an end to them all," he said.

"Yes, well, I am afraid I have my reasons," Bal returned evasively.

"Still, I would not have an innocent hurt for all the world. Not the boy and not your mate. Take care of her, Nate Cordoza, what you have is a precious thing."

"I intend to," Nate found the pained look in the Vampire's face to be oddly stirring and he found himself sympathizing with the man, *er*, Vampire.

"Yo Nate, cleanup crew is here," Daniel called to him and he turned his attention to where Luisa was patching up some of the scrapes and cuts the other Bears had received.

Luckily, as Shifters, scratches like that would not

have any lasting effect though they would take longer to heal. Bal inspected the wounds himself and assured the group that Shifter metabolism would purge the Vampire virus from their systems within a week.

As for the boy, a young-looking couple arrived with the rest of Bal's assistants. They chatted with the child who seemed happy to go to their home where he would learn about what he was becoming. Nate's heart still tightened in his chest for what the child would go through, but it was for the best.

They gave Luisa the proper paperwork from DYFS that would state the boy had been removed from Mr. Green's care voluntarily. They'd even hypnotized the man into agreeing. Not that Nate cared about the normal wretch, the guy didn't give a fig for little Jimmy.

"You do know his heart condition was fatal," Bal interrupted his thoughts, "believe it or not, the Hunter who bit him may have very well saved his life."

"Some life," Nate muttered.

"It can be difficult, that is true, but he will have a chance now. At any rate, I thank you and the Barvale Clan for your help," Bal extended a hand gripping Nate's with more strength than Nate had expected.

He saw in the Vampire's eyes this was not a challenge. More of a sharing of information. Nate's Bear grumbled but the man understood. The Vampire was sharing secrets here. Secrets other Shifters were not privy too.

Speculation and rumor. That was all that existed about Vampires even in the supernatural world. In Nate's opinion, there was a lot more to the secretive species than met the eye. But that was a problem for someone else to solve. He had a mate to take care of and the only thing he wanted to do right then, was to get her home.

"You about ready," he sidled up to Luisa and nuzzled her from behind loving the way she relaxed against him. Her complete trust in him was a gift he promised himself he would never take for granted.

"Mmm. Yeah, I'm exhausted," she said, and he could see in her face she was. Without hesitation Nate reached out and swept her up in his arms, Cinderella-style.

"Nate!" She giggle and buried her face in his throat.

"Um, sir?" Locke interrupted.

"What is it?" Nate said humoring the Bear even though he wanted nothing more than to hightail it out of there. The feel of his soft curvy mate in his arms sent pleasure spiking through his blood, stirring him in ways he'd rather not have the man witness.

"Alpha Devlin wanted me to tell you the cleanup was about done. He, uh, he said to take your, um, *pretty little mate* home," Locke's face burned red as he spoke, and Nate took a moment to enjoy the man's discomfort.

"What did you call my mate?"

"Not me! It was the Alpha! I swear, sir, I would never disrespect you or your mate-"

"Easy Locke, I'm just kidding with you. You can tell Marcus I plan on doing just that."

The Polar Bear Shifters were new to the Clan and after working with them a few months he could see they were going to be an asset. Still, it was fun to mess with them every now and then.

"Nate quit teasing him and take me home," Luisa said.

"Yes," he carried her to where her car was parked and placed her inside.

"So," he said as he turned the engine.

"So," she returned.

"I want you to know you made me the happiest man on Earth before," he felt his face warm as he spoke.

"Did I?" She smiled.

"Yep. But we still have a few things to discuss."

"Like what?"

"Well, the usual I expect," he bit back his grin as she sat up straighter, worrying her lower lip.

"For example, Italian or Chinese food?"

"Oh," she smiled as she realized where he was heading with this conversation, "Chinese."

"Okay. Are you an early bird or night owl?"

"Depends."

"Me too. This one's a little tougher," he frowned, "are we living at your place or the cabin?"

"The cabin?"

"Well, I'd like to call it our cabin since I've been fixing it up with you in mind," he knew he was blushing then.

"The cabin," she confirmed, "I loved my childhood, but I want to live in our house. *With you.*"

Pleasure filled his heart at her shy confession. He turned his eyes on her knowing his Bear was shining through them.

"Final question," he said with a hint of a growl in his throat.

"What is it?"

"Will you marry me?"

A few seconds ticked by and Nate stopped the

car, worried he'd drive them into a ditch if he kept staring at her. She hardly had any expression on her face at all. Then she smiled. And it was like the sun shining down on him. A moment later and his arms were full of his mate as she clung to him kissing his cheeks, his eyes, his mouth.

"Well?" He said between long, delicious swipes of her tongue.

"Yes," she said.

It was all he could do to get them home in one piece. Luisa did not move from his lap and kept on torturing him with the most exquisite little kisses and nips. He thought he'd burst if he couldn't bury his cock inside of her soon.

The second he had the car in park he leapt out of the car with her in his arms. Twenty seconds later and he laid his mate out on his bed. No, it was their bed now.

"Welcome home, honey," he growled as he stripped them both of their clothes.

"Yes, *home*," she moaned, and he wiggled beneath him.

"I love you, Luisa Sposa, and right now I'm gonna show you how much when I claim this sweet little body of yours all over again," he said and took her mouth in one long hard kiss that left them both breathless.

"I love you too, *sweet mate*. Now show me," she said.

His Bear roared happily at her use of the word mate and his cock grew even harder. Nate had never wanted her as badly as he did just then. Wanted her, loved her, with everything inside of him. Every curve, every dimple, every sweet sigh and moan. And he was going to prove it to her over and over again. For the rest of their lives.

Lips locked, he felt as if their very souls were meeting in the long intimate kiss. Her legs wrapped round him in that secret embrace that lovers shared. He pushed slowly, softly inside the silky heat of her tight little pussy. *His pussy now.*

She moaned at his invasions, savoring the penetration as she gripped his ass with her hands. *Strong little hands*, he thought as he swallowed her harsh sounds.

He tucked them away to be savored at a later date, with all the other little things he loved about her. Her sheath tightened its grip on his cock, and he flexed his hips instinctively finding her g-spot and stroking it with every thrust. *Swivel, thrust, swivel.* Again he repeated the motions, allowing the rhythm to take them both to new heights and pleasures.

His mouth found her breasts, suckling her plump nipples as she pulled on his hair and cried out. *Swivel, thrust, swivel.* Harder and faster, again and again he pushed until their heads were up against the backboard of the bed. He couldn't get close enough. Needed to be closer, deeper, harder.

"Luisa," he growled his fingers digging into her hips, mouth finding that spot on her neck where his canines had broken skin only hours before.

Her pussy tightened in response, choking his dick in a hold so strong he almost lost it completely. She was close, but he needed her to get all the way there before he could allow his own release.

"Come for me," he growled the command and bit down, reaffirming their bond. It was all the permission she needed. He felt her sex tighten and vibrate along his shaft.

"Nate!" Luisa moaned his name as she came on his cock.

"Mine," he growled, bathing her womb with his seed. Coating her in his scent and claiming her for all the world to see.

"Mine," she echoed and stared into his eyes.

The warm amber of her she-Bear peeked out at

him before returning to their usual deep chocolate brown. He'd never felt happier or more complete in his entire life.

"Guess we're not barely mated anymore," she teased and kissed his nose.

"I beg to differ, honey. I'd say we were very *bearly mated*."

Laughter filled the room as he teased and tickled his pretty little mate. Soon they were touching and kissing again. He'd never get enough of her, that was for damn sure. *Mine.*

EPILOGUE

Christmas that year was a major event at the Barvale Clan Den. With the four Devlin brothers mated, though technically one was a Cordoza, the house was full of love and laughter.

Clary the housekeeper gave out special batches of her famous Christmas *stollen* as gifts while managing to prepare a holiday meal that could feed, well, an entire Clan of Bear Shifters. Even with the new Polar Bear transplants taking up space under the tree trying to put together new baby toys for Mia and the Alpha's new son. The Den was open to all Clanmates, especially during the holidays.

Mia was toddling around the tree with her father close behind while his wife Lacey admired their newborn nephew, Jordan. Marcus hovered nearby, anxious to have his son back in his or his mate's arms. Papa Bears were very protective indeed, Luisa noted as she watched her sister Krissy waddle out of the bathroom, her pregnant belly protruding from the red maternity sweater she wore, Taylor close behind.

All was well with the Devlins' and she couldn't be happier. The plain gold wedding band she'd insisted on glittered on her finger as she sat beside her sexy new husband. They were just about to exchange gifts.

She felt sweat bead on her forehead as she waited for it to be their turn. She had a whopper of a surprise for her mate. They'd driven down to Maccon City after Thanksgiving and had gotten married by a local justice of the peace, a Werewolf who was used to that kind of rushed service. She didn't care about the pomp, just the ceremony and they'd both agreed they didn't want to wait.

Of course, Krissy had been pissed, but a second later she'd burst out in tears of happiness. Pregnancy hormones could do that to you, Luisa knew as a doctor. She'd been so standoffish about her mating that it was a wonder to her that she could feel so differently now.

Nate was simply an amazing husband. She couldn't have asked for a better mate. He was kind, considerate, sexy as all hell. He never demanded she choose between her work and him, in fact he was so supportive of her career he'd built her a home office and medical examination room.

She was already able to help her Clan in more ways than she ever expected through her profession and he was right there next to her all the way.

Any worries she had about their incompatibility evaporated the second she had decided to accept their mating and opened her heart to him. After all, the universe had chosen him for her! She knew now that they'd never have gotten it wrong!

As the gifts were being handed out, she bit her lip at the small box as she handed it to her husband. All this time she'd been worried, she'd never stopped to think if *he* was ready for this step. Fear suddenly gripped her heart and she felt her pulse speed up.

"Hey, honey, it can't be that bad," he said flashing a wide smile at her that usually made her panties uncomfortably wet, but right now she was too nervous for words.

"Luisa, I promise I'll love it, even if it is the ugliest tie in creation," he joked as he unwrapped the rectangular box.

She couldn't speak, could only watch as his head cocked to the side as he tried to make sense of the little plastic stick she'd placed inside.

"Are you? *Are we?* Luisa! *Wooheee!*" He shouted and lifted her up, quickly gentling his hold as he settled onto the couch with her in his lap.

The others in the room voiced their concerns and asked questions, but she was too overwhelmed by his reaction to notice. She tightened her arms around his neck.

"Everybody! We're gonna have a baby!" The room erupted in applause and shouted congratulations. Of course there were more tears from Krissy, but Luisa didn't pay any attention to them her eyes were on the deep set mossy green ones she loved so much.

"Are you truly happy about this?"

"You've given me so much, honey, I can't possibly tell you how happy I am."

"I love you," she said.

"But now I'm a little nervous," he began, and her eyebrows furrowed.

"Why?"

"You're giving me a baby, honey, and my gift, well, it just can't compare."

"I'll love it, I swear it," she said sitting up, but he held her firmly in place.

"I don't know," he began, but she took the oddly shaped package from him and wiggled a little in his lap, loving the proof of his desire as it hardened against her backside.

"If I don't like it, you can make it up to me later," she whispered and kissed him quickly watching the flash of desire that filled his glittery eyes.

She'd never get tired of seeing that look on his face, she thought as she bit her lip and ripped open the package. Her heart practically stopped when she saw what was inside.

"You? When did you-" one hand covered her mouth as she took in the beautiful watercolor in its simple wooden frame.

He'd painted her. Nate had painted her using soft colors and short strokes of his skillful hands. She looked beautiful in the picture. Her hair shorter than it was now and she was wearing a white bathing suit, sitting on the shore of Lake Ursa.

"I painted this right after I first saw you at Marcus' and Leya's bonfire," he murmured against her neck.

"You did?"

"Of course I did. I knew you were it for me even

then. Couldn't get you out of my mind, so I painted this. Hung it in my room so I could just look at you."

"Oh my God, did you know I was jealous-"

"Jealous of what, honey?" His concern showing in his loving gaze.

She could see his Bear pacing behind his eyes. He never wanted his mate to feel anything other than happy. She knew that deep within her soul.

"It's silly really, but I wondered why you never asked me to model for you," she whispered her guilty secret and looked up at him through her growing bangs.

"Honey," he said and pressed a kiss to her lips, "I have drawn you a million times since I first saw you. Memorized every inch of you, Luisa. Hell, I could draw you with my eyes closed."

"You can?"

"Of course I can. You're my mate, honey, I want you all the time, see you all the time in my head even if you're not standing next to me, love you so much," he spoke in low tones that made her toes curl.

"Nate, that's beautiful," she whispered, "everything is beautiful. You, Christmas, the tree, the painting," she felt tears sting her eyes as her heart threatened to burst out of her chest.

He took the painting from her and placed it

gently against the couch ignoring the *oohs* and *aahs* of everyone around them. He turned Luisa gently in his arms, watching her for any sign of discomfort while he framed her face in his large callused hands.

"You are the most beautiful thing I've ever seen, and I love you, honey girl, so much it scares me sometimes," the raw honesty in his voice touched a chord inside her and she trembled in his arms.

"I love you the same way, Nate. Forever," she echoed his statement and crushed her mouth against his.

"Let's get out of here," his green eyes glittered as they stared at her and only her. Luisa caught her breath.

The intensity in his gaze had chills running up her spine and after waiting a bit, they made their excuses and headed home with a carful of gifts from the brothers and their wives and boxes of goodies and leftovers from Clary.

"You take care, son," Iggy Devlin wrapped his arms around Nate and squeezed briefly before letting him go and kissing Luisa on her forehead.

Both men trembled slightly but let each other go before too long. Christmas had a magical way of letting water pass under newly built bridges and she felt the promise of their future relationship bud right before her eyes.

It was a good thing too. Her baby would have something she and Nate never did, a whole family. A support system in place to help love and educate all their future children. And she'd want more. Just as much as she wanted this one.

Luisa knew the embrace shook her husband and she held his hand as they'd said their goodbyes to everyone else. Hours later they lay in their bed, bellies full of good food, hearts full of love and laughter, she turned to him.

"Hey there, honey girl," he said and twirled a lock of her hair around his finger. They were still a little bit sweaty and her body was relaxed and sated from their long bout of lovemaking.

"Hey yourself, husband of mine. I was just thinking," she began.

"*Mmmhmm*," he snuggled closer to her, wrapping his big body around her, making her feel both protected and loved.

"I never thanked you."

"For what?"

"For being patient with me."

"Hush now. I'll always wait for you."

"I know. You proved that. I just wanted to say I'm glad you don't have to wait anymore."

"Me too, honey," he smiled and kissed her again and she opened up for him like a flower in the sunshine. Body, mind, heart and soul, Luisa was his. Just as he was hers.

The two of them *bearly mated* forever.

The end.

EXCERPT FROM CODE WOLF

"Are you fuckin' with me?"

"No, Randall, I assure you I am not fuckin' with you," Rafe Maccon eased his immense frame back into his oversized, black leather chair and narrowed his ice blue eyes at his Third and one of his oldest friends. How long had he known the man sitting in front of him?

Randall had come to Maccon City when Rafe was about ten, he looked the same then as he did now. Tall at six foot three inches, muscular, and more than a little intimidating to the Wolves under him with his long beard and equally long dark brown hair.

Rafe, however, was the Alpha. He was more amused than intimidated by his surly friend.

"A vacation?! What the fuck am I gonna do on a vacation? Come on, Rafe, this is bullshit!"

The door to Rafe's private office flew open and in strolled a very happy, very pregnant Charley Maccon, Rafe's wife. The Alpha's eyes glowed as they landed on his positively glowing mate. She wore a long, flowy dress. The shade was a pale-yellow color that, Randall admitted to himself, looked damn good with her creamy complexion and curly dark hair.

Their Alpha Female was quite something. There wasn't a Wolf Guard in the place who wouldn't lay down his/her life for her.

"Well, maybe you should consider a vacation to be a relaxing experience, Randy," she dropped a kiss on Randall's cheek and walked past him, over to her husband whom she kissed full on the mouth.

The way his Alpha's eyes homed in on her when she opened the door was nothing compared to the hungry gaze that followed her across the room.

Randall had noticed it took a while for Rafe to get used to his mate's habit of greeting everyone with a kiss or hug. Wolves were protective of their mates, but Randall thought his Alpha was doing an exceedingly good job of hiding his tension. Werewolves did not share very well.

Charley; however, had stood firm. That was the way she was raised, and she wasn't going to change for any, how had she put it? Neanderthal brow-beating husband, regardless of how cute his ass was!

Randall had no direct knowledge if the "cute ass" statement was true or not. And he didn't want to know. He liked Charley though, had from the beginning. He was musically inclined and often took to one of the common rooms to strum his guitar or play a few keys on the piano.

HAVE YOU MET MY DRAGONS?

The Falk Clan Tales are my stories surrounding four Dragon Shifter brothers and how they find their one true mates.

Each brother's chest is marked with his rose, the magical link to his heart and his magic. They each have a matching gemstone to go with it.

She's given up on love, but he's just begun.

In *The Dragon's Valentine* we meet the eldest Falk brother, Callius. He is on a mission to find a Castle and his one true mate, one he can trust with his diamond rose....

His heart is frozen; can she change his mind about love?

In *The Dragon's Christmas Gift* our attention shifts to Alexsander, the youngest brother of the four. He has resigned himself to a life alone, until he meets *her*.

Some wounds run deep, can a Dragon's heart be unbroken?

The Dragon's Heart is the story of Edric Falk who has vowed never to love again, but that changes when he meets his feisty mate, Joselyn Curacao.

She just wants a little fun, he's looking for a lifetime.

We finally meet Nikolai Falk and his sexy Shifter mate in *The Dragon's Secret*.

**Now available in a boxed set.*

EXCERPT FROM THE ENFORCER

The moon would soon be full. Isabeau looked at the night sky and pulled the hood of her ivory sweater up over her fiery red curls. She passed between the red and sugar maples, a few tall beech trees, and a lonely pine when a low growl sounded next to her. She reached out to touch the thick fur of the adult she-Wolf who walked beside her through the forest trail.

"It's okay Artemis, let's finish our rounds and get home."

As she walked around the perimeter of her land she chanted an ancient language that few would be able to identify fortifying the wards around her large animal sanctuary. That was what the mortals around her thought it was, and for the most part they were correct.

To them, Isabeau Rose had just arrived in town a few years ago with the deed to five-hundred acres of Northern New Jersey farmland. Within a few months, she'd transformed the abandoned horse farm and the woods around it into a series of habitats for wild animals that were injured or discarded. Creatures that needed a haven for rehabilitation.

She had a main house for herself that boasted ten-bedrooms and six-full baths, an indoor pool and spa, two stables, one for her horses, the other for more exotic wildlife, two large red barns, and a state of the art veterinary clinic on the grounds.

"Out late, aren't you?" Beau turned around to find the source of the unfamiliar voice. She lifted her hand to calm Artemis who was ready to pounce on the intruder.

"Who are you?" she demanded.

"The real question is what are you doing out here so late? Surely your wards don't need reinforcement at this time of night, not out in this quiet New Jersey forest, Sorceress Rose?" The dark stranger spoke with an unearthly calm to his voice that put Beau on edge.

This was no mere mortal. She used her keen

sight to see him despite the darkness and almost gasped aloud. His face was perfect, except for a thin silver scar that ran from his left eyebrow to his chin. His eyes blazed cerulean blue fringed with impossibly dark lashes. They were carefully masked to hide his emotions.

EXCERPT FROM SHIFTER MOUNTAIN BY C.D. GORRI

Keeton's Mountain Lion hissed angrily as he boarded the plane for the States. Three months on Moongate Island did nothing to repair his faith in people. Shifter or human, they pretty much sucked.

True, he was no longer being blackmailed by the sniveling cretin who'd been part of his last black ops assignment. Fucker had stepped on a landmine deep in the jungles of a place Keeton was not at liberty to name. Not even in his own head.

Fucking hell.

Yeah, it meant he could return home now, but to who? Keeton had no family waiting for him. His few friends were back on the island, but that was no place for his inner feline. The beast craved the hills and valleys of the New Jersey forests he called home.

He'd bought a hundred acres of forest off the beaten paths of New Jersey's Panther Mountains years ago. Even commissioned the building of a cabin deep in the woods. The design was environmentally conscientious and entirely sound. Two stories high, it had its own generators, additional solar paneling, and wind turbines for power, and indoor plumbing.

He wasn't an animal, for fuck's sake. But even if Keeton was going to avoid people, he didn't have to be uncomfortable doing it. Eyes closed, he sat seemingly at ease, but he was keeping tabs on every living thing around him on the plane.

Once a soldier, always a soldier, his two commanders, Callan McGregor and Landry Smyth, had said that often enough. Both men were Shifters, a unique Alpha and Omega pair who'd completed their Triad once they'd found their mate in Sage Freeman, a smart mouthed human female. That had been Keeton's cue to leave the island he'd called home for eighty-nine and a half days.

They hadn't kicked him out or anything. On the contrary. But he was restless and antsy. The island could no longer contain his need for isolation.

Memories of the disgust on Bruce Taylor's face when he'd seen Keeton lose control of his shift during a particularly bloody battle were forever ingrained in his brain. The human male had been a new recruit in the special ops task force where Keeton had served his country for the last five years in secret.

Dismantling dictatorships and stopping atrocities the likes of which he could hardly put a name to before they could ever see the light of day had been his job, and blackmail was his reward.

He'd kept the fact that he'd unwittingly told the secret about Shifters to the human from Callan and Landry until the night Bruce had died believing Keeton was the only one of his kind. The two men had investigated his claims, making sure that he never downloaded or emailed the proof he'd recorded with his phone the night Keeton lost control.

The half a million dollars he'd sent to Bruce's offshore bank was nothing. He didn't care about the money. It was simply the point of it all. The man had not trusted Keeton because of his dual nature. And he'd lost his life as a result.

"We need to stick to this route, Bruce," he growled at the human who'd become increasingly toxic to their two-man operation.

"Think I'm gonna trust a fucking animal. I'll go this way," the man argued.

After a few more minutes of trying to convince him, Keeton threw his hands up. His beast scratched at his skin, the animal sensing something was not right. The sounds of the explosion and Bruce's bitter cry rang in his ears, but he died before Keeton could ever hope to reach him.

It was his fault. He was the reason Bruce had died. After pledging his life to help save lives, he'd brought death instead.

Keeton was better off on his own.

EXCERPT FROM CODE WOLF

"Are you fuckin' with me?" "No, Randall, I assure you I am not fuckin' with you," Rafe Maccon eased his immense frame back into his oversized, black leather chair and narrowed his ice blue eyes at his Third and one of his oldest friends. How long had he known the man sitting in front of him?

Randall had come to Maccon City when Rafe was about ten, he looked the same then as he did now. Tall at six foot three inches, muscular, and more than a little intimidating to the Wolves under him with his long beard and equally long dark brown hair.

Rafe, however, was the Alpha. He was more amused than intimidated by his surly friend.

"A vacation?! What the fuck am I gonna do on a vacation? Come on, Rafe, this is bullshit!"

The door to Rafe's private office flew open and in strolled a very happy, very pregnant Charley Maccon, Rafe's wife. The Alpha's eyes glowed as they landed on his positively glowing mate. She wore a long, flowy dress. The shade was a pale-yellow color that, Randall admitted to himself, looked damn good with her creamy complexion and curly dark hair.

Their Alpha Female was quite something. There wasn't a Wolf Guard in the place who wouldn't lay down his/her life for her.

"Well, maybe you should consider a vacation to be a relaxing experience, Randy," she dropped a kiss on Randall's cheek and walked past him, over to her husband whom she kissed full on the mouth.

The way his Alpha's eyes homed in on her when she opened the door was nothing compared to the hungry gaze that followed her across the room.

Randall had noticed it took a while for Rafe to get used to his mate's habit of greeting everyone with a kiss or hug. Wolves were protective of their mates, but Randall thought his Alpha was doing an exceedingly good job of hiding his tension. Were-wolves did not share very well.

Charley; however, had stood firm. That was the way she was raised, and she wasn't going to change for any, how had she put it? Neanderthal brow-beating husband, regardless of how cute his ass was!

Randall had no direct knowledge if the "cute ass" statement was true or not. And he didn't want to know. He liked Charley though, had from the beginning. He was musically inclined and often took to one of the common rooms to strum his guitar or play a few keys on the piano.

CONNECT WITH C.D. GORRI

Follow me here:

https://www.facebook.com/Cdgorribooks

https://twitter.com/cgor22

https://www.instagram.com/cdgorri

https://www.bookbub.com/profile/c-d-gorri

Visit my website to find out more about my supernatural world also known as the Grazi Kelly Universe and sign up to be a subscriber!

https://www.cdgorri.com/newsletter

OTHER TITLES BY C.D. GORRI

Other Titles by C.D. Gorri

Paranormal Romance Books:

Macconwood Pack Novel Series:

Charley's Christmas Wolf: A Macconwood Pack Novel 1

Cat's Howl: A Macconwood Pack Novel 2

Code Wolf: A Macconwood Pack Novel 3

The Witch and The Werewolf: A Macconwood Pack Novel 4

To Claim a Wolf: A Macconwood Pack Novel 5

Conall's Mate: A Macconwood Pack Novel 6

Her Solstice Wolf: A Macconwood Pack Novel 7

Werewolf Fever: A Macconwood Pack Novel 8

Also available in 2 boxed sets:

The Macconwood Pack Volume 1

The Macconwood Pack Volume 2

Macconwood Pack Tales Series:

Wolf Bride: The Story of Ailis and Eoghan A Macconwood Pack Tale 1

Summer Bite: A Macconwood Pack Tale 2

His Winter Mate: A Macconwood Pack Tale 3

Snow Angel: A Macconwood Pack Tale 4

Charley's Baby Surprise: A Macconwood Pack Tale 5

Home for the Howlidays: A Macconwood Pack Tale 6

A Silver Wedding: A Macconwood Pack Tale 7

Mine Furever: A Macconwood Pack Tale 8

A Furry Little Christmas: A Macconwood Pack Tale 9

Also available in two boxed sets:

The Macconwood Pack Tales Volume 1

Shifters Furever: The Macconwood Pack Tales Volume 2

The Falk Clan Tales:

The Dragon's Valentine: A Falk Clan Novel 1

The Dragon's Christmas Gift: A Falk Clan Novel 2

The Dragon's Heart: A Falk Clan Novel 3

The Dragon's Secret: A Falk Clan Novel 4

The Dragon's Treasure: A Falk Clan Novel 5

The Dragon's Surprise: A Falk Clan Novel 6

The Dragon's Dream: A Falk Clan Novel 7

Dragon Mates: The Falk Clan Series Boxed Set Books 1-4

The Bear Claw Tales:

Bearly Breathing: A Bear Claw Tale 1

Bearly There: A Bear Claw Tale 2

Bearly Tamed: A Bear Claw Tale 3

Bearly Mated: A Bear Claw Tale 4

Also available in a boxed set:

The Complete Bear Claw Tales (Books 1-4)

The Barvale Clan Tales:

Polar Opposites: The Barvale Clan Tales 1

Polar Outbreak: The Barvale Clan Tales 2

Polar Compound: A Barvale Clan Tale 3

Polar Curve: A Barvale Clan Tale 4

Also available in a boxed set:

The Barvale Clan Tales (Books 1-4)

Barvale Holiday Tales:

A Bear For Christmas

Hers To Bear

Thank You Beary Much

Bearing Gifts

Also available in a boxed set:

The Barvale Holiday Tales (Books 1-3)

Purely Paranormal Romance Books:

Marked by the Devil: Purely Paranormal Romance Books

Mated to the Dragon King: Purely Paranormal Romance Books

Claimed by the Demon: Purely Paranormal Romance Books

Christmas with a Devil, a Dragon King, & a Demon: Purely Paranormal Romance Books

Vampire Lover: Purely Paranormal Romance Books

Grizzly Lover: Purely Paranormal Romance Books

Christmas With Her Chupacabra: Purely Paranormal Romance Books

Purely Paranormal Romance Books Anthology

The Wardens of Terra:

Bound by Air: The Wardens of Terra Book 1

Star Kissed: A Wardens of Terra Short

Waterlocked: The Wardens of Terra Book 2

Moon Kissed: A Wardens of Terra Short

*Now in a boxed set and in audio!

The Maverick Pride Tales:

Purrfectly Mated

Purrfectly Kissed

Purrfectly Trapped

Purrfectly Caught

Purrfectly Naughty

Purrfectly Bound

<u>Dire Wolf Mates:</u>

Shake That Sass

Breaking Sass

Pinch of Sass

Kickin' Sass

<u>Wyvern Protection Unit:</u>

Gift Wrapped Protector: WPU 1

<u>Standalones:</u>

The Enforcer

Blood Song: A Sanguinem Council Book

Spring Fling (co-written with P. Mattern)

<u>EveL Worlds:</u>

Chinchilla and the Devil: A FUCN'A Book

Sammi and the Jersey Bull: A FUCN'A Book

Mouse and the Ball: A FUCN'A Book

<u>The Guardians of Chaos:</u>

Wolf Shield: Guardians of Chaos Book1

Dragon Shield: Guardians of Chaos Book 2

Stallion Shield: Guardians of Chaos Book 3

Panther Shield: Guardians of Chaos 4

Witch Shield: Guardians of Chaos 5

Vampire Shield: Guardians of Chaos 6

<u>Howl's Romance</u>

Mated to the Werewolf Next Door: A Howl's Romance

The Tiger King's Christmas Bride

Claiming His Virgin Mate: Howls Romance

<u>Twice Mated Tales</u>

Doubly Claimed

Doubly Bound

Doubly Tied

<u>Hearts of Stone Series</u>

Shifter Mountain: Hearts of Stone 1

Shifter City: Hearts of Stone 2

Shifter Village: Hearts of Stone 3

<u>Accidentally Undead Series</u>

Fangs For Nothin'

<u>Moongate Island Tales</u>

Moongate Island Mate

Moongate Island Christmas Claim

<u>Mated in Hope Falls</u>

Mated by Moonlight

<u>Speed Dating with the Denizens of the Underworld</u>

Ash: Speed Dating with the Denizens of Underworld

Arachne: Speed Dating with the Denizens of Underworld

Asterion: Speed Dating with the Denizens of Underworld

Hungry Fur Love

Hungry Like Her Wolf: Magic and Mayhem Universe

Hungry For Her Bear: Magic and Mayhem Universe

Shifters Unleashed Boxed Sets

Check out these amazing anthologies where you can find some of my books and the works of other awesome authors!

Midnight Magic Anthology (Water Witch)

Rituals & Runes Anthology (Air Witch)

Island Stripe Pride

Tiger Claimed

Tiger Denied

Tiger Rejected

*Tiger Tales: Island Stripe Pride Tales Books 1-3

NYC Shifter Tales

Cuff Linked

Sealed Fate

A Howlin' Good Fairytale Retelling

Sweet As Candy (single edition coming soon)

<u>Coming Soon:</u>

Hungry As Her Python: Magic and Mayhem Universe

If The Shoe Fits: A Howlin' Good Fairytale Retelling

Chickee and the Paparazzi: FUCN'A

The Wolf's Winter Wish: A Macconwood Pack Tale

The Hybrid Assassin

For Fangs Sake

Tempted By Her Protector: WPU 2

Alien Protector: WPU 3

Elvish Protector: WPU 4

Thrilled By Her Protector: WPU 5

<u>Young Adult Urban Fantasy Books:</u>

Wolf Moon: A Grazi Kelly Novel Book 1

Hunter Moon: A Grazi Kelly Novel Book 2

Rebel Moon: A Grazi Kelly Novel Book 3

Winter Moon: A Grazi Kelly Novel Book 4

Chasing The Moon: A Grazi Kelly Short 5

Blood Moon: A Grazi Kelly Novel 6

*Get all 6 books NOW AVAILABLE IN A BOXED SET:

The Complete Grazi Kelly Novel Series

Casting Magic: The Angela Tanner Files 1

Keeping Magic: The Angela Tanner Files 2

<u>G'Witches Magical Mysteries Series</u>

Co-written with P. Mattern

G'Witches

G'Witches 2: The Harpy Harbinger

G'Witches 3: Summoning Secrets

ABOUT THE AUTHOR

C.D. Gorri is an International Bestseller and Award-Winning author of steamy paranormal romance and urban fantasy. She is the creator of the Grazi Kelly Universe.

Join her mailing list here: https://www.cdgorri.com/newsletter

An avid reader with a profound love for books and literature, when she is not writing or taking care of her family, she can usually be found with a book or tablet in hand. C.D. lives in her home state of New Jersey where many of her characters or stories are based. Her tales are fast paced yet detailed with satisfying conclusions.

If you enjoy powerful heroines and loyal heroes who face relatable problems in supernatural settings, journey into the Grazi Kelly Universe today. You will find sassy, curvy heroines and sexy, love-driven heroes who find their HEAs between the pages. Werewolves, Bears, Dragons, Tigers, Witches,

Romani, Lynxes, Foxes, Thunderbirds, Vampires, and many more Shifters and supernatural creatures dwell within her worlds. The most important thing is every mate in this universe is fated, loyal, and true lovers always get their happily-ever-afters.

Want to know how it all began? Enter the Grazi Kelly Universe with Wolf Moon: A Grazi Kelly Novel or pick up Charley's Christmas Wolf and dive into the Macconwood Pack Novel Series today.

For a complete list of C.D. Gorri's books visit her website here:

https://www.cdgorri.com/complete-book-list/

Thank you and happy reading!

del mare alla stella,

C.D. Gorri